Once in a
Pink Moon

Once in a Pink Moon

LUANNE C. BROWN

FROG TALE TRILOGY - BOOK 1

SEQUOIA GROVE BOOKS

SEQUOIA GROVE BOOKS

The Frog Tale Trilogy, Book 1: *Once in a Pink Moon*

2022 by Luanne C. Brown

Published by Sequoia Grove Books
WWW.SEQUOIAGROVEBOOKS.COM

Printed in the United States of America
ISBN: 979-8-9856912-0-7

Collages by Luanne C. Brown:
Ranya, Queen of Frogs, page 34
Salmon Falls River, page 132
Little Nora, page 281
Poe, the Raven, page 323
Pink Moon, page 450

First Edition
10 9 8 7 6 5 4 3 2 1

Pay close attention
To the spaces between things
They are not empty.

'Haiku 2" by Alan Riley

Drastic measures are inescapable.

Road to Survival by William Vogt

The author respectfully, and with gratitude, acknowledges that she works and lives within the occupied territory of the Puget Sound Salish peoples.

The Watcher: A Vow

Four Nights till Pink Moon
Before the Stroke of Midnight
Salmon Falls

THE NIGHT AIR vibrated with expectation, as if the world were on the brink of something terrible and new. But no one was paying attention except for the fog, who always seemed to know everything, and the creature who commanded it.

Moving out from a Pacific Northwest forest dense with cedar, fir, and pine, the fog engulfed a white clapboard church perched on a hillside that overlooked the town of Salmon Falls. Then, as instructed, it spilled over the edge of the hillside and blanketed the houses below.

Obscured by the mist, the creature walked toward the church dragging a sack with one hand. With the other it pulled a platform filled with an army of frogs. Some were injured in battle, others by a mystery disease. When they reached the base of the church stairs, the larger creature stopped.

Other frogs emerged from the fog and joined them, surrounding the platform. Then they all donned hooded mantles of mourning finely patchworked together from bits of cloth, moss, and satin ribbon the color of dead leaves.

The creature gave a whistle and all sounds and movement stopped. It hobble-hopped up the steps dragging the sack. And as it ascended, the frog chorus began to sing a mournful dirge. There were no words to the song, but the melody and five-part harmonies could coax tears from a stone.

When it reached the top of the stairs, the creature poured out the contents of the bag in front of the church door and began sorting everything into piles, humming along with the tune in a ragged voice.

With a deep sigh, the creature finished the task and brushed a long lock of lifeless hair strung with beads and carved bone back under its hood. Then it laid a bouquet of pond fronds on the middle pile and said, "Rest in peace, beloved largetoe."

The creature tried to leave but felt a tug on its cape, which had caught on a nail head at the base of the railing. With an impatient tug, it wrestled the fabric free then leapt several feet to the ground, landing beside the platform of frogs with a thump that shook the ground.

On a low branch of a stately red cedar, an unusually large raven called out, "Four nights to Pink Moon. Four nights to Pink Moon."

The creature tilted its head up and said, "Don't you think I know?"

But the raven continued to chant.

"Quiet, I tell you. This Pink Moon is no threat to her. She lies safely in her bed. Crying her eyes out. They *will not* get to her. Believe me."

"Some fine Watcher you are," the raven said.

"When I want raven wisdom, I will ask for it."

"What will be will be," the raven said, then flew away.

"Good riddance," said the hooded figure.

All the frogs removed their mantles, but the creature's hood remained. Then they all melted into the forest. The fog trailed behind, leaving the sky once again sparkling with stars.

The church bells chimed midnight and below, streetlights winked in the darkness as the town continued to sleep, unaware. Dogs barked. A far-off coyote howled. And in the distance the raven cawed, "Four nights to Pink Moon," and hoped that someone would heed his warning.

2

Nora ◉ The Funeral That Never Was

Three Days till Pink Moon
Early Morning
Salmon Falls, A Church

"Gran, you can't kill that *Eratigena agrestis*."

"Don't, Nora, just . . . don't. It's a plain old hobo spider, and it's in my way." Gran's voice was tight. "And why is this trash here? Who does that?"

Mickey, our Sheltie, whined as he pranced on a leash by my side. He never liked it when anyone was upset.

Someone had complicated my father's funeral by piling garbage at the entrance to the church, blocking the way inside. Everyone in town knew that Dad was a dedicated environmentalist. Still, it was hard to figure out if his memory was being honored or disrespected by the odd jumble of items greeting us.

I gently scooted the spider into my hand and placed it on a rhododendron bush towering beside the church.

"Whatever you do today, little hobo," I whispered, "stay out of Gran's way."

Gran shook her head. We did not see eye to eye on saving spiders and other things. Raising an eyebrow in disgust, Gran used her stylish black pumps to bulldoze the assorted trash over to the side of the landing where some fell to the ground.

"Gran, you're littering. Dad would hate that. Besides, it was all nicely sorted into compostable, landfill, and recyclable items. You're messing it up."

"Don't talk to me like that, young lady." The pert plume on her black hat wagged at me like a scolding finger.

I stared at the ground. "Sorry, Gran."

"And where is *your* hat? Sunburn leads to skin cancer, and your pale Scandinavian skin puts you at risk."

She had a point. It wasn't even noon, and the Pacific Northwest sun was already beating down on us with an intensity that felt unnatural for an April morning. But that's climate change for you. It's a bitch.

"And why didn't you wear those black mules I got you? They matched your pencil skirt and blouse perfectly." I had gone for comfort, not style. With huge feet like mine, I could barely wear regular shoes, let alone those with no backs, high heels, or pointy toes.

Fussing about my appearance—and hers—was Gran's way of dealing with the raw pain of what we were going through. I wanted to hug her fiercely for caring so much, but any tender gesture on my part might turn each of us into a sobbing mess. That's probably why she'd been keeping me at arm's length since Dad died. The chasm his death had left in each of our lives was like a gaping wound, but adding our individual losses together made it into a cavernous one that felt too big to ever heal.

"Tell me," Gran asked. "Is this one of your 'draw attention to the plight of the environment' stunts?"

"Me? Are you kidding? What if it isn't a stunt, Gran? What if it's a tribute to Dad? Done by someone who really knew how seriously he took littering and pollution?"

"That sounds ridiculous," Gran said.

"Maybe it was Recycle Rick. Where is he, anyway?"

"Rwanda, checking out how they recycle electronic waste," Gran said.

"Oh, yeah," I said, remembering that Dad drove Rick to SeaTac the day before he died. "Do we even know if he's heard the news about Dad?" I asked.

Gran shrugged. "I left him a message, but I haven't heard back." She picked up a bouquet of lily pads and their flowers tied with sedge, which had been left on top of the pile of waste. "So, whoever did this, it wasn't Rick."

A note fell from the bouquet. I picked it up. The writing was squiggly, like it had been written by someone with a shaking hand.

"Go ahead. Read it," Gran said.

And I did.

It's fine now to gather, remembering the man,
A true pioneer, no flash in the pan
Follow his lead, act in ways that will heal
To solve the big problems, summon his zeal
This natural world on which we depend
Was beloved of Henry. The All: Please defend.

I almost lost it when I read the last line. Those words "the All" were among the last my father uttered. I didn't know what he meant. Then or now. I folded the note and tucked it away inside my skirt pocket.

"Tribute or not—it looks like a mess, and I want this stuff out of here," Gran said and tossed the bouquet behind the open church door.

I tied Mickey's leash to the banister and did as Gran asked, moving the bulk of the pile behind the door as well. I'd take care of the rest later.

When I was done, I found Mickey sniffing around the banister. I bent to pat him and saw a piece of dirty fabric caught on it. Part of the recycled spectacle? I plucked it free and tucked it into my pocket with the note. As the daughter of a master recycler, I'd learned from Dad to never leave even one piece of trash behind.

People were starting to arrive, and we surveyed the gathering crowd.

"My goodness, what a turnout. Everyone loved your father, Nora." Gran said. "We both can take solace in that."

She was right. It seemed like the whole town was arriving. I nodded a welcome to the crew from our tree farm, friends from school, the librarian, the mayor, and members from our girls' softball team. I was one of the pitchers. Most everyone had already been to the house with flowers and casseroles during the week of mystery and pain since he'd died. But then, our small town was like that. For all the narrow-minded thinking I've seen in Salmon Falls, kindness and generosity usually won out.

"Now clear away the rest of this junk," Gran ordered. I placed my hand on her shoulder in a silent plea for her to relax a little. She brushed it away.

Mel Finley, our tree farm foreman, approached us. Head bowed, hands folded, he looked respectful and deferential—as always. But there was something about this guy that I never liked.

"About the favor you owe me . . ." Finley said.

Gran seemed to shrink before my eyes. Shoulders slumped, head lowered, she leaned against me for support. I put my arm around her protectively and raised myself to my full six-foot height.

"Gran's in no shape to do any favors for anyone," I said.

"No, no, Nora," Gran said so quietly I had to lean toward her to hear. Finley leaned in, too. "Mel here is the one doing the favor—for me. And for you."

I scowled. This sounded like a flat-out lie to me, but now wasn't the time to question her about it. Wondering about this 'favor' as I worked, I finished pushing the junk out of the way and Mickey helped, soft-mouthing some of the fabric and putting it behind the open church doors where I'd been stashing things. When it was all out of sight, I dusted off my hands and gave Mickey a treat for helping.

Leaning up against the banister for a moment, I caught my breath and felt a deeper loneliness than usual well up inside. I touched the brightly enameled green frog pin on my blouse for comfort. It had belonged to my mom, and I'd worn it as my way of bringing her spirit to Dad's funeral.

The pin depicted a roundish frog face wearing a golden crown with two sparkling red crystals for eyes. Mom had been a herpetologist and had devoted her life to two things: first, to our family, and second, to preserving frog populations in the wild. It comforted me to touch it.

Some of my friends made their way up the steps to greet me. We were all around the same age—but most of them were graduating from high school in a few months. I still had another year to go since my parents had kept me home for an extra year before starting kindergarten. We'd been hanging out together since our T-ball days and had played on the same teams for years, coached by my dad and Will's grandpa. I had a mean arm when it came to fastballs.

Kameela gave me a warm hug. "You doing okay?" she whispered in my ear as I clung to her. I nodded, hoping her kindness wouldn't set off a crying jag.

"I am so happy you're here."

She nodded. Her head was covered with a hijab made from the same printed material as her skirt. The colors looked beautiful against her dark skin, although I knew she was more of a ripped-blue-jeans-and-plaid-shirt girl like me. Kameela, whose family had come to the valley as refugees from Somalia, was the brains of our group of environmental activists—we called ourselves Mother Nature's Commandos.

Minh was next in the hug line. He, too, was dressed up for the occasion, wearing his older brother's suit, which was about a year too big on him. He still looked handsome, though, especially with the addition of an orange tie, which complemented his brown eyes. "Thanks so much for coming," I said after we'd exchanged a short hug.

Next came Will. Tall and slender with long jet-black hair, Will was a member of the local tribe. Shy but whip-smart, he was our technical genius and graphic artist. Our families were friends, especially his grandfather and my dad; our mothers, both gone now, had been close as well.

In fact, we'd spent so much time together over our seventeen years that Will was more brother than friend. Never much of a hugger, he made an exception today and gave my shoulders a squeeze. "The aunties sent more food for the reception. It's in my car," he said.

"They are so sweet. I'll be sure to thank them," I said. Will nodded.

One person was missing from our crew. Seth. Taller than me, he'd be easy to see in the crowd were he here. His dark hair and ginormous chocolatey eyes made him crush worthy. Some people thought he was broody. He wasn't. He was sad, frustrated, and impatient to get out of this town. Like most of us. And he had a good reason to go. His dad, Carl Kincade, was the meanest, most selfish man around.

Everyone hated the elder Kincade. Especially me. Having watched Seth grow up under his father's thumb made it hard for me to keep my temper when the man was around.

I gave up looking for Seth with a deep sigh.

"Nora, no worries, you're going to get through this," Kameela said, trying to inspire me with her confidence.

"We're here to help," Minh added.

"Anything you need?" Will asked.

"Only you guys—for now," I said.

They were all being so sweet. Since Dad died, we'd spent a lot of time together at my house. I tried to help Gran through the loss of her only child, and they tried to help me. And it gave Gran, who liked them all, the job of "grandmother-henning" a teenage brood.

But their awesomeness only made me feel worse. I still hadn't been able to tell them—or anyone else—about the night Dad died. The time would come when I couldn't avoid it. But that time wasn't today.

"Let's meet tomorrow," I said to my friends. "We have to finalize our plans for . . . you know."

"Nora," Kameela said. "We've been talking, and we think this crazy new scheme might be a step too far."

"A step too far for *you*?" I asked. "You're usually the audacious one."

Mickey whined.

"It's okay, boy," Minh said, bending over to give the dog's head a scratch. "We're not fighting. We're discussing." Mickey didn't look convinced.

"We've been rethinking the best approach to take," Minh said.

"You guys met without me?" I asked, surprised by the hurt in my voice.

"It wasn't a meeting—we ran into each other and got to talking," Kameela said. "That's all."

"But we had everything all worked out before Dad died," I said.

"Well, not everything," Will said. "There are tons of logistics to get through."

"And it's risky. Someone might get hurt," Minh choked out. "*We* might get hurt."

"The plan is good. It's safe. It's symbolic," I said.

"You've lost your dad, Nora. You aren't thinking straight," Kameela said, trying to comfort me.

"We *have* to do it. We have to," I said a bit too desperately.

My friends looked at me like I was nuts. Maybe I was.

"We've got to be realistic about what we can do," Minh said with his usual forthrightness.

"Minh's right. Our job is to help people see the cost of not acting," Kameela said. "That's how you change hearts and minds."

I wanted to continue to make a case for the stronger action we'd planned, but before I could, Gran approached us and grabbed me by the arm. "If I find out your little gang is planning any more eco stunts, you're all going to be in trouble." Her voice was sharp.

"Gran. Too harsh," I said.

She drew a ragged breath and let go, then patted the sleeve of my blouse as if to erase the tightness of her grip.

"Sorry, Will, Minh, Kameela . . . Nora." She looked at each of us as she said our names. "It's been a bad week, but your youthful enthusiasm isn't to blame."

We all circled around and gave her a hug. It only lasted a few seconds before she said, "You all are going to make me cry because of your kindness to this old crab."

With chuckles and smiles, we broke our circle.

"See you inside, Nora," Kameela said, and my friends filed into the church.

Only Will held back. "Nora, Mrs. Peters, my grandfather said he was sorry he couldn't come. His back is acting up."

"I hope he feels better soon, Will," I said.

"Yes, thank you, Will," Gran added. "Please give him our best wishes. I'll pay a visit soon if he's up to it."

"He'd like that, I know." Will smiled and followed our friends inside.

"Nora, I forgot my handkerchief in the car. It's in my big bag. Would you go get it for me?" Gran asked.

"Sure." I handed her Mickey's leash and started down the stairs.

I was almost to the sidewalk when a long shadow fell across my path. It was Seth's dad. Etched by time and anger, his face was never one I wanted to see. Particularly today. "Hello, Nora," he said in a gravelly voice that sent shivers across my shoulders.

He stretched out his knotted hand to shake mine, but I kept it at my side and took in the raggy blue jeans and flannel shirt he was wearing. Even in our backwater town of Salmon Falls, most people came today wearing their best—as a sign of respect for my dad. But not him. No surprise there. He respected only himself.

Kincade pulled his hand back, clamped it on the rail, and stomped a scuffed boot the color of dried blood on the lowest step. "You've gathered quite a crowd here. But who didn't love Henry?"

You, for one, I almost said. *And the person who killed him.* My head began to swim, and I had to close my eyes.

When I opened them, I noticed people pooling on the sidewalk behind him, afraid to pass by to climb the stairs. And there were more folks coming from the parking lot and the street.

Gran called out from the top of the stairs, "What are you doing here, Carl?" Mickey bared his teeth and growled.

"Got a delivery for you," Kincade hollered up. He waved a roll of papers at her, practically hitting me in the face with them. "I am assuming Henry showed you the originals before he died."

He thrust them into my hands and stepped back onto the sidewalk, still blocking the way.

"Nora, bring those papers to me," Gran said, her voice quavering.

I bounded back up the stairs and handed them over. She unrolled them and I read over her shoulder. "Deed of Sale?" I said, barely choking it out. I skimmed the page. It was hard to take in all that information, but it looked like it was for a deal between Kincade and Dad for our property. The house *and* the tree farm. No way. Absolutely no way.

"The deal's signed and paid for, and you have thirty days to vacate your property from the day it was signed," Kincade said, sneering.

I looked back at the paper, still not believing it was possible. It was dated the day Dad died.

Kincade turned and saw the people milling behind him.

"Get out of the way, Carl, we have a funeral to get to," an older man said.

"I'm not going anywhere until I say my piece," Kincaid said with a hiss, then addressed the crowd like some crackpot dictator. "As you all know, five generations ago the Peters family took advantage of my family when they were down on their luck, and they stole our property for a song."

Was he calling my family crooks? At my father's funeral? I started seeing red. "From what I heard," I said loudly, racking my brain for the details, "our ancestors bought the property for a *fair* price *before* the bank could repossess it."

"Shut up, girl," Kincade said.

The crowd gasped.

"For decades, I've been demanding that Henry sell me the timberland and the house where all the Peters—or what's left of them—live, all a part of my family's original holdings. But Henry refused. Until one day, he came to me and said he had a guilty conscience about how my family had been treated and wanted to make it right. I'm sorry he's dead, but at least justice for my family has been done. What was stolen from us is now returned."

Gran looked shaken. I was stunned. And it looked like everyone was taking him seriously. It was clever of him to make it seem like his lie was somehow Dad's idea. People believed Dad. They trusted Dad. Kincade was abusing that trust with his lie.

"You can't think Dad would really do this, Gran," I said. "You can't. He had so much invested in his plans."

"No matter how hard it is for us to understand, we must try to. For whatever reason, Henry changed his mind, and we must respect his wishes."

What was going on here? The Gran I knew would have told Kincade to stick those papers where the sun didn't shine. But instead, she caved—without even a fight.

But her caving seemed to come at a cost. Hands shaking, she lost her grip on her clutch, and it flew down the stairs and landed a few steps above Kincade. It popped open on impact and its contents spilled out: lipstick, keys, hearing aid batteries, wallet, and a yellowed buckskin pouch, the sight of which tweaked a faint memory.

"Nora, my purse," Gran whispered harshly.

I scrambled back down the stairs for the third time to get her things, but Kincade swept the pouch up before I could get to it.

"That doesn't belong to you," I called out, my voice sharp as a steel spike.

Kincade's eyes burned with anger as he looked up at Gran. "It does now," he said with a sneer.

People in the crowd were getting impatient with Kincade.

"Hey—give that back to Nora."

"You can't steal that from Ellie."

"Thief."

Kincade turned to the crowd and laughed, then tried to push his way through to the street, but like a soccer scrum, the mourners locked elbows and stopped him.

I spotted Pastor Lackerby pushing his wife's wheelchair toward the crowd at a faster-than-usual clip.

"Pastor Lackerby! Pastor Lackerby!" I called, feeling a bit like a tattletale.

The crowd let them through.

Kincade didn't move.

The pastor and his wife stopped in front of Kincade.

"Goodness, Nora," the pastor said. "Whatever is the matter?"

I pointed at Kincade. "He stole something from Gran." I wondered if my words sounded as petty to others as they did to me.

"Girls have such vivid imaginations, don't you think, Pastor?" Kincade said, swiveling his vile head my way.

I wanted to say, *Neanderthals like you could use some imagination.* But it didn't seem fair to Neanderthals.

Just then, Seth arrived on his bike.

I felt a wave of calm pass through me. But it didn't last.

Seth made his way through the crowd toward us. "Dad—what are you doing?"

The crowd grumbled and various people spoke out.

"He's taking Ellie's purse."

"And land."

"Give everything back, Carl."

"Haven't the Peters suffered enough?"

"Carl Kincade, stop acting crazy."

Kincade glared at everyone, then yowled in pain and grabbed his shin.

"Your wife kicked me, Pastor," Kincade said like a pouty toddler.

Heads swerved toward Mrs. Lackerby, who smiled at me like an angel. "Must have been one of my muscle spasms."

The pastor looked from his wife to me, then to Kincade, a confused smile on his face. "Let's get inside the church, shall we?"

The pastor pushed his wife toward the ramp until she said, "I'm sure you meant to tell Mr. Kincade to return Ellie's property to her, didn't you, dear?"

"Yes, of course," the pastor said. He faced Kincade with a frown. "Who was it who said, 'Thou shalt not steal'?"

Kincade's scowl deepened. "They stole first," he said, continuing to act like somebody who needed a full-time babysitter.

That was it. I was taking no more of his crap—and at my dad's funeral too. "Why is everything about you today, *Mr.* Kincade?" I asked with a sneer. "Today is my father's funeral and yet you insist on humiliating me and Gran in front of all our friends by calling us thieves. Couldn't you have come to discuss this in private *after* we bury someone we dearly love?"

Kincade looked like his head might explode.

"Instead of focusing on what we supposedly stole from your family, you could be feeling grateful for all that you have—like a wonderful son for one thing," I said. I looked at Seth, who blushed at my comment. "You also have our property—apparently—though I can tell you one thing. Despite what Gran says, I'll be looking into everything about this 'sale,' as you call it. Because it sounds like one great big lie to me."

Kincade sneered, looked at my grandmother, and said, "Is that what you think, Ellie? That this sale is a lie?"

Gran, sweating, swallowed hard. Her nervousness made me nervous. "Why, no, Carl. If Henry wanted to sell, it was his right. I respect that."

"As well you should," Kincade said with a sniff.

Before I could go on the attack again, Seth stepped in front of his dad, and said, "Let's go."

"After your father returns Gran's pouch," I said.

A sly smile appeared on Kincaid's face. He stepped toward me and dangled the pouch. "This? You want this?"

Before I could say a word, something zipped between Kincade and me and snatched the pouch out of Kincade's grasp. It was a bird. A raven . . . who shot up higher in the sky, the pouch dangling from its beak, then flew in a circle around us.

We all stared at the bird, mouths open. It took another pass and swooped down so low that it flew right back between the same space that still separated Kincade and me. A whoosh of air blew my bangs away from my forehead. I reached out my hand and he dropped the pouch right into it. I clenched my hand protectively into a fist.

The crowd gasped. And so did I as we all watched the raven disappear into a flash of sun. My father had made friends with a raven. He'd called him Poe. Could it have been this bird? He had come and gone so fast I never had a chance to identify him by the squiggly mark on his beak—a scar left from some horrible accident. My dad had found him critically wounded and at death's door and had nursed him back to health. Ever since then, they were buddies. And he'd been hanging around more than ever since Dad died.

The pouch had landed hard with a bit of sting. I opened my fist to look at it. Something rolled out of the pouch. I dipped down, scooped my other hand under it, and caught something that sparkled green in the sun.

Everyone started talking at once. I whipped my head from person to person until I was practically dizzy.

"Nice play!"

"Good catch."

"Way to go, Nora."

I pressed my catch protectively to my chest, accidentally hitting it against my mother's frog pin. I felt a click.

When I lowered my hand to look at the object, I heard a rip. My mother's pin had torn off my blouse. No, wait a sec. The pin setting was still attached to my top. But the frog medallion itself was gone. I gulped. *I cannot lose that. I cannot.* I looked down at my feet to see if it had fallen. Nothing. My heart sank.

Then I looked more closely at the object I had caught. It was a green egg-shaped stone. Maybe serpentine? Somehow the frog medallion had inserted itself into an indentation that fit it perfectly. Could the day get any weirder?

The fit was so good that when I tried to get the medallion out, the top half of the stone split into thirds and fell open, revealing a huge golden pearl the size of a giant jawbreaker. It lay on a bed of narrow strands of grey-green lichens—*witches' hair* we called it. It was then I realized that the egg-shaped stone was really what my gran would call a jewelry casket.

I looked up to see everyone's reactions, but no one had noticed. That's because they were frozen. Not icicles-dripping-from-the-nose frozen, but frozen as in not moving. Mouths open, sweat drops stuck on cheeks, arms in awkward poses. The sway of skirts had stopped mid-swish. Even Gran was stuck in time. The frightened expression on her face broke my heart.

What was this thing that made time stand still for everyone but me?

I examined it more closely. Its golden surface was dotted with veins of gold that encircled darker spots like the ones on Jupiter. Big for a pearl and so outrageously beautiful I was mesmerized.

And then, the surface of the pearl began to move. The darker spots swirled, and the golden veins pulsed.

A jolt of energy shook the air. It was so powerful I grabbed the railing so I wouldn't fall over.

The air filled with the fragrance of wild roses and berries warmed by the sun.

A white light flared from the pearl and changed the world in front of me into a sight I'd never seen.

The nearby stand of Douglas firs pulsated with rainbows of light and bowed my way as if honoring the object I held in my hand.

Was I losing it?

I tried once more to disengage my mother's frog medallion from the jewelry casket, and when I couldn't pop it out, I pressed it in. With a click the lid closed, obscuring the pearl. But I still couldn't get the medallion to disengage from the egg. It seemed stuck there like an on/off button I didn't dare mess with now.

The sweet fragrance faded.

The trees stood tall once more.

Birds fled.

The pace of the world returned.

I put the jewelry casket into the pouch and shoved it in my pocket.

An air of confusion hung over the crowd like they were waking up from an intense nap. Shaking his head as if to clear it, Kincade pushed through the crowd, calling for his son. "Seth, you better come or there will be hell to pay for both you and your mom," he said without any sense of embarrassment and got into his beat-up truck.

The color drained from Seth's face, and he dashed over to me. We hugged.

"I wish I could stay," he said. Then he kissed me. On the forehead.

I kissed him back, but I could only reach his cheek. We'd been dancing around getting closer for a while, but now wasn't the time for big steps, especially with half the town watching.

"Seth!" Kincade barked from the street, the anger in his voice rising above the noise of the crowd. Seth and I parted, and I ran back upstairs to Gran, still feeling Seth's touch. I dropped the pouch back in her purse and noticed that her face had turned pasty grey. She panted, then grabbed and tugged at her upper left arm. She looked me right in the eye.

"Reggie? Is that you?" Gran said.

Reggie was my mother, who died when I was ten.

"You disappeared."

Disappeared? A cloud of confusion swirled around my head.

"How could you leave Nora and Henry? I will never forgive you." She panted out the words. "Never."

Then she collapsed into my arms.

My stomach tumbled over itself. I cried for help.

I held her closer. The papers Kincade had thrust on us were now lying on the landing, quavering in the breeze. The rustle of paper made me think of a snake slithering through the grass.

Minh appeared and helped me lower Gran to the cold cement. He made sure her airway was clear and checked her pulse while I kneeled, helpless and trembling beside them. I could tell by the relief on his face that Gran was still alive. He gently tucked his suit jacket under her head. Kameela was already talking to the 911 operator.

The noise around me sounded muffled. Even Mickey's howls seemed distant. Will tried to quiet the dog, but Mickey was inconsolable. I closed my eyes and silently pleaded with my grandmother. *Please don't die. Please. Don't leave me alone.*

Panic ratcheted my chest muscles ever tighter until it felt like my heart might burst. One thing was for sure—there would be no funeral today. And I desperately hoped that tomorrow we wouldn't be having two.

The Veil of Mist is parted
Ancient trees step aside
Frog Mountain beckons
Palay gates open wide

3

Vizzard ❧ A Whiff of the Past

Three Days till Pink Moon
Dew Time (Morning)
The Palay, Quarters of the Grand and Glorious Vizzard

ORNING SUN THE color of hive-ripened honey streamed through a round opening carved eons ago into Frog Mountain.

"Your Grandness, it is time to wake," Clarenso said.

Balarius, the Grand and Glorious Vizzard to the Court of Ranya, Queen of Frogs, heard his aide's voice, but nothing in his pain-wracked body would move.

"Most Prodigious Master of Metaphysics," Clarenso pleaded, "it is already Fly Time. Her majesty expects you."

The vizzard, languishing on his side, groaned, and snuggled deeper into his cedar bough–lined sleeping nest. His goodnight tonic had deepened his slumber, but his old bones and depleted spirit craved more rest. Perhaps what he desired was eternal sleep in the Big Pond Beyond. When the Well of White Light willed it, it would be so.

"I have prepared your steeping pool. All awaits. But you must hurry."

With reluctance, the vizzard opened his one good eye and peered at the little transparent frog hovering over him. Oh, how Clarenso's gold-flecked collar ruffle sparkled in the morning light. His snappy livery featured a silk frogklath cape dyed the color of raspberries. On the back of his cape was the embroidered handprint of the queen. The captivating impact of his uniform distracted one's eye from the unsettling transparency of Clarenso's body.

But how could the vizzard judge others by their freakish looks when his own appearance sent hordes hopping in all directions?

"You are quite the wonderful sight, Clarenso. Your magnificence astounds me." The vizzard pushed himself onto an unsteady arthritic elbow.

"Munificent one, I only reflect your light."

The vizzard's chuckle abruptly stopped as a sudden wave of energy engulfed his body, and a tantalizing fragrance of wild roses and sun-warmed berries filled the air. But it was spring, not late summer. The scent sparked an ache in his chest that made him long for . . . what? He waved his hand through the air, the withered webs between his fingers fluttering. He captured a twisp of energy and blew it, all shimmering and bright, into a nearby snail shell and plugged the shell opening with a pussy willow bud that had fallen to the floor. He rolled the shell up in the sleeve of his garment. Where had he felt that energetic vibration before? Where had he smelled that elusive fragrance?

Memories flooded over him.

That fragrance told him one thing: A sacred promise had been broken. Whatever the cause, the most powerful magic in the world was now on the loose in unknown hands. And whosoever held it had the power to either destroy the frog world or create it anew.

Clarenso rushed to his side. "Your Amazingness, what has happened? Have you taken ill?"

"Did you feel that?" Balarius asked.

Clarenso's bulging eyes squinted with confusion. "Feel what, Your Astonishingness?"

"Nothing gripped your gut as it did mine?" The vizzard clutched his portly belly. "What about that fragrance?"

"Your Tremendousness, I felt nothing, saw nothing, smelled nothing." Clarenso leaned in closer with a concerned look. The vizzard shooed him back.

"Look, even my bouquets have responded to the energy flair," the vizzard said, pointing to the vases exquisitely carved from elkhorn that graced the short tables on both sides of his sleeping nest, now overflowing with beautiful blooms.

"But, but . . . how did they flower so quickly? It was only yesterday that I placed the hard buds of balsam, pussy willow, and forsythia in those vases." Clarenso said. "Blessed Vizzard, what in all that is sacred is going on?"

The vizzard did not know how to answer his aide's question, so he ignored it.

"I must attend to Her Majesty," Balarius said. "My sticks, please, so I may raise myself from this tomb of a bed."

Clarenso fetched the walking sticks. "Your Marvelousness," he said with the required sign of respect (a dip of his head) as he presented them to the vizzard.

The rattlesnake tails fastened to the tops of the sticks buzzed ominously as Balarius threaded his hands through the loops of braided hide that made them easier for him to use.

With protests from joints and sinew, he raised himself onto his two back legs. He glared at Clarenso, and the vizzard's admiration for his aide grew, for Clarenso did not flinch at the sight of his freakish self-inflicted condition. Balarius had long regretted his youthful application of potions to master the feat of walking on two legs like a largetoe, or human, as they were known to some. Not only had it set him apart from all other frogs, it caused him excruciating pain with every step.

Balarius rested his forehead against one of his walking sticks to collect his thoughts. He longed to ask his aide one more time, but he knew that too few were sensitive to the sway of the Golden Pearl of the Forest.

"I believe I will forgo my morning dip," he said. "The queen will be impatient for my arrival. My chronical cape, please."

While he would never call himself a fashion frog, Balarius loved attending court wearing this cape, which highlighted important life events.

He tapped his foot impatiently and turned, with some pain, to see his aide staring out the circular opening that overlooked the Plaza of the Blazing Sun.

"Am I boring you, Clarenso?"

"So sorry, Your Grandness. A band of refuge seekers from my homeland is expected today, and I hope that my nephew, Wink, will be among them. He is the last surviving member of my clan and is afflicted with health problems, like so many of our kind these days. I fear he is not strong enough to withstand the hardships and dangers of the journey."

"Then you must wait at the plaza for his arrival."

"But I must attend to you, Your Cleverness."

"I can tend to my own needs for a little while. And when Wink arrives, bring him here so I can welcome him."

"How kind, Your Greatness."

"Yes, yes. Now go."

Clarenso draped the magnificent cape across the vizzard's sloping shoulders and fastened the frog-shaped clasp carved from rare dragon bone stone. Then he went to look for his nephew.

When Clarenso had gone, Balarius studied the public pictograms on the outside of his cape. What a life he had lived. Battles. Rebellions. Triumphs. Tragedies. He had the urge to whirl about like the wind and let the cape with its fine fabric and embroidery billow out like a cloud around him. But alas, his infirmities made that impossible.

Inside the cape, the most personal of life events were recorded—those that held great joy, shame, longing, and the deepest secrets. He knew exactly where to find the private pictogram of the event that was now on his mind. His sister, the queen, had a similar pictogram on the inside of her chronicle cape, for it was an act they committed together and a shame they shared. And they had not discussed the incident even once since it occurred.

He closed his cape with a snap. No time for that now. His sister needed him. Had she felt the wave of energy and smelled the fragrance of the Pearl too?

"Oh, Well of White Light, bless you for granting us one more chance at salvation with the return of the Pearl," he said. "And may this be a sign that you forgive us for what we did so long ago."

He shambled off toward the Ruling Room fully awake and filled with fear.

4

The Queen Ranya's Command

Three Days till Pink Moon
Warming Time
The Palay, Ruling Room

"Simeon!" The voice of Ranya, Queen of Frogs, echoed throughout the large empty chamber, known as the Ruling Room, even before she was in view.

Simeon, a blue poisonous frog who served as her majordomo, peered into the hollow tube that the queen would soon be emerging from and called down to her. "Yes, Your Majesty?"

"Where is the vizzard?" she said, her voice getting louder as she rose from her chamber on the stone column that carried her, already ensconced on her throne. "Does he not know what *now* means?"

Simeon scampered backward as the queen rose through the floor in all her resplendent glory, sitting on an ornate throne carved in the shape of a lily pad flower. It was specially made from red jasper to help her maintain justice in her heart and imbue her with strength and stability. The throne itself sat on a cylindrical stone column. This system for transporting the queen, named by Azzie when he was barely a tad, was known as the queen's up-downer. It was a series of hollow tubes with moveable stone columns that carried her on her elaborate thrones (created from rock, crystals, and gems that enhanced her energetic powers) up to and down from various levels of the Palay.

Double-dipping before her, as Simeon was required by court etiquette to do, he said, "He is making his way to the Ruling Room, Your Majesty."

The queen lowered her voice and motioned Simeon closer, but not too close. One touch from her aide and even she would die.

"And my son?" She shifted her great girth to a more comfortable position on her unforgiving throne.

Simeon cleared his throat. "Prince Azzumundo is being sought throughout the Palay."

"I wager he is either composing an inharmonious chorus for us to endure or recovering from a late-night hop," she said. "*Why* will he not give up those follies and have more passion for being a prince?"

Her agitation rustled the spring azure butterflies that decorated the spiderdown cape she wore. Their soft blue wings outlined in black flickered as they rose in a cloud, then resettled. "Thank you, my beauties," she whispered to the insects. "You at least respond to my mood. No one else even notices."

She adjusted her flower crown that was fashioned from the same red jasper as her throne. Even though the crown helped unleash her passion for her role as queen, today the weight of it felt excessive.

"Shall I read the List of Losses while we wait, My Queen?" Simeon asked.

Nodding, she closed her eyes to listen. This was the most heartbreaking part of each day.

"The misted waterfall toad, the yellow-banded frog, the black-spotted golden frog, the variegated tan and brown frog . . ."

The name of each family of frogs landed like a blow on Ranya's back. She had failed to help her own kind survive in today's changing world. But what could she do? While all powerful in her own realm with sway over certain elements of nature, she was not omnipotent. There were other forces at play and the problems were too big to solve using her powers alone.

". . . the splendid poison frog, the white-nosed bush frog . . ."

With each name, the queen pictured their beauty, uniqueness, and habitat, the destruction of which had most likely contributed to their demise. But it wasn't just the loss of place—there were too many deadly toxins in the water and a mystery malady that was maiming and murdering too many of her subjects, sometimes wiping out whole populations.

". . . the booroolong frog, the fringe-limbed tree frog, the Taita Hills warty frog . . ."

And hers wasn't the only species being challenged. It was the whole Earth, with fires blazing, floods raging. Water was being used up. Homes everywhere were being grabbed from the trees, plants, animals, insects, and amphibians (including her beloved subjects) who lived there. Soon, there would be too little habitat left for too many creatures except for the selfish largetoe.

After the tenth name, Ranya could take no more and struck the bottom of her red bixbite-tipped scepter on the floor. Simeon's hands flew to his ear pads to block out the sharp reverberations, and the giant maple leaf, where the List of Losses was written, drifted from his hands down onto the fine mosaic tiles made from marble and precious stones.

"That is enough for today. Post the names at the entrance to the Puddle of Tears. And let me know who comes to pay homage to the fallen."

"Yes, Majesty," Simeon said. He picked up the leaflet and placed it reverently in a box fashioned from the wood of holly, where previous lists were stored. When full of leaflets, which would be too soon, this box would be stored in the Library of Losses located inside the Puddle of Tears, which was a location within the Palay where naturally dripping water had formed a forest of stalactites that looked like they were crying. Simeon never relished a visit there. The grief emanating from the place was palpable.

The hiss of rattlesnake tails gave their warning. The vizzard had arrived.

"You are late," she grumbled.

"Deepest apologies, Your Highness." Balarius shuffled forward.

"Simeon, check the room for Lord Raeburn's spies," she commanded. "I swear someone lurks in the shadows."

The vizzard, now in front of the throne, sniffed the air. "No unwelcome eyes or ears are present, Your Majesty, Raeburn's or otherwise."

Ranya's eye ridges arched. "You think I misjudge Raeburn?"

"I think no such thing," the vizzard said, straightening his bent body as much as he could.

"That stub-tailed frog will have my head on a pike if I am not careful. And yours as well."

"Come, Sister. Let us not squabble like taddies."

"Your words say one thing, Brother, your eyes another. Be careful, two-footed one. You are not indispensable, blood or no blood."

Ranya cast another furtive glance around the room and lowered her voice to a throaty whisper. "Did you feel the energetic rumble? Could it be the Pearl?" she asked.

"So, you think the Pearl has been found?" Prince Azzumundo asked from a patch of shadows to his mother's right.

Ranya flinched. "You startled me, Azzie," she said, using her son's pond name. "Did you feel it too?"

"I did," he said. "I am only guessing what *it* was, since no one in any of our lifetimes has ever felt its force."

Ranya glanced around the room until her eyes met those of her brother. But they both quickly looked away from each other. What Azzie had said was not true. The force of the Pearl had been felt—by her, her brother, and one other—so very long ago.

"The less we talk about it, the better," she said. "For us all."

"But why, Mother?" He moved to the edge of a light mote created from one of the lumitubes above. The harsh flare of sunlight reflected on his face, obliterating his handsome features.

And for a moment, Azzie appeared to be faceless, like a ghoulish idilon, those zombie-like frog soldiers of her enemy, General Oddbull. Visions of these creatures haunted the dreams of little tads everywhere.

"Is it not the dream of every frog to find the Golden Pearl of the Forest so we can perform the *true* Ceremony of Renewal and restore order to the All?" Azzie asked. He tossed his favorite snack, a fly-larvae puff, into the air and caught it with a flick of his tongue.

"It was probably an aberrant energy flare. As the webs connecting all life on the planet continue to fray and break, we must expect such anomalies, do you not think, Brother?" Ranya asked.

Before his uncle could respond, Azzie said, "I think we need to chase down the source of the flare to find out where it came from. Perhaps it will lead us to the Pearl."

"Our faux Ceremony of Renewal is already scheduled," the queen said. "We do not need the real Pearl or the real ceremony."

"Are you saying that you think the most reverent ceremony between the animal world and the world of the largetoe, the ceremony designed to remind the dominators that they are our equals—not our superiors—is a sham?" Azzie asked.

The queen did not reply.

"If you do not believe in it," Azzie said, "why am I taking my time to do a reenactment? You and your brother have tortured me for sun cycles to prepare for this bogus ordeal."

"Come now, Son, you know we frogs love spectacle," the queen said. "It quiets the masses, at least for a time. And the frogs in the Hinterlands need it most of all at this moment, with their numbers dwindling and their homes disappearing. That is why we are staging it so far from the traditional ceremonial grounds in an unspoiled venue. We must retain their loyalty to my throne, and the faux Ceremony of Renewal serves that purpose."

"Much better for me to suffer than your subjects, Mother," Azzie said.

"Exactly," the queen replied.

"Mother, I insist. Let us cancel the fake pageant and let me search for the Pearl of the Forest. If it truly still exists, it could solve everything."

"You exaggerate, Azzie," the queen said.

"Do I need to remind you again that the real ceremony—and the Confab of the All that follows—are the cornerstones of cooperation between the natural world and the largetoe? And Prince Ponte-Fricani ruined it when he disappeared eons ago after stealing the Pearl and changing himself from a frog prince into a largetoe prince, the exact opposite of what is supposed to happen.

"Since then, there has been no opportunity for largetoes to renew their connection to the All by bringing one of their kind together with representatives from other species and the elements, to discuss solutions that will enhance the health of the Renewee's local environment—lessons that other willing largetoes in other locations could learn from. It used to work. But doing nothing? Not even trying?

"Look where that has gotten us. The whole world is disintegrating before our eyes. Species of all kinds, including our own, are dying out. The spiritual essences of water, earth, fire, and wind—the Elementos—are being taxed almost to a point beyond redemption.

"Do you not agree that no matter how and where this energy flare originated, if it is connected to the Golden Pearl of the Forest, we should track it down?" Azzie asked. "That is, if only we had a way."

"I *may* have a way," said the vizzard softly.

The queen glared at him.

"Sister, if the Pearl has resurfaced, it is much better to find and control it than to let it fall into the hands of someone who may use it against us."

Azzie tossed his head upward and shook it in disgust. "You are so wrong, Uncle. But that is not unusual."

"Azzie," the queen snapped. "Respect your elders." Then she pondered her brother's suggestion. "Oh, very well. It vexes me, but you do make a point."

The queen could tell her brother was trying to hide his aston-
ishment that she had just agreed with him. It did not happen
often, so she could hardly blame him.

"I harvested an energy twisp during the event," the vizzard
said. He removed the snail shell, which pulsated with energy,
from his cuff and held it up for all to see.

"Why, of course. Uncle can magnify the energy twisp and
beam it outward," Azzie said. "It will seek itself. Then your
airtilliers can follow its web strings, which will lead them to the
source of the emanations—the Pearl."

The queen suppressed surprise at her son's creative proposal.

"Good ideas should not go to waste, Mother."

"And it is a most excellent idea, Your Highness," said the
vizzard, addressing the prince. "You could lead them yourself."

"I would entertain that possibility, but for one thing."

"What is that, my son?" the queen asked.

"If you get the Pearl, you will surely squirrel it away and not
use it for what it was divinely designed to do."

"And what if I command otherwise?" said the queen through
gritted snout.

"How many contradictory commands can one queen issue?"
Azzie asked, prodding the queen's fury. "Go to the faux ceremony—no, go in search of an energetic flow. Make up your
mind, Mother."

There was a collective gasp at the prince's impudence; the
queen tightened her mouth.

"But then who will lead the search for the disturbance, Sister?"
asked the vizzard.

"I will, Father," said Princess P'hustalinka as she advanced
toward the queen's throne. This magnificent yellow-green frog
with stripes down her side wore a protective bodysuit of polished

mica plates woven into a weft of mycelium, with copper-hewn plates covering her vital parts. She was commander of the queen's own guards. Her elite fighting group, the Zons, composed only of female frogs, followed in lockhop behind.

The princess, whose pond name was Linka, stopped beside Prince Azzie.

Azzie groaned. "Why her?"

"Because your *cousin* never lets us down," said the queen.

Linka double-dipped before the throne. "My aunt, My Queen."

"Rump kisser," Azzie whispered to Linka.

"Aquaphobe," Linka said in a low blow that referenced Azzie's fear of water.

"Why can you not be more like her, Azzie?" the queen asked, turning toward her son.

Azzie did not respond.

"Be on your way, Cousin. Leave the boring details to me. It is your right and privilege," Linka said with more than a hint of sarcasm.

"May you find the Golden Pearl of the Forest and put it to the use it was intended for," Azzie said.

The queen rustled uncomfortably on the throne, sending the butterflies into a swarm above Azzie, who swatted them away. He bowed to his mother and, before the butterflies could resettle, withdrew.

"No doubt His Highness is eager to prepare for his journey, Your Majesty," the vizzard said.

The queen sighed. "No doubt."

"May I begin now," Balarius asked, "or would you like to invite your subjects who wait beyond the great doors to this room to join you in wishing my daughter and her Zons well on their journey?"

"*Her* Zons? Never forget, Brother, they are my troops. And I wish to keep this expedition a secret for now. No sense stirring up hopes when only disappointment may result."

"Yes, Majesty," said the vizzard.

"Now, Linka," the queen instructed. "I want you to find what caused this energy flare. Was it truly the Pearl? Let me know who possesses it. And do what you can to get it back into my hands."

"Yes, Your Majesty."

"This journey may lead you beyond the protection of the Veil of Mist into the ever more dangerous world of the largetoe. I give you my leave to go where you must. May your journey be a successful one."

The queen waved her scepter at the dome of the Ruling Room, and it opened with the sound of stone grinding on stone.

The vizzard removed the energy twisp from the snail shell he carried and broke off a small piece, which he cupped in his hands. He blew on it, and tiny red sparks spiraled upward until they found a pathway out of the dome. He handed the snail shell to his daughter.

"Take what is left and use it sparingly when the energy of this first thread dissipates. It will, with luck, help you find the source of the emanation we felt this morning," the vizzard said. "If you still haven't found the source when all the energy is gone, you must dip the twisp into the Web That Connects All Things. As you know from your training, that is a hazardous proposition."

Linka took the shell and tucked it under the wristband she wore on her forearm. "I will be careful, Father. You have trained me well in all things."

"May the Well of White Light keep you safe and return you to me, dear daughter," Balarius said.

Linka nodded her thanks to him and made a clicking sound. Several large fruit-eating bats fluttered down from the ceiling and landed in a circle around the queen's throne. Brownish black with fox-like faces, these bats had sought refuge at the Palay from their home in the east, where they were being captured and killed in large numbers. They had sworn to serve the Zons in exchange for refuge.

"Squad One Zons, mount," Linka commanded.

The designated Zons inserted their webbed feet into the stirrups of saddles made from the inverted skulls of the horned lizard. Their hewn copper armor glimmered in the light from the opened dome. Long battle ribbons in colors unique to each Zon streamed from the tips of the pikes on their helmets. Knots in the ribbons recorded every kill.

"Remaining squads will stay to guard our queen," Linka commanded. Then she leapt onto her own mount, Myth. "Zons, away!" she cried.

Brandishing infinators, their highly sharpened figure eight–shaped fighting blades, Linka and her contingent bolted through the open dome. "For the Queen. For the All," they cried.

The dome closed once they were clear.

The queen snapped her head toward an echoey sound emanating from the shadows. "Azzie? Is that you?"

"I hear nothing, Your Majesty," the vizzard said.

A band of nerves tightened along the queen's neck and shoulders, confirming a presence. She slashed her scepter in a circle, casting balls of red light into the farthest reaches of the Ruling Room. But the only movement came from a sow bug attempting to wriggle away through a crack in the wall. Her tongue shot across the room to catch it, and a second later she was smacking her lips.

"Sow bugs make mighty spies," she said, "and delicious snacks."

"Remember, Sister. Interrogate first. Then ingest," the vizzard joked.

"I think we know where this little morsel came from. Do we not, Brother?" She turned to her majordomo. "Simeon, I am unwell and will take to my chambers for the day. Please cancel Court."

"But, Your Majesty, the hordes will be disappointed," Simeon said.

"They must learn to live with disappointment as have I," the queen said. "Arrange a demonstration of the Royal Aqua Team Synchronized Swimmers. And be sure to have Cook prepare some opulent snacks. Perhaps some buttercups filled with congealed boll weevil bouillon, ladybug larvae paste on toasted mallow leaves, and jubilee June bug pudding. Simple things that she can whip up quickly. And have some samples of what she serves sent to my sleeping nest."

Simeon cleared his throat nervously.

The queen knew Cook would have a fit at such an order. But everyone was there to serve the queen's wishes, no matter how quixotic. And serve they would.

"Tell them not that I take to my nest, but that there is an urgent matter of state that requires my full attention."

"But, Your Majesty, I implore you to remember that you serve at the pleasure of your subjects," Simeon said.

The queen cast a withering glance at Simeon. "We will reconvene at Warming Time tomorrow."

With a flick of her scepter, her throne sank from the Ruling Room, taking her to her sleeping nest below. The croaks and calls of thousands of frogs chanting her name outside the doors echoed against the walls of the up-downer. Her subjects were not happy to be denied an audience with their queen. She closed her ear pads to the sound of their demands for justice, blessings, and condemnations and wondered if she was truly unwell or simply feeling sorry for herself yet again.

5

Nora ◎ More Bad News

Two Days Till Pink Moon
Early Morning
Salmon Falls, The Hospital

A BRANCH SNAPS IN the distance. I wake to the sound, scramble out of my sleeping bag, and crouch low to the ground.

Someone—or something—moves toward me. Is it bear or bear hunter? I can't see in the still-faint, pre-dawn light.

"Nora? Where are you?" It's my father. Relief flows through me at the sound of his voice.

A gunshot booms from beyond my sightline; its sound echoes between the surrounding mountains in an eerie way that leaves me dizzy, disoriented.

A thud shakes the ground. I run toward the vibration.

The sky lightens enough for me to see that it's my father who has fallen. I go to his side and drop to my knees, cradling his head in my arms. "Dad."

"Nora," he whispers through clenched teeth.

My eyes freeze on the blood that pours from his chest. I try to scream but no sound comes out. I press down to stop the bleeding. But it continues to ooze between my fingers—warm, but not for long.

"Who's out there? Who did this?" I yell.

Someone crashes through the brush. Whoever makes the sound is not coming to help us; they are running away.

As the sound fades, it's only Dad, the trees, and me.

"So much to say," Dad chokes out.

"No, Dad, save your strength," I urge, not knowing if I should leave him to get help or stay by his side. If only our cell phones worked in these mountains, I could call for help.

"Nora. Much will change. Pink Moon coming. Take the chance to save . . . the . . . all. You must . . ."

His words stop. His eyes go blank. I squeeze his hand, but the softness and warmth of life have fled, replaced by the feeling of leather and ice.

His last words burn in my brain. What does he mean?

I want to stay with my father's body, but I must find out who shot him. I dash for my sleeping bag and cover his body. Not his face. I can't bear to cover his face. I make a pillow for his head from my jacket—and run, my heart breaking as I leave him behind.

I pull my mountain bike from the bushes nearby while mumbling, They will pay. They will pay.

The growing light casts distorted shadows low to the ground, making it hard to judge the size of a rock or the depth of a dip. The shooter must be heading to the access road west of us.

I pivot around low branches, roll down a rock or two in the middle of my route, and skid around fallen branches from last week's windstorm yet to be cleared.

I burst through the last of the trees to see the dust cloud fading on the road ahead. I missed him.

Then I hear another shot—to my right. Another bear baiter?

Tree shadows lengthen, looking more like prison bars. Will I ever escape this nightmare?

I ride toward the sound of the second shot, which seems to have come from the opposite direction.

I find my father's parked car. But through the tears, I see no one else is there. Like a deep ocean wave trying to suck me from solid ground, I am pulled back to the spot where he lay. In my head I know he is beyond help. But in my heart, I don't want to leave him lying cold and alone in the rising light of day. But I can't go back to him—I must get help.

When I found the courage to open my eyes and dry my tears, I looked up to see Sheriff Ardith Heinze.

It took me a second to realize where I was: in the hospital. Gran and I had been there since yesterday, after she collapsed before my father's funeral even got started, canceling the whole thing.

"You okay, Nora?" the sheriff asked quietly.

I nodded, slowly coming back to reality. I had had many a nightmare since Dad died, but this one was the worst ever because it was true.

"Why don't we step outside so we don't disturb your grandmother?"

I shivered. It could only mean one thing: more trouble coming my way.

We left Gran sleeping peacefully, plugged into more than one lifesaving machine.

Sweat trickled down my face. My jaw ached from clenching. But I followed her like a good little girl, backpack slung around my shoulder.

In the hallway the sheriff motioned toward the empty visitors' lounge. She pointed toward a chair. I sat.

"Can I get you a cup of coffee or breakfast?" she asked, a soft smile on her face.

"No thanks, Sheriff Heinze." I wouldn't call her "nice." It wasn't her job to be nice. But I knew her. And liked her. Who wouldn't like Will's aunt? She'd been a tribal police officer before running for sheriff of our county.

"Will tells me you've been having a hard time, what with your dad's death and now your gran. Your family is good people. I'm sorry for your troubles." She paused. "I know you talked to another officer right after your dad died, my vacation fill-in. His notes indicate that you didn't have much to say. That both you and your grandmother were pretty much in shock when you got the news. Any chance you'd be willing to talk about it again? To me?"

I had just been through it all in my dream. Did I really have to go through it again? Her eyes were on me. Waiting. Reluctantly, I nodded.

"So why were you and your dad up the mountain so early the morning that he died?"

I shuffled through my backpack and took out a piece of white paper folded in thirds. It looked like a worthless piece of paper in my hands, but looks can lie. I handed it to her. She read my father's name on the front, made from letters cut and torn from old newspapers and magazines.

Then she opened it and read the collaged words inside. "Bear baiting. Dawn. Sequoia grove."

"Looks like a ransom note from an old movie," I said. "And when I found this on our doorstep, the glue was still wet."

She paused for a moment. I think she wanted me to jump in with more information. But I was too busy shaking inside to talk.

"I take it the note was referring to your grove of sequoias up the mountain."

I nodded. Practically everyone in town knew where the grove was. It was an unofficial summer picnic site and tourist attraction on part of our tree farm. We didn't take kindly to trespassers. No tree farmer does. But there was little to do but post "no trespassing" signs.

"Forward-thinking, that ancestor of yours," she said. She was referring to Virgil Wallace Peters, my great-great-great-grand-father, who in his wisdom had planted thousands of sequoia seedlings back in the day.

"We aren't sure if he knew that sequoias grew here eons ago when the earth was warmer, or if he just liked the trees," I said. It was a family mystery; we had no documentation, only imagination, to solve it. Since signs of climate change have been around for more than the last two centuries, we liked to think that he knew the climate would shift again as the earth warmed, so that sometime in the future, these prehistoric giants (and huge carbon sinks) might be a great choice to replace our western red cedars, hemlocks, firs, and other trees as they died out.

Whoever left the note knew all about these trees, which are now hundreds of feet tall. But why target bears on our property? Bears are everywhere up in the mountains, and some tree farmers allow hunters to come onto their property, lure the bears to a spot with cheap food, and murder them on sight.

Bear baiting is illegal in Washington state, but there is a loophole in the law that makes it okay to kill any bear suspected of destroying the bark on valuable timber. The bark blocks sugar-hungry bears from getting a quick sugar fix from the inner phloem of the tree. And damaged bark can kill profit by killing the tree. And while black bears weren't the only 'bark strippers' in the forest, they had the capacity of damaging up to 70 trees in a day.

Bear baiting is cruel, and every bear is assumed guilty. But trees were commodities that needed to be protected for profit. There were several ways, short of bear baiting, to modify their behavior, including providing food pellets to feed the bears at their hungriest in the spring.

Not everyone thought that was a good idea. But we did it anyway. We also increased plant diversity in the area so there were other sources of food for the bears. Dad always said that we depended on nature for our livelihood. The least we could do was be a cooperative partner. The downside of it, in addition to the cost and labor, is that it attracted more bears to our property. And someone had taken it into their head that they could butt into our business and kill them.

"So, someone summoned your dad there with a note," the sheriff said. "But why did *you* go?"

I shrugged my shoulders. "Seemed like the right thing to do," I said. "You know, Sheriff, do you mind if we finish up this conversation later? I *really* need to get back to Gran. The doctor will be coming in soon and I'm worried about what's going on with her health. And I want to get a lawyer too. Can I call you in an hour to let you know when and where?"

The sheriff gave a curt nod and handed me her business card. "Don't make me wait too long. We really need to discuss why you were there and why you haven't told anyone."

I got up to leave when a question for her popped into my brain. I said, "I wonder if someone was really baiting my dad and not the bears."

6

Azzie 🐸 Dark Winds Rising

Two Days Till Pink Moon
Dew Time (Early Morning)
Outside the Veil of Mist

PURPLE FLYCAPE STREAMING behind him, crown askew, Prince Azzie was surfing the breezes on a leaf, or burfing, as frogs called it. He had chosen his wardrobe carefully for the occasion. Nothing ostentatious. His flycape was dyed the color of the sky using a unique combination of cornflower blue, purple hyacinth, dogwood bark, and fruit, and it was finely embroidered with a depiction of what was about to take place: the Ceremony of Renewal. His crown was a modest ring of hammered gold embedded with glittery blue sapphire gemstones so that it would be easy for bystanders to see the jewels' reflections in the sky.

He was finally on his way to the new site of the faux Ceremony of Renewal, having snuck out of the Palay without his escort. His mother would be furious. But when he returned triumphant from the ceremony, all would be forgiven. His mother had somewhat of a short attention span when it came to disciplining him. And he was grateful for it.

He knew that to use the actual and more conveniently located ceremonial site for the fake ceremony would be sacrilege. That's why his mother had built a stand-in well beyond the Veil of Mist. It was in a still-hidden spot where it could be easily attended by field frogs (the designation for all frogs living outside the grounds of the Palay) from the surrounding Hinterlands. It was also, however, located deep in largetoe territory and Azzie had never even flown past the Veil of Mist before.

Moving forward, since frogs were so ubiquitous around the world, a new location would be chosen each year for the month of the Pink Moon. It would be the only way he could see as much of the world as he wanted to before becoming king. And why was this happening now? Azzie had just come of age, and from now on, it was his duty as the reigning frog prince to engage in the Ceremony of Renewal, fake or not.

There hadn't been a renewal ceremony since the Golden Pearl of the Forest had gone missing, long ago. This recent scheme of establishing a faux Ceremony of Renewal had been his mother's idea. She wanted to distract her subjects from their troubles, which were many and growing.

But Azzie bristled at the fact that his mother didn't even try to hold Part Two of the ceremony: the Confab of the All, which was a sacred meeting of all life forms in a secret place known only to frog royalty. Azzie didn't understand why his mother never called for a confab, and she always changed the subject or outright refused to discuss it the few times he'd asked.

As far as he could see, nothing could be accomplished without largetoe representation. They created the problems and it was on them to fix things. Surely, if they all ganged up on the largetoe and held them to account, things would have to change. Just imagine the chaos it would cause if all Nature rebelled.

And Linka and the vizzard always played into his mother's demands—never questioning her about anything. That's what a monocracy was, he supposed, but they were a family. And weren't families supposed to fight and discuss things?

But unquestioning devotion to his mother was not the only reason he was not fond of his cousin. He despised Linka's effort-less perfection and ambition. Nothing came easy to Azzie. But everything did to Linka. She was afraid of nothing and competed with him in all things, especially getting his mother's attention.

Even as tads they had not gotten along, although if their Aunt DeLili had ruled, he would never have had to worry about being king. And Linka would never be queen (something Azzie was sure she'd try to maneuver when the time came). His aunt's progeny would have carried the line of succession.

Enough of Palay politics. For the first time in his life, he had flown outside the ancient trees that bordered the inner sanctum of the Palay and through the Veil of Mist, where he had to endure a horrifying moment of *wet* before entering the Land of the Largetoe.

The contrast between the beauty of his home and the ugliness of the outer world was great. Particles with a leaden quality pockmarked the air and gave it the consistency of tree sap, which made it hard to fly through. The air around the Palay was always alive with a spectrum of colors that only frogs saw, like umba, esbue, tuw, pule, rue, and rink. Palay air was playful and danced when Azzie flew through it, whirling and twirling in patterns that made him laugh with delight. The lifeless air of the outer world was the color of yellow mud and markedly more difficult to command.

But it was not only the air that was so altered. As he flew over mountains, valleys, and plains, it was clear just how the largetoe had decimated the land. Forests gone, rivers dammed, towns and cities pockmarking the landscape. These sights made him ill.

And then there were the towns where largetoe dwelled in great numbers. Smoke and other offensive vapors were belched out of buildings and moving transport in alarming quantities. Could the largetoe see what they were doing to the All? Didn't they care?

Perhaps to cheer himself up he should compose an extemporaneous tune and sing it at the top of his lungs in his magnificent (if he said so himself) tenor voice to drive the darkness that gripped him away and fill the air with the beautiful colors of sound. He hummed a little tune, but it had no life, no verve. And lyrics wouldn't come. So, he flew on in silence and, with growing dismay, longing for his splendiferous home.

A plunge in atmospheric pressure pinched Azzie's flesh. He cursed his lack of a neck, which made it impossible to simply turn around to see what had changed in his surroundings. If he tried to look, he'd fall off his leaf. But the prickly sensation crawling up his spine was hard to ignore. Was he being stalked by a bird of prey?

His temples prickled, throbbed, then pounded as he traveled in suspense hopalometer after hopalometer. If only frogs could swivel their heads like owls.

When his terror built to a breaking point, he removed his crown and thrust it into a hidden pocket in his flycape and executed a loop-de-loop, which revealed a huge, dark, roiling cloud chasing him. It was the color of charred forest, with jagged bolts of blood-red lightning that sparked and sizzled at its center.

Contaminated currents of air whipped around the cloud center like thready tentacles, making the winds appear as if they were a dark, angry octopus in the sky with flashing, fury-filled eyes. He called to the little windlets that whipped along under him to pick up their pace.

He knew that if the cloud caught up with him, he would be dashed from his leaf and dropped into the great river that lay ahead. Azzie's lifelong terror of water, brought on by a bad first-breath experience, was an unfortunate affliction for a frog.

A blast of air from the dark mass struck him. He rocked side to side until he could steady himself, then, gripping the edges of the leaf, somersaulted onto an air stream that moved straight toward the churning mass of dark air.

"Do you know who I am?" he shouted.

"We do, and we demand your attention," the Dark Winds called to him in several dialects at once. The combined sound was high-pitched and grating, like bear claws swiped across slate. The stench emanating from the collection of polluted winds pinched Azzie's nose and made his eyes water.

Azzie hovered in place.

"What do you want of me?" he said, grateful for once to his mother, who had forced him to study so many dialects of wind language. There were few frogs, save himself and his mother, who would have understood what they were saying.

"We must speak with your mother."

"We?" Azzie asked.

"We are the collected fetid Winds of the Earth, sullied by contamination from the factories and farm animals and machines humankind has let loose, and we are on our way to demand that the queen do her duty."

"And what duty is that?"

"She is the Voice of Nature. She must lead the revolt against the largetoe. Destroy their homes. Drive them from the earth."

Azzie rode in circles in front of the winds, surprised by the strength of their anger against his mother. "That seems unfair. She is only one frog. How can she possibly solve every problem?"

The Dark Winds struck him with a sharp blow against his head. "She does nothing to resolve the matter between humans and the All. Nothing. While we all suffer. Winds are eternal, but the filth that we must now carry about is making us vengeful and full of rage. And it is your mother's fault. Why does she not insist that a real Ceremony of Renewal take place and not this folly which you are about to attend? We were not even invited to the proceedings—none of the Elementos were—nor were any other creatures. It's only for frogs and it's only for show."

The winds were whipping up an angry fire in Azzie's belly, but he was so dizzy and disoriented he couldn't settle on a course of action. Then the dense, acrid, angry air sucked him into its center and whirled him in a tight spiral. Round and round he spun, unable to escape the centrifugal force of the turbulence. Drops of blood formed on his skin from the pressure, and there was only one way to escape the clutch of the winds. But it, too, meant probable death and was the second most terrifying of all his anxieties: free fall. Did he have the courage to attempt it, the luck to survive?

Bloody tears flooded his eyes and ran down his face. He went limp and let his burfing leaf slip out from under him. Momentum propelled him from the vortex of the spiral to its edge and spit him out the other side.

He hung in the air for two strokes of a hummingbird's wing, then plunged toward the earth, his cape flapping around his face, making it impossible to see.

Azzie clawed at his frogklath, pulling it from his face, and called out to the winds as he fell. "Dark Winds, I am sorry for my bad manners." He ripped off his wrist band, made of rough-hewn silver and gold in the shape of a spiderweb with a fire opal spider at its center, and tossed it to the wind.

"Take this to my mother. She will grant you an audience."

The Dark Winds sucked in the bracelet without a word of thanks and blew off toward the Palay while the prince continued his fall.

Azzie stuck out his arms and legs and spread the webs on his hands and feet to slow himself and give him some control over his direction. When that didn't work, he fought to draw the corners of his flycape together to form a chute. But the cloak's clasp, a cracked geode the size of an overripe elderberry, pressed against his throat, nearly choking him.

Wheezing, he released the cape corners and fell faster. If only he had worn his arachnachute. But he was prideful about his burfing skills and refused to rely on this backup.

As he fell, images from his past flicked through his mind like gnats: missed ceremonies, cracking up with his cohorts during solemn rituals, sleeping during Royal Chorales as a tad back before his passion for composing seized him. So many occasions when he exhibited an irreverent lack of knack for ruling. Not much to show for his life. And all because his mother had disdain for his opinions and ideas. Her way was the only way, so why should he bother?

In the distance, a flock of purple martins tore across the sky. He called for help. The martins headed his way. The Mud-Mud-Muddy raced over half-submerged rocks below. He would die on impact. What would it matter if he died on earth or water? He would still be dead.

"Great Well of White Light, spare me such a death, and I will do my best to be the prince that I should be."

The Well always listened. But would its answer echo back to him in time?

7

Nora ◎ Bitten by the Past

Two Days Till Pink Moon
Morning
Salmon Falls, The Hospital

As I WALKED back into the hospital room, I heard Gran moan.

"Gran? You okay?" I asked and gently rubbed the papery skin on her arm, which was hot and dry.

She didn't answer, so I pulled a chair up and sat down, scanning her for any sign that she was in distress and needed more attention than I could give. The bruise on her face, still black and purple around the edges, was no longer hidden by her fantastic makeup job. She had fallen harder than she let anyone know.

I wanted to kiss the bruise to make it go away as she had done when I was little, but I was afraid it still hurt. So instead, I sang a song while a mash-up of life-giving machines played background music.

Sweet little tadpole
Resting in the pond
Soon your legs will grow
Then you'll be gone
Onto the land
Out of the water
At home anywhere,
My lovely little daughter.

My mom had sung it when I was little. And while the words to this song didn't exactly fit Gran's situation, it calmed me to sing it.

Memories of stories that Mom used to make up for me flowed back. Elaborate and wildly imaginative. What did she call them? If only I could remember. I treasured every little thing that had any association with my mother. Sometimes I would lie in bed at night and try to remember the sound of her voice until my heart and brain ached from the effort. But the memory of how she sounded was gone. Somewhere we had home videos of us together. But I hadn't been brave enough to watch them. Someday. When the pain of her loss wasn't so sharp.

But I did remember this song, and I remembered that Mom had been kind and loving and really, really cared about us all— even Gran, who was crusty on occasion to everyone. No one, even a woman as stellar as Mom, was good enough for her son, or so it seemed from the little remarks Gran had made about Mom through the years. It was a shame they'd never built a relationship on what they had in common: they both loved Dad.

Gran's eyes fluttered open.

For the first time since yesterday, I took a deep breath.

"Reggie? Is that you?" As Gran spoke, her speech slurred.

My chest tightened. Gran thought I was Mom again—and the thought didn't seem to please her.

"I kept your pouch because I *knew* you couldn't stay away," she said.

I was surprised by the note of sarcasm in Gran's voice.

"Purse," she said, her smile lopsided. "Been there all the time." She tried to wink, but her face didn't work right.

I fetched her bag from the bedside drawer and popped the clasp for her.

With trembling hands, Gran pulled out Mom's pouch. "Here."

She closed my fingers around it. My mother had always worn the pouch around her neck and tucked into her clothing. I pulled my hand away. The soft doeskin deepened the constant ache I carried inside.

"We've all missed you, Reggie. Even me. I'm sorry we weren't closer—my fault, mostly—but now that you're back, maybe we can mend things—for the girl's sake. Put it on and everything will be as it was," my grandmother said, growing more insistent.

I couldn't do it.

Gran's breathing quickened.

I placed the cord of the pouch around my neck to calm her down.

"There," my grandmother said with a sigh. "Promise kept. You said . . . never give it to Nora and I didn't. Instead, I kept it close to me, hoping someday you'd be back . . . and I could give it to you and make amends for how badly I treated you."

Just then Mel Finley stepped inside the room. Right when I was finally getting some answers from Gran.

Gran's eyes grew wide when she saw him. Was that fear or confusion? I wondered for a moment what the heck was going on between them. She had had a similar reaction at the church when they were talking. "Water," she croaked. Closing her eyes, she turned her head away. She wasn't up for visitors, especially Mel.

I picked up the empty water pitcher and headed into the hall, motioning Finley to follow me.

I closed the door behind us and headed to the water dispenser, but he blocked my way. "Is there something you need?" I asked.

"No, just wanted to check in on Ellie. See how she is."

"Well, you saw."

We stood facing each other in uncomfortable silence for a moment. Then I walked past him as I rounded the corner to the water and ice machine.

He followed, trying to catch up, but I managed to stay a step ahead of him so I didn't have to look him in the eye. For whatever reason, this guy was giving me the serious creeps.

"Nora, I'm a bit confused about something."

I placed the pitcher on the water dispenser, my back toward him, and pressed the fill button.

He tried to peer over my shoulder. I felt his breath and jumped to the side, spilling water on the floor.

"Whoa, Nora, I'm not going to hurt you," he said like he believed it. But I didn't.

"What are you confused about?" I asked, trying to get this over with as soon as possible.

I grabbed a mop from a cleaning cart in the hallway and handed it to him. He took it with a look of distaste and mopped up the water while he spoke.

"Do you know if your dad ever executed the papers on the conservation easement? I helped him prepare them and was wondering why he would have sold your property to Kincade when he had already prepared the easement."

There was something seriously weird about Finley. His words were meant to sound sympathetic, but his sentiment didn't match.

"Last time we talked about it, that was the plan. But then"—it was still hard to say this—"he died. And Kincade showed up with his papers."

"Maybe your dad left those papers lying around the house, or maybe he actually filed them with the county."

"Don't worry, we're checking into everything," I said.

"Good. I guess if he *didn't* file them that probably meant he was no longer interested in doing the conservation easement because he decided to sell, which would mean Kincade was right about the deal," Finley said.

I wanted to ask, *Whose side are you on?* but held back, feeling not for the first time that this guy, whom Dad and Gran had always depended on, was no friend of our family's. Dad and I had fought about Finley more than once. And Gran had always taken Dad's side. According to them, he was an asset to the family. I always thought he was just an ass and resented his irritation at anything I did or said.

"Kincade? *Right?* No. We'll get a lawyer and look into the whole thing."

I decided to keep to myself what I was *really* thinking: that if Dad *had* dated, signed, and submitted the easement papers before he dated and signed the sale to Kincade, that could mean Kincade's sale wasn't valid.

"Think you're pretty smart don't you?" he asked, trying to suppress a sneer.

"Why are you so interested?" I asked.

"Well—I worked for your dad, and I have an interest in keeping my job."

"Not an interest in helping our family?"

"Of course. Of course."

I didn't believe him.

"Let me know if you find those documents, will you?"

There was something patronizing about what he said and how he said it. Like his stake in this had more value than mine. Without Dad or Gran to talk me down, I snapped. "You're not going to have to worry about keeping your job with us any longer, Mr. Finley, because Gran told me to let you know that we didn't need your services anymore."

"Ellie actually said that?"

"Yes," I lied.

He threw the mop down. "She's going to be sorry she said that. It's time to pay up. And pay she will. You both will."

He stomped away.

A sense of relief flooded over me. I felt free. Well, pretty free. I'd have to somehow deal with running the everyday business now and go to school. It was a small price to pay to get him out of our lives.

With a full water pitcher, I headed back toward Gran's room. But I stopped when I heard voices inside. I peeked around and saw two women cleaning. I recognized Mrs. Hayashi, the mother of my friend Kikko. She was dusting. The other woman had her back to me.

"Poor dear," said the woman I couldn't see. Her voice, which was oddly familiar, sounded scratchy, like sandpaper on glass. "She deserves better than this. A dead son and a weird granddaughter."

Weird? Is that what people thought about me?

"Nora's a wonderful girl," Kikko's mom said.

I smiled. Her words were like a soft Band-Aid on my heart.

"And don't go talking in front of Mrs. Peters like she's already dead. She may hear you and understand you even if she *is* unconscious," Mrs. Hayashi said.

"Nora's mother was even a bigger piece of work."

I had to grit my teeth to stop from screaming at her.

"I thought you two used to be best friends," Mrs. Hayashi said.

"Us? Ha," said the other voice. "She's a liar. In fact, I don't think she's even dead. I think she ran away with another man."

Mrs. Hayashi gasped. "The Peters are all good people, and I won't have you talking that way about any of them."

Go, Mrs. Hayashi.

"But—"

"No. Enough of your wild theories," Mrs. Hayashi said, irritation rising in her voice. "Let's leave this poor woman to rest."

"You go on ahead," said the other woman. "I want to water the flowers."

"Don't be long," Mrs. Hayashi said.

I ducked into the next room, which thankfully was empty, until Mrs. Hayashi left. As her footsteps faded, I popped back into Gran's room and caught the other woman going through the drawers on the bedside table.

"Hey, stop that."

The woman whipped around. It was Seth's mother.

"Mrs. Kincade? What are you doing?"

Sarah Kincade's face turned bright red. "I . . . well, I work here," she said.

"And why are you going through Gran's things?"

"Don't be silly. I'm straightening." Her embarrassment drained to a pasty white and her face looked pinched.

"Maybe you were looking for this." I whipped out the pouch from around my neck.

Her eyes popped wide, and she reached out for it with a trembling hand.

"Did you come to get it for your husband? It's not enough that he's stealing our property," I said. "He has to take every last thing we own too?"

"You don't understand. Carl wasn't taking the pouch for him. He was taking it for me. I'm the one who made it. I'm the one who gave it to your mom."

That was a shock. I didn't even know they'd been friends.

"And now you want it back," I said, holding it up like a prize ribbon at the fair.

"I don't. Truly. But he's left me no choice. He wants it and that's it."

"Maybe he doesn't want the pouch—he wants what's inside," I said more to myself than to her. I should have probably kept that thought to myself.

Confusion crossed her face. "What's inside? That has nothing to do with me."

I wasn't sure I believed her. Could it be Seth's dad was so egotistical and controlling that he didn't really care about what she thought—he only cared about himself? If anybody asked me, I'd say yes. But who would ask? I felt sorry for Seth's mom.

Mrs. Kincade bowed her head. An anemic tear squeezed out of one eye and ran down her cheek. "I told Carl that the pouch had been a gift. It was so long ago, what did it matter?"

"But why say such nasty things about my mom? That really hurt. Surely you don't think they're true?"

She didn't say a word, but her face turned red, and her body seemed to shrink into itself. If she made herself any smaller, she'd probably disappear.

"You'd better leave now," I said. "And don't ever come near my grandmother again. As for the pouch, it's staying right where it is." I tucked it back inside my shirt and stepped to the side so she could pass.

"You won't tell Seth about this, will you?" she said.

"I don't know yet. I'll have to see."

Shoulders hunched, head down, she walked to the door and held onto the wall to steady herself. She pivoted to look at me.

"Things were not supposed to turn out this way." Then she hurried away.

Things? What *things*?

I rushed to Gran's bedside to make sure she was okay.

She was asleep. But her shallow, rapid breaths didn't seem right. I pushed the call button and waited for the nurse to come. I was getting seriously pissed at the Kincades. All the Kincades. Was Seth even my friend? It broke my heart for the thought to enter my head, but blood's thicker than water, so they say.

And money is thicker than blood. The Kincades thought they could take what they wanted because it was good for their pocketbooks, like some huge corporation taking resources from the earth to profit, without a thought about the cost to the environment.

Carl and Sarah Kincade were out to take everything from my family, down to something Gran carried in her purse. Greedy, greedy people. Greed destroyed. And I was not about to let that happen to what little was left of my family and what was ours. Time to fight back or go down trying. Even if it meant losing any future Seth and I might have as friends—or something more.

8

The Queen
One Frog Dreaming

Two Days Till Pink Moon
Warming Time (Early)
The Palay, Ruling Room

THE RULING ROOM was quiet. The queen had finished her morning meditation and was concerned that it had not left her overflowing with energy as it usually did. She was still not in top form after yesterday's stressful morning, even though she had kept to her nest for the remainder of the day and faithfully taken a regular dose of the tincture of termite she had prepared herself.

Had she not been queen, her tonics and tinctures, poultices and potions would have made her a famed healer throughout the queendom. But she couldn't publicly compete with her brother's talents lest she diminish his reputation, so she kept her concoctions to herself. When she did share them with her intimate circle, she always labeled the container with a stamp of her brother's hand, not hers. He knew, of course, and was happy to take credit for her brilliant brews.

She scanned the energy of the room, searching for a certain frequency: sow bugs. But she could sense none.

Ranya hated those traitorous balls of legs and antennae—available at a price to any scoundrel in the world. For all she knew, there were thousands hiding in the walls waiting to probe the room and sell their surveillance reports to the highest bidder. They were purely loyal to their stomachs, and even she, with her prodigious appetite, could only eat so many a day.

Using a jewel-encrusted mirror, Ranya examined the placement of today's fluff-of-milkweed crown, made with the finest shards of rod crystal and charcoal-colored diamond seeds. Her scepter was a golden facsimile of a milkweed stalk, topped with a milky quartz in the shape of a milkweed pod designed to complement her crown.

Today, she sat on her ametrine throne. The bottom was carved from a band of rich amethyst, and then fanning out behind her, the purple band blended with a band of orange, then yellow citrine. Ametrine always increased her energetic and intuitive connection to the Well of White Light and left her feeling like she alone could change the world.

There would be no holding back the hordes today. She would spend the morning granting supplications and applying justices. Time to begin.

With a wave of her scepter, rocks and islands of sand, mud, and earth rose from the floor. Some of the mounds sprouted toadstools of various heights, allowing courtiers to choose the most comfortable perch for themselves. Water sprang from the many fountains in the floor, which had a mosaic pattern in shades of green and blue that resembled ripples in a pond. The Ruling Room was ready to receive.

"Simeon, the doors."

Simeon nodded to the doorkeepers, who worked together to open both sides of the great arched door, and the horde poured in.

Lord Raeburn, a grand-tailed frog, was the first to enter. Queen Ranya resisted the urge to rub the scar from a gash on her shoulder, a gift from Raeburn delivered during battle practice as youths. The sight of him always made it throb.

He vaulted ahead of the pack and landed too close to the throne. The Zons leapt in front of him, infinators drawn.

"What an aggressive way to start the morning, Lord Raeburn," the queen said.

"Pardon me. But I had heard you were unwell, Your Majesty, and wanted to be sure for myself that you were fine. May you live a millennium more—although, surely, you are looking peaky today. Is your health in order? I do hope so," Lord Raeburn said as he tried to mosey past the Zons, who again blocked his way.

"Do not bother with your phony well-wishes. We both know you want me dead."

"And you do not wish the same of me, Majesty?"

"A dangerous question, Raeburn. Now, what outrageous demands will you assault me with today?"

"You make me sound like a greedy groundhog, Majesty."

"We both know that's *exactly* what you are."

"Very well. I will not disappoint," Raeburn said in his piercing voice. "I demand domain over the new dreaming pods that are about to start construction."

"What makes you think you have any chance to take on more dream power when you both neglect and overwork the dreamers you already employ?" Queen Ranya said.

"Your Majesty, it humbles me to point out your ignorance, but they are no longer called 'dreamers' because, obviously, they cannot dream. We younger crowd refer to them as CODERs, which stands for "converters of dream energy.""

"Presumptuous provocateur," the queen sneered under her breath. She refused to acknowledge his correction.

"And I must protest, in the strongest terms, your assertion that I overwork and neglect my crew. Your Majesty, I am appalled by such accusations. How could you accuse me, your most loyal courtier, of such heinous activity?"

The queen scoffed, taking a moment to notice the other courtiers gathering around Raeburn. "Do you think I do not know what goes on in my own Palay? Think again. This is your last warning, Raeburn. Your CODERs are to get immediate relief and going forth are not to be on duty for more than the already established time periods. And no dabbling in the dark arts. This is not the Maw of Malevolence. This is the source of dream energy for the entire world."

"For the entire largetoe world," Raeburn said. "Why we must supply those horrible creatures with the energy to dream so they can conjure up even more ways to destroy us is beyond me."

"Hold your tongue, Lord Raeburn, or you may not have one for long," the queen snapped. Then she indulged in the enticing image of using her own longer and more lethal tongue to decapitate him with one flick. She fought the urge to smile at the thought. "My decision is final. Lord Bumbleberry, in honor of your magnificent loyalty to the throne, I award you the soon-to-be-constructed dreaming pods."

The room was silent as all attention focused on the toadstool where the elderly Lord Bumbleberry blissfully snored.

A courtier prodded Bumbleberry. He cocked one eye open and smacked his giant toothless mouth. Spittle flew in all directions. Then his gracious lord fell promptly back to sleep.

The queen stifled a groan at her unfortunate choice and willed herself not to glance skyward in disgust. Courtiers chittered away.

"Another dynamic, forward-thinking decision, Majesty. I congratulate you." Raeburn feigned a demi-dip. "I suppose you will continue to award incoming refuge seekers to Lord Bumbleberry?"

"Need I remind you, Lord Raeburn, that any member of the Frog Clan unfortunate enough to lose their homes to largetoe destruction is welcome here. They are full citizens of the Palay, with all rights and freedoms granted them. They are not here for your convenience. And when they come, we treat them with the respect they deserve as members of our global family. I do not 'award' refuge seekers to anyone. They are *not* property. Members of the greater Frog Council are in positions of power and privilege—as you know. Some, like Bumbleberry, act with compassion for our new arrivals. You treat everyone badly, Raeburn. From your dreamers—CODERS!—to your own family. Why do you think I would make it easy for you to expand your ring of cruelty?"

"I do not have any idea what you are talking about, Majesty. I offer to feed and employ new arrivals like others in my position. Yes, my expectations may be different, but under the Rules of the Dream Charter, I have some leeway in how I get my CODERs to process the energy allotments to which I am entitled. We have the highest production records around," Raeburn said.

"And the highest incidence of dream madness, which comes from the overuse of our transformational power," the queen said.

"To call my practices a 'ring of cruelty' goes too far. I will not demand an apology, but do not forget—I can," he said. "And then you will be forced to deal with me on my level."

The queen's great body shook with laughter. "You? Challenge me? That's a step too low."

"I have the right to challenge you. But it is such a beautiful day, and I have other plans, so for now, your throne is safe." With palpable disdain, Raeburn moved away from the queen. His loyal band of followers crowded around him, whispering and nattering like a clutch of silly tads.

It was dangerous to underestimate Raeburn, she knew. His power-seeking ways would need to be curbed. If decapitation was too bloody, perhaps a little accident—a drowning for instance—might be in order. Such a tempting thought. Or maybe she should egg him on to that challenge he sought and devour him before it began.

Was it the thought of eating Raeburn that sent a queasy ripple through her formidable belly? Perhaps that third helping of sand-fly souffle she had eaten at fast breaking was to blame. Or anxiety over that mysterious energetic wave that had swept the world yesterday.

So many things to worry about, including the whereabouts and well-being of her son. Could their combined effect be taking their toll? The queen's head and shoulders pulsated with the rhythm of her heart. Then, in a moment of knowing, she understood the reason for her disquiet.

Another dream comes my way.

The coming of a dream always surprised and terrified Queen Ranya down to her webtoes. While all frogs could amplify and direct dream energy sent by the Well of White Light (which dwelled under Frog Mountain), Queen Ranya was the only frog gifted to *receive* dreams from the Well, a power given to *her* by the Well itself when she ascended the throne.

"Vizzard? Where are you?" she called.

"I am here, Majesty."

Wheezing, the vizzard moved to her side. "Dreamtime comes," the queen said.

"May the Well of White Light give you strength, My Queen," the vizzard said. She could see shock register on his face.

"The dreams seem to be coming faster and faster, Your Majesty," Simeon said. "And each one holds a more desperate warning."

"Without these dreams, the Royal House of Ranya could not warn endangered populations to leave their homes and make their way to the refuge of the Palay," said the queen.

"Only if they can get here," the vizzard whispered.

"My airtilliers do what they can to protect them on their journey. But there are only so many I can send," the queen said.

"It is both painful and terrifying to see General Oddbull and his Bulldoggies grow ever bolder and more powerful," the vizzard said.

"How is it that he knows our secret trails? And the times of transport?" the queen asked.

Sounds of a scuffle came from the back of the room.

"What is that?" the queen demanded. "I must know."

A Zon escorted a frog to the front of the room.

"Clarenso?" the vizzard exclaimed when he saw his aide at the Zon's side. "Are you the source of this terrible commotion?"

"This is my throne room. I will ask the questions," the queen said. "Clarenso, why are you caterwauling?"

"Grant me grace, Your Glory. We have news of a most devastating nature."

The queen's heart clenched like a fist. Her breathing grew shallower and faster. "What is it then? Do not spare me the truth."

Clarenso twisted the corner of his tunic, shredding the delicate fabric, and choked out his report.

"General Oddbull's Bulldoggies have captured yet another band of refuge-seekers and dragged them off to the Maw."

Horrified gasps filled the room, then the hubbub quieted.

"We do not know the details, Your Supremeness." Clarenso choked back a sob.

"Your nephew?" the vizzard asked.

Clarenso bit down on his clenched hand and nodded.

"This is grave. The Bulldoggies grow so strong; fewer groups now arrive at the Palay. And you know what that means," the vizzard said.

"Increasingly, our beloved brethren are being churned into the Maw and . . ." Ranya could not bring herself to continue.

"And made into idilons," the vizzard whispered.

At the mention of that terrible name, a full-body spasm seized Ranya, and particles of white light danced above her head. If only she could swim away from her duty. But she had stolen the throne from another. And she would take the punishment for her crime in the form of these soul-crushing dreams. She closed her eyes in submission. It could not be resisted. Nor was there time to clear the great room to give her the privacy she craved.

The dream had arrived.

9

Nora ◎ Mother Nature's Commandos

Two Days Till Pink Moon
Late Morning
Salmon Falls

I HAD SAID GOODBYE to Gran even though she was sleeping. I walked out of the hospital toward our rather pathetic downtown area and its stench of overcooked broccoli in the air thanks to the nearby papermill.

I'd broken into a run, maneuvering around broken pavement and missing sections of sidewalk. The morning air cooled my face and for a moment I simply existed in the world. But instead of feeling good, I felt pinched and achy.

Just running past vacant storefronts hurt. Breathing in the hints of papermill, which never seemed to clear the air, hurt too. Winter's leftovers—dry leaves, plastic bags, and other litter—tumbled down the street pushed by the wind. I snagged whatever pieces I could along the way, slam-dunking them into the odd trash can as I went.

I never got why people littered. It was like they couldn't see what was right in front of them. That was the goal of Mother Nature's Commandos: to get people to see the damage humankind was doing to the planet, with the hope that if they did, they'd stop. Unfortunately, more often than we liked, people weren't even aware of their behavior, and those who were aware weren't always interested in changing it. What would it take for them to see the light of truth? Or simply to care? We didn't know. But we kept trying to figure it out.

The dilapidated state of our main street made my heart ache, and I sat on a bench that had been part of a bus stop when our town had the budget for a bus system. All around me, the fabric of our town was frayed and worn. I felt frayed too. I took some deep breaths and sighed loudly to drain some stress away. There was no one around to hear or judge.

Closing my eyes and leaning back, I pictured meeting up with my friends. That always put a smile on my face. But there was one person I was nervous about seeing. Seth. After what his dad had done at my dad's funeral, I had no idea what I'd say to him if he were there. Should we even be talking, with all the legal stuff that was about to come down?

It had been fun getting to know him better since Minh had brought him into the Commandos. Even though we'd gone to school together since the beginning of our school days, we never spent much time with each other because of the history between our families, which was like the Capulets and the Montagues. But even though we were crushy toward each other, I had no plans to play Juliet to Seth's, or anyone else's, Romeo.

I wasn't ready to have an "us" story. I needed to know what my own story was before I got deep into someone else's. And I didn't want to change my destination in life before I even knew where *I* wanted to go. My mother had changed everything about herself—from where she lived to how she spent her days—just to be with my dad. I wouldn't be doing that for anyone. Not just yet anyway.

I couldn't deny I was attracted—okay, *really* attracted—to him. He was the only guy I knew who could discuss laminated root rot, water stress, and so many of the other challenges midsized tree farmers like us shared. We were just getting around to admitting our interest in each other slowly, since everything between us was a bit of a tangled root ball that went back over a hundred years to the rift between our families.

Enough ruminating. I continued on my way, unable to stop thinking about Seth as I passed more small-town blight.

When I reached what we jokingly called our "hideout"—a room in the basement of Minh's family restaurant that we were welcome to use when Minh wasn't working—I wasn't quite ready to put my own thoughts aside.

It had been a shock that the sheriff knew I'd been at the scene of my father's death. Though I did leave all my stuff up there when I ran after Dad's murderer. Didn't matter. They knew. And now everyone would know. And everyone would be talking about it all over town. That's the way small towns were.

I guess, in a way, Dad's death was my fault. I knew he wouldn't want me to think that, so I tried to keep from going there. But now others might think so too. And they might not be as forgiving. Except my friends.

They'd be finding out soon enough. And I would tell them about my crazy vision at Dad's funeral. Might as well get it all out at once. I was pretty sure they would understand and support me, but I've been wrong before.

Enough of my problems. Our local ecosystem had issues that were much more important to fix. And more than one solution would be required to make the needed changes. Tragically, there was no going back—climate change was well underway, even here. From earlier springs, to lack of snowfall, to weakened resiliency in too many species —it was just getting harder to survive with the negative changes happening all over the world.

All we could do was try to soften its impact. Would we be able to bring back the thousands of species that had gone extinct? No. Could we bring back habitats that had been destroyed? Maybe some. But we might be able to repair those still under threat and protect the too few pristine places left on Earth.

Our motto was "Give Mother Earth a Rest." Our message? "Stop the destruction! Stop!" We couldn't understand why the people who had all the power wouldn't do absolutely everything they could to save our future. We couldn't wait. Earth couldn't wait. We had to do everything we could. Now. And even though the problems seemed endless, we all believed that we were the solution. We had to be. It was our future and the future of the world we were dealing with.

We'd been doing lots of activism over the past year, with local issues like light pollution, plastic bag use, and other political issues where there were two sides: ours and theirs. And the only arrows in our quiver were things like texts and phone calls, petitions, marches. But there never seemed to be much of an impact. So we started a water testing program to track things like water temperature, alkalinity, and other measurements that revealed our water's quality. We were learning while making a difference. That felt good.

We also helped get a local plastic bag ban ordinance passed, but there were so many exceptions (like containers for hot food) that it didn't seem like a huge victory in the end. Single-use plastic was still going into the landfill at an alarming rate.

So we were getting ready to take more drastic action; however, we couldn't agree on what. Or where. Though we had decided that local was best. Before we moved forward, we had to deal with a bit of friction in our group. But we were determined to get to consensus with our relationships intact and our goals agreed on.

Okay. Time to face my friends. And Seth if he showed up.

The earthy smell of incense mixed with fragrant broth greeted me as I entered through the back door of Pho-Freedom, Minh's family's restaurant. It was the only pho restaurant in Salmon Valley, and the food was amazing.

I ran down the stairs to the basement and called out, but no one else was there. I stopped to pay tribute to Minh's family shrine directly inside the door. It was decorated with photos of Minh's relatives, pretend gold coins, fresh flowers, a five-fruit tray, and two statues set on a red cloth covering a beautifully carved mahogany altar. Minh had told us all when we began to meet here that the statue of the laughing man with a rounded belly holding a fan was of Ong Dia, the Land Spirit. The beautiful figure of the woman was the Holy Mother Goddess.

I respected Minh's tradition of honoring those who'd passed. I would honor my ancestors by keeping some Scandinavian traditions, like making my Danish grandfather's paper heart baskets and my Norwegian grandmother's lutefisk and lefse dinner on Christmas Eve. Cod cured in lye. What could be better. Many people thought it was gross, but I liked it—once a year. Properly prepared it was delicious with mashed potatoes, rutabagas, and tons of butter on a piece of lefse, which was a cross between a thin pancake and a tortilla made with potatoes. I hoped I would still have Gran around to teach me her secret for making it—and other family traditions.

When she was better, I wanted Gran and I to work together on making a bunad, a Norwegian national dress, to match her own, using the style from the Sognefjord area where our ancestors came from. We usually made the trip to the Ballard area of Seattle every May 17 for the Norwegian Constitution Day parade, which brought out hundreds of people in traditional dress. Gran always walked in the parade with Dad and me cheering her on from the sidelines. And when I had my bunad finished, I'd march with her.

I smiled at the thought. Then a twinge of emptiness, longing really, passed through me as I wondered about my mother's family: her parents, siblings, grandparents, aunts, uncles, cousins. I didn't even know what part of the world they were in or how they celebrated birthdays, what holidays they had, what foods they ate, how they dressed—all parts of Mom's heritage, *my heritage*. I guess now that Dad was gone, I could go ahead and get my DNA tested. That would help tell my mother's story. A few years ago, I wanted to do it, but Dad asked me not to. He was uncomfortable with online privacy risks or something like that. But now that I was on my own, I *could* do it. After I got over the feeling that I was betraying Dad.

I had barely gotten to the couch at the back of the room when everyone but Seth arrived. The huggers hugged and we got down to business.

We always began our meetings holding hands in a circle, like we'd learned in co-op preschool, and offering a spoken land acknowledgement. It was Kameela's turn, and she uttered the words we'd agreed on many meetings ago to make sure that we gave honor and gratitude to the people of Will's tribe, past and present, and to the land itself.

Then Will did an invocation that was sacred to his tribe. Today he added a request and asked blessings for Gran's speedy recovery. What a kind thing to do. His words brought tears to my eyes. Kameela's too. Even Minh was sniffling.

After that, we stood together for a moment in silence, then took our seats.

"Anyone know if Seth's coming?" I asked.

"I don't think so," said Minh. "His dad is being a jerk again."

"He's pretty much a monster as far as I'm concerned," I said. Mouths dropped open.

"I'm talking about his dad. Not Seth."

There were a few chuckles.

"So, what's up with that whole land sale thing?" Will asked.

I shrugged. I didn't really want to trash Seth's dad in front of friends any more than I just had.

Will continued, "I'm thinking your dad would *never* do that."

I agreed and asked him if he'd told his grandfather about this yet.

"We haven't really discussed it. He's still in pain with his back," Will said.

"I know Dad relied on his opinion. They'd made some plans together for training local kids from the tribe and the town as foresters and technicians in the research facility they were hoping to fund."

"Your dad was pretty convinced that planting sequoias and redwoods as carbon sinks was a good regional answer to climate change," Will said.

"Not the only answer, but yes."

"When he's better, can I come over and talk to him?" I asked. "Or maybe you can discuss it with him."

Will nodded again. "One way or another, we'll find out what Grandfather thinks."

I smiled my thanks.

"I'm confused," Kameela said. "You think that Kincade's lying about the fact that your dad sold him everything?"

Kameela said the words I'd been afraid to say. They were serious allegations and I had absolutely no proof, except for this knot in my gut that had been there since I saw the documents.

I shrugged.

"But what about those papers he handed you so dramatically at your dad's funeral?" she asked.

I shrugged again. Why couldn't I just say it? *Kincade is trying to steal our land.* But the words would not come out of my mouth.

"Maybe your dad changed his mind about the conservation easement," Will said.

"I don't know," I said, wishing I had stayed informed about the details. I fought back surprise tears. I should know what Dad had been thinking. I should have taken more of an interest. While I'd always been somewhat involved in our family business, it was Dad's priority, not mine. If we ended up still *having* a business, that would have to change.

"Or maybe he already filed them with the county," Minh said. "And wouldn't that make the sale to Kincade impossible?"

"I checked the county's tax records online last night to see if any changes to ownership had been made, and nothing had been updated yet," I said.

"Okay. We're here to help, Nora. Don't forget that," Kameela said. "Now let's get on to the other topic we have to discuss," Kameela said. "Operation: Pink Cloud."

I heard some moans and saw some shrugs.

"That doesn't sound good," I said.

"To be honest, Nora, like I said before, some of us are getting cold feet," Kameela said.

"That's understandable," I offered. "It's a risky thing to do. But we all know why we made the decision, and we made it together."

"Nora, it's a big deal. We'll be breaking laws," Minh said.

"Sometimes you have to push the boundaries. Don't we want people to wake up and *really see* what's happening to our local environment? If we don't act soon, more animals, more plants, more locations will be hurt. Earth is dying, and it's going to be a horrible death."

"Maybe . . .," Will said. "Maybe that's expecting too much from a bunch of broke teenagers who live in a deadbeat town at the edge of nowhere."

"Doesn't that mean we have nothing to lose? The worst that can happen is that no one pays any attention to what we're doing," I said. "The best that can happen is that we end up doing some good. Maybe even a lot of good."

"Except for the fact that putting something in someone's gas tank that produces a big pink cloud without their knowledge or permission is against the law," Kameela said. "And because it's against *state* law, we could be putting not only ourselves in jeopardy, but all the kids lined up to help us. Our families could get in trouble too," Kameela said.

"Okay. No one should take risks that make them uncomfortable or endanger anyone they love," I said. "The people doing the harm should be the ones who are uncomfortable. Not us."

"Everything is almost ready to go if we change our minds," Minh said. He had concocted a recipe for a powder we'd put into gas tanks to color the car's exhaust pink. But we still hadn't figured out how to get it into enough gas tanks to make an impact people could see.

"I've worked up a plus-minus analysis of the situation and its potential outcomes at this moment," said Kameela, our awesome list maker. She showed us a list of bullets in two columns. There were more items on the minus side than the plus.

She gave us each a printout of her work. Basically, the list of positive outcomes that might result from pulling our little pink cloud caper was remarkably short. And the list of negative options was way too long, although it could be said that having "go to jail" on any list of outcomes could be a deal breaker for some.

I guess we weren't at that point where we were willing to risk everything yet. And what about the laws that existed to repress activism? Those should be broken for sure. It sounds all heroic to say you'll do anything to stop this bad thing or that bad thing, but when push comes to shove—it was scary too.

All of a sudden I was so tired everything hurt. I dropped onto a nearby couch and couldn't even open my mouth.

Based on our discussion and Kameela's list, we decided as a group to let ideas marinate and come up with another plan. But the question hung heavy in the air: How could we get people to see what we saw and felt so clearly—that Earth was dying, and it was our fault?

Kameela sat down beside me. I leaned my head back against the couch. My tears were quiet as they fell. Kameela patted my arm and Minh moved to sit on my other side. Will pulled a rickety chair up in front of us all and sat there leaning forward.

Strangely, it would be easier to tell everyone the details of my dad's death without Seth's being present.

I looked at the clock. It was almost time.

"There's something I'd like you all to know. Got time to listen?" I asked.

Everyone did.

But before I could begin, there was a knock on the door.

10

🐸 Linka Zeros In

Two Days Till Pink Moon
Warming Time (Late)
West of the Veil of Mist

"Steady now, steady," Linka said to Myth, the bat she rode. Sajay, Jineta, Trep, Roya, and Mura had followed on their bats, having left most of their sisters in service behind at the Palay to guard the queen. They had followed the web string of energy activated by the vizzard into the realm of the largetoe where it disappeared.

"I'm doing my best, Princess, but the headwinds are fierce," Myth replied, straining to fly into the stiff wind.

Linka quickly rechecked the remaining energetic twisp in the bag her father had given her. Its red glow and sparkle were dimmer each time she checked.

"I am going to have to dip into the Web That Connects All Things," she said.

"But you could lose a body part—all your body parts. And mine as well," Myth objected.

Linka placed a reassuring hand on him. "Trust me, friend."

"Sajay," she called to her second-in-command, "lead everyone at least a hopalometer out in case something goes wrong. If it does, return immediately to the Palay."

Without a question or gesture of dismay, Sajay gave the order and the Zons departed. When they were a safe distance away, Linka broke off a piece of the energetic twisp. Then she strummed the Web That Connects All Things by moving her other hand in a slow, sweeping arc through the rather dull particles of living air that surrounded her. Myth bucked the wind to hover in place, with difficulty.

Like a flycape shaken in a lazy breeze, the net-like structure created with all the colors of the universe rippled outward beyond the horizon. Once it resettled, the light of one of the web strings shone brighter than the rest and vibrated with the energy pattern of the twisp Linka held in her other hand.

"Myth, let us follow that energy line until it fades," Linka instructed, summoning the other Zons to trail behind. They followed the web string for several hopalometers, riding the breezes that tumbled over the landscape. Signs that the largetoe had trampled the earth were plentiful. Great stretches of barren mountains stuck out like a sore web digit. Rivers of deadened colors flowed sluggishly toward the ocean, which Linka could smell but not see. And the air was like mite mush to fly through.

Linka nudged Myth to land in the top of a swaying evergreen tree and gave a silent hand command for the other Zons to land as well. When they had settled on surrounding branches, she said, "We have to go deeper into largetoe territory than expected. And the deeper we go, the more careful we must be."

The Zons dipped their snouts.

"Fight in the Light. Die in the Light. Go to the Light," they said as one, brandishing their infinators.

"Myth, away!" she cried, and Myth took to the air.

They soared over a low set of foothills into a valley dotted with largetoe dwellings on either side of a meandering river. The web string's energy waned until it petered out and disappeared.

A sense of foreboding settled over Linka. She could not return to the Palay without the Pearl. Her pride would not allow it. And the almighty prince would never let her forget it. The Pearl had been missing for a long, long time, and if she were the one to bring it back to the Palay, she would make her mark on history. But what could she do if the other end of the energetic thread couldn't be found?

Sprinkling the last of the twisp in the air, she plucked a web string one more time.

"Fly, Myth, fly," she said, and they followed the glimmering line that led farther away from the Palay than she had ever been in her lifetime.

11

Azzie 🐸 Death Floats

Two Days Till Pink Moon
Warming Time (Late)
East of the Veil of Mist

DROPPING FROM THE sky like a boulder, Azzie looked down to the spot where death waited. Should he call out to Aquatessa, his least favorite Elemento, to reach out with watery arms to save him? Before he could decide, he felt a swoosh of air beneath him, and he landed hard on the back of a purple martin. He clung to its feathers with all his might.

"Back off with the grip—do you mind?" chirped the bird.

In front of Azzie sat a frog with leopard-like spots wearing a red flycape with golden grape leaves embroidered along the edge, the emblem of the FAFA (Flying Army of Frog Airtilliers).

"Commander Frago at your service, Your Highness. Welcome to our skies. We are riding on the back of the most noble Sage, who serves us at his own pleasure."

"Thank you, Sage. I am sorry for hurting your feathers," Azzie said.

"Think nothing of it, Your Highness," said the bird with a bob of his head.

Frago was twice Azzie's size and flew in the lead position in a squadron of five frogs, all mounted on purple martins.

"You saved my life, Frago and Sage. I am most grateful," Azzie said, eyes still wide with disbelief. The prince tipped his head to the other squadron members, whose mounts dipped their wings in respect.

"You were late for the ceremony, My Prince, and we were worried about your safety," Frago said.

"I am very, very grateful for your concern."

"Doing our duty. Right, Sage?" Frago patted his mount, and the sleek bird responded with a jerk of his head. The other flyers formed a protective circle around Frago and the prince.

Duty. Yes, duty was paramount. It meant following orders, even if one did not like those orders. Unexpectedly, Azzie regretted his resentment toward his mother. Had she been right all this time? Was "duty" everything? Because a squadron of FAFA had been doing its duty, Azzie was alive. Alive.

Azzie drew a deep breath until his lungs vibrated with joy. His whole body tingled. Even the clouds, the sky, and the treacherous Mud-Mud-Muddy pulsated with a beauty Azzie had never really noticed and taken in before. Perhaps there were other things in life he had been missing too.

The squadron banked to the left, following the curve of the great river, then took a sudden dip down to skim the tops of the waves.

The proximity of the water doused Azzie's exuberance. His world turned gray. Exhaustion hit and his hands trembled. Azzie willed them to be still but failed. He calmed himself with a deep breath and put on his best imitation of his mother's regal smile. It wouldn't do to let his mother's subjects know their prince was a fraidy-frog.

He must try to do better. He had promised the Well of White Light that, if spared, he would try. The old Azzie would have commanded Frago to turn around and take him back to the Palay, where he could find a forgotten chamber to hide in for the rest of his days. But the new Azzie had a duty to do, and duty, as his mother and the vizzard never ceased to point out, came first. It had never made sense to him before, but after his plunge toward death, it now did.

"Your Highness, if you do not mind, I want to show you something on the way to the ceremonial grounds," Frago said.

Azzie turned the corners of his mouth into the broadest grin a frog could manage. "Frago, I owe you my life. Take me wherever it is you want me to go, but let us not forget, my mother's subjects await." That answer seemed regal enough. Perhaps he had a knack for ruling after all.

They flew in a northeasterly direction over grasslands and another range of mountains then approached an area with a variety of budding trees. Small lakes dotted the land in a leapfrog pattern.

"Your Highness, please." Frago handed him an extra-long flyrein attached to his mounthorn. "I could not help but notice your nervousness flying above water. This should assure your safety."

Azzie secured himself and wrestled against his inclination to hang his head in shame. What must Frago think of him? Not much. But then, Azzie had done nothing to earn that respect, so it was only fair.

Frago directed Sage downward, toward one of the small lakes with a tiny island in the middle. Anxiety grabbed Azzie's gut and began its familiar slow twist.

"Steady, Prince. You must be able to see the surface of the water."

Azzie recoiled and considered ordering him to fly away until he remembered his vow moments ago: to help Frago no matter what the request. What a rat he was.

"You have my trust." Azzie closed his eyes and gripped the mounthorn until his webs turned a pale pond-scum green.

They flew in low over the lake. "Your Highness, open your eyes. Look down. Look down."

Azzie inhaled and did as Frago asked.

Dots appeared before his eyes: dots of white, yellow, and green floating on the surface. Dots? He came all this way for dots? Perhaps Frago wasn't as trustworthy as he . . . *Wait*. He took a second look.

Oh, no. Those dots were frogs. Dead frogs. All. Kinds. Of. Dead. Frogs. Covering the surface of the lake. Floating. Bobbing. Spinning in the wind that played across the surface of the water. As far as his eyes could see. Azzie clamped his eyes closed until he could bear it no longer. He took a second glance, seeing that it was much worse than he had originally thought.

For they weren't merely dead.

He saw one frog with three legs . . . another frog with two forearms growing out of one elbow joint . . . conjoined frogs that shared one pair of legs . . . some with two heads . . . others with extra legs and toes . . . others were limbless. There were boils oozing with pus, and blood covered their bodies. The sight was both heartbreaking and revolting.

Desperate helplessness overwhelmed him. The scale of devastation was so great he couldn't absorb it. The suffering sucked the breath out of his lungs, drained the blood from his heart, left his limbs limp and weakened, and altered his soul forever. What kind of world was it where such things could happen?

He clung to the mounthorn with what little might he had left, grateful for the lashing and fearful his body would crumble under the pain. And then he caught sight of movement.

"Look, over there," he said. "The floating log. Circle it."

Frago nudged Sage to comply.

On the log, a frog stared up at them with one eye that bulged three times its natural size, and the other a sunken socket.

She had five arms on one side and four on the other. Twisted around each other, they seemed to be strangling her.

Sage and the other flyers circled above the deformed frog.

"Can we help?" Azzie called from above.

From the log, the frog struggled to speak. "You are kind, but the only help is a swift death."

"There must be something we can do," Azzie said. The torment of her suffering pierced his heart.

Frago shouted down to the poor twisted frog. "Tell his Highness what happened. He must hear the truth."

"A few sun cycles ago, we, the infirm, deformed by poisons in the water where we were laid and born, the neediest of all frogs, were being brought to the Palay by a mercy caravan to tell the queen of our plight. We had heard the group ahead of us had been captured by the Bulldoggies and dragged off to the Maw. Even though General Oddbull captured healthy frogs with vital lifeforces and was not interested in ones with infirmities like ours, we were still afraid.

"So we took a detour to this lake, where we planned to wait until we got word from our guides letting us know we could move on. We did not know it at the time, but the contaminated waters of this lake hastened our doom. It did not take long for many of us to fall ill with excruciating sores popping up everywhere.

"Most died. The truly unfortunate, like me, have suffered as witnesses to it all. You cannot help those who are already in the Maw's grip. And you cannot help those who are dead, but please, find out why this has happened to us. Why do some of us have these deformities from the time of our birth and metamorphosis? Why do others die of the terrible plague? How is any frog safe with such pestilence about?" the frog said.

Azzie said to the dying frog, "I will do all that I can to ensure the suffering stops with you."

"You have my gratitude. Now, please, release me from my agony."

"Your Highness?" Frago said. "I await your order."

Confused by the question, Azzie stared at Frago, then realized that as the superior officer, it was up to him to order the death of the frog.

Dizzy from flying in circles, Azzie shook his head. How could he order one of his mother's subjects to die? He could not. And yet, the next time their eyes met, he knew it was his only choice.

"I am sorry for your suffering," he said and nodded to Frago, who gave a hand signal to one of his flyers. "Thank you for your story."

The flyer broke formation, dropped closer to the frog, and removed his flaktal, a polished disc with a sharpened edge, from its holder. Azzie, knowing what was coming, kept talking in a soothing voice, trying to hold the attention of the deformed frog below. Her eyes widened with fear.

The flyer released the disc.

With the sun glinting off its whirling edge, the flaktal flew straight to its mark, making a whistling noise as it went.

The deformed frog heard the noise and closed her eyes. Her shoulders relaxed. She felt relief at the oncoming sound of her demise.

The flaktal sliced the frog's head off, then skipped across the water. The flyer veered off to catch it.

"No, let it go," Azzie shouted. "It might carry the disease to others."

The flyer reared his mount upward and let the flaktal skip across the water like a flat stone and sink beneath the waves.

"May she find peace in the Great Pond Beyond," Azzie said. "Please, can you land on the shore, so I can compose myself?" Azzie asked. He had seen quite enough.

"Stop," boomed a croaking voice from the shore. "Do *not* land."

Sage swooped closer.

A hunched figure the size of a bear two seasons old crouched on a rock above the lake.

"Go away," the creature said, batting a hand in the air. It wore a tattered cloak with a raised hood.

"Who are you?" Azzie cried.

"That doesn't matter."

Azzie wanted to ask, *what* are you? But his courtly manners forbade it. How was it that the creature spoke Frog but didn't look Frog?

"Do not land. If you touch anything in the vicinity, you might die too."

"But what about the dead? We must send them on to the Big Pond Beyond."

"I will collect and burn the bodies, although it may do no good. Whatever killed them may yet spread."

"Will that not endanger you?"

"Death would be a welcome relief, young Azzumundo. You look so like your father."

"Did you know him?"

The creature nodded. "Yes, at one point in time, we were known to each other. Now please, go."

"What is your name, so I can thank you for your service to my mother's queendom?"

"I do not exist. Tell everyone to avoid this place, which from now on will be known as the Lake of the Dead."

"Your Highness," Frago said. "The ceremony . . ."

Azzie nodded and watched as the creature followed their departure, tilting its head back until the hood tumbled off. Azzie gasped at the sight and averted his eyes at the horror. Webbed, colorless, moss-like hair, hooded eyes, a frog snout . . . and a humanoid head? What kind of unnatural creature could this be? Loping toward the surrounding forest, the unfortunate being disappeared in the trees.

Frago and his flyers veered off in the direction of the cere-monial grounds.

"Frago, send one flyer forward to cancel the Ceremony of Renewal. Some of your flyers must stay here and patrol the lake so that no interlopers carry away this disease. I will speed home to tell my mother what has happened. This terrible news should come from me, not an emissary."

"The Ceremony of Renewal must go on, Highness. No need to tell your mother of this place. She already knows."

Azzie froze. "I do not believe you. If she knew, she would have done everything to fix the problem. And I am sure she would have told me."

Frago shrugged. "Permission to speak without reprisal?"

Azzie considered the request and had to grant it.

"Perhaps she did not want to interfere with your busy social calendar."

Azzie's face burned with shame. "What do you know about my mother's decision-making process?"

"Only what she has told me," Frago said.

A wave of jealousy washed over Azzie.

"And why have we not met before?"

"It is as your mother has commanded. And I must obey, to a point. The queen wants to keep the grave problems we face as a species a secret. I do not agree."

"But you risk treason," Azzie said, his mouth dry.

"Your mother risks the Queendom of Frogs. She risks everything by not doing her duty."

"None of us are perfect."

"I do not mean to be harsh," Frago said, "only honest."

Azzie's will sagged. "I do not think I can go on, Frago. This has all been too upsetting."

"We will be at the ceremonial grounds shortly. Time to put your crown on. Your subjects are counting on you to be a grand reflection of themselves."

Azzie gulped and withdrew his crown from the inside pocket of his flycape, where he had placed it earlier in the day, and put it on his head.

"I believe it would be best if you flew in on Sage solo," Frago said.

"I beg your pardon?" Azzie's eyes widened with alarm.

"Your subjects are expecting a show of courage. I will dismount and turn Sage over to you. He is an easy flyer and knows what to do."

"Dismount? Mid-air?" Frago's instructions confused Azzie.

One of the other FAFA flyers dropped under Sage. Frago handed Azzie the flyreins and, with a nod and a wink, executed a tidy mid-air somersault and landed on the flyer below.

The squadron veered to the right, and Azzie flew solo straight toward the solid limestone wall of the cliff that shot into the sky.

"Frago!" Azzie cried out. He tried to steer Sage away from the cliff, but she wouldn't budge from her course. A beam of hot yellow sunlight hit his eyes and he couldn't see. And for the second time that day, he prepared for a fatal impact.

12

Nora ◎ Anything Goes?

Two Days Till Pink Moon
Just Before Noon
Salmon Falls, Pho Freedom

INH OPENED THE door, and I could tell he was surprised—and uncomfortable—when he saw who was standing outside. It was Sheriff Heinze in uniform. And there was an older Hispanic woman dressed in black dress slacks and a royal-blue suit jacket. I recognized her as someone I'd seen around, but I didn't think she lived in town.

"Auntie," Will said. He got up from his place on the couch and gave her a hug.

"May we come in?" the sheriff asked, looking directly at Minh, who nodded.

The other woman followed. "Which one of you is Nora?" she asked. I raised my hand and stood up.

"Violetta Bravo here. Maddy Ramirez called and asked me to come by."

"Yes. My family is friends of the Ramirez family," I said. I had called their house after I talked to the sheriff because I knew they had a lawyer in the family.

"I don't usually make house calls, but anything for Maddy," Violetta said.

"I really appreciate that," I said.

"Do you have a dollar?"

Puzzled, I went into my backpack and found one. I handed it to Violetta.

"Great," she said. "Consider that a retainer for my legal services. Now let's have a chat."

Violetta motioned me to follow her into a corner and asked if there was anything she should know about my actions regarding my father's death. Something that might implicate me in his murder. "I didn't kill him, if that's what you mean," I said. "But I . . . I do feel responsible for his death," I said softly, realizing that this was the first time I'd said those words out loud.

Then she asked me some questions about what had happened. I told her quickly, whispering the whole time so the others couldn't hear. The sheriff and Will were chatting in a warm family way. Violetta listened intently and took some notes. When I was done, she said, "Look, this is unusual. I don't think this is the best place to have these discussions. Here. Among your friends, I mean."

"Please, I need their support," I said.

"I'm not sure you understand the risk," Violetta said.

"I'm eighteen. Well, almost. This is the way I want to do it," I said.

Violetta faced the sheriff and said, "You can ask your questions." Then she turned to me and said, "I'm here to protect you, so if I stop things along the way, I'm just doing my job."

I had a deer-in-the-headlights feeling. Like I wanted to crawl away and hide for good. But at the hospital, I'd promised the sheriff I'd tell her my story. Could I trust her? It seemed like I didn't have a choice.

"Do you mind if I record this?" Sheriff Heinze asked. I looked at Violetta. She nodded.

"It's okay with me," I said.

The sheriff remained standing, took out her phone, and set it to record. Violetta pulled up a chair beside the sofa so she was close but not uncomfortably so.

"Uh, Nora? What's going on?" Kameela asked.

"There's something that I have to tell you all—something the sheriff wants to know about too, so I invited her to come."

"Go on, Nora," Violetta said quietly. "We're listening. Take your time."

I told everyone everything.

. . . The note.

. . . The trip up the mountain.

. . . Waiting.

. . . My dad getting shot.

. . . The worthless chase.

. . . The second shot.

I held nothing back.

By the time I was done, my heart was pounding. It was hard to breathe or speak.

Kameela came over and gently hugged me. "How awful for you," she said. "And your poor dad."

"He didn't deserve to die—and I don't even know who did it," I said, leaning against her for support.

Tears spilled down my cheeks. Kameela handed me a handkerchief. It was beautifully embroidered with red and pink roses. It looked like a piece my mother might have done. I would have rather stared at the handkerchief all day than tell the story I had just told.

"Nora, that's terrible. I'm so sorry," Will said.

Minh got a can of mango juice from the fridge, popped it open, and handed it to me.

I downed it in a few gulps. "Thanks." My friends gathered around me. "Sorry I didn't tell you all this before," I said. "It was too hard to talk about."

They all said it was okay, which I really appreciated.

"Did you tell your grandmother what happened?" the sheriff asked.

"No, she wasn't home, and by the time she got there, someone had already told her, and she was hurt."

"Tell me more," she said.

I nodded. "Apparently she collapsed when she was told the terrible news and hit her face. She was already so upset when I finally saw her, I pretended I didn't already know. And I haven't told her the full story yet."

"Nora, do you want to take a break?" Violetta asked. "Maybe finish another day? I know this is very upsetting."

"Maybe that's best," I said, feeling like a mashed-up potato.

"Yeah, let's stop now, Ardith," Violetta said. "It seems like she's getting tired. I'm sure she'll be happy to answer any more questions you have during your investigation. You know where to find me when you want to get in touch with her."

I leaned over and whispered in Violetta's ear. She nodded.

"Sheriff Heinze, can you tell me what *you* know about who killed Dad?" I asked.

"We're working on some avenues that I can't really discuss," she said. "But we'll get the person who did it. I promise you that."

And I would hold her to that promise.

13

The Queen
The Dream Arrives

Two Days Till Pink Moon
Fly Time (Early)
Palay, Rainbow River

As wisps of the dream clutched the queen's body, she could no longer speak, yet she was still aware of all that surrounded her. The dragonflies on her cloak departed and were replaced by a swarm of small black dreaming moths.

With a twitch of her webbed finger, the queen signaled her readiness to Bacareno, the court caller. Bacareno expanded his magnificent yellow throat with a deep breath and issued a commanding bark.

"Zons, your queen summons you to protect her."

The Zons who had remained behind to guard the queen marched from the far reaches of the chamber. Protection was vital during dreaming when even a graze could kill the queen.

Linka had drilled the Zons in their duty, and the queen sighed with relief as they circled her ametrine throne and struck the curved end of their infinators against the smooth granite floor. Each instrument of destruction sounded a different tone, and together they produced a deep, dissonant, awe-inducing chord that reverberated from their circle making hearts tremble.

Wisps of the dream applied light pressure to the queen's skin.

The Royal Mister sprayed her with eucalyptus-scented water, which he blew through a cattail stem riveted with fine holes. Dehydration during dreaming could also be fatal.

She inhaled the soothing scent, which reminded her of warmed pine needles. The mist falling on her skin cooled her fears but did not wash them away. Surrendering her will to anything, even a divine dream, was a challenge.

Bacareno called out, "All quiet in the Ruling Room. Ranya, Magnificent Queen of All Frogs That Flourish in the North, South, East, and West and in Water, Sand, and Mud receives a Dream."

The royal femnuras (adult female frogs) and memnuras (adult male frogs) of the Court stopped their gossip and the room fell quiet.

"Your Majesty," said Balarius. "Calm and center yourself so the dream can enter."

The queen heard the vizzard's words and emptied her mind.

Her exhaustion, forgotten.

The coldness of her throne, ignored.

The echoes of her subjects' demands, silenced.

Anxious thoughts about her son, gone.

The terrible secrets she had kept from her subjects, vanished.

She became a vessel.

Bright rays of spectral colors danced around her head, and as the cool mist settled over her, she entered the void to receive the dream.

In the space between here and there, she heard her brother's voice. "You are doing well, Ra."

She would chide him later for the use of her pond name.

"Breathe. Deep. Long," he continued. "Draw power from the heavens and the earth. Bask in the void and open to the Flow."

Ranya moaned and was engulfed by the Dream.

The vastness of primordial space emerges in the void. Multicolored clouds, clotted from stardust, dance around a sun-colored proto-planetary disk.

A star forms anew.

In accelerated time, clouds elongate into ribbons, whip around each other, and coalesce into a vast sphere of dancing colors. This gleaming astral body looms large, pearlescent, and lonely in the silence of space.

Rays of molten white light burst forth from the heart of this new place, cracking its lustrous surface. Light blooms as the star explodes, filling the space around it with billions of glimmering pieces.

One angular chunk, brighter than the rest, hurtles solo toward a distant iridescent planet.

Time and space bend. The chunk enters the atmosphere of the blue-green planet. Molten, it lands in the center of a great lake that evaporates upon contact. A mushroom cloud of mist billows upward, outward, and then clears, leaving a huge crater that houses this piece of star.

Time flows in waves that undulate faster and faster around the fragment, polishing its surface. The volcanic earth beneath it vibrates and pushes the piece of heaven upward until, now shining like the moon, it rests on a high mountain peak. A forest sprouts around it and grows ancient in the span of one breath.

And the object, now spherical, its edges smoothed by the forces of time, sits on a moss-covered stump cradled in a nest of green clover and surrounded by a forest vibrant with life. The air sparkles and fills with the music of nature as the ground teems with life.

The pink pearlescent point of light shines in the darkness and rises to hang over Frog Mountain, home of the Palay, heart of the Frog World, like the full moon. Beautiful.

The vizzard, ever alert to the queen's state of being, watched with growing alarm as the color of her skin changed from bright green to grey green.

Particles of darkness swooped in and fell in soft folds, veiling her from the crowd. The vizzard inhaled sharply. *The Cloak of Quietus*, an emanation that forecasts death, fell over the queen.

A feral croak shatters the tranquility of the place.

The Pearl's unique swirls of color whirl into a face—the queen's.

Plummeting from the sky, the Pearl lands atop Frog Mountain and crushes the Palay.

Surviving frogs flee the rock rubble that once had been their home.

The queen's grim expression fades from the surface of the Pearl as the sound of her death croak shifts from thunder-like to high-pitched and grating. The Pearl rolls to the edge of the mountaintop, then teeters and falls over a cliff.

Down it rolls, sucking the lifeforce out of the forest in great ribbons of color. Emerald green from the majestic trees, blue from the rapids that course down the mountainside, ivory from the alabaster cliffs that define the mountain's frog shape from a distance, and orange from the vein of iron ore that runs under the heart of the mountain.

The Pearl swells as it sucks in so much life.

Waiting at the bottom of the hill is a figure, a female largetoe, radiating a white light from within.

The Pearl rolls toward the figure, who extends a hand. White light shoots from her palm and shatters the Pearl into a billion pieces.

"No!" the queen screamed, wrenching herself from the dream. She did not want to know the dream's end and had to be free of its grip—now. As she opened her eyes, the tangle of black filaments from the Cloak of Quietus disintegrated.

Disoriented, she looked about the Ruling Room into the upturned faces of her subjects.

"What vision has so shaken you, Your Majesty?" Lord Fountainblower called out. "Another tragedy?"

"Which clan is next to die?" Lord D'graff demanded.

The queen returned to the present and took in the panic in the room. How would she tell them that the dream had foretold not the death of a clan, but of them all? And at her hand.

She sent out a flow to calm the panic, both theirs and her own.

"I do not understand what the Well told me. I saw the Golden Pearl of the Forest . . ."

Murmurs about the Pearl wafted through the courtiers.

"And a largetoe girl—a femtoe—who . . ." The queen's throat pinched. How could she tell her courtiers, with their mouths agape, that she had dreamt of their destruction?

"What happened then, Your Majesty?" asked another.

Again, she studied their trusting faces. They counted on her protection. It was her only job, and she had failed. The weight and heat of her shame burned her like molten rock.

"It is all such a blur," she said and buried her face in her hands.

"Let our queen rest from her ordeal," the vizzard said. "I will give her a rejuvenating tonic, and she can tell us more on the morrow."

"But what about the Cloak of Quietus?" a courtier spit out.

Sister and brother looked at each other with alarm in their eyes.

"At sunset, I will issue a call to assemble the Frog Council," the queen said. "When they arrive, I will tell you all at the same time."

The room erupted in fear.

"Hush now!" Bacareno boomed.

The room quieted except for some uncontrollable sobbers who migrated to the edge of the gathering.

Terror clutched the queen's throat. She timidly patted her shoulders, afraid to find them draped in the veil of death. But it was not there. The cloak meant death would visit soon. But would it lay claim only to her or to the entire Frog Clan?

14

Azzie 🐸 False Promises

Two Days Till Pink Moon
Fly Time
Outside the Veil of Mist

"Hold tight," Sage said. Azzie grasped the flyreins and fought to see beyond the bright light. Passing from sunlight into shadow, Azzie saw a cliff immediately in front of him. He shaded his eyes with one hand. If he was going to die, he wanted to see it coming.

Let it be over swiftly.

Collision seemed inevitable. Sage tucked his wings tightly against his body and, right when Azzie was sure they would slam into the rock, flew through a crevice in the limestone bluffs that Azzie couldn't see.

They wove through the jagged crevice in the yellow rock until Sage broke through to the ceremonial grounds on the other side.

Tears welled in Azzie's eyes, and relief flooded through his veins. He lived again.

Chants of, "Az-zie. Az-zie. Az-zie," boomed from the crowd. His audience perched on seats carved in circles into the steep rock walls that formed an oval-shaped amphitheater. Red pennants with the queen's symbol festooned the place.

At the center of this amphitheater stood a statue representing a female largetoe six hundred frogs high. Azzie recoiled at the sight. Although he hadn't ever seen a real largetoe, their form appeared as hideous as the acts they perpetrated against the All. Thank the Great White Light that the figure in front of Azzie was not a real femtoe.

Her flowing gown was made from red daisy-like fire wheel flowers with yellow tips. Her face was composed of birchbark, clusters of purple morning glories for eyes, shelf fungus carved into a nose, chokecherry lips, and a sharp chin made of twigs bundled into a rounded point. Her head was covered in bristly sunflowers, and yellow-flowered vines cascaded in braids to the ground. On the top of her head was a wreath of ivy, twisted red willow twigs, and the small white flowers known as tadpole breath.

Around her neck hung a chain made of yellowed sedges with a golden pearl-like object hanging from it. It was covered in buttercups with vibrant veins of violets and wild roses that swirled in crazy patterns over the yellow.

The vizzard had rehearsed Azzie to near exhaustion. But what if he flubbed?

The crowd's chants continued. "Az-zie. Az-zie." And their stomping web feet made the ground tremble. But even above the din, Azzie could hear the vizzard's gravelly voice in his head: *Remember the rules. Remember the rules.*

Rule One—what had that been? Oh, yes. *Play to the crowd.*

Azzie had scoffed at this directive. It seemed foolish to pretend. What was the point? There was no magic to this ceremony. It was all an act—a sham. A hollow dream. And to what purpose? Azzie didn't know. Ritual gestures would never restore what had been lost.

But now, on a day when he had twice been saved, Azzie cast aside his doubt and committed to the performance. His all for the All.

"Okay, Sage, Frago said to trust you, so let us do this." Azzie patted Sage's neck. Sage gave a great downbeat with his wings and launched into a virtuoso flight. Swooping up, down, and all around, Sage wove his way around the amphitheater three times. Azzie waved and painted what passed for a smile on his face.

Rule Two: Partake of the potion with panache.

Azzie grasped the small jade amulet that dangled from the chain around his neck. He held the amulet high for all to see. The air vibrated with the crowd's hunger for pageantry as they chanted, "Drink it. Drink it."

Azzie whipped the lid off the vial and waved it around.

The crowd cheered.

He held the vial to his lips.

The crowd hopped up and down in unison and created a driving beat.

Head thrown back, Azzie downed the vial's contents, which was Merely Dew, a popular drink made by many vendors in the Plaza of the Sun, and his favorite.

The sweet, fermented mixture of honey and dew slid down his throat with a pleasant sensation that both fortified him and reminded him of home.

The crowd went crazy, doing belly bumps and flipper slaps.

Rule Three: Pucker like you mean it for the kiss.

Kissing, like smiling, did not come naturally to any frog, but as the crowd's chants shifted to "Kiss her . . . kiss her . . ." Azzie knew it was time. But he was not sure how Sage would get him close enough to the statue's chokecherry mouth for the kiss to occur. During his many rehearsals he had been burfing, which gave him more control of his position. Doing it on the back of a bird was at least twice as hard.

He needn't have worried. Sage knew his part and acted with no direction from Azzie, flying to a small platform—another trick of the eye—positioned under the statue's lips.

And there, Sage perched, waiting for Azzie to do his thing.

Whoever thought of kissing? The Grand and Glorious Vizzard had forced Azzie to spend hours in the Hall of Reflection trying to purse his lipless mouth into the shape the vizzard had described to him. Absurd. And painful. At least it wasn't a real largetoe.

He puckered his lips as best he could and touched them to the cool red chokecherry lips on the statue. The crowd cheered. There. Done.

"Let us go, Sage."

The bird hopped from his perch, took a nosedive, then cruised around the amphitheater in ascending loops, past the enthusiastic crowd, until they were high in the sky, where they joined Frago's squadron, which was circling the grounds.

From this vantage point, Azzie could see an army of frogs at the top of the amphitheater ready to push aside a boulder that was holding back water from a higher elevation.

With grunts and groans aplenty, the frogs above worked as one, stacking themselves on one another's backs to form a wall of frogs as high as the boulder.

Finally, they moved it enough to start a trickle. More frogs joined in, pushing harder and harder, and the trickle turned into a torrent. The freed water traveled down a hollow log positioned directly over the head of the statue and washed it away until there was nothing but a pile of mud surrounded by a pool of debris.

Frogs pushed the boulder back into place, shutting off the torrent. The amphitheater was silent. A femnura, chosen by acclamation, should emerge from the rubble for all to see. This female frog represented the transformed largetoe, who, as the story goes, would dwell among them for three days to learn the glories of all things frog.

Time ticked by. Why wasn't she doing her part, whoever she was?

The crowd began to grow restless. Azzie watched as Frago directed his flyers to descend. One by one, they shot toward the ground, with Frago leading the way. Sage strained at the flyreins to follow, but Azzie held him back, panicked by the sight of all that water below.

"Why is the water not draining?" a bystander bellowed.

"She is pinned under by debris!" another frog shouted.

"She might drown if she does not get air!" a third frog cried.

"Surely she knows how to keep water out of her lungs," another frog said.

"But only if she does not panic," someone else added.

Do not panic, do not panic, do not panic, Azzie pleaded silently. But even he wasn't sure if he was talking to himself or the little femnura under water.

Soon the crowd was yelling for the femnura to be saved. "Save her! Save her! Save her!" they chanted.

Panic sparked every nerve in Azzie's body. Every nightmare about drowning he'd ever had raced through his mind. His first and last instinct was to flee, but Sage resisted his tug at the flyreins and would not allow Azzie to force his beak upward.

The urge to turn flippers and hop back to the Palay like a little tad wailing for his mommy overwhelmed him. Every part of his body sizzled with electricity. Azzie flicked the flyreins more viciously in the direction of the Palay.

How he hated himself. A parasitic panic had invaded him, and he couldn't shake it off until he remembered the vizzard's words:

It's not true. Your mind is telling you a story that is not true.

Azzie took a deep, shuddering breath and tried to let the panic go. He patted Sage's neck apologetically.

"I am sorry to be unkind. You will want to return to help Frago, I know."

Azzie loosened the flyreins and let Sage take the lead. The great bird headed down toward the floor of the amphitheater and landed in time for Azzie to see Frago pull a frightened young femnura from inside the hollowed-out rock, where she had waited for the water to drain.

Azzie turned pink around his ear pads. He should have been the rescuer, the hero, but he had been the coward and the fool.

The poor, sweet thing had almost drowned, and he had done nothing. Nothing. He approached the femnura as Frago draped his cape across her shaking shoulders.

"You are lucky Frago is not a fraidy-frog like your prince. I am so sorry I deserted my duties and left you in danger. What is your name?"

"I am Nunya, Your Highness. Tell me, why could we not do it the normal way, with a real largetoe?"

Prince Azzie smiled. "That is the way it should be, but as you know, Prince Ponte-Fricani stole the Golden Pearl of the Forest many sun cycles ago. So even if we had the girl—and the real potion—no Pearl means no transformation. My mother says reenacting is better than forgetting, but it is not as good as the real thing." Azzie turned to Frago. "Frago, you are more prince than I. Thank you for your valor. My mother would thank you too."

Frago bowed and whisked Nunya to safety.

Home tugged at Azzie. He couldn't wait to return to the Palay. And yet, he feared facing his mother. The day had been a disaster, and he had only himself to blame.

What would his mother say when she learned that he had failed her yet again? Azzie did not want to find out.

15

The Queen Ranya's Decision

Two Days Till Pink Moon
Fly Time
Palay, Rainbow River

IN A CAVERN deep inside the Palay, Ranya floated on her back in the calm, colorful waters of the Rainbow River trying to wash away the effects of the dream—but everything she saw reminded her: from the constellations of gold specks on her massive green belly to the sense of doom that hung around her shoulders like a leaden shawl.

To distract herself from despair, she wondered how her son had comported himself. She could find out in an instant by tapping into the Web That Connects All Things. But she held back. Word would come soon enough. She prayed the words would be of praise.

She dove underwater and gazed at the bands of different-colored phosphorescent algae that grew up the sides of the cavern.

Even the protective membrane that covered her eyes couldn't dull the magnificent colors with midnight blue on the bottom to the rich purple of a late-summer grape to a startling band of teal ending right below the water's surface.

Ranya poked her head above water. The colors shimmered more brightly as they crept up the rock walls. A rich esbue with overtones of cranberry transitioned to blackberry red. Then came salmon pink, copper, turquoise, and a particular shade of umbau that mimicked the midnight sky covering the roof of the cave. Stalactites dripping from the ceiling were studded with golden selenite crystal clusters that glowed with the soft light of a distant galaxy.

Usually, the beauty of the place soothed her, but the gnats of hopelessness and despair invaded her thoughts until she noticed Simeon clinging to the cavern wall.

"The Elemento Aquatessa would like an audience," Simeon told her.

"Aquatessa? She is always welcome," Ranya replied.

Aquatessa's awareness merged with the water surrounding the queen and bathed her in an embrace of genuine affection.

"I am sorry to disturb your private time, Your Majesty, but an event of grave importance has occurred."

"Yes?"

"I've experienced the power of the Golden Pearl of the Forest, and it's in the possession—"

"Of a largetoe girl," the queen said, her voice as hollow as the center of a reed.

"Why, yes," Aquatessa said. "Perhaps I might have spared myself this journey."

"I only knew the news loomed," Ranya said. "Not when it would arrive, or what exactly it would be, although based on my dream I had my suspicions."

"Ah, I heard tell of your dream. If you don't mind my saying, dear friend, you seem less than overjoyed."

"In my heart, I have always been indifferent to the existence of the Pearl. It seemed like a tall tad tale. A story we tell to give us hope and to mask the pain. It was never real to me. That changed later when I discovered it could serve as a tool to purchase my heart's desire. Now I am afraid of what will happen to me and my queendom if it is found," Ranya said.

"How disturbing," Aquatessa said.

"I foresaw my death and the destruction of the Palay at those awful webless hands of a girl," Ranya said. "That goes beyond disturbing, and that is why I ask you to find her and take her life."

Agitated whirlpools formed on the surface of the water.

"Calm yourself, Aquatessa. Perhaps now you will understand why the girl must die. Her existence jeopardizes the Palay. Will you help me make it so?"

"I am not an assassin," Aquatessa said.

"You have been known to destroy millions with your power," Ranya said. The water around her cooled precipitously, and she shuddered from the shock of the rapid change.

"Only when other forces combine to make it so. There are immutable laws that govern the behavior of the Elementos. I cannot change those. When Bortos, my brother of the Winds, is riled, he pushes me about. Or when Magmo is upset and causes volcanoes to erupt, I am forced to move again. And then there are the largetoe, as you call them. They bring on their own misery by clearing the land so nothing can stop my flow and pave over surfaces with impenetrable substances. Why am I to blame?"

"I should have known you would not help." Ranya's voice grew as cold as the water as harsh memories of Aquatessa returned. She had once asked Aquatessa to help rehabilitate her son by allowing him to feel peace and tranquility in her presence. But the spiritual essence of water had refused, saying Azzie's fear was of his own making, not hers, and when he was ready to confront it, she would be there to support him. But she would not conspire to make it so.

Aquatessa calmed and warmed her surface. "Let us not quarrel about the past," she said and swirled about Ranya to soothe both their tensions away. "I would help you with almost anything but what you ask. It is between you and the girl. She is my child, as are you. And in *this* situation, I will not choose one over the other. Besides, I have grave matters of my own to deal with," she said. "I am ill, my friend. Terribly ill."

"I have sensed so for some time, Dear One," Ranya answered gently. "It must be the poison from the largetoe that is released into your magnificent rivers, channels, lakes, lagoons, and seas. It is the garbage they spew into you, the radioactive matter, the plastics that break down and poison you and your children, including my subjects and myself."

"Can you concoct one of your powerful cures that will declutter my veins and help me to ripple and run, billow, break, flow, and surge with the exuberance I once had? I am so weighed down by all the foreign substances I am expected to carry."

Ranya was silent for a moment. "I have no cure for you. Only time, and the cessation of befoulment. But how do we stop the largetoe from that?"

"Since I am eternal and cannot cease to exist, I will only come to know greater pain and suffering as my condition worsens," said Aquatessa. "But it is the suffering of all who depend on me as the Bringer of Life that hurts most."

"I can briefly soothe that kind of sorrow," Ranya said. She asked Simeon to fetch an ampoule from her robe, which lay folded on a flat rock. When he delivered it to her, she withdrew the stopper and poured the contents into the water.

"Ahhh," Aquatessa sighed. "It *does* soothe." She enjoyed the reprieve from her pain, then said, "I will grant you a favor in return, my friend. What shall it be?"

"Lead Linka to the girl."

"And then stand by as Linka kills her?" Aquatessa said.

The queen shrugged.

"Again, you want treachery," Aquatessa said. "I will grant your first request—to find the girl—but nothing more." Then she swirled around Ranya in an embrace. "We do not always agree, old friend."

"But we always love each other," Ranya added before she sank beneath the water. There she projected her message to Linka in a series of thought bubbles, which Aquatessa carried with her as she departed.

After Aquatessa was gone, Ranya positioned herself over one of the many stone platforms scattered underwater, like hopping stones in a creek bed. Simeon placed her bathing robe across her shoulders. With the power of her desire, a stone pillar below the lily-shaped platform carried her upward toward the hole in the ceiling. She looked forward to landing on the level of her sleeping nest. It had been a challenging day, and it was time to rest.

Everything depended on Linka. Or had she set a task too hard for even the greatest warrior princess ever to live? Perhaps the better question was whether she had set the *right* course.

Oh, Well of White Light, guide Linka's hand. Give her the courage to perform the impossible. To kill a largetoe many times her size and bring the Pearl back to me so that I can destroy it before it destroys us all.

When she was finished with her exhortation, she called Simeon to her side.

"Fetch my brother. Tell him I desire his counsel on the subject of my recent dream."

Back in the cavern, an aquatic sow bug released herself from the wall and floated down the Rainbow River to a designated meeting spot where she would report the conversation she had just overheard to an enemy of the queen's.

16

Nora ◉ Dance Water Dance

Two Days Till Pink Moon
Early Afternoon
Salmon Falls River

THE SHERIFF LEFT first. But before Violetta walked out, I asked her if she could help me with a real estate issue. She said she wasn't the person to handle something like that, but she had an associate who could and handed me a card with a name and number on it. Come Monday, I'd give her a call and see if I could get some legal advice about this messy real estate situation we found ourselves in.

Then it was time for all of us to leave. As we walked out the door, Kameela asked, "You sure you don't want to come to my place and hang out?"

"No, I really want to go for a swim, but thanks. Why don't you come with me?"

"I'm not much of a swimmer."

"You can wade. Or we can at least walk through the woods together and catch up. I want to hear what's been going on in your life," I said, eager to get out of my own head at least for a little bit.

Joining arms like characters from *The Wizard of Oz*, we veered toward the forest that ran along the edge of the river. We walked in silence for a while, aware of the change in sounds and smells as we left town and wound through the woods to the river. The rumble of cars and trucks on asphalt gave way to a rustle of wind through the mixed deciduous forest. The slap of our running shoes against pavement transitioned first to crunch on gravel, and then to thud on forest duff, leaving little clouds of dirt in our wake. Soon, the *shack-shack-shack* of a stellar jay and hollow sound of a pileated woodpecker attacking a dying tree punctuated the air.

The air smelled different too. Town air had hung heavy with cooking grease, and sugar from the doughnut shop blended with diesel and paper mill. On a bad day, fumes from the oil refinery farther down river by the ocean would be blown our way. But once we entered the woods, the smell of green was everywhere. It was a relief.

"So tell me, my friend, what is going on with you?" I asked, adding my voice to the sounds of nature that continued in the background.

Kameela's eyes sparkled as joy and happiness bubbled out of her. "Oh, nothing much. Just got an early acceptance from Stanford."

"You what?!" I shrieked with joy. Kameela joined me in what we called our happy dance—which basically consisted of jumping up and down while screaming.

"Why didn't you say anything?" I asked when we ran out of breath.

"I've told people individually—except for you. So now every-one knows."

"Your parents must be beside themselves with pride."

"And a little worried too. My scholarship covers almost every-thing—it's the 'almost' they're worried about."

"Let's do some more grant research—scholarships from environmental organizations. We probably missed a few the first round."

"Don't worry about it now. You've got lots on your mind."

"Hey—you and everybody else have pretty much carried me on your backs since Dad died. Time for me to help you."

"I wish you would come with me in the fall. You'd love the place, and their writing program is first-rate."

"It will have to be next year, maybe," I said, wanting with all my heart for it to be 'now'.

"That's what I get for hanging out with juniors," Kameela said.

We giggled and did a happy dance encore while some birds circled above, squawking and cawing like they were part of the dance.

A chill shuddered through me, and I glanced around to see what was behind us.

"What's the twitching about?" Kameela asked. "A new happy dance step?"

I shrugged. "Sometimes I get a creepy sensation." I rubbed the back of my neck to get the tingling to go away. "Like someone's watching me. I call it my 'ghost in the forest' feeling."

"Anyone ever tell you that you're nuts?" Kameela asked, a smile on her face.

"Yes, you. All the time."

We laughed and moved on down the path, passing a stand of birch—not a common tree around here.

"Maybe it's the *Betula pendula* watching," I said. The birch trees had straight white trunks and were marked with black eyebrow-like arches with eye-like knots at the center.

"Show-off," Kameela said. "Hey, don't run into that giant *Picea engelmannii* up there." Kameela gestured toward an Engelmann spruce up the path.

We had a friendly ongoing competition: Who knew the most scientific names for the flora and fauna we came across in our rambles in the woods. We'd been competing for years, and there was an imaginary tally we kept adding to as time went on. It was a game my mother had gotten me interested in when I was little. As a scientist, she said that using Latin names was a good way to know that everyone was talking about the same thing. I guess learning her language was a way of keeping her close to me. Kameela usually beat me—but not always.

Salal leaves crunched under our feet. "What's up with this?" I said, bending over to pick up a handful of dead leaves.

Kameela wandered off the path. I followed. The crunching got louder.

"Look," she said. The floor of the forest should have been covered in dark green salal with shiny leaves. This time of the year, there should have been clusters of small round berries—dark purple. But instead, most of the salal was dead.

"That's not a good sign," I said and stooped to get a closer look. The evergreen plants' leaves were indeed crunchy and brown, with a grey overcast, instead of being shiny and leathery to the touch. I crumpled a few of them, the sharp edges of their shattered shape poking into my hand. "What's killing them?"

"Nobody seems to know," Kameela said. "Some say it's the year-after-year drought we've been having, which means the dying salal might be a new sign of climate change. What's even more worrying is what might be happening to the rhizomes and mushrooms that are supposed to be protected by the shade of the salal. If the salal is dying, they might be dying too."

Kameela and I stood beside each other, heads down, jointly experiencing the pain of real evidence of a sick environment in our own backyard.

"You know that epic stand of sword ferns on the other side of town?" she asked. "I heard that was dying back, but I haven't been able to check it out yet."

Kameela, a dedicated phenologist, took some pictures to record the scene. I knew that later she'd share them on a national phenology website that helped people track local seasonal changes across the country. The information was used to try to understand how climate change is impacting the change of seasons and how in turn that impacts when plants bloom and animals reproduce, among other things.

"You know, I hardly dream anymore, but when I do, I've been having nightmares about this," Kameela said. "What if things get as bad here as they did in Somalia? I keep dreaming we'll run out of water, or some horrible disease will start killing all the trees and plants and animals. And then where will we go? That's why my family is here. Not in Somalia. I feel like people are running out of places to go."

I gave Kameela a hug. "That's what we're trying to stop. That's why we're Commandos. We're fighting as best we can with our hearts and our brains to make people pay attention to what's already happening. To notice the salal dying. To notice that trees are dying off in our very own forests—the hemlocks, the western red cedars, even the big-leaf maples are all fighting against the effects of an already changing climate. To notice the increase in forest fires—although that's a more in-your-face sign. To notice the decline in insects and birds and frogs. We just have to figure out what will get their attention and make them realize what's at stake."

"And we won't give up until we do," Kameela said, growing a smile.

"And we won't give up until we do," I repeated.

We gave each other a high five and returned to the path. We continued in silence until we reached the small pebble beach with bigger rocks to perch on. It was upstream from the town, so I could swim in clean water before it ran past the plant. Whenever I needed to clear my head, this is where I came.

Arms linked, we stood at the curve of the river and surveyed the beauty around us. From the glorious mountains in the distance to the heron resting not too far away. We were lucky to live in such a glorious place.

When we parted, I lowered my backpack to the sand and stuck my mom's pouch inside it for safekeeping. Then I took off my shoes.

"Sure you won't join me?" I asked Kameela.

"You're crazy. It'll be like swimming in ice cubes. You do your polar bear thing. I'm going to head home. Mom will be worried and there's no service out here," she said, taking her phone out to check. Living with a huge range of mountains between us and civilization made it hard to talk from too many places.

"What if I drown?"

"Right. Miss Fish drown? Not a chance."

"Some lifeguard you are," I said, taking off my pants.

"Hey, no flashing body parts," Kameela said, her back already to me.

With no one to offend, I took off my shirt, ran for the river, and did a shallow dive, squealing with shock as I hit the icy water. When I came up for air, Kameela was out of sight.

Several strong strokes against the current washed away the top layers of hurt and pain caked all over me—body and soul—and left me with the deeper questions I couldn't scrub away.

These questions and others swirled in my head until they formed a whirlpool that threatened to suck me under. More than I could probably ever answer. I swam upstream as fast as I could against the current. It felt good to stretch into my strokes and experience the power of my legs propelling me through the water. When I was tired, I let the flow of the water carry me back to the beach.

I climbed out of the water and felt the temperature drop as a band of dark clouds gathered on the horizon. Nothing new for this part of the country, but I would have to get home before the storm arrived.

I was mid-crouch, struggling to get my dry jeans more than halfway up my not-so-dry legs, when a murder of crows flew in circles above me cackling a warning.

Someone—or something—was coming.

The hairs on the back of my neck stood straight up. I froze and immediately toppled over like a bowling pin.

"Hey, Nora, it's me," Seth called from the edge of the woods. "I ran into Kameela on the path. She said . . . you were . . . naked," Seth said, mouth agape.

"Kameela said I was naked?" I asked, growing redder by the moment as I scramble to right myself like a graceless turtle stuck on her back, arms and legs flailing.

"No, no. You *are* naked. Well, half naked."

"Will you stop saying the word 'naked' please?" I said, tugging my pants on the rest of the way and sitting up. I covered my top half (yes—breasts!) with one arm and reached out with the other one to grab the sweatshirt Seth had taken off and was handing to me, his eyes politely averted.

"Sorry—I didn't mean to say 'naked' so many times," Seth said.

"There you go again."

"I meant 'swimming.' Kameela said you were swimming. Yes, 'swimming,' that's what she said."

Sweatshirt on, I laughed.

Seth joined me.

"Let me help you up, Nora. I won't look. I promise you." Seth was still looking away as he came close enough to extend a hand.

I took it and he hauled me to my feet. "I'm dressed, silly."

He peeked at me. And we laughed some more.

"I figured you'd come for a swim and brought you this," he said, holding out a greasy paper bag.

I gave him a gentle shove.

"Hey. What's up with the shove? I thought you were the nonviolent type," Seth said.

"I think I'm mad at you."

"You're mad at everything when you're hungry. Eat."

"How could you not tell me about the 'deal' between our dads?" My irritation sounded whiney even to me. But I couldn't help it.

"I told you. I didn't know much before you did," he said. "He could be planning world domination for all I know, and I'd never hear a thing about it."

"I still can't believe—in fact—I never will believe that your dad isn't cheating somehow. And lying. And . . ."

"Hey, whatever happened to innocent until proven guilty?" Seth asked. "Even for him, that should be the case. I don't know that he cheated, but I don't know that he didn't, either."

"Well, it doesn't make sense to me that Dad was planning to convert the land to a conservation easement—and then he does a 180 and sells to, let's face it, 'not his best friend.'"

"And then he gets killed," Seth said softly.

"Yes. And then he gets killed," I whispered. I stared at the ground, whisked backward in time.

"Nora? You okay?"

I nodded, still distracted by my thoughts.

"Sit down, Nora," Seth said gesturing to a large flat rock with room enough for the both of us. For once I quietly followed instructions and dug into the rice, refried beans, and chicken tostada.

Seth sat down beside me. I offered him some food, but he shook his head.

"There's something more in the bag," Seth said. "Take a look."

I checked and saw a clamshell container full of cherry tomatoes.

"Don't worry, the container is recyclable," Seth said.

"But of course," I said. "Would a Commando buy anything that wasn't recyclable?"

"Not if we can help it."

I opened the container and popped one into my mouth, relishing the explosion of wonderful tomato-ness as I chewed. "Thanks, Seth." I'd been a jerk for being short with him. He was one of the few people who cared enough to notice what I liked.

We were silent as I ate. But our silence didn't mean there was nothing going on between us. There was a definite vibration, like we'd been magnetized and couldn't resist being drawn together. It was overwhelming.

Seth jumped to his feet and paced. "So where did we end up on Project Pink Cloud?" he asked, turning down the rising temperature between us.

I rushed through the details and ended with how the Commandos had taken a giant leap backward from anything resembling a plan. When I finished telling him that we were failures in the 'change the world' department, he shook his head.

"Better to not do anything that creates more problems than it solves, that's my motto," Seth said.

"You're good at staying out of trouble, Seth. Guess you have to be . . ."

"With a parental unit like Dad?"

"I mean, it seems like just breathing around him can get you in hot water," I said.

Seth was silent. I could tell that my snarky remark had hurt him. I guess I hadn't realized how much he cared about his dad. But why should I be surprised? Love is love. And sometimes it doesn't matter that the person you care for isn't loveable. Finally, I broke the bubble of silence that had ballooned around us.

"I'm sorry. That was thoughtless of me to say." I touched his arm. "I've been wanting to thank you for standing up for me at my dad's funeral. Thank you for bringing me food. Thank you for being you.'"

Seth nodded, not meeting my eyes.

"How are you anyway?" I asked. "Like 'all' of you. Not just the parts I can see—the inside parts too."

Seth sank back down and sat on a rock. "On the 'miserable' scale, I'm at least a seven."

I joined him on the rock. "Let's see if we can get that down to a three. Think about the short time you have till you graduate, and then you can get out of here."

"That makes it worse since I'm not going anywhere."

"What about college? What about becoming an engineer?"

"Dad won't give me the money my grandparents saved for me. Says he needs it for the business."

"Isn't that illegal?"

"Darned if I know. Doesn't matter anyway. I can't leave my mom. One of these days Dad's going to go too far."

"That's so awful. I wish there were some way I could help, Seth. Maybe you should run away . . . and take her."

"I've suggested that, but she won't come."

"I know it seems hopeless right now, but maybe good things will happen, and it'll all work out."

"Thanks. We'll see. How's your gran?"

While he listened to my answer, he stood up and searched for skipping stones. I joined him and soon we were battling for who could skip a stone the greatest number of times.

"What is it about your family and mine?" I said as the battle heightened. "At the hospital today, your mom said some pretty ugly things about my mother."

"Oh, geez. I'm so sorry, Nora." Seth kicked the sandy gravel with the toe of his running shoe.

Must be tough to have two strange parents. Still, it was better than having none.

"She said that Mom ran away with another man. That she was still alive. And Gran practically confirmed at least the 'not being dead' part when she was delirious and thought that I was Mom."

"How's that possible?" he asked. "We were both at her funeral. We both saw her buried."

"But I never saw her body," I said.

Seth's eyes widened. "You were a kid. Who shows a kid the body of their dead parent? It means nothing that you didn't see her."

"But it could," I said. "It *could* mean that she *never died*."

"Look, I can totally understand why you want your mom to still be alive." I could tell he was trying to be sensitive. "But wanting something impossible won't make it happen."

That was when the worst idea—ever—popped into my head.

"There is one way to prove it," I said. Goosebumps raced along my arms. I gulped and leaned forward. Seth leaned in too.

"What?"

"I have to dig up my mother's coffin."

Seth looked at me like I was nuts—then laughed. Just a chuckle at first, but then he really got going and the chuckles became a roll of laughter. Soon, he was laughing so hard he had a few tears running down his face. Finally, he stopped, caught his breath, and wiped his face with the back of his sleeve.

"Whoa. Thanks, Nora. I haven't laughed so hard in, well, ever 'cause I thought you said you were going to dig up your mom's grave."

I wasn't smiling.

"Grave. Your mom's grave. Dig it up. That's what I thought . . ."

"Exactly," I said, standing up, hands on my hips, daring him to guffaw one more time.

He drew himself to his full height and waved his arms like he was trying to erase my words. "No, no, no. Nora. No. That's against common decency—not to mention the law. It's pretty much the most horrible thing I've ever heard," he said.

"More horrible than Dad getting shot and Gran getting sick or us losing our land?"

"Okay, okay. I get your point. Yes, that's all horrible. But grave 'un-digging' is going too far."

"*I'm* going too far? Wonder if you'd say that about your mom who was ransacking Gran's things at the hospital—probably trying to steal *this*." I held out the pouch.

Seth gasped, then raked his fingers down his face like my words were too much. He walked away.

I went after him, reaching him in a few long strides and catching his shoulder with my hand. He stopped and faced me.

"You hate my dad, I get that. Most times I hate him, too, but he's still my dad. But my mom? She's gentle and good to me. Weak, maybe, because she can't leave a man who is so cruel to her. But leaving is not that easy to do. What I don't understand, Nora, is if you hate *them* so much, how can you even like me?"

Oh, man. I had made a mess of this. Big time. "Sorry, Seth, really. I was only trying to tell you what happened. I don't really hate anyone—well, I guess you're right about your dad and me—but I don't get your mom. First saying those things about my mother and then trying to steal something she must have known meant the world to me."

"That doesn't sound like her, Nora. My dad must have put her up to it."

I shrugged. Not an excuse in my book, but I kept my mouth shut.

"Can you show me that pouch? I'd like to see why everyone is making such a big deal about a shriveled-up piece of doeskin," he extended his hand, palm open.

I handed it to him reluctantly, baffled and frustrated by my pendulum of emotions swinging from attraction to distrust. Is that what love was? He weighed it in his hand and held it up for closer examination, then handed it back. "Doesn't look like much to me," he said, without a lick of interest at what was inside.

"So, your dad only wants the pouch?" I asked. "He doesn't care about what's inside?"

"He never said anything about what's in it to me. Just said, 'Bring me that pouch.' Like I was his servant and not his son."

I loosened the cords and tipped it upside down. The jewelry casket tumbled into the palm of my hand, and I stuck it in my pocket so I could examine the pouch. I held it up to the sky for more light—but I couldn't really see anything interesting. It was old, well-seasoned doeskin, and the beading was beautiful.

I turned it inside out. There was a lining made from faded red calico. But that was all there was to it.

"Here. Take it." I said handing him the pouch.

Seth's eyes widened.

"If your dad wants it so badly—take it to him. It's not worth fighting over. The land—our land is something on a different scale entirely. I won't be so nice about making sure he never gets that. But the pouch? He can have that now."

I put it into Seth's hands. But he didn't look at it. He was staring at the jewelry casket in my hand.

"What is that thing anyway?" he asked.

The grey skies disappeared, and a sunbeam returned, poking through the branches of a red alder tree growing close to the shore. I thrust my hand into the yellow light to give a closer look. The jewelry casket sparkled with golden flecks embedded in green stone which was more mottled than I had noticed at first.

"Looks like a rock to me," he said.

Ah, no. It didn't look like that to me at all. "What about this?" I said and pressed the frog medallion that was still stuck in the indentation on the surface of the jewelry casket. The top popped open, exposing the pearl to the air. "How many rocks have something like that inside?" I asked and looked up to see if Seth was as impressed as I was, but the Seth I knew wasn't there. Oh, his body was, but he had a vacant look on his face. He was frozen in time and space like he and everyone else had been at the church.

Like before . . .

. . . the swirls on the pearl pulsed until the colors blurred.

. . . a jolt of energy shook the air.

. . . the air filled with the fragrance of wild roses and berries, warmed by the sun.

. . . prismatic light burst from the pearl and the world grew quiet.

No birdsong, no wind rustling the trees. Even the sound of the river disappeared. Had the world gone silent last time as well? In the moment I couldn't recall. Light shot out from the pearl like lasers and with a swoosh, the water rose from the creek and slammed onto the rocks drenching us, while the rest of the creek bubbled, boiled, and roiled so fast that mist rose.

I snapped the egg shut.

The bubbling stopped.

The creek ran smooth.

The sounds of the forest returned.

The mist cleared.

"Nora? You all right?" Seth asked, his voice wobbly. "Hey, how'd I get so wet?"

"Did . . . did you see that?" I asked.

"See what?"

"You didn't see the water?"

"Well, I *see* water. It's right there in front of us."

I shook my head to clear my brain. "How did you not see what the water did just now?"

"Water flows. It drops. It doesn't do much else. What are you talking about, Nora?" Seth said slowly, like he was questioning a crazy person.

"It danced."

Seth looked at me like I had lost my mind.

"Watch," I cried desperately. I opened the pearl to the air once more.

This time there was no 'frozen time' and with a ferocity that sucked the oxygen out of my lungs, the creek burst into motion, at first bubbling and boiling like before, then spouts sprang up with an intensity that made the water seem alive and jumping out of its skin. And there I stood, my eyes riveted to the sight, breathless, on the rim of that bubbling cauldron which pulled me toward it.

I snapped the jewelry casket shut again.

The creek quieted.

"See? See?" I asked. Seth shook his head like he was clearing a cloud from his brain.

"Nora, you're honestly terrifying me. What are you doing? What do you want me to see?"

"This green egg—when I open it—has a pearl inside that makes the water dance." I felt like a child. I sounded like a child.

"That stone?"

"Yes," I said, holding it up for him to see.

"Nora, it's a rock."

"Here. Put your hand in mine so we're both touching it," I said.

Seth did as I asked, and I had a second of happiness at his touch. I pressed the frog again. Time didn't stop for Seth. He saw what I saw as we both watched the water dance.

When the wonder of it all became overwhelming, I closed the jewelry casket. Life around us resumed. Was there a rule that if you opened the Pearl twice in quick succession, time didn't stand still? I'd have to remember to try that out at another time.

We looked at each other, unable to talk for a few moments. Then Seth said, "I don't know what that was or what it means."

"That pretty much sums up my feelings too," I said. "But there are two more things I want to know— why did my mother have this 'thing' and what, if anything, did she use it for?"

"I'm not sure I want to know," Seth said. "But I do know this pouch belongs around your neck—not my dad's." He handed it back to me. "Keep it and I'll make sure he doesn't ask for it again."

Because Seth wanted me to take it, I did. And who knows. Maybe he was right.

I shoved the jewelry casket back in the pouch and placed the pouch around my neck.

It was time to go.

As we walked away from the river, Seth said, "What time tonight?"

"Tonight?"

"What time tonight are we digging up your mother's grave?"

Linka 🐸 Orders from Headquarters

Two Days Till Pink Moon
Fly Time
Outside the Veil of Mist

L INKA HAD JUST finished talking with some field frogs who had given her a frightening report on the decline of their local population, but the field frogs had no clue about the largetoe she was seeking. There were simply too many about and it was very hard for the field frogs to distinguish one from the other.

Cruising above a river, now, her body ached with exhaustion edged with despair. Both sets of her eyelids were tired, and her head pulsed with frustration. She could tell by the slow dip of Myth's wings that he was tired as well. Plunging into the Web That Connects All Things had taken its toll. And they still hadn't located the Pearl.

She weighed using the last of the energetic twisps. Once that was gone, and if she had not found it yet, the Pearl might be lost forever more. The desire to admit defeat and return to the Palay prickled her webtoes like she had frog fleas.

But she couldn't muster the energy to return home. She was tired. Myth was tired. Her troops were tired.

"Zons, refresh yourself in the river below. Then, Mura and Jineta, you ride to the south and survey the territory for danger. Trep and Roya, you fly to the east. Then you all can join us five hundred hopalometers upriver after your patrol of those areas. Sajay, you come with me," Linka commanded. The other Zons whooped with delight, directed their mounts to nosedive into the river and back out. Pumping their dripping infinators in the air, they flew off as Linka had directed.

When they had gone, Linka heard the water whisper to her. "Princess P'hustalinka . . ."

The call came from beyond the stand of willows around the next curve in the creek. Linka nudged Myth in that direction. Sajay followed.

"Who summons me at such a time?"

"It is me, Aquatessa. Elemento of Water."

Linka looked at the river and saw a wildly beautiful and fluid face constructed of whirling eddies for eyes and water tumbling over rocks for long flowing tresses.

"I am blessed to see you," Linka said as she hovered over the portion of water imbued with Aquatessa's presence.

"I know the location of the Golden Pearl of the Forest."

Linka's veins fizzed with joyful energy.

"The queen asked me to lead you to the largetoe who possesses it. She sent these thought bubbles to guide you."

Linka stripped her armor off, secured it to the saddle with the flyrein, and did a graceful flip off Myth's back into the water, plunging into the middle of the thought bubbles which whirled below the surface.

In an instant of condensed time, Linka absorbed the queen's message:

I send you greetings, dear Linka.

Aquatessa will lead you to the largetoe.

Try to retrieve the Pearl, but if you fail, gather some-thing that contains the girl's essence and send it to your father. I have already instructed him to prepare a vial of the most potent Golden Death he can make. If he has something with her essence, he can make it even stronger. The potion will be delivered to you when it is ready.

Linka surfaced, refreshed yet confused. What should she do? She had been trained to unthinking allegiance, but this order left her queasy and questioning. It was one thing to protect the queen from imminent threat. But to follow this order had far-reaching consequences—where could it lead?

And just because her kind were killed wantonly by the largetoe, was that a moral reason to kill one of them simply for something the queen wanted to possess? Kill in defense—yes. Linka had no moral problem with that. But there was something about the queen's order that left her questioning her very purpose.

"Where is the femtoe now?" Linka asked.

"I will take you to her." Aquatessa rose into a tall wave and carried Linka along. And because water knows all, Aquatessa said, "She is around this bend in my flow and carries the Pearl inside a protective casket made of resistance rock in a pouch made of deerskin and beads."

Linka signaled to Myth who swooped in through the wave and emerged with her once again on his back.

They followed Aquatessa's flow.

Following Aquatessa, Myth cruised low along the surface of the water while Linka donned her armor. Sajay followed, keeping a protective eye on her commander's back.

"You may not sense it if the Pearl's casket remains closed," Aquatessa said. "But trust what I know about largetoe. They keep their riches at hand. And the more valuable the item, the closer they keep it. She will either wear it or keep it within reach unless she is careless enough to lose it. And if that happens, we are all lost, for even I cannot track it unless the casket is opened. Track the girl and you'll soon possess the Pearl. You have my word. Now I must depart."

Linka bid Aquatessa farewell and rounded the bend in the creek. There, on a rock beside the water, stood a towering femtoe. Images of her kind, painted by the Muse Division, had always been shocking. But they did little to prepare her for the terror of being in their presence.

Linka's stomach contents filled her mouth at the sight. She spit the bile into the wind. If it hadn't been for Aquatessa, they might have flown in circles forever less than a quarter of a hopalometer from here.

How many frogs would have to boil to create enough Golden Death to take down a creature of that size? Linka wondered. She landed in a nearby tree to observe the girl and wait for her troops to find her.

18

Nora ◎ Barber-ous Behavior

Two Days Till Pink Moon
Early Afternoon
Salmon Falls River

FTER SETH AND I parted ways, I followed the river toward home until I came to a big rock jutting out over the water. I sat down for a rest and removed the pouch from my neck, dangling it in front of me like a pendulum. Could I use it to divine my future? Or maybe I should toss it in the water and be done with it. But my mother's hands had touched it and that made it sacred to me.

I wondered about the object inside the green jewelry casket. Did it have more powers than I'd already seen? Did it have anything to do with why she wasn't here? Or maybe she really was dead—lying in her coffin. I would know soon.

Streaks of black and green sliced through the air around my head. I stood up and tried to block my face and knocked the pouch against the side of my head. A second later, something yanked my hair. And then whatever had attacked me was gone.

I stared into the creek and saw a short tuft of white hair sticking up in my reflection. My streak of white hair had been stolen.

By what? A flying barber?

I threw the cord back around my neck and tucked the pouch inside my shirt for safekeeping. The outside world was getting weirder by the minute. Time to get home where things were quiet, sane, and lonely.

Linka ⚜ A Hairy Problem

Two Days Till Pink Moon
Fly Time (Late)
Salmon Falls River

L INKA, HER FIST full of largetoe hair, repositioned her infinator on her back and soared high into the sky on Myth. "Python piddle," she mumbled under her breath. Sajay had been tasked with grabbing onto the string of the pouch that contained the Pearl and Linka was supposed to fly in and cut it. But Sajay had grabbed the girl's hair instead. And, in the heat of the moment, Linka had cut it off without realizing their mistake.

They flew on to where they had arranged to meet the other Zons, who were waiting for them in a tall tree.

"Toadation and thunderation," Linka cursed again.

"We failed," Sajay said, her eyes cast down in shame. The other Zons were quiet.

Disappointment—not at Sajay but at herself—pressed on Linka's shoulders. She had bungled her strategy. And the Pearl was so close. But the only thing Linka had come away with was this swath of disgusting largetoe hair.

At least she got a living sample of the beast herself for the dose of Golden Death—although she was still disquieted by that notion.

"Sajay, it was my failure, not yours. Return to the Palay and give this *hair*, I think they call it, to the vizzard. Tell my father I am well and that we are following the largetoe in question."

Sajay didn't move.

"Sajay? What's wrong? You are trembling."

"The largetoe. She was ugly, so ugly. How could the Well of White Light create a creature so vile and terrifying? Even my training did not prepare me for the impact of seeing one in the flesh."

"Steady yourself, femnura, and fly as I have commanded you. We do not judge creatures by their appearance. We value what lies in their hearts and their acts toward their own kind and others."

"Then given the failure of so many largetoes to protect the All, are they all not ugly?" Sajay said.

"All species possess their own kind of beauty. And there is good and bad in every group. Now fly back to the Palay. Jineta, you should accompany her."

"Fight in the Light. Die in the Light. Go to the Light," they said in unison with infinators raised in the Zon salute.

Sajay and Jineta flew off on their mounts toward the Palay, the strand of hair from the largetoe in Sajay's possession. Meanwhile, Linka and the rest of her Zons stayed on the trail of the largetoe who carried the Pearl.

20

Raeburn 🐸 The Maw of Malevolence

Two Days Till Pink Moon
Fly Time (Late)
The Maw

*E*VIL OOZED THROUGH the air as Raeburn, riding a vulture for hire, approached the Maw of Malevolence. This trip would either clinch the queen's demise and assure his takeover of the throne, or it could prove to be his downfall. Never before had one of the queen's subjects visited the Maw and returned to tell the tale. But he must be quick. The queen would expect to see him at the Convocation of Winds later today. And as much as he abhorred his ruler, she was still in power for the moment, and it was best not to call too much attention to his disrespect.

The landscape below was a vast, rocky wasteland devoid of plant life and pockmarked with holes that bubbled and belched toxic gas. General Oddbull ruled this territory and its emanations of Darkness, and no frog, except perhaps a few, lived by choice within its borders. Most inhabitants were prisoners who would never escape. And Raeburn might just be the only frog brave enough to make the arduous journey. But then, his own bravery did not surprise him.

Spurred by the queen's Divine Dream (and the appearance of the Cloak of Quietus perhaps predicting her death), Raeburn had requested and been granted this meeting. Through the spy channels that he had set up some time ago, he reported to the general on the routes of refuge seekers to the Palay.

The general owed him—big time—and he meant to collect. He traveled here in secret without his usual retinue of young frogs, who were almost as eager for power and change as he. Either it would prove foolhardy or the smartest thing he'd ever done, for without Oddbull's assistance with his big plans, he would never go from Lord to King to Resplendent Dictator of the World.

Aflame with the promise of a darker tomorrow, Raeburn directed his vulture to descend through the dense, dark cloud that hovered above the Maw and cast it in perpetual shadow.

As they emerged on the other side, he spotted Oddbull's warriors, the Bulldoggies, flying in circles below him. They were using helpless captives as targets for their aerial drop-net training. Raeburn instructed his ride to make wide circles around the Maw so he could scope out the site.

The Maw itself was impossible to ignore. It was so big, so deep (at least it appeared that way), and so rank in smell, it resembled a fatal wound. Bulldoggie convoys were arriving from all directions bearing captured refugee frogs who had been driven from their homes by disease or loss of land due to the largetoes' passion for destruction.

This was all due to Raeburn himself, who knew every route they had undertaken, thanks to the sow bug spy network that had infiltrated the Palay under his guidance and patronage.

Plus, he had other accomplices of the web-footed kind. His sycophant Kon oversaw capturing any messengers delivering news of the current route refugees were taking to the Palay. Kon would then relay these messages to Oddbull, who used them to easily capture the helpless and exhausted wayfarers. Such easy pickings, it was a wonder the queen hadn't twigged into Raeburn's scam.

Raeburn instructed the vulture to land near the great bridge made of a large, petrified tree trunk that spanned the Maw's opening. Around the Maw's circumference was a line of liths. These giant frogs, goliaths of the amphibian world, acted as guards to the Maw and its commander.

When they landed, the cries of terror from the great pit assaulted Raeburn's ear pads. Always prepared, he removed his skullcap, which he had decorated with painted cactus needle spikes, and untucked the ear pad protectors so they could perform their intended function. He put his cap back on, dismounted, and adjusted his new moleskin mantle, also armed with spikes to make himself a less tasty morsel.

Assured that he looked his finest, he approached the bridge. Halfway across was General Oddbull himself. Raeburn caught a glance at his back, visible through the figure-eight openings of the infinators from which the clamshell-shaped throne was made. *Oh, how it would vex Princess Linka to see her weapon of choice used this way*, Raeburn thought with glee.

The throne was obviously built to swivel and move back and forth across the length of the bridge, pushed by Bulldoggies. Raeburn readied himself to face the general, trying to suppress his joy at being here. Everything about this place invigorated him, and he longed to issue a croak of joy that would rock the world.

But he knew he could not. Had he tried, he would only have managed an embarrassingly hoarse burp at best. (Secretly, Raeburn suspected that his lack of croak, along with the small tail-like protrusion on his rump, were part of a family curse, for he was descended from the most reviled frog in history, Prince Ponte-Fricani. It was for this reason—or so he told himself—that his family and he were so despised and despised everyone else in return.)

Now on the ground, he couldn't help but notice the vile stench, which reminded him of a mélange of fermented frog, rancid pond scum, and various harsh, metallic fragrances. Breathing in the noxious air with relish, he watched some liths come dangerously close to him as they forced a group of captured frogs over the Maw's edge.

The surge of screams as they disappeared made Raeburn's brownish skin ripple with a delicious feeling of terror and glee. He carefully approached the edge of the great pit and watched as the newest additions were absorbed into the churning mass. It was mesmerizing. What a perfect ecosystem of self-perpetuating malice.

As soon as they were inside the pit, these once lively amphibians had their lifeforce, vim, and verve extracted through the osmosis of evil, and they were less than shadows of their former selves. They had become idilons, vaporous blue zombie-frogs. Now and forever. Or at least that was the belief.

Raeburn noticed a transparent frog, a recent metamorph, clinging to the edge of the Maw using the strong suction cups on the underside of his flippers.

"Please, please, do not make me go!" the young frog cried.

"Over the edge with you," said a lith with a droopy eye and body armor formed from arrows threaded through his own skin. The lith stabbed at the little frog's hands. But the transparent one dodged each staff strike, sliding closer and closer to Raeburn.

"Oh, Great Lord," the little frog implored Raeburn, "I beseech you. Save me from the Maw."

Raeburn bristled at the interruption. "Give me one good reason I should. I do not even know your name."

"Wink, sire. My name is Wink. My uncle, Clarenso, is aide to the Grand and Glorious Vizzard." Raeburn contemplated the pros and cons of compassion. *What could it hurt to help this well-connected wee one?* "Liths, spare this frog. This Wink. I will compensate your master."

Wink leapt to Raeburn's side. "Thank you, Great Lord. My uncle will be indebted as will I."

Raeburn heard a heavy rumble. "Get behind me and stay there. You are not safe yet," Raeburn whispered.

Raeburn's revery was interrupted when the general swiveled his throne to face him and spoke in a voice so deep, the bridge rattled with every word. "With your pretty skullcap, I can see that you think very highly of yourself, do you not?"

Raeburn stifled a gasp as he took in the magnitude of Odd-bull's incredibleness. Clearing his throat, he said confidently, "I admit to a keen sense of my own elevated destiny—and fashion."

"Personally, I worry more about what goes inside my body than what is on the outside," Oddbull said, and he laughed so hard the chains of frog bones piercing his lips and face clacked together with a ghoulish sound. His infested flesh quivered with each fiendish guffaw until the bridge beneath them undulated like an ocean wave from the force of his laughter.

"Come, my friend. Come closer," Oddbull said.

Raeburn gulped and leapt onto the bridge but didn't advance. Wink followed.

"Who is that tender transparent morsal accompanying you?" Oddbull asked.

"He begged for my protection before being tossed into the Maw, and I granted it."

"You did what?" Oddbull shrieked, with such force Raeburn worried that the general's foul breath would melt the quills from his skullcap.

"Please, calm yourself. We will be partners in this venture I am about to propose. That gives me the right to do as I please," Raeburn said.

"Your bug-brained act of generosity comes at my expense," Oddbull said.

"You may add it to my balance when our negotiations are through," Raeburn said, then he instructed Wink to wait at the top of the wall surrounding the Maw until it was time to go. No one must hear the conversation that was about to occur.

Raeburn felt more at ease once Wink had withdrawn. Whenever he was nervous, Raeburn's head itched like he'd been bitten by a thousand mosquitos. He longed to rip off his ridiculous skullcap and toss it in the pit, but pride prevented him from removing it.

"How, dear sir, does this whole Maw thing work?" Raeburn asked, trying not to stare.

"Are you an ignoramus?" Oddbull bellowed. "Tads everywhere should know this tale."

"The queen controls the inflow and outflow of information. We know what she wants us to know," Raeburn said. "There are rumors, of course, but I only know you are the queen's greatest nemesis. Next to me. And that is why I am here. To seek your help to destroy the queen so I can take over the throne."

"An interesting idea. We will contemplate," Oddbull said.

"Before we do, I feel that it is in my best interest to better understand what you are all about," Raeburn stated.

"It is simple, really," Oddbull said. "As the queen sits atop Frog Mountain, directly over the Well of White Light, I sit above the Maw, its geological and metaphysical opposite. The Maw extracts lifeforce from the captured frogs as you have just witnessed. This lifeforce, in liquid form, drains down through the Maw's central vent, where it pools in a now-dormant magma chamber. Then, after a period of fermentation that infuses maximum evil into every molecule, the goo flows out through empty lava channels that circle the globe."

"How delightful," Rayburn said, clapping his hands.

"And with all the new holes being dug deep into the earth by the largetoe for the extraction of precious minerals, gasses, and oil, our evil goo has many places to emerge and cause havoc. For once it emerges from the ground, it vaporizes. And when inhaled by humans, it fosters bad moods, evil deeds, unkindness, cruelty, greed, despair, jealousy, depression, anger, resentment, prejudice, hate, and pettiness.

"The only deterrent to our malevolent mist is the dream power that the queen's CODERs create. But with the decline in the number of field frogs to relay that dream energy, it is hardly a fair contest anymore."

"Malevolence holds more sway than love every time, although I find it interesting that the balance of Light and Dark in the world as a whole comes down to frogs," Raeburn said.

"Delicious, is it not?" said Oddbull, smacking his lips. "Inferior largetoes prefer to believe in aspirations like kindness, compassion, and equality, where everyone has equal power to pursue their dreams. We proudly power superior despots, dictators, and demons, and they do the rest."

The general was more philosophical than Raeburn had expected.

"Thankfully, largetoes are lazy about making their dreams come true. Evil is easier. It is second nature for most creatures to put themselves first, and in that inclination alone lies fertile ground to increase the authority of darkness. Love is vastly more difficult. It requires a willingness to sacrifice one's own well-being by putting the needs of others in first position," the general added.

"Who would do that?" Raeburn said, laughing.

General Oddbull joined Raeburn in his merriment. "When we love, we are weak, vulnerable to pain," he said.

"And hate makes us strong," Raeburn added.

"I will eat to that," Oddbull said. As he spoke, he plunged his arm into the Maw and pulled out a handful of idilons, which he waved about with a bloodthirsty croak. Raeburn sighed with envy at the sound of Oddbull's voice.

Writhing, some of the idilons escaped the gigantic frog's grasp and fell back into the Maw with screams and moans. With a slurp, Oddbull vacuumed the squirming bodies that remained in his fist into his cavernous mouth. Then, remembering his manners, he offered a flailing frog torso to Raeburn, who declined. Oddbull stuffed it into his mouth and reached for another handful.

"You do not know what you are missing," Oddbull said, shaking his head with delight at the flavorful mouthful. Bloody debris from his frenzied feast flew in an arch. Raeburn hopped backward to avoid being hit.

Then a burp from Oddbull shook the air. "Now that I have partaken of a snack, tell me why you are here."

"I want you to help me depose the queen, as I have already stated," Raeburn said. "It is my divine plan. I shall do it. With or without you."

"You are a bold one."

"Think of your hunger for power, General. With my plan you could assuage it."

"One does not crave what one already has, my good frog. I already have power, more than you and even more than the queen."

"But what if I were to tell you that the foundation of your power may be threatened?"

Oddbull stopped mid-chew, then shook his head in denial. Ropes of bloody saliva flew in all directions.

"You are as foolish as you are finicky, my friend. I am confident in the balance of power as it stands now. In fact, every sun cycle my power grows. With more frogs losing their homes, they have no choice but to make their way to the Palay. Their weakened health from deteriorating environmental conditions, the strain of traumatic loss, and the harshness of the journey to the Palay make them easy prey."

"But things have happened that you do not know about," Raeburn said. "The queen has had another dream."

"A dream? Tell all."

"She has not yet shared details, but the rumors, thanks to my faithful network of spies, say that it foretold of the coming of a femtoe who possesses the Golden Pearl of the Forest."

"The Pearl has been found?" Oddbull's jaw dropped. A half-chewed idilon crawled out between a gap in Oddbull's teeth and landed on the ground beside Raeburn.

Raeburn kicked the twitching idilon back into the pit and ignored Oddbull's question on purpose, especially since he wasn't sure of the answer himself.

"How do you plan to use this information?" Oddbull asked.

"I want your Bulldoggies plus your idilons from the Maw, a million strong, to march to Frog Mountain to unseat our monarch."

"You want to use my idilons as warriors for your cause?"

"It is *our* cause."

Oddbull looked skyward, a contemplative expression on his face.

Raeburn could tell Oddbull was thinking about his request and that such deep thought was painful to a brain so used to easy satisfaction.

"The idilons have never been free of the Maw. How will I manufacture evil without their presence here?" Oddbull asked.

"They will bring their negative energy along with them, extending your reach as they suck up and destroy all the lifeforce in their path. I'm quite surprised that you did not think of this before," Raeburn said in his most convincing voice.

"Oh?"

"The power, the freedom, the food you will get for helping me will exceed your seasonal take many times over. When we breach the Palay's fortifications, the number of Palaysians available for the picking will more than compensate for a temporary downturn in volume. And that is only phase one of my plans."

Raeburn flicked idilon bits off his mantle. "Come to think of it, perhaps my offer is too generous."

"Not at all, Raeburn. Overrun the Palay and depose the queen?" Oddbull asked. "Then what?"

"Then we move on to the world of the largetoe and overtake it with frogs of every remaining kind. I have an accelerated breeding plan that could create enough frogs to take over the entire world in less time than you imagine. There are already experiments underway," Raeburn said, rubbing his hands together. "And once we have used the masses to rid the world of largetoe vermin, you can eat whatever you like. Maybe you can even eat largetoes."

Oddbull's eyes bulged with interest. He shook his massive head, whipping the ever-dripping ropes of blood-pink drool about. "I must have time. And more idilons."

"I will leave you with more routes of the refuge seekers, although it is getting harder to abscond with this information as I think the queen grows suspicious."

"You have done well, supplying me with this information. I owe you something for that. But I am no traveler. How will we find our way?" Oddbull said, reluctant to admit any shortcoming.

Raeburn removed his skullcap, taking care not to prick himself, and took out two small leaflets hidden inside.

"Easily solved. I brought directions." Raeburn unfurled one of them—a specially prepared lily pad with a notated map to the queen's home. "I have even designed a platform to facilitate your travel," he said, pointing to the other leaflet. He put them both down in front of him and kicked it toward the general. There was no way he'd endanger his life by getting within Oddbull's reach. What if he presented too tasty of a morsel to resist?

Examining the drawing, Oddbull pondered the notion. "How would we gain access to the grounds once we were there? No one has ever challenged the queen's power in her own territory."

"Trust me. I know the weaknesses of the Palay," Raeburn said. "And the queen, for that matter."

"The risk is too great," Oddbull said. "If we failed, it would mean the end of us both."

"Land-hungry largetoe have made you lazy," Raeburn observed.

"And I am grateful to them," Oddbull said. "I have little incentive to help you, my grand-tailed friend."

"What can I grant you when I am King of Frogs?" Raeburn asked. "Is there nothing you have dreamed of having?"

"There is one thing," he said. His long, spear-like tongue snaked out of his mouth to lick the slobber from his bulbous lips. "The queen herself. Nothing tastes better than a fricassee of enemy."

Raeburn pondered the general's request. He had his own plans of revenge against the queen, but perhaps the sacrifice was worthwhile.

"She is yours," Raeburn answered, his smile bright.

"Are you not forgetting one thing?" Oddbull asked.

"And what would that be?"

"The refuge seekers' routes," Oddbull said.

Raeburn fished a third leaflet out of his hat and gave it to the general. He climbed aboard the vulture, then they picked up Wink and departed.

"Don't forget—you owe me for that one," Oddbull called after them.

Not long after Lord Raeburn's departure, Oddbull summoned the head of his field troops.

"I want Bulldoggie patrols sent out in all directions. I want the Pearl. It will be mine, no matter what—or who—has to be sacrificed to get it."

21

The Queen Convocation of Winds

Two Days Till Pink Moon
Sundown
Plaza of the Setting Sun

AT THE TOP of Frog Mountain was an open gathering place called the Plaza of the Setting Sun. The queen sat under the Crystal Contemplation Dome at the center of this spot deep in meditation. Her white-quartz throne was configured to look like clouds. Her cloak, woven in spun gold threaded with precious gems, depicted the setting rays of the sun. She looked about to see members of her court gathered round. Azzie, of course, was on his mission. But where was Raeburn? Somewhere plotting against her no doubt.

The countdown crow cawed, "Sundown. The Convocation of Winds must now begin."

Nervousness rose in the queen's throat, tearing her from her meditative state. But before she brought her full senses back to the outer world, she prayed:

May I act with wisdom and restraint.
May I put the needs of others before my own.
May I deserve the title Queen.

Her ability to summon the Elementos themselves and their minions was a sacred gift. Aquatessa, the Essence of Water; Igneo, Fire's Heat; Magmo, Spirit of Rock; and Bortos, Wind's Fury, were the essential elements—the Elementos.

With a wave of her scepter, today tipped with a blazing emerald, the queen opened the dome, which unfurled like a budding wild rose. The hum of the crowd crashed over her like a stormy wave. Almost every inhabitant of the Palay had gathered in the plaza to watch the coming phenomenon. A crowd lingered around the Pool of Water Shining Bright, while others gathered in the Swampy Swamp, a wild and natural habitat that surrounded the more highly groomed pool.

Bacareno ordered the burfers in training from the sky. These young flyers were cruising overhead, practicing their lessons from the Royal School of Burfing. Trailing banners and flags of various colors and weaves, they enlivened the sky with their dives and loop-de-loops. But even the most experienced flyer could not withstand the collective force of the winds the queen was about to summon, and their safety was paramount.

A halo of brightly colored pygmy hummingbirds, unique to the Palay, swooped in and hovered above the queen's head: a symbolic touch designed to give her summons wings.

Bacareno opened his white-rimmed mouth and cried, "Ocie, ocie. Let the summoning begin."

Raking the space above her head with her hands, the queen drew sparkling white energy from the sky. She inhaled, held her breath, then spoke in tones both long and low.

"To Bortos and his winds of the east, west, north, and south, hear Queen Ranya's plea. Send your sons and daughters forth. Bring my council to me."

Her hummingbird crown carried her invocation into the sky, releasing pouches of fragrant violet petals as they flew.

There was silence. A spring breeze from the south wafted in, but before its cousins from the other directions could follow, threads of the Dark Wind, the same amalgam of blustery air that had accosted Azzie, coalesced into tentacles and dove toward the queen with unleashed ferocity.

The air filled with high-pitched sounds, like rocks being rent apart. The crowd covered their ear pads to protect them from the piercing noise.

Queen Ranya drew her cloak about her and willed the dome to snap shut.

"Zons, to the sky!" she commanded. She watched as they mounted their bats and took flight.

But as the Zons attacked, the Dark Winds split into even finer strands that wrapped themselves around each Zon and her mount and whipped them about.

Other tentacles thrashed the Contemplation Dome then grabbed hold and rocked the dome above the queen until the crystal shattered. The queen was exposed to the full fury of the wind, which gathered itself into a ball and whirled in front of her, shredding her cape with its force.

"Who gave you permission to enter?" the queen boomed with a tone that matched the ferocity of the wind.

The Dark Winds dropped an object in front of her. Simeon scurried forth, picked it up, and handed it to the queen.

Ranya gasped at the sight of it. It was Azzie's wristband. She had given it to him herself.

"My son invited you?"

"It was not an invitation but a promise. He promised that at the sight of this object, you would admit us and hear our plea."

"And what did you promise for such a token?"

"We promised to spare his life," the Dark Winds said. "We have no use for baubles. We need a queen who will stand up for us."

"Exactly what is it you want?" the queen demanded.

Dark Winds wailed and moaned as if they were singing all the notes from a complex chorus all at once.

"We are the Winds of the Earth, poisoned and befouled by the largetoe. As the Voice of Nature, it is up to you to lead the revolt against them. Destroy their homes. Drive them from the Earth. As queen, you must take your place at the front of the advance as the All rebels against the largetoe scourge."

"What would you have me do?"

"Your duty. Speak for Nature. Speak before the dirt and the filth we are forced to carry chokes you. Largetoe have left no spot untouched on Earth. If you do not act, then we will take our revenge on the entire planet, shredding everything on Earth to bits. Even now, we gather our forces from all directions. Act now or we pity you all. You've had chances to stop them. You had a chance to stem the tide of destruction, but you willfully ignored it. You weren't even willing to bring us all together to try to solve these problems on our own. No, instead, you insisted on a fake Ceremony of Renewal and wouldn't even give us the choice of participating in the sham. You are supposed to be the voice of Nature, but you only speak for yourself."

"Do not threaten me, Dark Winds. I rule with the advice of my council. I am calling on your milder, better-behaved cousins to fetch my Frog Council. Winds of good heart, appear before me," the queen commanded.

Winds from the north, south, east, and west arrived, whirled around their rebel cousins, and caressed Queen Ranya.

"We have not abandoned you," the north wind said in a soothing voice.

"We will honor our ancient contract," the south, east, and west winds said in unison as they circled her protectively, pushing the Dark Winds back.

"Change *must* come. Radical change. We have warned you!" screamed the Dark Winds, then they disappeared with a great *whoosh*.

The queen could barely repeat her request for the *good* winds, as she would evermore call them, to bring her Frog Council to her. She paused, waiting for her hummingbirds to release their violet petals in tribute to the winds.

"My hummingbirds, where are they?"

The vizzard approached, his head bowed. He opened his hands to reveal the dead bodies of the queen's well-loved pygmy hummingbirds, who had been bashed by the Dark Winds.

The queen stifled a sob.

Murmurs of regret and sadness wafted through the Plaza.

The Zons, armor in tatters, landed. Their fine skin and the skin on the wings of their mounts showed signs of bleeding and bruising from their battle. One of the Zons collected the tinier-than-tiny hummingbird bodies from the vizzard and spirited them away.

The queen remained silent.

The crowd recovered from their shock, straightened their tattered cloaks and collars, and brushed away the dust. Those who were injured received help.

They looked to their queen. But she said nothing.

"Act for the good of the All," one frog cried, and others joined in like ripples across a pond. Soon, everyone on the Plaza was chanting the phrase.

Queen Ranya raised her scepter and spoke. "Worry not, my subjects. All will be well. Four Winds, you may depart with my message to the council."

The winds departed.

The queen said to the crowd, "Return to your sleeping nests while we await the council."

And they did, grumbling to each other about the outrageous behavior of the Dark Winds. Some even complained about the queen.

"She avoids responsibility at our peril," the queen overheard one frog say.

"What are we going to do if the Dark Winds return?" said another.

"We're doomed," said a third frog.

The queen clamped her jaw shut. It was best not to respond.

And then at the worst possible moment, Azzie returned.

The crowd booed. Word of his shameful behavior at the Ceremony of Renewal had arrived earlier.

Queen Ranya abandoned her son to the cursing crowd and descended into the center of the Palay on the stone pillar that held her throne.

Night fell and the queen's spirit plummeted into dark territory.

Nora ◎ Dirty Business

Two Nights Till Pink Moon
Evening
The Peters' Family Cemetery

IT WAS NIGHT. Late. We were on the grounds of my family cemetery at the far end of our acreage. Ironically, it contained the graves of both Peters family members going back to the mid-1880s and some earlier graves that belonged to the Kincades. Simple stones marked each grave. They were strangers to me, even though I carried their blood in my veins. The only person I'd known besides my mother (if she was here) was my grandfather, who was buried ten feet or so from where we were about to dig.

The hiss of the kerosene lantern I'd brought from our barn annoyed me as much as the sickly smell it gave off, like one part drying oil paint mixed with one part natural gas. Its weak yellowy light poured onto the dark ground around my mother's grave, making it look like we were seeing it through a window-pane blurred by time.

Both Seth and I wore baseball hats backward and had taped our cell phones, in flashlight mode, onto the hats like miners' lamps so we could see where we were digging. I even had a flashlight in my back pocket. Every bit of light was necessary, since the night sky was cloudy most of the time, preventing the moon, which would be full tomorrow night, from helping us out.

I silently asked my ancestors to forgive me for what I was about to do and removed the vases that sat on top of the grave. The flowers in them were all dead. Been a while since Dad and I visited, so I offered Mom an apology as well.

I drove my shovel into the flat earth near the gravestone, which read *Regina Peters* with the date of her death. I had never noticed before that her birth date wasn't there. I wondered why not. Also missing was her last name before she got married. *Maiden name* was the term, but I hated that throwback to medieval times.

My digging set off Mickey. He barked and raced around us, even butting me with his nose trying to herd us away from the spot. Too late to change my mind about bringing him. He'd been stranded in his outdoor pen since after the funeral and I mistakenly thought he'd relish a field trip.

I wished Mihn had stayed home. Without even asking me, Seth had brought him along to "make things go faster." I hadn't planned on telling anyone about this little escapade.

"I don't feel good about this," Minh said. "It's not right. If I ever dream again, I'll probably dream about this, and it'll be another nightmare."

"Kameela says she doesn't dream much anymore—and when she does it's always a nightmare," I said.

Minh nodded.

"Same with me," Seth said.

What was up with them? I wondered. Then I remembered that the same thing was happening to me. Hardly any more dreams. But the ones I had were always bad. Must be a sign of the dark times we were in.

"Minh, I'm sorry, but it's something that I've got to do," I said.

I was aware not only of his disapproval (and Seth's) but of my ancestors' disapproval as well, despite my apology to them. It was like there were spirits gathered around the air above us, shaking their fingers and scolding me. I knew what I was doing was shocking. I would never be able to unsee what I might see. In fact, there was no good outcome to this deed. Either I saw an empty coffin, or I saw my mom's skeleton. Both nightmare sights for different reasons. But I had to know.

"Let's get the headstone out of the way first," I said.

Minh stared at me, the horror in his eyes growing. He reached out to touch it, then pulled his hand back like he'd been burned.

"I'm sorry, Nora, Seth, but you're on your own."

He backed away from us like we had some disease. Then he bumped into another headstone, jumped a few feet in the air, and ran back the way we had come.

I began to cry.

"You can go too, Seth," I said between sobs and sniffles, ashamed of involving anyone else but myself in this ghoulish plan.

"You know me better than that. Let's get it done."

I wiped away my tears and we worked together in silence until we were ready to remove the headstone. It wasn't that big, but it was still heavy, and it took effort on both our parts to get it loose and then to move it safely out of the way.

Seth and I took turns with the dirt. First one of us would use a pick to loosen it in a big circle over where we thought the coffin might be. Then the other would come behind and shovel it away. There was no real easy way to do it.

Thankfully there was little chance of anyone stumbling in on our dig party because, number one, we were on my family's property, and number two, we were far away from anything but the dirt road that led there.

"Why are you helping me?" I asked Seth.

"Shut up. I'm digging."

"You don't have to."

"Yeah. You've told me a hundred times."

Not only did we have to clear the dirt over that space, we also had to clear space around the coffin so we had a place to stand while we raised the lid. But we had to reach the coffin first. After what seemed like hours, the hole was deep enough so that only our heads stuck out. My teeth were chattering from the cold and every part of me hurt.

I'd been avoiding telling him about what had happened the night my dad died. Now was the time.

I used practically the same words to describe the horrible scene to him that I'd used before, and he was every bit as shocked as everyone else had been.

When I was done with the story, I stopped digging and looked at him. There was compassion and sadness on his face.

"Nora, that's terrible. Why didn't you tell me?"

I shrugged.

"Let's stop this. You need a break. We can come back tomorrow. Finish up."

I ignored him and kept on digging, with fury this time.

He was staring at me, then, after a bit, he got back to digging. Time passed. And the night made noises beyond us. After a lot more digging, we heard a *thud*.

We'd hit the wooden coffin.

The air chilled unexpectedly like the door to an icy hell had opened. We looked up from our work and saw a ground-hugging fog as it snaked around the other gravestones and head straight toward us. When it passed over our heads, it muted the lantern's light.

The hair on the back of my neck froze into micro-icicles.

Mickey growled.

A moan came from deep within the fog. It was like no other sound I'd ever heard—was it an animal in pain? Or a monster from hell?

"Leave the dead alone," the voice hissed.

All the warmth in my body drained out through my feet. I swallowed hard. "Who are you?"

"The guardian of dead secrets. Now go. Let the past sleep in peace."

The shadow lurched toward the grave.

"Seth, duck!" I yelled, instinctively covering both our heads. Whoever—or whatever—it was leapt across the opening. Fabric grazed my hand and tangled in my fingers.

The figure landed with a thud on the other side, and we heard steps with an uneven cadence head into the forest beyond.

Mickey tore after it.

"Mickey! Come back here!" I said, calling for him. By the time I'd scrambled out of the hole, both the grave jumper and the dog were gone.

"He'll be fine. He knows where he lives," Seth said reassuringly.

I climbed back down the hole, taking the lantern with me.

"Who was that . . . that jumper?" Seth asked.

"Or *what* was it?" I asked. "Some homeless guy? Your dad in disguise?" I shook the shivers off and looked at what I'd caught—some ragged fibers knotted together in a wad. I shoved it in my pocket for a later look.

"You can't blame everything on my dad, you know," Seth said. "Besides, he's too egotistical to disguise himself. When he does something bad, he wants everyone to know it's him. Not to mention, he could never jump like that."

We both snorted with slightly hysterical laughter.

Finally, the top of the coffin was cleared of dirt.

It was time to open it, but I didn't rush to do the deed.

Seth moved to the same side of the coffin as me, and I handed him the lantern so I could use both hands. He held it high.

I opened the simple metal clasp and raised the lid, which moved easily.

Before I looked down, I stared up at the sky. I couldn't see the stars, but they pulled at me. I wanted to be on another planet. Then the ripening moon bashed through the clouds and added to the lantern's light, casting sharper shadows everywhere.

With a deep breath and pounding heart, I looked inside.

What I saw ripped my breath away.

It was filled with rocks.

Seth and I looked at each other.

"My mother must be alive. Alive!" I shouted. I hugged Seth with joy and he hugged back tightly. For a moment I was happy. Then I began to shiver and shake. Seth's embrace kept me from falling to the ground.

If she wasn't dead, where was she? *And why,* I thought with a surge of anger, *had everyone I loved lied to me, including her?*

I propped the lid open with the shovel and fought the urge to crawl inside. But the urge got too strong and I didn't even know why. Was it to be closer to where I had imagined my mother lay? She wasn't even there.

My phone battery was dead, so I took off my hat and got out my flashlight. Then despite Seth's urging, I stretched out on the bed of rocks. I didn't know which story to believe. My family's story—that Mom got sick and died—or Seth's mom's story—that she ran away. Or was there another explanation that only she could tell me. . . if I ever found her?

"Hey, come on, get out of there," Seth said.

But I wasn't ready to go. My life had shifted catastrophically yet again. What's worse? Being without a parent because they're dead? Or being without a parent because they don't want to be with you?

"I will find her, Seth. Wherever she is. And when I find her, I'll tell her how much I hate her."

"You don't mean that."

"I don't? Watch me." I scanned the interior of the coffin with my flashlight and spotted something sticking to the underside of the lid.

23

Will O' The Winds

Various times around the globe

DEEP IN A teakwood forest, a Malaysian tree frog, Lady Li, sensed the queen's call. She had a mere tick to find the right leaf for her journey and to put on her best flying cape.

"Oh, Well of White Light, let me choose wisely."

Her hand was guided to a sturdy broad teak leaf. She hopped on, and a moment later the whirlwind breeze sent by the queen lifted her into the sky.

On the great plains of the desert, Gindjurra the Magnifico, sensed the reverberations of the queen's call in his bones. He dug his puffy, round, pale-yellow body deeper into his favorite termite mound with his small head. *Drat. Not again.*

What awful situation could warrant another trip from his dark, cool home into the glare of the sun and the gale-force winds required to move his rather large body about?

"Never mind, love," said his mate, Lucia, who was burrowed in cozily beside him. "You will be back before I realize you are gone. Always are."

"This is true, but circumstances for our kind grow treacherous, and I fear more the reason for the trip than the trip itself," Gindjurra croaked.

"Now, now. The council has never failed us before, nor has the queen. Come, my sweet, let us return to the surface so the spiders can fit you with enough arachnachutes for your journey. They have been working on them full-time since your return from the last summons." Lucia grunted daintily as she propelled her body forward. "I have even woven you a special reinforced flying platform out of eucalyptus leaves and branches to make your journey more comfortable."

"Very well then. Must be ready for the willy-willy when it blows by." Gindjurra practiced squinting before he moved into the hot light cast by the sun down under.

Lord Yan refused to open his eyes as the typhoon blew around him. The harsh winds that had carried him into the eye of the storm had already shredded his burfing leaf. He had an ugly picture in his head of his red-and-black-mottled belly hanging out for anyone to see. He would have a word of complaint with the queen when he arrived at the Palay. It was unnecessary to send such powerful winds to carry him forth. If he were huge, like some of his fellow council members, force would be required. But he was so light and small that a mere zephyr would suffice.

He would have preferred to remain in the cool, damp darkness of the bamboo forest, but who dares to refuse the queen's call?

While Lady Li, Gindjurra the Magnifico, and Lord Yan were being whipped up into the sky by winds under the queen's command, there were countless other council members from all over the world who took to the air as well. Lord Shaba from Ruska, Lady Ranocchia from the Peninsula of the Boot, Lord Dofedi El-Gabal from the Land of the Pyramids. Lady Batrachas from Many Islands in Bright Blue Water, Lord Oscar-froskur from the Land of Ice, Lady Keewada from the Ouaddaï Highlands, Lord Byang from Bangala—and more. Not all would survive the perilous journey. The queen would do all she could to keep them safe using her powers that stretched beyond the Palay. But as everyone knew, she was not infallible.

Azzie ~ The Heart of the Matter

Two Nights Till Pink Moon
Late Swarm Time
The Palay, Chantry Cavern, and Beyond

AZZIE MADE HIS way from his quarters above the Royal Academy of Burfing where he worked as an instructor as part of his royal duties. One day, when he was king, he would automatically be the Most High Commander of the FAFA. It was vital that he be an accomplished flyer by then so he would have the respect of those he commanded. Ironically, once he assumed that title, he would not actually be able to fly anymore because of the girth he was destined to gain.

Maybe that was why he was so restless and longed to flee royal duties. There would come a day when fleeing was not an option. He had seen the toll it had taken on his mother, once a most active frog, to become so large she could only move with assistance. It was a pity that she could not even leave the Palay. (Although he was rather grateful, as she had not seen his shameful behavior yesterday.) He dreaded being in the same state.

Getting back to a regular schedule was the best thing to do until his incident of shame was dealt with—or forgotten. But every scheduled student had canceled their nighttime flying lessons, probably reluctant to be associated with him.

He was a total and complete failure. Everything terrified him, from the dead frogs he'd seen floating in that mountain lake, to his humiliating show of cowardice at the faux Ceremony of Renewal, to his terror of answering his mother's summons later today. He was a fraidy-frog, yes, but so was she for not facing the challenges of her kingdom head-on.

On the other side of the Veil of Mist, he had blamed the largetoe for what he had seen. They must know, they must see what they are doing to the world. So why weren't they doing everything to stop and reverse the damage?

But his own kind wasn't without fault either. His mother and other royals, himself included, knew of the heart-wrenching, life-threatening problems their kind were experiencing. Why weren't they using every tool at hand to try to change things? Were they complacent cowards or were they simply uncaring? Or maybe they didn't want to be inconvenienced?

Why wasn't everyone—largetoe, amphibian, animal—asking *What can I do? What should I do for the greater good of the All?*

Azzie barely had control over his own behavior so it was unfair to expect others to control theirs, but perhaps he could exert some influence on his mother, and she could work to influence others. But all this would have to wait for his meeting later in the day with the queen.

He was almost late for his other duties as shift supervisor in one of the many dream pods relegated to the depths of the Palay, right above the Well of White Light. There was one question that had never fully been answered by even the wisest of frog philosophers (at least to Azzie's satisfaction): Why had the Well divined that frogs were the creatures to convert the Well's energy to frequencies that would inspire those two-footed demons to dream?

And why did the largetoe ignore any obligation to return the favor and gift back something to the world of amphibians in gratitude for what they received? Instead, they used this gift to dream up monstrous acts. On that he and Raeburn agreed.

But this was not the time for deep philosophical thoughts. He had a job, one of many, to do and even though he could have asked someone else to work this shift, he didn't. Because princes don't ask for help. They did their duty, even if frogs like Frago thought he was a shirker. Yes. He was a party frog, he admitted that, but he was still young. Hopefully it would be a long time until the crown even passed to him, if indeed it ever did.

Before yesterday, Azzie would have stuck out his tongue and given the world a great big raspberry. Before yesterday, duty was a lot of hooey. Today, he only wanted to do the right thing—though he was not sure what the right thing was.

A gong sounded three times. Azzie entered Chantry Cavern and turned down Tourmaline Tunnel Run which led to the dream pod he supervised. Tourmaline Tunnel was one of several tunnel runs. There was Rose Quartz Crystal Run, Tiger's Eye Run, and Amethyst Run, and they were all named for the rock they were carved from. Every type of rock found in the depths of the earth grew out of the Well of White Light below them and snaked across the globe.

As usual, the vast channels of water flowing on either side of the tunnel sent prickles of anxiety through his body. Would his fear of water ever unclench his soul? There were only a few last-shift stragglers to nod to—if they dared to even meet the prince's glance. No formalities down here. He liked that. He had risen to his position on his own merit. In the pods, all frogs were equal. He entered the southern sector and passed Dream Pod Stellarus and Dream Pod Trinitarium. The next one, Dream Pod Centurion, was his.

Centurion, like all the other pods, was shaped like the bottom half of a gigantic basin and was already filled with designated CODERs.

Two gongs. He had arrived barely in time. As he darted into the pod, he slammed into Lem, the chantry commander. There was only one reason Lem would be here: trouble.

"Excuse me, Your Highness, I mean Azzie," Lem said, remembering Chantry protocol. "There seems to be a serious problem in the eastern sector."

"The eastern sector?" Azzie said. "What kind of *serious* problem?"

"It is best that I show you."

Azzie's mind whirled with distractions. Would he be able to solve this problem *and* make his meeting with his mother on time? She would not tolerate tardiness, and he was already in deep pond goo with her.

"I cannot leave the pod unsupervised," Azzie said.

"I will get a replacement for your pod work so you can come with me now," Lem said.

"Better get us each a pika to ride. I must be back here by end of shift," Azzie said, a ring of new-found confidence in his voice. It was a good sound.

Lem gave him a nod and left to rustle up some rides and a shift supervisor to replace Azzie.

After Lem left, Azzie got down to work. The CODERs settled into their nests, lined with beautiful mosaic patterns crafted from transmitter rock. The room glowed with pale yellow light emanating from the phosphorescent moss that covered the ceilings with star-shaped pieces cut away. It created the illusion of a yellow sky populated with dark stars.

The final gong sounded, and a beetle began to roll its ball of dung around the top edge of the pod. When it returned to its starting point, the shift would be over.

The frogs entered their meditative states, then the head chanter began the chorus with a series of low, discordant croaks. The jangled energy between uttered notes felt like it was a requirement to jump-start the cycle of conjure-transform-release. Other frogs joined in, sounding discordant at first to "wake" the energy in the Well and draw it forth. There were a few frogs that were rhythm keepers who used sturdy sticks on the rock floor to set a driving beat.

Azzie scanned the pod for problems. That was his job. Was everyone awake, hydrated, healthy? Were all the reflective surfaces shiny enough to magnify the vibrations? Were the nests clean and tidy? Was the outside air that was brought in through a honeycomb of channels fresh with the right moisture content? His blessed father used to say, *Dream pod supervision is not for amateurs.* His father had even written the training leaflet on pod supervision, which Azzie referred to frequently.

Moving up and down the gentle slope of the pod's pathways, Azzie gently shook a young metamorph awake. Inexperienced meditators often fell asleep. Then, an older memnura got woozy when the steely energy from the Well of White Light seeped up into the nests, called by their chanting. Azzie had one of the other CODERs bring him an acorn top full of water to cool his head. The misters would eventually make their way to every room, but there were always those frogs who needed more moisture than the rest.

As the beat quickened, the pattern of croaks became more complex, and the light in the chamber transitioned from steely cold to vibrant silver to warm, pearlescent pink to an almost hot, dusty rose. That's when the spontaneous harmonies began—the most beautiful of sounds—sounds that were of the Earth, of the Well, yet they were sounds that were cosmic, celestial, divine.

When the chorus reached its crescendo, the energy vibrated with enough force to flow from the vents in the chambers to the many tunnels that ran under this level of the Palay then out into the world. The energy would head off in a direction based on a complex equation of the type of dream energy being generated at the moment and those places on Earth that required that energy, as well as the availability of what was known as field frogs (so named because they worked outside the Palay for the good of the All) to summon and relay vibrations best suited (and most needed) for their geographic location.

The chamber became quiet once more and returned to its pale glow. CODERs were served energy balls made of fly larvae and honey, coated in crushed dandelion seeds while a light, rose-scented mist was blown about the chamber by the misters who had finally arrived. That is one improvement Azzie would like to have in their operations. With all the refuge seekers arriving, perhaps they could create teams of misters for each pod. He would bring that up with Lem and see if they could come up with a new strategy for trying (again!) to convince his mother that this was a prudent move. He did not know her reason for not wanting to enact this policy, but as queen she did not have to give one.

How different this kind of energy was from the red-hot flare he and his mother and uncle had experienced that fateful morning a few sun cycles ago. That had been a heat hot enough to make flowers bloom and berries ripen in but a moment.

Azzie sighed with pride as the next cycle began. It always took him a round or two to adjust to the cacophonous first segment, but once his ear pads warmed to the sound, it got easier, and the ear pad covers he usually brought for the first round were no longer required. He may not like that his kind was obligated to supply dream energy to the clueless largetoe, but he was proud they did it well.

"Sir, Pender will serve in your stead while you accompany me," Lem said.

Azzie greeted Pender and thanked him for helping. Then he quickly updated him with a report that pointed out a few potential problems to keep an eye on.

Azzie watched Pender in action for a few moments until he was confident this replacement was up to the task.

Pender took over the job with ease and Azzie prepared to leave.

"The pikas are waiting over there," Lem said, pointing to one of the more extensive interconnecting tunnels. Azzie followed Lem out and they each mounted a brown, furry pika and urged them forward down the steeply pitched ramp that wound its way deeper into the earth.

Moving swiftly through the maze of tunnels, with huge dreaming pods branching off in all directions, Azzie and Lem were accompanied by sounds of frogs singing versions of the song of dreams. Some pods specialized in sending out energy that fueled artistic endeavors, like writing, music, and other arts. Other pods specialized in emotional, physical, spiritual, and scientific energies.

But most pods were less specific and contributed their own dream energy to the global mix. Azzie's pod was explicitly directed toward musicians and composers. While technically it wasn't fair to be that specific, Azzie had his own inclinations in that direction and had naturally attracted CODERs who had a similar affinity. Sometimes things simply worked out that way, and until someone broke them up, Azzie was content to let it be.

Besides, it was not like they were depriving anyone else of dream energy. It was plentiful and free for the taking for any largetoe who was receptive to a particular wavelength. Too bad more largetoe were not so inclined. There would be fewer problems in the world if more of them put the creative energy made possible by the Frog World to use instead of the destructive energy that came from the Maw of Malevolence.

Finally, they reached their destination at the deepest part of the Palay.

They dismounted and entered the huge cavern, which was unlike any of the others. There were no frog choristers here. This cavern had a different purpose, perhaps more vital and sacred than all the rest.

Made of perfectly clear quartz crystal, stalactites dripped from the egg-shaped dome. At the center of the great space was a milky-white lake. In the center of that was a beautiful fountain where a crystal mass pulsed with red light. It was the Auraventricalus—the heart of the Palay.

There were no living frogs here, only beautifully and accurately rendered statues of male and female frogs that no longer graced the Earth—struck in lively poses and placed around the edge of the lake. Carved from crystal and gemstones in appropriate colors to match the once-alive frogs, they were true works of art. Beneath each pair was a crystal casket containing their fertilized eggs, which waited in suspended animation. And there they would stay until the Earth was restored and these species could be reintroduced. Then Azzie remembered the true name for the eastern sector. It was the Crystal Egg Cave. The most precious cave of all.

Azzie looked about for a recognizable problem. "Lem, everything looks perfectly normal. I know you would not drag me here without a good reason. What is it?"

"Wait. Listen."

Azzie paused. In the quiet it was easier to hear a little sound like ice cracking in spring. But there was no ice around to make that sound. He looked along the edge of the room where wall met floor and saw intermittent piles of fine crystal shards collecting in the seam. The crystal substructure of the cave was full of microfractures.

He calmed his heart so it would not pound its way out of his chest.

"What is going on?" Azzie asked.

"We suspect a negative feedback loop may be forming."

"A *what*?"

Lem sighed, his impatience showing. "Because of the decline of our energy transfer pods in the field, thanks to the decline in frog populations everywhere, there are not enough frogs to pick up the dream energy from the Palay and relay it to the largetoe. Since it has no way to get to its ultimate destination, it circles back and returns home to the Palay."

"I noticed the great silence when I was in the outside world. No grand frog choruses at dusk or dawn. Just the sounds of other species. It was sad and disturbed me, but I did not think of this as a repercussion," Azzie said.

"It points to a dark future. If too much energy reverts to the Palay, it could cause the Crystal Egg Cave to collapse, and the whole Palay could implode."

"So, it is not *that* serious," Azzie said, trying to lighten the mood.

Lem stared back, a solemn expression on his face.

Azzie cleared his throat and adopted a more somber demeanor.

"For now, the energy is pooling around the outskirts of the Palay and seeping back into our lowest area—the Auraventricalus. Returned dream energy levels are climbing, based on the increased frequency in the number and size of the shard piles we are finding."

"How long until the problem becomes irreversible?"

Lem shrugged his shoulders. "It may take many thousands of seasons to develop, or it could happen tomorrow."

"Lem, why did you *really* bring me here? There is nothing I can do to help, especially right now. I am in the proverbial brackish, slow-moving backwater pond when it comes to my mother. She is not going to listen to anything I say. Now or maybe ever."

Lem looked at him with serious eyes.

Azzie swallowed hard. "You want me to be the one to tell the queen."

Looking away, Lem mumbled, "*Someone* has to do it."

"And someone will," Azzie replied, although he already dreaded being the messenger.

"I urge you not to wait. There is talk of new dreaming chambers, which will only make the matter worse. If anything, we need to close down several pods to let the overabundance of dream energy dissipate."

"Very well, Lem. Let us return to our jobs, and I will put it on my long list of disasters to discuss with Mother." Azzie's already tight jaw ached even more. If it got any tighter, it might, like the very foundations of the Palay, crack.

25

Nora  Homecoming

SETH AND I were cold and bone tired from digging up and reburying the coffin that never held my mother. I carried a little package from inside the lid, not sure I even cared what was in it.

We replaced the headstone and smoothed over the restored earth that covered the site, then walked back across my family's hay fields, using our lanterns to light the way. We walked home in silence, both a little shocked, I think, about our actions and what we'd discovered.

What we'd done, what I'd wanted us to do, had been reckless. I guess if I thought my mother was *dead*-dead I wouldn't have done what we did. Because if it had gone the other way, and she was *dead*-dead, I would have been left with a different kind of nightmare for the rest of my life: the sight of my mother's decayed body. But at the end of day—or I guess the end of tonight—what had I gained?

All I really knew for certain was that her body wasn't in the coffin—but it wasn't empty. Did the package hold more clues? What mattered most was that my mother's body wasn't there. Did that mean she was still alive? That was the answer I was craving. That is what I wanted to hear. That she was living somewhere. Somewhere where she could be found.

I snorted at my own selfishness. It really was all about me, wasn't it?

Seth looked at me funny but didn't ask. Probably as sick of me as I was of myself.

Along the way, we both called for Mickey and listened for any whimpers he might make in case he was stuck somewhere, but he didn't come, and we didn't hear a thing. When we arrived at the back door, I gave one last call.

Seth said, "There's a chance that Mickey is chasing down, well . . ."

"Whoever jumped over my mother's grave?" I filled in.

Seth nodded.

"I hope whoever it was doesn't hurt him," I said.

Seth kicked the dirt. "He'll come home. And that's where I'd better head now."

"I never would have managed this without your help," I told him.

Seth looked at the package I was carrying.

"Let me know what's inside when you open it?"

"Sure. That's the least I can do."

Seth touched my cheek. "You've got some dirt here." He gently brushed it off.

"You've got some too," I smiled, and I returned the gesture. We moved closer to each other, so close we were breathing the same air.

"Goodnight, Nora."

"Goodnight, Seth."

We stood there like two idiots looking at each other. I took a deep breath for courage and moved to kiss him when a car entered our driveway, its headlights making it impossible to see. Kameela, Will, and Minh got out and walked up to us, looking solemn.

"Nora. This is an intervention. Seth—we'll deal with you later," Kameela said. "Can we go inside and talk?"

I knew better than to resist. "Sure, follow me."

We all went inside and stood around the kitchen island. I put the tea kettle on to give myself something to do, but Kameela wasn't having it.

"So, Minh told us what you and Seth were up to tonight," she said. "You want to tell us your side of the story?"

"Side? I don't have a side," I said. "I had to find out if my mother was dead and buried or if there was a chance she was still alive. Digging up her grave was the only way I could be sure."

"Digging up a grave is against the law, Nora! You could get in real trouble," Kameela said.

Everyone was silent.

"Archaeologists do it all the time," I said.

"Not the same thing. We're worried about you. We care," Will said. "We want our old Nora back. The girl who gets into good trouble—not bad."

"We're trying to protect you. Keep you safe," Minh said. "I know you're probably mad at me for telling the others, but if you'd shared your thoughts with us before going out there, we could have talked you out of it."

"Do you not get it?" I cried. "I didn't *want* to be talked out of it. I had to know. And now I do. And I wish I didn't."

The Commandos exchanged looks then looked at me, waiting for an answer.

"The coffin was empty," I said. "Empty! Except for whatever this is." I showed them the package.

Mouths fell open.

"That means . . . what?" Will asked.

"You know, Will, I don't really know what that means. It could mean a bunch of things. I haven't had one second to figure it out."

Kameela said, "Let us help you."

I grabbed some paper and a pencil and handed them to Kameela, queen of lists.

While I poured tea and got out some dessert (a white cake with coconut frosting, chocolate chip cookie squares, and Nanaimo bars that friends had made for Gran and me), Kameela wrote down a question at the top of the page: *Why is the coffin empty?*

As we ate, we brainstormed a bunch of answers that ranged from "my mother isn't dead" to "someone stole her body and replaced it with stones." From there we came up with a list of potential reasons for each one, starting with why she would have faked her own funeral. That's the one that nagged at me most, maybe because Gran mistook me for her. She wouldn't have done that if there was no chance my mother was still alive. Would she? And worse than that, it meant that Gran had known all this time that we were living a lie.

Had Mom done something bad? I knew she'd been sick, but I never knew how sick until Dad told me she was dead—or did he say 'gone'? He must have said 'dead' because of the whole funeral thing. Right?

Had she gone someplace else for help and not been able to come back? Had she run away with another man—or woman?

But she loved Dad. She loved us both. Nothing would convince me otherwise.

Gran must know more than she's telling. But how could I demand answers when she was so sick herself?

It must have been something terrible to make her fake her own death and abandon us.

"You know," Minh said, "there might be a lot of answers in that package." He didn't have to point. We all knew what he was talking about.

"That's probably for Nora to look at when she decides the time is right, don't you think?" Seth said. He'd been quiet the whole time, probably worried I felt ganged up on. But I didn't.

"Thanks, Seth. I want to open it. I do. But for some reason I'm scared of what I'll find. I think I need to wait until tomorrow."

There was disappointment on their faces. I think they wanted to see what was in the package even more than me. But I couldn't do it tonight. "I really appreciate that you all care so much," I said. "And next time I have earth or mountains to move, I promise to ask for your collective help. Okay?"

It was still early, but we were all tired, so with hugs and forgiveness all around, my friends left. Seth was the first to go, and as he hugged each of us, I'm pretty sure he hugged me a little closer and tighter than everyone else.

Minh said he'd give Kameela a ride home and they took off. Will asked, "Do you want me to help you look through your dad's papers to see if he has anything about the sale?"

"Do you mind if I put that off until tomorrow?" I asked. "I gotta get some sleep."

"Sure. Let me know if I can help," Will said, and then left by the back door the way the others had.

After everyone was gone, I closed the door and leaned against it. The house shuddered. And so did I. Everything in the world seemed to be sitting on a shaky foundation. Even this house, which had stood here for such a long, long time.

A knock at the front door interrupted my downward spiral. What now? I threw my backpack over my shoulder and walked through the living room to the old part of the house, which was basically the foyer made from the three walls of that precious family log cabin Kincade was always ranting about. The back wall of the cabin had been taken off when the rest of the house, including the second story, had been added on in the 1930s. To say that this architectural feature gave our house a unique quality is an understatement.

"Nora? You there?"

It was Mel Finley. I could tell by his voice and the shadow he cast on the clouded glass pane that made up the front door.

My heart pounded. What was he doing here so late in the evening? Was he here to give me bad news about Gran? I had called the hospital before Seth and I took off for the cemetery. She'd been resting comfortably.

Then I remembered with a chill. Gran had been afraid of Mel at the funeral. Maybe I should be afraid, too, especially after I fired him. Taking a deep breath for courage, I opened the door.

"Nora, I'm here to apologize for my snarky behavior at the hospital and to give you this." He thrust out a square-shaped bentwood box that I knew contained my dad's ashes.

I stepped back, my stomach swirling tight. Finley took that as an invitation to step inside.

"Pastor Lackerby asked me to return this to you. Guess he hadn't heard I wasn't working for you anymore."

Guilt weighed on my shoulders. Not for firing Finley, but because I hadn't given Dad's ashes even one thought.

"Ellie had been quite specific about not wanting your dad's ashes to spend even one night in the mortuary, so Reverend

Lackerby has been keeping them at his house. He wanted to bring them here himself, but his wife is feeling poorly."

I felt ashamed, but I couldn't stand the thought of having the ashes in the house. There was something about them that made me seriously shaky. Maybe it was thinking about the violence of how a human body became ashes that freaked me out. Or maybe it was imagining all that my father had been being reduced to ash.

Finley urged me to take the box. It was made from one piece of red cedar that had been cut, steamed, bent, and painted to form a box with a tight lid. We'd commissioned it from a master artist in Will's tribe. It was a work of art. But I still hated the thought of what was inside and couldn't bring myself to touch it.

I unzipped my backpack and motioned for Finley to place the box inside.

Once he did, he stood back, smoothed his greying hair, and said, "I would like to get my old job back." Finley said it like he was pretty sure that all he had to do was to ask.

I was silent for a moment, pretending to consider my answer, when I knew what I wanted to say the moment I heard his request. "You tell me what favor Gran owes you, and I might try to get her to reconsider." I was surprised at my anger toward him, but why shouldn't I be mad?

"Nice knowing you." He reached for the door and opened it.

I stepped back, shocked by the force of his response.

"You won't have much work when your property's handed over to Carl. Maybe I should ask him for a job."

"Maybe you should," I said, stepping to the side to open the door wider and motioning him outside with a sweep of my hand.

"Find someone else to do favors for your family," he said with a sneer as he marched out the door.

I wanted to tell him what a favor he was doing us by getting out of our lives for good, but why poke that boil.

I slammed the door. I held my backpack at arm's length, my stomach clenched doubly tight by what it contained and the ugly nature of my exchange with Finley. There was something about the whole favor thing that left me teetering on a dangerous edge. Something I couldn't describe but felt a lot like a black hole.

Dad's office door tugged at me. I should probably go in there and look for the original easement papers, but I was pooped—emotionally and physically. Tomorrow would be better. Right?

I climbed the stairs, pausing outside my father's bedroom. I hadn't been inside since he died. I forced myself over the threshold and had a good look around. Not a thing had changed. It was as tidy as could be except for the pair of khakis pants that hung expectantly from the top of the open closet door.

I placed my backpack on Dad's bed. I would leave it there for the night so I wouldn't have to remove (as in *touch*) the box with his remains.

"One more night at home, Dad. In your bed, where you belong," I said. "Tomorrow I'll bury your ashes next to Mom's empty coffin. Wish you would have explained all that to me."

I noticed a small box wrapped in the Sunday comics that was sitting on the bedside table. I read the tag: "Happy birthday to my Nora." My birthday present.

That's Dad for you. An early shopper. Gran must have found the package hidden somewhere and put it out on his bed.

What day was it anyway? I counted on my fingers. My birthday was tomorrow.

I tore through the wrapping. It was a heavy-duty pocketknife with all the bells and whistles and my name was even engraved on it. It also had a leather case. I'd like to say I felt thankful. But I felt sad. Everything he'd touched in life was now sacred to me, so I tucked the tag with his handwriting on it into an easy-to-reach outside pocket on my backpack and pulled out the package I'd removed from the empty coffin. It seemed right to use this gift from Dad to open the mysterious object that had something to do with Mom.

I cut through the plastic carefully to find a couple of layers of brown paper wrapping and folded them back. Under that was a piece of cloth embroidered with a woodland scene wrapped around what felt like a book. It was held in place with a gold ribbon. Tied up in the bow was a bunch of dried lavender—one of my mother's favorite scents. Only an echo of its fragrance remained. I ached to trace the embroidery stitches my mother had made and to open it but held back. Everything my mother had touched in life now felt just as sacred as everything my dad had touched.

Her hands had wrapped it and taped it to the inside of the empty coffin. I didn't want to contaminate this sacredness. So I rewrapped the book without ever touching it and tucked it, along with the knife, into the other pocket of my backpack.

I realized then that I was afraid. Really afraid. Shoulders-hunched, jaw-clenched afraid. People don't disappear for no reason. It had to be something big and bad and life-changing that made Mom exit our lives. Was it something twisted up with *her* family, *her* home country? Why didn't she ever talk about those things?

And what if there was some piece of information inside the book that destroyed the way I viewed my world? Some earth-shattering revelation that cast a negative light on everything I knew and loved. Why don't secrets ever reveal good things? I guess sometimes they do. But I doubted that was the case here.

Both Kareema's and Minh's parents had told them stories about their home countries, and their homes here had small items of value that they'd brought with them. They also had family photographs. Why didn't Mom have even one little thing—like a picture of her mother, her father—anyone she was related to?

Then it occurred to me—while the pouch was from here, what was inside it might very well be from Mom's place of birth. Had she known the pearl was magic? If so, why did she leave it behind? And why didn't she ever want me to know? I was afraid to step outside the circle of knowledge about my mother into the potentially wide-open pages of this book. In the end I decided that I got a gift from each of my parents tonight. For the moment, I'll be thankful for that.

Leaving the backpack and all the preciousness it contained on Dad's bed, I took a shower, laid out my clothes for tomorrow, and put the pouch around my neck. At least nothing bad would happen tonight. I was home. I was safe. I was alone.

26

Linka Guards the House

Two Nights Till Pink Moon
Dark Time
Largetoe's Nest

T HE MOON SHONE down on Linka and Myth as they glided across the night sky, followed by the three remaining Zons from her contingent. How was it possible that they'd only left the Palay this morning?

Track the girl and you'll soon possess the Pearl. Aquatessa's words reverberated in Linka's ear pads. Of course, an Elemento was never wrong (Linka hoped). They had followed the largetoe to her dwelling, then patrolled the area for escape routes if required.

"Land there," Linka directed Myth, pointing to a large madrona tree, one of many that grew in the area. Linka was curious to get inside the place and observe the habits of the two-footer for herself. She had learned many things about their kind when she attended lectures on largetoe culture and customs at the Frog College of All Knowledge but observing them in their natural habitat was an opportunity few frogs from the Palay had experienced.

Maybe tonight would be her chance. Once she was sure it was safe, she planned to go inside and rescue the Pearl. She instructed Mura, Trep, and Roya to take turns resting their mounts and patrolling the area while she watched over the house.

Several largetoe had come and gone at different times. And now another one approached. Or was it a femtoe? Linka still had difficulty telling them apart. There was something different about this one, who moved like a spider stalking prey. But unlike the spider who acted out of hunger, Linka sensed that this largetoe had malice on its mind.

The intruder paused under the young magnolia tree, yet to burst into bloom where Myth hung upside down from a branch. Linka peeked through his wings, which were wrapped around her holding her upside-down body in place. Perhaps sensing their presence, the intruder looked up.

Did the largetoe see her?

Apparently not.

The largetoe moved in to the house. Linka followed, a wave of revulsion passing through her. Even though it was against the frog ways to judge based on appearances, she found their differences almost too much to digest. This one carried an odor that assaulted her nostrils more than the femtoe with the Pearl. Maybe it was whatever was in the large vessel it carried, which sloshed with the sound of liquid inside.

Linka heard a tinkling noise, like ice being shattered. The largetoe had broken what Linka knew to be a window because they had something like that at the Palay too. The largetoe reached through the window, unlatched the door, and entered the house, moving with the stealth of a snake in the grass.

With a series of whistles and clicks, Linka ordered Roya to stay vigilant on patrol and instructed Mura and Trep to wait for a bit then follow. She and Myth flew inside the largetoe dwelling. Once there, Linka directed Myth to fly high and close to the walls.

Unseen by the intruder, they watched as the largetoe poured a trail of liquid across the floor.

Imminent danger to the girl was in the air. And if *she* was in danger, the Pearl would be as well. Linka left the relative security of Myth's back and scrambled along the wall after the largetoe, waiting for her chance. When it came, she leapt from the wall onto the top of its head and dropped to its nose, swiping first on one side and then on the other with her spinning infinator.

The largetoe stifled a cry and dropped the vessel it was carrying, splashing foul-smelling liquid everywhere. With flailing arms, the two-footed abomination struck Linka away and sent her, flying into the wall.

Linka barely managed to cling to it with her suction cups. A rising cloud of fumes from the liquid hit her like a barrage of porcupine quills. She signaled Mura and Trep, who had just arrived, to flee, but their mounts were immediately overcome by the fumes. One crashed against the door and the other against a window.

Linka's heart sank. She wanted to help them, but her head spun, and her limbs quivered. Losing her grip, she slid uncontrollably down the wall toward the puddle of poison. Linka struggled to reattach her suction cups to the wall, but her body wouldn't respond. She dug the spikes on her armor into the wall to slow her descent. Whatever happened, she could not land in the puddle of toxic liquid that shimmered below her—it was certain death.

With her snout, she punched a sparkling green jewel on her forearm guard. A three-pronged hook with a woven vine attached shot out from the wrist apparatus and embedded itself in the wall above her. She jerked to a halt and dangled over the rainbow-colored slick below.

The intruder took a stick—no, it was called a match, if she remembered correctly—and it made fire.

Linka called out to Myth, then kicked herself outward to try to reach the largetoe, but it was too far away. She swung back and hit the wall, hard.

On his way back outside the house, Myth tore past Linka with the two Zons, Mura and Trep, on his back. They were coughing and gasping for air from the fumes of the toxic liquid.

Below Linka, in the middle of the room, the intruder struck the match against a rough surface.

No flame appeared.

The intruder said something Linka didn't understand but said it in a way that reminded her of her favorite curse word: squamatadoo, which was lizard dung. But instead of making her smile, a taste like pickled worms rose in her mouth. She didn't want there to be any similarities between her kind and the largetoe. They were evil. All evil. With no redeeming qualities. Not all her kind believed this. But she did. And she would not be convinced otherwise.

The largetoe struck the match again.

The head of the firestick broke off and fell to the floor.

Linka sighed with relief as she dangled in place.

Myth returned. "Bulldoggies have been spotted by your patrol. They are close."

Bulldoggies! Linka's blood turned glacial. How she hated Bulldoggies and their commander General Oddbull, who seemed to have a special vendetta for Zons.

But what would bring Bulldoggies here? They usually stuck to raiding bands of migrating frogs and tending the Maw and were as loathsome as largetoe in her opinion. Had they found out about the Pearl? But how? Linka swallowed her fear, but it stuck in her vocal sac like a bolus of desiccated dung beetle.

"We will deal with them if we survive," she said.

By this time, the intruder had ignited a match. "Igneo, extinguish yourself!" Linka commanded. But the flame burned high and bright.

"Myth, the fire stick—put it out."

Myth tore down toward the largetoe. His great leathery wings rolled puffs of air toward the flame and snuffed it.

The intruder grunted in surprise and flung its arms around to ward off the bat.

"Myth, swoop in below me, and I will jump on."

Myth dove under Linka, but the grappling hook was stuck too deeply in the wall and wouldn't disengage. She fumbled with the catch on her forearm guard, but it was stuck too.

The intruder lit yet another fire stick and held it between trembling fingers.

"Myth, hurry!"

The intruder dropped the burning stick and fled. The liquid ignited, and a sea of flames pitched and rolled throughout the house with a blast of heat hot enough to sear spots off frog skin.

"Igneo. By order of Queen Ranya—you must desist," Linka decreed as she swayed helplessly. Smoke engulfed her. Her body was wracked with coughs.

A monstrous skull-shaped face with gaping holes for eyes and a cavernous V-shaped mouth formed from the flames and smoke. "I obey your summons, Princess, but I refuse to deny my nature. You ask too much, Little One," Igneo hissed. "The queen's days of power are waning. She no longer commands my respect or the respect of every Elemento as she once did."

"I wager your sister, Aquatessa, would not agree," Linka said.

"I care not for the weakness of my sister. My brothers Bortos and Magmo stand with me against the queen for her refusal to use her voice to defend the All. Why should we honor her?"

Fingers of flame crawled up the walls, closer to where Linka hung.

"I have as many reasons as there are grains of sand in a desert, Igneo. Perhaps you could calm down and we will discuss them one by one."

The flames subsided, then burned hot again. "You think you can trick me?" Igneo hissed, and he doubled his size and intensity.

"A little frog like me, trick an ancient wonder like you? Impossible." Linka continued to try to free herself. But nothing was working.

"Release yourself into my tender care, little one." His laughter rocked the house. "A sacrifice of a royal frog will cool my flames."

With a slash of her infinator, Linka called to Myth and severed her forearm below the elbow joint. She tumbled through space like a lemming over a cliff.

Myth dove below her.

For a breath Linka was numb. Then a white-hot pain gripped her.

She strained to catch Myth's reigns with her one good hand as he flew past her into the rising thunderhead of fire and smoke. But they fluttered beyond her grasp.

"Igneo, perhaps you will get your wish," Linka said through a gritted snout. She fought against the pain from her self-amputation as if it were her most hated enemy. She landed on something that was stuck to the wall. It was faces—largetoe faces, framed in wood. A whole family of them. Pictures. That's what they were called. She was grateful they were there.

Still fighting to regain control over the suction cups on her remaining limbs, she slid down the smooth surface of the large-toe faces. The closer she got to the fumes, the more they stung her eyes, and she couldn't see anything but the long, dark path that led to death.

Regret washed through her heart for all she would leave undone. It would not be long now. "Great Well of Light . . ."

"Save your prayers for another time, Your Highness," Myth said as he again fluttered below her.

Linka released her grip, pushed out from the wall with her mighty legs, and landed awkwardly on the bat's back.

"Groark!" Linka cried victoriously. Exhilaration flooded her body, the pain of her lost forearm momentarily forgotten. She righted herself, inserted her feet into shell stirrups, and secured herself to the saddle. Never mind the hot tingling in her spine from the hard landing. Never mind the sadly parched state of her skin. Never mind the missing hand. It would grow back, but it would take a very long time—up to four hundred days—and she would be vulnerable until it was whole and fully functioning. Would the queen replace her as leader of the Zons if her weakness were a threat to the queen's safety? Linka drove the thought from her mind. Most importantly, she was alive. That was comforting enough for now—as long as she stayed that way.

"Don't be too proud, little one," Igneo roared. "I will have my sacrifice of royal frog yet."

"Up!" Linka commanded Myth, patting out smoking patches on the bat's hide. She unfurled her long tongue for the harder-to-reach places and grimaced at the taste of burnt fur. "You are badly hurt," she said.

"I am fine." Proving otherwise, he dipped sharply to one side, then overcorrected in the other direction.

Linka clung more tightly and tried to ignore the throbbing in her stump, which oozed blood.

"Whoa, Myth, take it easy. You fly like you have been drinking too much fermented dew."

"But I am flying, Your Highness. And you are safe. That is all that matters."

An intense heat pulsated against Linka's back.

And no matter which direction Myth took, Igneo sent up billowing towers of smoke and fat columns of flame. "You are mine!" roared the Elemento.

Linka spun her infinator a powerful spin and punched a hole through the smoke with the air stream. Like a needle through frogklath, they threaded their way to the top of the stairs using the spinning infinator to help them see.

With the house now burning, there was no time to search for the Pearl. Linka would have to trust Aquatessa's word that the girl would have it close by, which meant that to save the Pearl, she'd have to save the girl. The taste of bitter disgust on her tongue was even worse than burning bat fur.

Nora ◎ Fire!

Two Nights Till Pink Moon
After Midnight
Home

I MUST HAVE FALLEN asleep with the light on, 'cause when I opened one eye, I had no trouble seeing the frog sitting on my nose and staring at me. I bolted upright in bed. The frog fell into my lap and jumped away.

My nose hurt with a dry, achy itch. Smoke! Was I having another nightmare?

A moonbeam shone through the window illuminating fingers of smoke that rose through the floorboards.

My. House. Was. On. Fire.

Help. I needed help. There was no point in trying my cell—it rarely worked from home. I picked up the house phone and dialed 911, wishing not for the first time that we lived closer to town.

The line was dead. Then the light went out.

Blue jeans on. Sweatshirt. Feet stuffed into boots, I slung my leg out the window and once again came eye to eye with the frog, which was now sitting in the windowsill and staring at me.

"You better get out of here, froggy." It leapt onto the roof.

That's when I remembered.

Dad and Gran!

I had to wake them up, get them both out of the house!

No. Wait.

Gran was in the hospital, sick. And Dad was dead, his ashes across the hall.

I couldn't leave without him.

28

Linka 🐸 Bring on the Bulldoggies

Two Nights Till Pink Moon
Late Dark Time
Largetoe's Nest

INKA JUMPED TO the peak of the roof and watched for the girl to emerge from the window. But the girl had not followed. She called for Myth, who answered right away.

He had been circling the house since escaping, nursing his burns and staying out of reach of Igneo's flames.

"Should I fly inside and shoo her out?" Myth asked, fluttering in place above Linka.

"No, it would put you in too much danger."

She whistled for the remaining Zon, Roya. But there was no response.

"Where is Roya?"

Myth didn't know.

"Mura? Trep?" Linka asked.

"Safe for now."

"And your burns?"

"They are nothing," Myth replied, although Linka could see by the strain on his face that was not true.

"I am sorry about members of your camp, Myth."

"They served the queen well."

"Indeed, we will honor them in safer times. Now, fly out and find creatures sympathetic to the queen to assist us. But do not be gone long. I may need another rescue."

Myth widened his circle, his wing strokes faltering from time to time, until Linka could see him no more. Then she closed her eyes and summoned her awareness. The promise of a solution tugged at her.

Eyes open, she spotted a leaf floating in a clogged rain catcher along the roof's edge. Water. Linka needed water to drench Igneo's passion for destruction. And she knew how to get it.

Linka made a mighty leap from the peak of the roof and landed with a splash in the rain catcher. She dipped a hand into the water and touched her forehead.

> *Aquatessa, Spirit of Water.*
> *Think of me, please, as your very own daughter.*
> *Keep Igneo, despised brother, from causing me pain.*
> *Please, Aquatessa, send me some rain.*

There. Linka had asked. But would Aquatessa heed her call? The perpetual enmity between these two Elementos gave Linka hope.

Linka sensed movement behind her and ducked as a black-berry-thorned bludgeon cut through the space where her head had been.

A bullfrog three times Linka's size attacked her from above. Linka dodged his blows by slogging backward through the mass of rotting leaves in the rain catcher. From the gaping frog jaw crest on his armor and his humongous size, Linka knew he was one of the enemies Myth had warned her about.

"Well, hello, Bulldoggie," Linka said, and she deployed her infinator with her remaining hand.

"Hello, Zon. Put your puny infinator away. It is useless as a weapon against us as this proves," he said, waving a Zon helmet about.

Linka's heart sank. The helmet sported Roya's color. She leapt up the incline on the roof, then spotted another Bulldoggie waiting for her along the roofline.

"What are you two doing outside your normal zone of terror?" she asked.

The bullfrog in the rain catcher leapt after her. "Do not tell her, Xeron," he said to the Bulldoggie above.

"I will not tell her anything, Drengo. But if we do not get in that house and find the Pearl, we will not be able to go back to the Maw without having our innards eaten for fast-breaking by the General himself."

Linka chuckled. Bulldoggies might use their size as a weapon, but she never had to worry about being defeated by their brains—the wart heads. So, General Oddbull and his Bulldoggies were also after the Pearl. She had to alert the other Zons and the queen to a spy in their presence. But first she had to either avoid a fight . . . or win one.

29

Nora ◎ Ashes to Ashes

Two Nights Till Pink Moon
Deepest Night
Home

BY THE TIME I made it to the hallway, the smoke had thickened so much, I had to drop to my knees to catch a patch of clear air. I crawled past the collection of family photos that lined the hall. I wanted to rescue them all, but it was the pictures or me.

I scrambled inside my father's room and shut the door behind me. My eyes burned and watered. I wouldn't last long. I had to—*had to*—leave. I thought of trying to use the pearl in some way to help me out of this situation, but it had caused the river water to go wild. I couldn't risk making the fire burn higher and hotter in response to it. I would have to get out of here on my own.

After being momentarily distracted by my thoughts, the tendrils of smoke seeping in under the door quickly reminded me I needed to get moving. I grabbed my backpack and dragged it across the bed by one of the straps. But when I hoisted it onto my shoulder, the bentwood box spilled onto the floor, landing on its side, top skewed, with *most* of the ashes spilled out.

"No! No! This *can't* happen!" For a moment the room was clear of smoke and the temperature had plunged so low I felt a chill. I could see. I could breathe. How it happened I didn't know or care. The relief was overwhelming.

That feeling only lasted seconds, until I heard a grinding sound like bone on bone. Low and eerie, it was as if an ocean of sand were scraping against my eardrum. Then my body began vibrating until the marrow in my bones quivered.

A different kind of magic must have been at work that had nothing to do with the pearl's power because a breeze appeared from nowhere and swept the grit and ash up off the floor into a whirling funnel that resembled my father, Henry Quentin Peters.

And then, the specter spoke.

30

Linka 🐸 Two Foes to Go

Two Nights Till Pink Moon
Deepest Night
Largetoe's Nest

YTH SWOOPED IN above Linka, his voice shrill with worry. "Princess, are you okay? Help is on the way."

"Hear that, Bulldoggie?" Linka sneered. "Soon you will be outnumbered."

"Too little too late, Princess," said Drengo, advancing. He puffed his chest out and a sly look overtook his face. "Have a little accident?" he said, nodding toward her missing forearm.

"A little slip of my infinator. Nothing to worry your empty head about."

Two big drops of rain fell.

More, Aquatessa. More.

The rain fell faster. Igneo hissed, his rage dampened.

Drengo threw his bludgeon at Linka while Xeron dropped a net made of sticky-spider web.

Linka ducked as the bludgeon whizzed by and popped back up right in time to grab its handle. She whipped it over her head and caught the web on its barbs. With a twisting leap to the side, she brought the web down over Drengo and hammered his head with a blow so hard the blackberry thorns embedded into his skull.

Drengo yelped with pain, his arms and legs tangled in the web. Myth swooped in from above and used his claws to drag Drengo to the edge of the roof, where he let the Bulldoggie go. Drengo plummeted with a screaming croak that faded as he fell, landing with a splash in a rain barrel.

"That *should* take care of him," Myth said.

Now, Linka thought. *Where was that girl, and did she still have the Pearl?*

31

Nora ◎ From Beyond the Grave

Two Nights Till Pink Moon
Deepest Night
Home

INSIDE MY FATHER's bedroom I was scrunched against the wall, trying to slow my breathing as I watched long ribbons of ash spin out from the fingers of the specter before me. The ribbons curled into tourniquets around the smoke and held it back.

"Dad," I croaked, my voice ruined from the smoke. "I'm so sorry! Can you ever forgive me?"

"You must listen, Nora. I can't hold back the smoke for long." His voice, though familiar, sounded distorted, as if he were talking through water from the moon. "You must do one thing for me: Take my remains . . . up *there*, above the steppes to the Nexus."

"The Nexus? Where's that?"

"The place where it began. The place where it will end," he said.

"But how will I find it? I've never heard of it."

"Start at the Flying Demon Tree and the path will open for you."

At least I knew where that was. It was a start. "Dad, I have so many questions."

"When we are up there, together, everything will be revealed. But beware on your journey," he said, waggling an ashen finger in warning. "Anything from your mother should never go to another—especially if that other is 'frog'. And whatever you do—make sure it's in the best interest of the All."

There was that term again. If only I knew what it meant. But before I could ask, my father's form crumpled with an explosive rush that temporarily dampened the fire.

I dropped to the floor, and, with sweaty hands and gritted teeth, I quickly gathered the ashes into a pile. I scooped them into the square box and replaced the lid, which was lying upside down at my feet. In life, he had been warm and smelled of the outdoors, with hands calloused, shoulders broad, arms strong. In death, his body had been cold like a stone. How could such a man, his body, mind, and spirit, now be reduced to grey powder and grit? And how is it possible that I talked to his ashy ghost?

I finished my grim task, then rubbed my hands together and ground the ash into my arms. He was a part of me now—forever.

I stuffed the box in my backpack.

Smoke closed in around me.

32

Linka 🐸 One Less Foe to Fry

Two Nights Till Pink Moon
Deepest Night
Largetoe's Nest

XERON LEAPT TOWARD Linka, one leg extended, and delivered a kick that knocked her up onto the glass of the window. She clung to it, but her suction cups still weren't working right, and she slid down to the flat part of the windowsill. As she did, she saw that the girl was no longer inside the room.

Xeron rammed her with his snout, flipping her off the ledge outside the window and onto the roof. The speed and force of his movements sent shock waves through Linka's body and left her amputated stump throbbing. She willed her body to go limp.

"Give it to me," Xeron demanded, advancing on her.

Linka quickly righted herself. "You will get nothing from me but this." She used her good hand to extract a two-pronged dagger, an orb plucker designed to take out both eyes at once, from inside her chest armor. This lethal weapon was forged in the bowels of the Palay by the Zons themselves, who had a whole corps of weapon makers. Linka threw it at Xeron, but her injury left her unbalanced and she missed.

"You will have to do better than that," Xeron said, sarcasm dripping from his words. "General Oddbull wants the Pearl."

"You cannot take what I do not have, you brainless bag of gelatinous mush."

"Oh, Princess, you wound me."

"That is the idea," Linka said and looked up over Xeron's shoulder. She smiled at the most beautiful sight she had ever seen: an owl diving in for the kill above Xeron.

"What have you got to smile about, Princess? Looking forward to the warm greeting from the General before he rips you from web to head?"

"No, I am looking forward to seeing the greeting you are about to get."

A shadow fell on Xeron.

"Huh?" He looked up and hopped in a half circle to see what was coming. It was a snowy owl, replete with full body armor. The owl slammed into Xeron's back, pinning the bullfrog to the roof. Its talons ripped through the bullfrog's massive body and out the other side.

Xeron cried out in agony.

"Die, enemy of my queen," Linka said to the Bulldoggie. Then she issued a kill order to the owl.

With that, the owl ripped Xeron's body open with his talons, setting his guts free.

Linka almost took pity on the Bulldoggie, whose face contorted then went blank. But then she remembered how many of her kind had been captured and tortured by the General's troops, and her compassion vanished. Linka shut her nostrils at the foul stench that engulfed her.

"Smell that, Xeron? It is your entrails. May the stink haunt you in the Great Pond Beyond—if you ever get there."

She looked to the owl, her broad mouth breaking into a smile. "Thank you, mighty owl, for answering Myth's plea for help. How are you called?" Linka asked, dipping her head in deference to her savior.

"I am Noble."

"Could you grant me a ride? I must circle this house and find the femtoe."

"I have no saddle for you. How will you hold on with a missing forearm?"

"Let me worry about that," Linka said. "And if you do not mind foregoing Bulldoggie to break your fast, I would appreciate it if you would carry him to a place I designate, where I will ask you to let him go."

"Of course, Your Highness. Hop up."

And Linka did, although it was an awkward hop. Linka whipped a cord out from one side of her armor and, with permission from Noble, threaded it gently around the owl's breast. She then snapped it to a hook on the other side of her armor. It was a crude but effective means of staying put when unexpectedly hitching a ride in battle.

"Be on the lookout for other Bulldoggies. He said they were coming."

The owl took a quick look around. Then, with a downbeat of his wings, Noble rose from the top of the house, his talons gripping the dead bullfrog.

When they were well above the flames, Linka leaned over and asked Noble to release the dead weight he carried.

Noble let go of his bloody cargo and a greedy flame rose to accept it.

"Igneo. Here is your sacrifice of frog. Now quell your flames." Linka refused to indulge in a smile at the thought of defeating this Elemento. But she couldn't prevent a wave of smug satisfaction from brightening her mood.

But instead of lessening, the fire roared higher and hotter into the sky. "You got your offering, Igneo," Linka said as they flew, circling high above the house. "Hold to your part of the bargain."

"Bargain? You broke that bargain when you summoned my sister," Igneo said, his voice crackling with anger.

"I should get double favors for giving you a frog three times as big as the one you asked for."

"It was you, tender *you*, I wanted. Not a thick-muscled Bull-doggie."

"Waste no more of my time, Igneo. If the femtoe dies by your flame, you will not only have your sister and the other Elementos to answer to, you will have to answer to the queen."

"I tremble at the thought," Igneo said, and he laughed so hard the flames danced.

Noble descended on the other side of the roof. Linka spotted the girl inside. "There is the window, Noble," Linka said, pointing to the one she wanted.

"There's fire inside," Noble squawked, back flapping his wings to fan the smoke away.

"It is our one chance to save the Golden Pearl of the Forest before it is forever destroyed. You must dive, Noble, dive," Linka said. And together they plunged into the black billowing clouds of smoke and the shooting flames that fought for survival against the pelting rain.

"I will not let you in," Igneo said, growing higher and hotter. And the higher he rose, the harder it rained. It was a pitched battle between Elementos that neither wanted to lose.

Noble retreated above the cloud of smoke that engulfed the house and circled the area to regain his breath.

"Oh, yes, you will, brother." A soft voice with the hiss of rain falling on fire spoke from the skies. It was Aquatessa, and she finally released a deluge.

Igneo roared. "You have made an enemy today, Zon." His flames retreated, but the smoke increased.

Noble treaded the smoky air.

"Inside," Linka urged, motioning toward the window. She clenched her legs around him more tightly. "Noble, you *must* fly inside."

The great owl hooted in dismay.

"Noble, please. Be brave. We must save the femtoe to save the Pearl."

Noble nodded and dove into the veil of smoke and through the open window. Linka's heart missed a beat. There, on the floor, lay the crumpled body of the girl. Was she dead? No. She was still breathing. If there was only a way to find the Pearl on the girl, she could leave the girl to die. But the best way to get the Pearl out safely was to have the girl carry it.

"Do you have a pellet to regurgitate?" Linka asked.

"On her? Your Highness, no."

"Then peck her on the head. Or poop on her if you like."

"Your Highness. Please."

Linka rolled her eyes in disbelief. She didn't have time for owlish sensitivities. "We need to rouse the femtoe."

Noble landed and delivered a swift peck to the femtoe's head.

The femtoe groaned.

"Peck her again."

Noble did.

The femtoe sat up and rubbed her head.

"To the window, Noble, show her the way."

Noble hopped up to the windowsill and waited. Linka peeked out between feathers to see the femtoe grab her belongings. She didn't look worthy of the trouble Linka had gone to—but then was any largetoe worth saving?

"To the skies, Noble," Linka commanded. "We must find a path and figure out how to lead this femtoe to safety before Igneo reignites his ire."

33

Nora ◎ Out on a Limb

Two Nights Till Pink Moon
Deepest Night
Home

HAD A BIRD pecked my head, or had I imagined it?

I jumped up, tasting blood, and headed out the window onto the flat roof over the porch that ran along the second floor of the house. In the distance I heard sirens. Somebody must have noticed the fire down in the valley and called it in. Help was on its way.

The ground looked a million miles away. It was raining enough to slow the fire down, but not put it out. Smoke continued to billow, making it hard to see where I should go.

An owl hooted from a big tree at the back of the house. His huge yellow eyes summoned me like beacons. I moved toward him.

A sore spot pulsed on my head. I felt it and looked at my fingers. Even in the dim light of dawn I could see the blood. Diluted by rain, it was running into one eye, stinging it shut.

Confusion swirled in my brain about what had happened moments ago, and I felt discombobulated. I felt for the pearl. It was still there, in the jewelry casket in the pouch around my neck.

No way was I losing that. I patted my backpack to make sure Dad's ashes were inside, slung it around one shoulder, and made my way across the roof, which was mossy and slippery in places.

"Nora," someone called.

I looked down. I could barely see through the smoke, but I recognized the voice. It was Will. Relief flooded through me.

"We're here to help, Nora, the whole family," Will said.

"Get the hoses from the garden," I heard Kameela yell.

The sirens got louder.

Minh said, "Don't worry, Nora. There are more people on their way."

"Do you have a ladder so we can get you off the roof?" Seth said.

"It's all the way up at the barn. I'm going to climb down the tree," I shouted back, unwilling to wait another minute to get my feet on solid ground.

I grabbed the overhanging branch of the giant, gangly, big-leaf maple that shaded the house on hot days. I had always loved this tree, despite the ocean of broad yellow leaves I had to rake up in fall. And now it was saving my life. But the dense smoke was making it hard for me to find my way down.

The owl hooted. I moved in its direction and saw a frog on one of the forks of the branch—the same frog I'd seen earlier? Its bright-green skin with copper flecks glowed with a light from a different world. I hadn't noticed before that it was missing an arm.

The frog jumped down a few branches until it sat at my feet. It appeared the frog wanted me to follow, as it seemed to blaze a trail along the shortest and easiest route through the tangle of the tree, never getting so far ahead of me that I couldn't see it. I had the urge to thank it for its help—but I resisted.

I heard my name again.

I wanted to yell back, but I was too focused on following the frog through dense branches until I reached the main trunk of the tree. "Here, up here!" I yelled, finally finding my voice again.

The sirens were on top of me, and I heard airbrakes. Then the sirens died. A woman called out orders. Help from the fire department was here.

"She's over here—in the back of the house," someone said.

All I had to do was climb down to the ground. I fought my way through the newly budded leaves, my eyes riveted to that little frog that never moved out of my sight.

As smoke snaked down the tree trunk, my eyes watered. I couldn't see above or below. But the frog, which glowed with a light of its own, acted like a beacon and led me to the lowest branch, which was still too high from the ground to jump.

The frog didn't move any farther down the tree trunk. Was it stuck?

I couldn't leave it behind, although it may well have gotten loose without my help. It squirmed in front of me, its foot caught in a groove in the bark. I don't know how, but I knew it was in pain. I moved closer and teased its delicate foot from the bark with one hand and tucked the frog into my shirt pocket, hoping that it wouldn't get smushed.

"Nora, the firefighters have a ladder," Minh said. "They're putting it against the tree."

"Can you see it?" Kameela asked.

I could. All I had to do was swing onto it and climb down.

Within seconds, I was on the ground being swathed in a crinkly emergency blanket. "Thank you, thank you." It was all I could say to *everyone*. I'd been in the worst trouble, and my friends and their families—a bunch of townsfolk—had come to my aid. Without them getting the ladder, I might have risked a jump and broken something. And without the owl and the frog, I might have died the most horrible of deaths before even getting to the tree.

My friends led me away from the house to the ambulance, where I got examined by a paramedic who said her name was Trish. She was kind and thorough. When it came to examining my hands, I saw that not only were they covered in soot, they hurt like hell. And they weren't the only things that hurt. I had other small burns on my arms as well other places on my body. Funny thing about burns though; they don't like to be ignored, and now that I knew about them, they began to hurt worse than before. Trish cleaned and treated them, and the pain was somewhat eased.

As she worked, she asked me questions. I guess I answered them, but I don't remember what was said. It felt and smelled like there was still a cloud of smoke hovering around my brain, making it hard for me to sort out what had just happened.

How could everything that ever meant anything to my family—our home—be gone? It was hard to tell how much damage the structure had suffered. The entrance to the house—that sacred log cabin that Kincade valued more than his son and wife, was smoking rubble. Some walls remained and the upstairs had not collapsed yet. It was too much to take in. I guess they call that shock.

After lying on the stretcher for a while, my eyes shut tightly so the tears wouldn't leak out, Trish said they would take me to the hospital for follow-up care.

"No, I can get there on my own," I said and got off the stretcher. If Gran heard I was in the emergency room of the same hospital she was in, the shock might kill her. Hearing about our destroyed home would be devastating enough. I wouldn't do anything to pile onto that message.

"If you're sure," Trish said. "The choice is yours."

I nodded, thanked her, and joined my friends who were huddled in a circle close by.

The frog wriggled inside my pocket. I wanted to check on this little lifesaver, but I wanted to do it alone.

"I need some time to myself," I told my friends. "I'm going to walk to the hospital."

"You are absolutely under *no* circumstances going to walk to the hospital on your own," Kameela said.

"You're nuts if you think we're going to let you do that," Will added.

Seth reached out and gently took my hand. "Nora, please. Let us help."

"You guys ganging up on me again?" I asked, touched by their concern.

"It seems like a lot to put yourself through on top of everything else," Seth said. They were right, of course. They usually were. I just needed some time—even a little—to be by myself and try to figure out the feelings whirling through my head like a hurricane of smoke.

"Okay, okay—I need to look around and take everything in," I said, realizing that I had to square away the picture of *now* before I left. I had to be able to tell Gran about the damage, for one thing. She'd demand every detail. And I had to know myself, for another. I had already seen the damage to the back of the house. Now I needed to walk toward the edge of the plateau where the house sat and look back on it from there. The only way for me to believe that all of this had really happened and wasn't a nightmare was to take a real hard look at the truth.

"Sure," Seth said. "You go on. Take your time. I'll be waiting for you right here. Want me to take your backpack for you and put it in the car?"

"I got it," I said.

The others left. I slung my backpack over my shoulder, careful not to squish the frog, and took off toward the edge of the plateau to catch my breath. It felt good to know that Seth would be waiting for me when I got back.

The Queen 🐸 Shame Reigns

Two Nights Till Pink Moon
Deepest Night
The Palay, The Queen's Private Chambers

GREAT THICK AND thorny vines of dread rose from the floor and slithered across Ranya's body. She was about to deliver the most painful message of her reign.

"Your Majesty, Prince Azzumundo is here," Simeon said.

"I will see my son soon enough," the queen replied. "Let him wait. I crave a moment of inner calm before the turmoil our meeting is sure to bring. I remember when I left the Palay before my last transition. Upon my return, I almost fell from my burfing leaf when I saw Frog Mountain from a distance. It looked like a giant frog, sitting on flat earth, its eyes bulging with beauty—and on its head a crown of ancient trees. I had never explored the upper regions of the Palay until then, and I found these rooms abandoned. Imagine my delight when I realized that the upper eyelids of those great eyes formed a canopy to keep the sun at bay, while the lower lids protruded far enough to form this very balcony where I now sit."

"Very clever discovery indeed, Your Majesty."

"Yes, Simeon, I seem to be the cleverest frog ever, except for when it comes to my son." The queen closed her eyes and breathed deeply to a countdown from dexicum to wahedicum:

Dexicum: How could her son have shamed her so?

Nintentum: To be a leader he must be known for his courage and strength, as was she.

Octophoricum: Was there no way to help him restore his reputation?

Sabatentos: Doubtful, given his past performances.

Seso: Without an exemplary character, he could not rule.

Phalangicum: But what of her reputation? Had she not acted falsely to gain the throne?

Fortos: Yes, but none—but one—knew. No, make that two.

Talentos: So, it is not truth that matters, but appearances.

Dosicum: Even when it comes to family? Especially so.

Wahedicum: The appearance of family solidarity must be maintained. So, in the family's best interest, Azzie would remove himself, at the right time, from the line of succession. For what was best for the family was what's best for the queendom.

After her last deep breath (and thought), Ranya, less relaxed than before her countdown, opened her eyes and signaled to Simeon that it was time to bring her son into the room.

Azzie entered. "Mother, I bring you greetings from your subjects outside our blessed Palay."

"Let us not be disingenuous with each other, my son. I received report of your performance at the Ceremony of Renewal. My shame of you knows no bounds, and for that reason, I must tell you that you will never reign in my place. When the time comes, I will pass my crown to Linka. She will be queen."

Azzie's gaze shifted to the floor, and he swayed a bit at the shock of the news and the cruel, insensitive way it was delivered. The queen's heart torqued to see her son in such pain.

"You cannot be more ashamed of my behavior than I, Mother. I do not know how to feel about your decision. I have lived my life not wanting to follow in your hop-steps. But now that my wish has come true, I cannot imagine not being king one day. And you know my disdain for my cousin. She will be croaking about this for the rest of my life. If only I did not suffer from my lifelong affliction, things might have been different. I might have been the son that you wanted, the son you deserve."

"At what point do you dig deep and find the courage to over-come this problem?" The queen hated the terseness of her voice. But it was who she was.

"Perhaps never. Although I will not stop trying."

"I remember your First Breath Day, when your gills were finally absorbed in your growing body. You were about to start using your lungs and move up from the brooding pond."

"With respect, Mother, my uncle has told me this story many times," Azzie said.

"It truly was only a small moment when your foot became entangled in pond weed and you could not exit the water imme-diately to take your first breath. Your uncle untangled you. And the next moment you were fine. Breathing like you were born to it. You were never even in danger of drowning—because you still could absorb air from your skin. And yet that moment of fear has changed your destiny."

"I admit I held a grudge against my uncle since the beginning for neglecting me in that moment. But I got water in my newly working lungs. It was a strange, unsettling sensation and that was all it took, especially for a fragile first-breather like me, to panic. Water in the lungs kills. Uncle should have been focused on me. His attention should not have been diverted by Linka, who also transitioned on that day and who, as usual, needed no help from anyone."

"You make too much of but a moment."

"I do not deny I have made an anthill into a termite mound, but I take full responsibility for this problem as my own. If I could see a way forward, I would take it. But the fear and panic linger and are paralyzing. No one experiences the ill effects of my failings more than I."

"Be that as it may," said Ranya, "frog kings do not reject the comfort of water, the nourishment of water, the protection of water. To deny those things is to deny your very essence as a frog. My subjects, who would have been yours when I pass to the Great Pond Beyond, will not tolerate such an affront to their very nature. You had a chance to prove yourself worthy of taking over my reign, and I fear you will never regain their positive opinion. That is why I have come to this decision."

The shadow of defeat fell over her son's face and his dejected sigh broke Ranya's heart. But what was a frog queen to do? She had denied the truth long enough. Her son was not fit to rule. Linka was.

"As devastated as I am to disappoint you, Mother, there are bigger problems than who will take over your reign. While on my travels, I saw a terrible sight—one that you know full well."

"Oh, tell me, which terrible sight was that?" Ranya said. "There are so many we could choose from."

"The Lake of the Dead. And I want to know how you can ignore it."

"Lake of the Dead? I know of no such lake in my territory."

"It is outside the Veil of Mist, in the land of the largetoe," Azzie said.

The Queen snorted in surprise. "It is no reflection on me to ignore harsh realities that cannot be changed," said the queen. "That is in the land of the largetoes. Not my realm."

"But you know all realms are interrelated and you know you are supposed to be the Voice of Nature," Azzie declared. "If you do not speak and act with authority, how can things change?"

"All realms have ceased to listen to each other. What can I be expected to do?"

"Everything you can," Azzie said with more passion than he'd felt for anything in a long time. "We may live in separate realms, but we do not live on separate planets."

"Oh, that we would," the queen said, her eyes closed as if in supplication to the Well.

"And you did not see the cruel nature of these deaths. These frogs must have suffered terribly because of the changes inflicted on them by poisons in the waters they were born in—and with the addition of pests and unnatural debris, which gets added to their home over time. I saw one frog who was in absolute agony. We had no choice but to end her suffering and set her free for the journey to the Big Pond Beyond. How could you know these things and not act with compassion to help your subjects?"

"The harm is done. The suffering, inevitable."

"Surely there is *something* we can do. *We* did not make those poisons. *We* did not make that debris."

"What exactly would that be? Kill every largetoe on the planet? We do not know what is causing these problems. We are not even sure if the largetoes are at fault."

"How can you say that? If you had traveled more recently into the land of the largetoe, you would know the truth instantly. One look at the dullness, the grime, the lack of vibrancy in the air, and you would sense it deep in your webs that they are at least a major part of the problem. And it is not only causing problems out there. We also face devastation inside the Circle—at the Palay."

"Our home?" The queen's face registered immediate alarm.

"The very structure of the Palay is in jeopardy."

Wisps of her recent dream circled her head. Was it already coming true? If so, had she done anything to make it so? "But the Palay is made of rock. How could anything but an earthquake destroy it? And Magmo would never do that."

"We are creating too much dream energy, and there are not enough frogs in the field—since too many of them have them died or migrated—to relay it to the largetoe."

"What do you know of the largetoe? You have never even seen one."

"I have seen firsthand the effect they have had on the All. Surely they can learn to live as part of this world without destroying or degrading it. Just look at the decline of our own kind. Can we not lay that directly at their webless feet? Whether it is from the theft of our brethren's homes or the filth they pour into water and air, largetoe are not getting enough energy to help them dream up solutions to these big problems or these problems would not be there. It is a vicious, interdependent circle."

"How can we stop what we are meant to do?" the queen asked.

"We do not have to stop it. We can modify our output, at least while the cycle is unbalanced. Do you not see, Mother? If we continue to put dream energy out there that cannot be used, the dream energy returns home. Even now, it is pooling in the very foundations of the Palay."

"You have proof that this is true?"

"Proof? You want proof?" Azzie approached her with a clenched fist extended and asked her to hold out her hand, which she did. He released his grip, and a shower of fine rock shards fell into her open palm.

"This," he said, motioning to the pile on her hand, "is why there can be no new dreaming pods, Mother. They will only add to the problem."

The queen brushed her hands off, letting the shards fall to the floor. "Explain this . . . dirt."

"When the unused dream energy returns, it vibrates the bottom strata of the Palay, and this vibration is chipping away at Frog Mountain's structure."

"You are wrong. You must be wrong. How can we halt progress?"

"Mother, you are not listening. How can it be progress if it causes us to hop toward our own destruction? More dreaming pods mean more dream energy that has no place to go. I say we cut down on active CODERs until we resolve this problem."

"That is simply not possible. Dreaming is our part in the Grand Design."

"Then we need a Grand *Redesign*, Mother, or there will be no Palay. It will happen. Maybe not in your lifetime or mine. Or maybe it will all be over tomorrow. No one knows. But why take even the smallest chance?"

"The dream. Perhaps it was the meaning of my dream," the queen said, more to herself.

"You had a dream in my absence? Why wasn't I told?"

"I have not revealed all of its deeply disturbing contents to anyone. That is why I called the Frog Council to me. Some have already arrived, but many more will come in the next two sun cycles. I would like you, as a gesture of courtesy, to greet those who have come the farthest at the Gathering Glen."

Azzie nodded his snout. "I am happy to do so, Mother."

"I will reveal my dream to everyone at once."

"You will not even give me a preview?"

"Let me say that I thank you truly for sharing your knowledge with me. You have given insights into the problems revealed in the dream. But I suspect that when Linka retrieves the Pearl and kills—"

"Kills *who*, Mother?"

"There is a femtoe who happens to possess the Golden Pearl of the Forest. Linka will kill her," she said. "Your uncle is preparing his Golden Death potion now, which Linka will deploy, returning the Pearl to me once the girl is dead."

"Mother, I urge you to reconsider. Do you not see the poetry of it all? A femtoe has the Pearl. Let us convince *her* to become the Renewee. It is the perfect opportunity. The perfect time—if we can get her to the true Renewal Grounds for the full Pink Moon."

"That is totally unsuitable. We do not take any old largetoe as our Renewee. They must be kind, compassionate, courageous. Seekers of truth, bringers of change."

"How do you know she is not like that? Perhaps the Pearl has chosen her. There must be *some* reason why she has it in her possession. If you have Linka kill her before finding out more, you kill the possibility of fixing these problems that threaten to destroy us."

The queen was silent, locked in a battle with her fear. Would she ever be able to admit that her dream foretold that *she* would be the one to destroy the Palay? If only she knew what her future self would do to cause the destruction. And if she couldn't tell her own son the truth, she would have to lie to the council.

"Mother, you told me that I must learn not to be a coward, but you must learn not to be a coward as well. Whatever you do, do not let Linka kill the girl. At least until the Frog Council meets. And allow me to determine a safe level of operation for the dream pods."

"I deny both of your requests. Even now, the vizzard prepares the means of death for the largetoe. You are as bad as Lord Raeburn, Azzie. Neither of you listen."

"The same could be said of you, Mother," Azzie said.

"And please, do not discuss my decision to have Linka succeed me—with her or anyone else. I will decide to hand down my decision when the time is right to do so."

"I only ask that you warn me first, Mother, so I do not have to live in constant anxiety about the timing of my diminishment." Azzie gave his mother a double bow and took his leave.

"Oh, son, you forgot this," Ranya said as Azzie neared the door.

He turned, a quizzical look on his face.

Ranya tossed him the wrist cuff the Dark Winds had dropped at her feet as they departed from their destructive visit. He caught it with a snap of his hand, placed it back on his wrist, and left without another word.

Ranya wondered if her son could be right about her duty to do more to solve the problems of the world. It wasn't her fault things were this way. The world expected the Queen of Frogs to be the voice of the All. It was a role she had rejected from the first. Why couldn't the world take care of itself?

No, she thought. She was not wrong. How could she be? She was queen. The largetoe girl had to die. The real ceremony would never happen. Relief washed over her and she could breathe more easily.

35

The Vizzard Gone Yesterday, Hair Today

Two Nights Till Pink Moon
Deepest Night
The Palay, Corridor of Exalted Rulers Long Dead

I N HIS LABORATORY, Balarius sat as no other frog could sit (cross-legged) at his workbench. He mixed a tincture of lemon balm, lavender, and his personal favorite, chamomile, into half an oyster shell and handed it to Wink, Clarenso's nephew who had shown up at the Palay half-dead and apparently alone, with no answer as to how he got there.

"Drink this and don't worry if you gag a bit. Nasty stuff, but effective in calming the nervous system. Then tell me how you escaped the Bulldoggies," Balarius said.

Clarenso stood nearby wringing his hands.

Wink drank the brew and grimaced. "I am sorry, Great Sir," he choked out. "But I cannot explain."

"He will not tell me a thing, Your Grandness," Clarenso said. "I have no explanation for my nephew's behavior. Please forgive him. He is young. Frightened. Far from a home he will never see again. And at a loss for family except for me."

"Now, now," said Balarius. "Clarenso, leave Wink to walk with me. I have an errand to do in the Hall of Exalted Frogs Long Dead. There is more I want to know of his experiences and perhaps I can help him, gently, to recall."

Wink looked at his uncle with desperation as Clarenso departed. The vizzard suppressed a sigh. It hurt to be an object of fear among the young.

"Let us ramble together," Balarius said to the young frog. With some effort, he rose to his feet and, walking sticks in hand, led the way out into one of the grand corridors that connected the main rooms of the Palay on this level.

Channels of fresh mountain water flowed down either side of the wide corridor, which was dotted with tidbits like dandelion flowers and floating bowls of delicacies like deep-fried flies and night worms stuffed with funnel mushrooms and thyme to munch on for passersby. Fine mosaic tiles depicting a tropical mountain stream covered the floor of the corridor, with its surrounding jungle covering the walls.

Balarius helped Wink onto a floating platform tethered by his door for his easy travel. Using a walking stick as a punting pole, he steered them through the rapidly moving water. After they had gone a little distance through the winding corridors, Balarius spoke.

"Now tell me, little one, who and what has frightened you so. You impress me as a frog with a stout and honest heart. I know you would not lie to me unless you have been coerced to do so.

My wise father said, 'Saying nothing is the same as lying.' But one of the advantages of being a vizzard is that I can always see a lie. Please, share your burden with me now."

As they ventured further down the corridor, Wink relented and told him the story of how he and his party of refuge seekers had been captured by the Bulldoggies, and how Lord Raeburn rescued him as he was about to be thrown into the Maw.

"Raeburn at the Maw. Interesting. And you promised him you would do anything to repay him for saving you."

Wink nodded, his entire body quivering like an aspen leaf in a brisk breeze.

"Now, now," Balarius said. "All will be well. Together we will figure this out. Who is your greater loyalty to? Lord Raeburn or your queen?"

"My queen, Great Lord. It must be so."

They reached a junction in the corridor where the channel took a sharp right and headed for a common area. There, Balarius pulled the floating platform to a stop, lashed it to one of the intermittent resting posts, and disembarked. "Your uncle will be waiting for you at the end of this channel. When he has settled you in his comfortable quarters, not those of Lord Raeburn's choosing, please send him to me in the Corridor of Exalted Rulers."

Wink kissed the hem of the vizzard's cloak. "Lord Raeburn knows of our meeting, kind sir. What shall I tell him about it?"

"Since you seem like such an honest sort," Balarius said, "I will not ask you to lie like Raeburn has. Simply tell him the truth. Do not compromise yourself anymore. Only do what seems right and good in your soul. Then, come and tell me what that is. And be sure that Raeburn knows about this visit and future ones. It is always better to meet another's treachery with your own truth. Now, off with you, young sir. I have work to do."

Wink dove off the platform and swam in the direction Balarius had indicated.

Balarius chuckled to himself as he walked the remaining distance to the Corridor of Exalted Rulers Long Dead. *Wait until I tell the queen that Raeburn has been to the Maw. The audaciousness of that frog. What other plans does he have?* He would have to find out.

Balarius shuffled his aching bones down one side of the corridor. There were no water channels here to allow close viewing of the portraits, which had been painted by the greatest frog artists of this or that reign and hung on the silk-covered walls, woven in a pattern of the most delicate bamboo leaves. There was Queen Soffinatta, King Milostonae, King Garruchian. Most of the great ones were there. Rulers who acted in the best interest of their queendom or kingdom and themselves.

But they weren't alone. The untalented, the infirm, and the unfulfilled were there as well. So many portraits. He knew the exact one he was looking for. But his last visit here had been so long ago, he wasn't sure where to find it.

"Your Fabulousness, I am here," Clarenso said.

"Ah, Clarenso. Thank you. I need your help finding the portrait of our beloved Queen DeLili."

"Gladly, Sir," Clarenso said, and he scampered up the wall, leaping from one portrait nameplate to another as fast as he could.

The vizzard toddled after him.

"Here, Your Inquisitiveness," Clarenso cried. "I have found her."

It took a few moments for the vizzard to join him, and when he did, he stood in front of the portrait.

"If ever you wanted an example of the promise of greatness thwarted, it is here. Who knows where the queendom would be if the kind, the gracious, the brilliant Queen DeLili had not met an early demise?"

"She indeed looks . . ." But the aide hesitated.

"Unusual?"

"Yes. And capable." Clarenso gave his uncharacteristically small compliment in a hurried fashion. "And those eyes."

"We are such a varied species, Clarenso. Do you not think we should love all our kind?"

"Your Brilliantness, I am not one for withholding love based on looks, but if you forgive me, hair on a frog is disturbing."

"We have both been known to startle the masses, Clarenso. Certainly, you will forgive this femnura for startling you."

Clarenso bowed before the vizzard's greater wisdom.

"And now, this is what I want you to do." Balarius removed the tuft of hair Linka had sent from his cloak and handed it to Clarenso. He recoiled at the sight.

"Come now, take it. Then climb up the wall and compare it to the color of the hair tuft in the portrait. I must know if they are similar."

Clarenso's hand quivered, but he followed the vizzard's request and held the real-life sample up to the painted one.

"It is hard to tell, even for my own keen eyes. Perhaps," Clarenso said. "Or perhaps not."

The vizzard tapped one of his walking sticks three times on the mosaic floor, which captured the image of water racing over rocks. Instantly a lek of fireflies appeared, congregating above his head. He pointed a webbed finger to the portrait in question and the lek surrounded it, illuminating the dark upper regions of the frame.

"Yes, I can see now, Oh Clever Clarity Seeker. It appears that it might be a match—not an exact one though, color-wise. But close."

"I will accept *close*, Clarenso. You may climb down and thank you for your keen eyesight. My own fails as we speak."

"May I ask what this means, Oh Great One?"

"Of course, you may, but that does not mean I will tell you."

The transparent frog flushed pink as all his vessels gorged with the blood of embarrassment.

"I did not mean to cause you any mortification," said Balarius. "I must weigh the value of keeping this discovery to myself."

"Of course, Wise One. You know best."

"Now off with you. See to your nephew. He's a good tad, and I have much to consider."

And Clarenso withdrew.

Alone, Balarius slapped the piece of hair, with the roots so white they were almost blue, against his thigh. Was this a wild hunch on his part? A mere sight evaluation was, of course, not proof of anything. Further tests would be required, but in his heart, he knew he was right to pursue the possibility that the femtoe his daughter had found might, in fact, be part frog.

36

Azzie 🐸 Frogs on the Boil

One Day Till Pink Moon
Sunup
The Palay, The Vizzard's Laboratory

SHOCK REGISTERED DOWN to the bottom of Azzie's webbed feet when he saw the long line of Poisonous Ones that stretched down the corridor outside the vizzard's double door. That sight could only mean one thing. The femtoe was as good as dead, unless he could convince his uncle otherwise. A sense of urgency twanged away at his tendons till they vibrated at a discordant pitch.

One of the double doors opened and the vizzard poked his head out. He surveyed the long line of volunteers with satisfaction. "Thank you. Thank you all for coming. You serve the queen well with your presence here."

But the vizzard's smile faded when he spotted Azzie.

"Nephew, how fine to see you. It has been an age since you have paid me a visit." His words sounded light, but his expression darkened. It was always like this when Azzie saw his uncle, who, for all his power, could not release himself from the burden of guilt over Azzie's affliction. Or perhaps it was really because Azzie still held him responsible for it.

"I see you are busy, Uncle. But if you could spare me a few brief moments, I have an urgent matter to discuss."

"Come in, come in. I always have time for you." His uncle opened the second door to give Azzie a wide berth around those waiting in line. Azzie moved past them, grateful that the Poisonous Ones all complied with the Palay rule that they must wear shibshibs, slippers made from miniature rubber tree plant leaves. These leaves were grown in the Palay conservatory for this express use since the queen could hardly allow poisonous frogs to roam the corridors and create trails of poisonous frog goo wherever they went. Only those frogs who did not excrete poison through their feet, like Simeon, were exempt.

"I see you are already working on Mother's plan," Azzie said as he made his way through the other door.

"Oh, she has told you," the vizzard said.

"Let us say we discussed it with a great deal of heat," Azzie said.

"Do you mind waiting, dear nephew, while I select the volunteers I wish to work with and send the rest on their way?" his uncle asked.

Azzie suppressed a sigh of annoyance and gave his permission with a curt dip of his snout.

The Poisonous Ones filed in.

"I will take you and you," the vizzard said, pointing to a golden frog and a black frog with thick irregular yellow stripes. "Azzie, these fine residents of the Palay could kill several largetoe at once. I am working on an amazing killing formulation, the best there is, and it surely will not fail."

Azzie's alarm grew with every selection.

"You, the handsome yellow frog with black legs and the tadpoles on your back," the vizzard called out.

The frog in question nodded to the vizzard. "I excuse you from this call to duty because of your tads. Return to your nest and rear them safely."

"But we wish to serve the queen. All of us," the father frog said.

His little ones nodded their agreement, with echoes of high-pitched cries. "We want to help. Let us help."

"You are all too precious to risk in the preparation process, dear tads. But I promise you, your time will come."

The tads cheered as the largest one said, "We get to boil later. Yay!" But the poor father frog had a distinct air of dejection about him as he departed with his family to return to their quarters.

"That handsome memnura," said the vizzard, "expels poison that causes torment with fits, spasms, and paralysis of the lungs and muscles. He would have been an excellent choice, but rearing tads comes first."

Azzie wandered over to inspect the cauldrons on the hearth while his uncle continued with his selection.

"You, the reddish-brown fellow with the yellow side stripes and mottled legs, please make your way into my lab." He faced Azzie. "Worry not, Nephew, for all the pain I can cause with my special poison brew, I have no wish to make the femtoe suffer. This frog has a poison that, while deadly, is also a painkiller that works two hundred times better than any other."

"Very interesting indeed," Azzie remarked.

The vizzard spoke to the remaining crowd. "I have what I need for today. Please go back to your appropriate habitat. Thank you, one and all."

Disappointed, the unchosen frogs departed, and he closed the other door behind them.

"On to the fun," he added with some satisfaction. "Now, fine fellows, all, we will start the extraction process. Please select a cauldron on the hearth and hop into it."

Some of the poison frogs rocked nervously on their webbed feet. Others shook. But the pure yellow frog kicked off his shibshibs and hopped into the first cauldron. Others followed, selecting from the ones that remained. "I promise I will not harm you. I will heat the water until you sweat. Then I will harvest your poison," the vizzard said in soothing tones. "Young Wink, will you please strike the flint to start the fires?"

Azzie noticed, with a start, a young frog in the corner by the hearth. Azzie had missed him because of his translucence.

"Your Highness, this is Wink."

Azzie dipped once. The young frog returned Azzie's dip twofold then lit the hearth.

"He has endured a terrible experience at the Maw," the vizzard said.

"And he survived?" Azzie asked.

"Obviously, Nephew."

Azzie blushed. "I have never heard of anyone's escape from that death trap."

"He may be the first. And you will never guess who his savior was."

Azzie shrugged.

"Lord Raeburn."

"Raeburn? At the Maw?" Azzie asked.

His uncle nodded.

"Mother should brand him a traitor for consorting with the enemy," Azzie said.

"In due time, Nephew. In due time," the vizzard said. "Now, with the frogs on the boil, tell me what you need."

Azzie moved closer to his uncle and lowered his voice. "I must speak to you in total confidence. It is dangerous for me to say what is on my mind and dangerous for you to listen."

"Wink, will you be kind enough to fetch more wood? You know where it can be found."

After Wink left the room, Azzie peered around the corner to make sure the young frog wasn't eavesdropping. A heavy mantle of dread shadowed him. What he was about to say to the brother of his mother was nothing short of treason.

He cleared his throat and began, in a whisper, on the off chance the frogs, each in their own pot, might hear over the hiss and crackle of the twig fire. "I am asking you to prepare an ineffective version of the Golden Death, one that will not actually kill the girl with the Pearl. I have asked Mother to spare the largetoe so that we can have an actual Ceremony of Renewal. She has refused. But if the girl does not *really* die, perhaps we can convince Mother that this is a portent in favor of an actual ceremony."

His uncle froze.

Azzie's heart skipped like a flat pebble across water. Had he gone too far?

"You are asking me to go against our queen's orders?"

"I am asking you to consider which course of action leads to the greater good. I do not know why Mother wants this femtoe dead. I fear that if she kills her, with your help, we may lose our last hope of turning our decline around. As you know, the Frog World is deteriorating rapidly. We cannot afford to wait for the next Pink Moon to make this happen. It appears that the All is conspiring to bring these forces together at *this* time. Should we not at least try our best to pay attention?"

"I should report our conversation to your mother, and she would be justified in punishing you. But since you are my beloved nephew, I cannot."

"I do this not to betray her. I do this to serve her subjects, and the All, in the most beneficial way I can."

Breathing heavily, his uncle went to the large window that overlooked one of the many lush gardens surrounding the Palay. Steadying himself with his walking sticks, he faced Azzie. "I will keep your words secret and give them serious consideration. I owe you that much. For now, that is all I can say."

"Thank you, Uncle." Azzie inhaled deeply, through lungs and skin, and for a moment he knew what it was like to be a normal frog, not a panicked, fearful one. "I wonder if I could impose on you for one thing more."

The vizzard's soulful glance told Azzie his uncle's patience had almost evaporated. With a weary sigh he said, "First I must check the frogs."

Wink came back wearing a head harness connected to a travois stacked with small branches and twigs.

Azzie's fear blossomed into frustration. Perhaps his mother was right. Governing did not suit him. Linka would make a better monarch than he. Why, then, was he compelled to prove his mother wrong?

His uncle checked the temperature in the pots where the selected Poisonous Ones lounged and chitter-chattered. "Frog boiling is a tricky business," the vizzard said in a whisper to Azzie. "They would stay until they all boiled to death, and they would not notice that anything was amiss."

"It is much like how we live our lives every day, failing to notice all the little things around us that are no longer how they once were," Azzie said.

His uncle's eyes widened, and he cocked his head to the side as if in deep consideration of Azzie's words. Then, returning abruptly to the moment, the vizzard spoke to the young transparent frog. "Wink, once you have stoked the fires, please offer our guests snacks. There are crunchy katydids, some grub granola, and pickled fire ants."

"Oh, thank you, dear sir," the yellow frog chirped, clapping its hands together excitedly. "I adore pickled fire ants." Other frogs down the line of cauldrons clapped too.

"It is the least we can do. We are deeply grateful for your help."

They all chimed in:

"It is nothing."

"We are so happy to serve the queen."

"Anytime you need us, we are here."

Balarius returned to his nephew's side. "Now, what else did you have on your mind?"

"Merely to consult with you about a creature I saw."

"Creature? What kind of creature?"

"It was the size of a young bear, only hunched. It spoke in our tongue but was not a frog. And oddly—it had a long shock of hair."

Balarius stroked his snout, pondering the list of characteristics Azzie had given him. "Hair?"

"Yes, strung with colored threads, beads, and bones."

"Hmm. Did you notice the color of its eyes?"

"I did not, Uncle. There was too much else to see and take in."

"And where did you meet this unfortunate one?"

"Frago took me to a lake where many of our kind were dead and malformed. It was a horrible sight."

"Hmm. Hmm. Wait for me in my study, beyond that doorway there," Balarius said as he pointed toward an inner archway. "I will be with you shortly."

Azzie made his way into his uncle's study and tried to be patient. After a few moments, however, his curiosity instigated some poking about. There were so many fascinating things to see.

He was drawn to a wall with cubby holes carved into it. Each cubby was labeled for its general purpose: "Potions for wart removal," "Letters to Great Aunt Peragonia," plus cubbies dedicated to the records of vizzards gone by. Within each cubby were stacks of leaflets with tags that identified their specific purpose dangling from each stem. "Recipe for warts and boils bigger than a blueberry," for example. One caught his eye. It read, "Contracts: Queen DeLili's reign." There were several leaflets in that cubby, but one called out to him. It was written on a eucalyptus leaf, which was very unusual.

He picked it up and sniffed it. The eucalyptus fragrance was faint but still present. The tag tied to the leaf stem said "Queen DeLili's pre-dethroning agreement."

Curious, Azzie read it. Its contents were startling.

He tucked it inside his cape a moment before his uncle entered the room.

37

Vizzard ❧ Feature Creatures

One Day Till Pink Moon
Sunup
The Palay, The Vizzard's Laboratory

"Welcome to my library," Balarius said, pointing above him with pride to vines that stretched across the room in all directions. There, more leaflets were arranged by subjects, such as Amphibology, Ecology, Chemistry, Embryology, and Metaphysics. "My current reading list," he chuckled, pointing upward.

"And what about these leaflets over here?" Azzie asked, gesturing to the wall of cubbyholes.

"Oh, those are very historical documents. Nothing of interest to younger generations such as yourself."

"What is it you wanted me to see?" Azzie said as he perused some of the titles hanging from the ceiling. *The Ecological Legacy*

*of the Largetoe, The Metaphysics of Metamorphosis, Mutation of the
Species, Environmental Decline Over the Eons*, and more.

Balarius pointed to the wall across from the cubbies where several drawings hung. "These are reported creatures that have resulted when two different groups of animals have mated or been bred artificially. Your creature, I hate to say, sounds like a cross between an amphibian and a mammal."

"How is that even possible?" Azzie said.

"There are many strange largetoe experiments."

"Whatever for?" Azzie asked.

"I know not. I have my spies in various largetoe laboratories and educational institutions and have heard many distressing things. Frogs, especially the poor clawfoot frog, have become some of the victims of such madness."

"So, Uncle, you think the creature I saw could be an escaped experiment?"

The vizzard shrugged. "It would be hard to know unless I met it myself. Tell me now, was there any resemblance, even the slightest, between the creature you saw and any of these?" he said, pointing with a gnarled webbed digit at the framed drawings.

Azzie ambled by a picture depicting a long snake-like body with a protruding forked tongue and fins.

"This is a snish," said the vizzard. "A cross between a snake and a fish."

They moved down the wall.

"And this is a squirtle, a cross between a sea squirt and a turtle."

Azzie examined that picture up close. "The bright royal blue turtle-like body is beautiful, but how does it protect itself with the sea squirt-like tubules on its back instead of a shell?"

"Shoots out poison, I believe. If you look a little closer, there are notes on the drawings." With a flick of his hand, the vizzard tugged a hanging vine attached to a mica mirror in the lumitube to focus more light on the drawing.

"That is indeed what the drawing states, Uncle. A paralyzing poison in fact."

Balarius pointed to another drawing. This one was very tall and featured another snake-like creature standing on a curved tail with rings of brightly colored feathers in different colors, like yellow, turquoise, pink, and rue, set below a pair of wings that looked like irregular starbursts on either side. "This is a snerd, a cross between a snail and a bird."

Azzie recoiled at the sight.

"And this unfortunate thing is a furd. Notice the bird-like body covered in spotted fur. Without feathers, it cannot fly, and with its spindly little bird legs and the heaviness of its fur, I imagine, like me, it cannot walk far either. You see from the number of drawings that stretch along the walls of this room that there are many more creatures of unique design than anyone could imagine."

Azzie moved down the line of drawings, wincing with each new image. "And you approve of such things? You must since it would be you to brew the potion to transform the largetoe to frog and back again."

"Let me say in my own defense that I was born with an insatiable curiosity for the power of experimentation. In fact, you must come to my villa at the base of Frog Mountain sometime, and I will show you some of my work."

"I remember many happy times there as a metamorph, Uncle. Back when Linka and I were good friends."

"Those were happy days, indeed, Nephew."

And they had been, before Azzie recalled in a nightmare the neglect his uncle had shown him at his hatching. That hurt had clouded the rest of his younger days.

"Have you ever made the potion required for the Ceremony of Renewal?" Azzie asked, purposefully changing the subject.

"It has always been kept at the ready."

"So, if the right circumstances arose—where a girl and the Pearl were available—under a Pink Moon, of course," Azzie said, "we could try for an authentic Ceremony of Renewal."

The vizzard chuckled (a bit condescendingly Azzie thought).

"Do I sense a new trait emerging in you, Nephew? Tenacity? As you know, nothing of such magnitude could possibly happen without the queen's permission," the vizzard said. "And there will be eternal drought in the Big Pond Beyond before the queen will agree to such shenanigans."

"I do not agree with your position, Uncle, but the truth is always best. I wonder what the truth is in this case. Perhaps what I should have asked for was more time to make my case with Mother."

"For that, I would refer you to the one who delivers the ultimate blow."

"You mean Linka?"

"It has always saddened both your mother and me that you two were more enemies than friends. Perhaps, in your hour of need, you might reach out to her and find you have the best interest of each other in common. Here, a blank leaflet." The vizzard handed Azzie a poplar leaf. "I will include your missive with the poison pouch I am sending to my daughter." The Vizzard held up a pouch and placed another leaflet inside. "I have already prepared the instructions for administering the Golden Death potion which will soon be complete."

Azzie's skin paled.

The vizzard cleared his throat. "How indelicate of me. If I had any doubts about my daughter's loyalty to your mother, I would never allow you the chance to inspire my daughter to treason.

It is an impossibility. Perhaps once she knows your thoughts, she can inspire you to be a more loyal son. Now, be quick. I will soon summon a Zon to take the poison to Linka. We will let the Well of White Light decide who shall live and who shall die. I pray that among the dead will not be those I love."

After his uncle withdrew, Azzie took the leaf and held it to his forehead. Golden particles imbued with his thoughts flowed from his heart, through his mind, then danced their way into the cells of the leaf.

38

Nora ◎ Making My Way Back to Gran

One Day Till Pink Moon
Early Morning
Home

I WALKED TO THE edge of the plateau where our house had stood for over a century. I couldn't look back. Instead, I'd hold the memory of what it had looked like when it was whole. I looked out over the Salmon Valley, across the town below, and to the majestic purple mountains beyond still tinged with the pink rays of the rising sun. Looking at the beauty before me, I imagined I was inside my home, in the comfort of 'the familiar,' surrounded by those I loved. In the days to come, I would return to this spot and remember, but those memories were too painful to dive into now.

The frog I had saved (or had it saved me?) was wiggling hard in my pocket trying to get out.

"Hang on a minute, froggie," I said and stopped to look at the *Trillium ovatum* that had bloomed faithfully every year. It had been crushed by someone. Gran called that plant her faithful friend and would not be pleased. This early in the spring it was still white, but the color of the flower, if it hadn't been trampled, would have changed to pink and then purple over time.

Most of the footprint was indistinct, and I wondered if it was made by the person who had burned down our house.

I passed between the two great cedar trees, planted generations ago, marking the start of the downhill path. I leaned against the smaller one and drank in its quiet strength. I wanted to look back at my house, but I couldn't. My legs were as heavy as the trunks of these great trees.

Everything that happened last night clanged together inside my brain. My mom's grave was empty. Our house was destroyed. My father's ghost sent a message that still whirled through my head. *That which came from your mother should never go to another— especially if that other is 'frog'.*

What did he mean? I had an idea that might help me figure it out.

I rummaged around in my backpack for the container from the tomatoes Seth had brought me (was it only yesterday?), placed the frog inside it and snapped the lid shut. It was the perfect size and had ready-made holes, so the frog could breathe. And the lid was tight so it couldn't get out. There were even a few tomatoes for it to chomp on.

I removed the pouch from around my neck and poured the jewelry casket into my hand. This was something from my mom. And I had a frog. What would happen if I put the two of them together, contrary to my father's command?

I lay on my belly so the frog and I were eye to eye.

"Okay, frog. Let's experiment. What could Dad possibly not want to happen here?"

I touched the gleaming golden frog at the top of the jewelry casket, and it opened, revealing the pearl. As the pearl's surface started to swirl, time in the world beyond me slowed but did not stand still. Leaves in the nearby arbutus trees waved like lazy flags in the wind. Birdsong shifted from high, fast trills to sounding like someone put playback on half speed. But, as usual, I could still move at a normal rate.

The light from the rising sun softened into a wash of pastel colors. The frog looked different in this light. From what I could tell, it might be a Pacific tree frog, given its bright-green color and the mottled stripes down its sides. But beyond that it was unlike any frog I'd ever seen.

For starters, it wore a protective helmet, with a spike and colorful braided ribbons of grass dangling from it. There was also an armor-like vest and a lethal-looking figure-eight blade on its back. Even its skin sported brightly colored tattoos that enhanced the natural patterns of speckles and dots on its face. I shook my head to jog my eyeballs back in place. But the warrior frog was real.

"You and the owl saved me. Thank you," I said.

The frog winced in pain. It must have been in agony from the oozing burns and lost limb.

A nearby salmonberry bush reached out to me, inviting me to pick its leaves. I crushed the leaves until they were juicy, opened the top of the container and squeezed out a few drops of juice on the frog's injuries. "This will help."

The frog scrambled backward, then stopped. Nodding, it let me continue to treat its wounds.

Then it pointed at the pearl and in a crackly, croaky voice, it spoke: "Do you realize, largetoe, that you hold the most powerful object in the natural world in the palm of your weirdly unwebbed hands?" It looked at my fingers and shuddered.

So, the frog talked too. Right. I had gone from slightly weird to fully and certifiably insane.

I gave the pearl a closer look. I can't say it looked "powerful," but it was beautiful with its luminescent yellow-golden color and raised, burnished veins.

"This little old thing?" I said, trying to make a joke.

"Little? Maybe to you. Old? Yes. But it has power beyond anything you have ever known."

"And you want me to give it to you."

"Yes," the frog said.

"Ah. No," I said, wondering what astonished me more—that a frog was talking to me or that I was talking back.

"Frogs have a custom of not taking things that do not belong to us. That Pearl is ours. Return it."

"Perhaps before we argue we should introduce ourselves," I said, remembering my manners. "My name is Nora."

"Nora?" The frog pronounced my name with a kind of hiccup or croak where the *O* should be.

"I am Princess Push-ta-linka," she said slowly, like she was talking to someone who didn't have her brainpower. "I am Commander of Queen Ranya's own guards, the Zons."

"Queen Ranya?"

"Ignorant largetoe. I will educate you later if you live long enough."

"You—a little bitty frog with one arm—are going to kill me? I could grind you into the ground right now and save you the trouble of doing anything—ever." My strong reaction to this little green thing surprised me. I never even killed spiders. I couldn't ever kill a frog. Why was I being so cruel?

"You may dip your snout to me. Now," the frog said.

"Dip my snout? I think we call that a bow, and around here we don't bow to royalty. Frog or otherwise."

"Of course. Why would you? You respect nothing."

She had guts, that's for sure.

"You may call me Linka since my name seems to confound you."

"I had no idea there was such a thing as a frog princess."

"Typical largetoe narrowmindedness," Linka said.

"What is a large toe?" I asked. I tried to copy the way she said it, with a guttural sound where the "ge" should be.

"You are that—you are a LARGETOE."

"Do you mean human?"

The frog nodded.

"Why do you call us that?"

"Have you ever looked at your feet?"

"Not from your point of view."

"Of course not. Your kind is incapable of seeing anything from any other viewpoint but your own. Perhaps that explains your ridiculously wrong-headed stories about frog princes that do not even consider that there might be a frog princess."

"You're right. I never considered it."

"Ignorant and dangerous. Your narrow version of the All is remarkably close minded."

There was that phrase again. "What is the All?" I asked.

"Every single thing on the planet is imbued with vibrations, and those vibrations connect us to each other."

"I don't get it," I said.

The frog looked at me in complete disgust. "Every river, every rock, every mountain, every creature, every plant, every tree, the water, the air are all connected and that 'connected entity' is the All."

The disdain in Linka's voice was hard to take. "You're a pushy know-it-all frog, and I'm not sure I like you," I said. Then I snapped the pearl's casket shut, and the adorned frog I had been communicating with faded into a plain old frog.

Okay. So this pearl possessed the power to make ignorant and dangerous people like me see everything in a whole new light. It connected me to this frog. What else did it connect me to? And why would my mother have had it?

I reopened the jewelry casket and in the presence of the pearl, I could see the frog in all her glory once again. *But time didn't slow.* I wondered why.

"I am glad you changed your mind," Linka said.

I drew the pearl closer. I was giving it to no one.

"You are not going to give the Pearl to me," said the frog. "I clearly see that this is your plan."

"You are not wrong."

"Would you at least allow me to touch it?"

"Why should I do that?"

"It is a precious thing. A sacred object. To touch it is to receive a blessing from the Well of White Light—the source of all that is good in our world."

What could one little touch hurt? And there was such reverence on that bright little tattooed green face that it seemed heartless to say no. So I moved it closer to her.

The frog drank the sight in with a rapturous expression on her face, then slowly, reverently spread her hand and placed it on the pearl. The yellow-gold surface quivered and its veins bulged and began to flow with spectral colors that pooled into spots that grew and merged until the pearl itself was a swirling rainbow.

Then, the boundaries between pearl and frog dissolved as her hand penetrated its surface. As it did, an aura of the same rainbow light infused her body. Tranquility that had settled on her face was replaced with alarm, and she screamed in agony. I wasn't sure if I should rip the pearl away from her or what. But when I looked closer, I saw that, amazingly, her burns were fading, and her severed arm was growing back.

As the process neared completion, the little frog's cries lessened until finally she shuddered with relief and flexed her new webbed fingers and forearm slowly. "Praise be to the Well of White Light," she said in a voice that wobbled with exhaustion.

"Did you know that was going to happen?" I asked.

"No one knows all the things that the Pearl can do," she said.

"Every time I open it, it seems to demonstrate a different power. The first time, I saw strings that connected everything."

"You. Saw. Web. Strings?" She sounded very impressed.

"That's not what I'd call them but yes. It was crazy—like everything in the whole world was connected to everything else. Hey—that's just what you said the All was about. I get it now. And then the next time, I saw the water dance. And now, regeneration. That's not something you see every day."

The little frog was quiet for a moment, then said, "The Pearl just healed you as well."

I looked for the burns on my hands and arms. Gone. I felt my forehead for the sore that the owl had inflicted. Gone. The frog was right!

I poured some water from a bottle in my backpack into the container. She slipped out of her armor, jumped in, and doused herself. I poured more water over her head, and it seemed to refresh her. Then she tried to put her armor back on but her regrown arm seemed too weak for her to manage. I picked up the main piece of her body armor, which looked like a front and a back piece fastened together at the shoulder. Exactly how was this supposed to go on her body? I examined them more closely to find out.

What I saw was enchanting. The pieces were beautifully made from hewn copper. The front piece was decorated with what looked like a webbed foot, done in silver and what might have been ruby inlay. The back was unadorned except for a figure-eight piece of metal that had the sharpest edge I'd ever seen.

The bottom part of the eight was in a sheath, while the top half had no covering. I had to work extra hard not to slice my finger as I put the armor over her head. She instructed me to fasten it at the side with fiddley hinges and an attached pin that my fingers were almost too big to manipulate.

Then she jumped up onto the rock wall that marked the edge of our property. I didn't try to stop her.

She landed awkwardly, unable to support herself with her rejuvenated arm, and got right down to business. "I will grant you one wish in exchange for the Pearl," she said.

I got up and faced her on the wall. "I feel like I've just stumbled into the middle of a fairytale," I said with a chuckle.

"Call it what you like," she said. "It is an offer you will not get twice."

"So, you give me what I want, and you get the pearl."

"Exactly."

"Can you bring my father back to life?" I asked, trying to blink back sudden tears.

"No. If he is gone from this world, there is nothing I can do. It is an immutable law. Is there another thing you would ask in trade?"

Only one other desire swelled in my chest. "If everything is, as you say, connected, you should be able to find a connection to my mom—if she's still alive. Help me find her and it's yours."

"Is she lost?"

"Yes and no. She may be hiding—pretending to be dead."

"I must say, you largetoe are indeed strange. In our world tads do not mind one bit when their parents leave. Why should you even want to see your mother again?"

I said nothing.

"Do you have anything that belonged to her? Anything we could use to track her ness?"

"Her *ness*?"

"You know—her way of being in the world. Her energetic vibration. That which departs from her body when she dies. Your father's ness is mostly likely gone, although sometimes it takes a while for it to disappear completely. But if your mother still lives, then we should be able to find her."

I held up the medicine pouch. "This belonged to her, and the casket with the pearl inside it."

She was silent, then said, "How did the Pearl get into your mother's hands?"

I shrugged. "I have no idea. She wore it around her neck in this pouch every day of my life. Probably before too."

Linka reached out and touched the pouch, then quickly withdrew her hand like she'd been shocked.

"What is it?" I asked.

She hesitated before she spoke. "The buzz of your energy is mixed with other females of your line."

"And?" I said impatiently.

The frog dismissed my complaint and said defensively, "I am not sure I can tease the web string of your mother's out of this and follow it to its source. Do you have anything that she was the last one to touch?"

I glanced behind me at the smoldering ruins of our home. Yesterday I might have been able to dig through a box of her clothes in the basement. But today? I had nothing, so I shook my head.

"Think, largetoe."

"Boy, you *really* want this pearl, don't you? But who wouldn't?" I asked. "It's magical. It's mystical. And it can do so many things. Maybe I should hang onto it, especially since I have nothing that fits your request." My body buzzed with frustration. As crazy as it was, this might be my only chance to find my mother.

Then I got a spark of inspiration and pulled out the package I'd taken from my mother's empty coffin. With the fire and all that followed, I'd totally forgotten about it. "This . . . this, whatever it is, belonged to her."

"Open it," Linka said. "But be careful. Do not contaminate whatever is inside with your ness."

I unwrapped the package to discover that it *was* a book, and on the cloth cover there was an oddly shaped mountain with two figures standing on the top. A girl and a frog. There was writing in a script that looked like sticks arranged in different shapes. I could tell the embroidery must have been done by my mom. Her stitches were incredibly expressive. I could always tell what she had been feeling when she made them. These stitches said "loneliness" to me.

I set the book on the rock in front of the frog.

I could tell nothing from her expression. With no real lips to turn up or down, and prominent brows that looked too bony to furrow, I couldn't really tell what was on her mind. But that gasp indicated that something unexpected happened.

"What is it?" I asked.

"Nothing," she lied.

I snatched the book away. "You are free. Go. And don't come back. I will never, ever give you the pearl."

"What if I told you I knew where your mother was right now?"

My stomach dropped. In an instant, my desire flipped 180 degrees. Why should I want to find my mom when she clearly didn't have any interest in me? I picked up the book and my backpack and ran up the hill toward Seth, taking the pearl with me and leaving the frog behind.

39

Linka Betrayal or Bust

One Day Till Pink Moon
Dew Time
Largetoe Nest

LINKA FLEXED HER newly generated forearm. It ached as she watched the femtoe run away. Had she sensed Linka was lying when she claimed to know of her mother's whereabouts? She could have found the mother most likely, but it would have meant dipping into the Web That Connects All Things again, which was too risky. She was curious about one thing, though. How did her mother come to have a largetoe-sized book written in Frog? There was a familiarity to the energy vibration that Linka could not explain. Well, that wasn't entirely true. She sensed an explanation but did not want to consider what it meant.

She had hoped to lure the femtoe into trusting her and then take her to a place where she could wrestle the Pearl away from her. It hadn't worked out. Not yet. Linka would get the Pearl back. But other matters came first.

"You may come down to this rock now," Linka said.

Jineta and Sajay emerged from hiding on the branches of the nearby dogwood tree bursting into bloom. Their mounts flew them down to join Linka. After the two Zons dismounted, their bats returned to the tree.

"Commander, we are back from the Palay," Jineta said.

"We only arrived while you were talking to the largetoe," Sajay said.

"Yes," Linka said. "I noticed."

"We did not want to interrupt such a historical event," Jineta said. "Is she as horrible as you expected?"

"We do not speak in that way about others. No living creature is horrible. They may act badly, but each of us has the same intrinsic value as all others. That is a basic Frog Way and as a Zon, you are expected to embrace it."

Jineta bowed her head.

"No shame required, Jineta. Just acknowledgement that you are now more enlightened than you were before."

"I am. I am," Jineta said fervently.

"The largetoe saved my life when she could have left me behind to die. And she allowed me to touch the Golden Pearl and regenerate my arm instantaneously," Linka said, showing her Zons the proof. "She is difficult to deal with, yes, but also compassionate."

"What you say is true," a thready voice piped up. It was a root of the smaller cedar tree, and it wound its way up to Linka's eye level and swayed in the gentle breeze. "We know the girl."

Other fine root hairs, and some thicker ones too, broke through the ground and undulated in the air like dancing snakes, chattering their support of the girl.

"She is kind."

"She doesn't carve on our skin."

"She makes wreaths of our fallen leaves and branches."

"She watered our roots with her teacup when she was small."

A chorus of scale-like cedar leaves on a long branch talked in unison, each voice combining into a deep and resonant sound that reflected the age and strength of the tree. "She has a good and gentle heart and brings her pain to us, which we absorb gladly. As a little girl, she came often to rest her back against us, and throughout her life, she has gifted us with her tears."

"But . . . but she is a largetoe!" Jineta cried. "The most selfish and destructive creature in the world."

"Not this girl," barked the older, taller tree.

"How dare you talk to one of the queen's own Zons like that?" Jineta said.

A clash erupted between trees and frogs, both sides talking in their loudest voices, with neither side listening. A few overexcited roots wrapped themselves around some of the Zons, pulling them down to the ground.

"Zons, stop waggling with words," Linka said, although secretly she was impressed that the girl had received such high praise from the trees. They generally thought less of humans than even the frogs, thanks to the murder of billions of their kind at largetoe hands. "While we argue here with trees, Bulldoggies may be swarming along mountaintops nearby. Trouble is rising."

Linka called to Myth with a whistle-like croak.

"Your Majesty. Are you well?" Myth asked in his high-pitched voice as he sailed in and landed on a low-hanging branch. "Your arm. It . . . it—grew back so fast. How is that even possible?"

"Anything is possible with the Pearl, Myth. I will tell you the story when there is more time. How are our injured Zons?"

Myth whistled and Mura and Trep appeared, snuggled into the feathers of Noble the owl.

"Thank you, Noble. Are you available to take our injured Zons to the Palay?"

"It would be my honor," Noble said.

"What of our youngest recruit?" Sajay asked.

"Roya died following my orders last night and will be honored as a hero when we return to our headquarters," Linka said.

Dismay rippled through the battalion. Then Linka withdrew her infinator and raised it with her regenerated arm.

The other Zons, including several new arrivals perched in the surrounding trees, followed suit.

Linka led the Zon salute: "Fight in the Light. Die in the Light. Go to the Light."

The voices of these female fighting frogs reverberated with power.

When the sounds of their voices faded, Sajay handed something to Linka. "Apologies, Commander, for not giving you this missive sooner."

Linka accepted the pouch Sajay handed her and opened it to find a seed pod inside a crystal, with a note of caution and instructions on how to use it written out in her father's hand. Inside the seed pod was the smallest drop of Golden Death. The queen had ordered her to administer the poison to the femtoe who possessed the Pearl.

Linka drew a deep breath. Unseen forces pulled at her gut. How could she carry out these orders now that she owed a debt of gratitude to the femtoe?

It was against the Zon way to disobey the queen, and it was equally wrong to renege on a debt of gratitude, although in theory Linka had saved the girl's life as well—with Noble's help.

That should have absolved the first debt of gratitude. But then again, the girl had allowed Linka to touch the Pearl, which unexpectedly regenerated her forearm. Whatever the balance of their cosmic debt toward each other, killing the girl was not something Linka could morally do. But disobeying an order from the queen was equally unthinkable.

And other things tugged at her: There was a largetoe girl. She had the Pearl. It was almost the Pink Moon. How could this be merely a coincidence? Did the Well of White Light conspire to bring this person and the holy object together at the right time and place to perhaps reverse the course of this world's certain demise? And if that were so, why would the queen not seize the opportunity to make it happen instead of doing all that she could to prevent it?

"Jineta, you accompany Noble and his passengers back to the Palay with a small contingent of Zons. Sajay, take temporary command of the rest of the battalion and fly ahead. If you do not pick up the girl's trail immediately, send out searching parties in all directions. If she has the Pearl, we must not lose her. Keep your eyes open for Bulldoggies, whom I suspect are about. If Bulldoggies attack, the Pearl comes first. I will catch up to you shortly."

Everyone departed in a flight of leathery wings.

Linka waited until they were out of sight to remove a leaflet that had been folded into the bottom of the pouch. She touched the tip of the leaf to the middle of her forehead.

Golden particles shimmered as they traveled down the veins and stem of the leaf and into her mind. She heard her cousin's message in his own voice:

Cousin, your Zons report that you have discovered the Pearl in the possession of a largetoe girl. I also know that you are in receipt of a dose of Golden Death, prepared for the current holder of the Pearl.

I implore you not to deploy it. The girl may be our only hope to have a true Ceremony of Renewal. My mother has her own reasons for wanting her dead, of which I know nothing, and while it pains me to go against her wishes, it is not in the best interest of the All to carry out her orders to kill the largetoe.

Given time, I hope I can bring Mother over to my way of thinking. Do what you can to bring the girl to the true ceremonial grounds on the night of the full Pink Moon, along with the Pearl, and let us hope for the best.

Please forgive me for past wrongs. I hope that moving forward we may be allies. And when we are together again, let us discuss our aunt DeLili. I fear a great wrong has been done to her.

Astounding. Had Azzie read her mind? This unfamiliar gesture on his part filled her with warmth toward him. But she was still torn about what to do. Obey the queen and kill the girl, thereby killing any chances of a true Ceremony of Renewal? Or simply let the girl go if she could get the Pearl? But what good was the Pearl without the girl given the fast-approaching lunar event? At least her cousin had added a third choice that might be the most advantageous to the All. Get the largetoe with the Pearl to participate in creating a *real* Ceremony of Renewal.

The leaf she held was depleted, so with permission she plucked another one from an evergreen huckleberry bush and held it to her forehead. A band of golden light fluttered from between her eyes, and the leaf absorbed her message along its stem and veins.

She summoned a breeze:

Breezelet, breezelet,
Come this way. Please,
Take this leaf to the queen's Palay.
Into the keeping of the prince
To let him know I am almost convinced.
But I ask him, first, for the best of reasons.
Is there ever a season for committing treason?

A brisk breeze appeared. Linka tossed the leaf into the air along with a pinch of wild sage as a token of gratitude.

She whistled for Myth, who flew in low and landed. Linka jumped onto his back, and they were off. She could tell, however, from the first downstroke of his wings, that her beloved friend was not up to the journey. He needed to rest someplace safe until he could heal from the burns the fire had caused him.

She bent close to Myth's ear and shared with him what was in her thoughts, then summoned an image of the strongest, most invincible flying mount in proximity. Grabbing another pinch of sage, she released it into the wind along with the image in her mind of the perfect mount, knowing with complete confidence that a new mount would appear soon, and Myth could take his leave and find a place to rest.

The two giant cedars on the edge of the plateau tracked the diminishing vibrations of Nora's footsteps as she moved farther and farther from them into the valley.

"You made a mess of that," Taller Tree said to the other through intertwined roots. "Arguing with frogs. Royal frogs at that."

"At least I acted," Smaller Tree said, its boughs quaking with fury." You? You simply stood there."

"That's what trees do, my top-heavy friend. I am frightened for her. So sweet she was. Hugging and kissing us almost every day when she was little—even in the winter. And now, potentially terrible things await her," Taller Tree said. "If only I could walk, I would follow her, protect her, save her from the horror that comes her way."

Smaller Tree shuddered with disgust, its branches quivering. "Walk? Why walk when you can root talk?"

"Root talk. Of course. Your intuition runs deep, my friend. I apologize. You are not the sap I thought you were," Taller Tree joked.

And then together, the trees sent out a joint message through their roots:

> *Watch for our human.*
> *Kind she is, and sweet.*
> *Offer wayfinding*
> *To guide her two feet.*
> *Provide her with shelter*
> *And food she can eat.*
> *Web of tree roots and fungus*
> *That form a ring of life around us,*
> *Kindly spread the word to the world*
> *Do what you can to protect our girl.*

The earth glowed with yellow light the color of early spring maple buds as the message rippled out to the roots of the neighboring trees through the mycorrhizal fungal network that connects all things.

But it didn't stop there. Surging in ever-widening circles it spread out into the broader world. And by the time the trees' request had spread to the tiniest root hair of the smallest seedling to the most giant tree, every growing thing that plunged its roots into the ground knew of the cedar trees' request.

The trees both sighed, their great trunks creaking. They had done what they could to keep the girl safe. For while all rooted beings had heard the plea, there was no guarantee they would heed it. Trees could be fickle and although they knew what was expected by the greater community, their will was their own.

"Will she ever come back to us?" Smaller Tree asked.

"We must be patient," the other tree replied.

"Patient? That's what we do best."

The branches of the trees danced, and their leaves rustled with laughter.

Nora ◎ A Change of Heart

One Day Till Pink Moon
Early Morning
Salmon Falls Hospital

SETH DROPPED ME off at the hospital and headed home for a shower. He was still shaken from everything I'd told him about the fire, including the appearance of my father's ghost and my conversation with her high and mighty highness, Linka.

He didn't say he thought I was crazy, but he was probably thinking it. I know I was. In true Seth fashion, he promised to come back as soon as he could, even though I told him to get some sleep.

Sheriff Heinze was in the lobby, apparently waiting for me.

"Your friends are upstairs with your grandmother. They made me promise to get you examined right away," she said.

"It can wait. I'm really okay," I said. And, thanks to the pearl, I was.

"I'm worried about your safety, Nora. Are you up for a conversation?"

"Don't you have to get my lawyer out of bed first?"

"Not really. Given circumstances where your life might be in danger, we don't have to worry about that part of the law."

"My life? In danger?" I said, incredulously.

The sheriff raised an eyebrow. "Dad murdered. House burned."

Maybe she had a point. "Then let's do it, sheriff," I said.

"I think it's okay for you to call me Ardith," she said.

"Thanks, Ardith. But can we make it fast? I want to see my gran."

She motioned me inside a nearby office and closed the door behind us. I sat down in one of the chairs and was overcome by the smell of smoke emanating from my hair, clothes, and body.

"So, tell me what you know about the fire." Ardith took out her phone. "I'm going to record this."

I nodded.

"Please say 'yes' for the recording."

"Yes," I said.

"So what happened, Nora?" she asked.

"I came home, Seth and I hung out, then our other friends joined us for tea and cake. They left, I went to bed, and I woke up with the house in flames," I said, holding back on all the weird parts of the story, like the fighting frogs and talking ashes.

"Any idea how the fire started? Candle left burning? Iron on?"

"Do I look like I iron my clothes?"

She chuckled.

"I really don't know. I do remember the strong stink of gasoline, though—like someone had watered the house with it. But by the time the smoke woke me out of a dead sleep, the only thing I could do was leave through an upstairs window and climb down a tree. I'm lucky to be alive."

"Yes, you are. We'll be doing a full investigation, of course, so now would be the time to tell me about anything else I need to know."

My face flushed at her question and the back of my neck got hot and prickly. "You don't think I burned down my own house, do you?"

"Did I say that?" Ardith said.

"Tell me what you're thinking, please. I have a sick grandmother upstairs, and I barely survived the night—and I lost my house and every memory I ever made with my parents. I don't mean to be disrespectful, but the least you can do is to be honest with me."

"Look, Nora. Like I said, you might be in danger. Either you've got someone after you who wants you dead, or your family is the unluckiest family in the world," she said. "Let's share what we know and see what we can figure out. Work with me here."

I nodded, curious about where she was heading.

"Anything more you want to tell me about the fire?" she asked.

I shrugged. "If I think of anything . . ."

"Then let's go back to your dad's murder." Ardith got out a little notepad and tore out a blank piece of paper. She put it on the table. "I'm heading up to the murder scene later today, and I want to make sure I have the details of your experience nailed down."

"Why don't you just take me along?"

"I would, but I think you've been through enough lately, and I need some time at the site on my own."

I was too tired to argue. Besides, the thought of going back there made me a little sick.

While I waited, trying not to tap my foot, Ardith drew the surrounding mountain range in a few squiggly lines, then roughed out the positions of the nearby roads and our grove of sequoias. Then she drew a stick figure lying on the ground.

"I suppose that's my dad," I said.

"It's a representation of the situation, nothing more," she said. "According to the coroner, the shot that killed your dad was fired from about thirty feet. That indicates an intention to kill in my opinion."

Then she put an X on the paper below the body toward the bottom of the page.

"Let's assume that the shooter was somewhere here. Would you agree?"

"I didn't see anyone, but that's the direction I heard the shot come from, and it's the direction I took to catch up with whoever shot Dad," I said.

"Based on this, where would you say the second shot came from?"

"The opposite direction, closer to the road."

"That would be here," she said, making a circle to the left of the X. "How long after the first shot did you hear the second shot?"

I shrugged. My sense of time had been distorted that night and probably ever since. "I really couldn't say. Five minutes? No more than ten?"

"Let's go with what we know for sure," Ardith said and put another X to the left of the body. "Potentially, a second person was somewhere over here, and since your dad was already deceased, this shooter was not the one who killed him. Would you agree with that?"

"I guess I'd have to, but none of this is new information," I said.

"No, it's not, but it will help us both keep a picture of what happened, with reference points, when I revisit the site later this afternoon—so thanks."

Suddenly, it felt like a duty—my duty as a daughter—to accompany her, despite my fear of the idea. I pressed my case and asked again.

Ardith laughed. Not unkindly, but with surprise in her voice. "I am as committed to finding your dad's killer as you are. Let me do my job, okay? I promise to keep you in the loop if you promise me the same thing."

"Sure," I said.

Then she took her phone, took a picture of her drawing, and handed the original to me. "Hang onto this if you like. Look at it every so often and let me know if anything else comes to you."

I took the scrap of paper and put it in the same small section of my backpack.

"Wait. I just thought of something," I said. "This morning, I saw that Gran's trillium had been crushed. There's a footprint there, although part of it's fuzzy. You'll find it off the path that leads from the house down the hill, about halfway on the right side. The trillium was fine yesterday when I passed it, so whoever stepped on it did it after I came home in the late afternoon from the hospital and swimming."

The sheriff nodded. "We'll check it out. Who do you think might have set the fire?"

"Mel, maybe. He was angry at me for firing him. And he *was* at the house on the night of the fire asking me about Dad's original papers for the conservation easement, which seemed weird to me." I thought for a second. "Or maybe it was Kincade because of his bogus land deal."

"Whoa, back up here. You better tell me these stories."

So, I sang like a canary (as Gran would say), telling her about the documents and Kincade's claim to the property and Finley's treachery toward Gran. I didn't mention the part about the favor because I still didn't know what that meant. Probably nothing, but my instincts said to keep quiet about it. So I did.

"You know more than you think, especially for someone who's been involved one way or another in two major crimes in two weeks."

"I've been *the victim* of those crimes, Ardith," I said. "I haven't committed them."

"No, I don't believe you did."

It was a relief to hear her say that. And it made me want to say more. "One thing I've been wondering about is this nonsense that Dad would sell Kincade everything, including our home. I think Kincade made up the whole thing. It is not possible. Our house and the greater part of our land was never part of the conservation easement at all. Dad was only setting a small piece of our property aside for that. Yes, that part originally belonged to Kincade's family. But it was also the best acreage for him to use for his climate change project. And once the paperwork was done, Kincade wouldn't ever be getting it back."

"That sounds like more friction between your families than I realized," she said. "I'm pursuing all appropriate lines of inquiry when it comes to the death of your father. And I'll be working in cooperation with the arson investigator, who'll want to talk to you as well. And now, based on what you've said, I'll be extending my investigation into this land sale business. Where can we find you later?"

It was then that the full impact of our house fire hit me. I had no place to go. My insides hollowed out, and then I realized that my body may not have a home, but my heart did. "I'll be with Gran," I said.

"I'm not too worried that you're going to run off, but it would be nice if there were no more surprises. Sticking with your grandmother seems wise." Ardith and I stood up, and she opened the door. "By the way, were you aware that as of your eighteenth birthday, you'll inherit everything your dad owned?"

My legs felt shaky, so I sat back down. "How do you know?"

"Your grandmother told me."

There was something about that revelation that made the reality of my dad's death hit me like a boulder. Who cared about who owned what? I'd give everything away tomorrow if I could get him back. And how was I going to carry the weight of it all? I had plans and dreams of my own that I'd have to bury to take care of Gran and the tree farm. I was about to turn eighteen, but I felt like I was eighty.

The tears spilled out of me until I couldn't see. I hid my head in my arms and just let go. All the pain, the fear, the sadness since Dad died wouldn't stay dammed up inside.

Finally, the storm passed and I raised my head, remembering that I wasn't alone. Right in front of me was a box of tissue. I used it to mop up the mess my tears had made. Then I got up, looked the sheriff in the eye, and said, "No, I didn't know."

She nodded her head like I'd passed some test and said, "I'll be in touch, and if you need a place to stay, I'll help you find one. Now go get yourself checked out by a doc and see your gran."

"Thanks," I said, following her out into the hallway. "There are a few more things. Could you keep an eye out for our Sheltie, Mickey? I haven't seen him since before the fire. He wasn't there when the house burned. And I really need to find him."

"Take that worry off your mind for now. I'll tell the animal control folks and my officers that he's missing. Keep a watchful eye out for yourself and your grandmother. I'm going to station an officer outside her door for now. And the other thing?"

"Could you try to find out where Recycle Rick is? He was Dad's good friend, and he needs to know that Dad has died. He's somewhere in Rwanda."

"That's a pretty big country. Not exactly in my jurisdiction, but I'll see what I can do."

I thanked her. Then she left and I headed for the stairs. No doc for me. I ran smack into Mrs. Hayashi.

"Nora, we're all so worried about you."

"Thanks. I appreciate that."

"And we're all so sorry about your house."

I nodded, grateful for her kind words, but I couldn't really say more.

"If you don't mind my saying, you look like you could use some TLC. Why don't you come to the staff room? You can take a shower. I'll find you some clean clothes and get you some food."

"Thanks, but I need to see Gran," I said.

"Showing up smelling like smoke will only make her more upset."

"You're right. Thanks, Mrs. Hayashi. I appreciate that, and the kindness you've always shown me and my family."

I wanted to say more, but that would mean I'd have to explain that I'd overheard her sticking up for me with Seth's mom. It occurred to me, not for the first time, that most people, when given hard times, reacted with kindness and compassion.

And then there were those who imposed unkindness on others. (Kincade for one. He seemed to go out of his way to be cruel. Finley fit that mold too.)

But my friends and their families were kind. Mrs. Hayashi was kind. And Ardith was as well, for the most part. All the people who'd come to Dad's funeral, or left food, flowers, and cards at the house had been kind too. I would remember them always—with gratitude.

"Kindness counts," my mom used to say. "It's more important to be kind than critical." I'd try to remember that when it came to Kincade and Finley, but I had severe doubts I'd ever succeed.

I felt (and smelled) like a new person after a quick shower, a change of clothes, and a cafeteria egg salad sandwich Mrs. Hayashi provided. I didn't know whose sweatsuit I was wearing, but everything was warm and clean and pretty much fit, so I didn't care. I'd managed to scrub up my shoes, but my backpack was still "grody," as my dad used to say. I'd have to stash it somewhere so the smell wouldn't bother Gran. She had a nose on her like a hunting dog.

Wet hair and all, I bounded up the stairs to the third floor, where I found my Mother Nature Commando friends—minus Seth—standing quietly in front of Gran's closed door.

"You get checked out by a doc?" Minh asked.

"I'm okay. I really need to see Gran."

"We wanted to make sure you were okay," Minh said. "Do you want one of us to stay here with you?"

"I'll be okay. Isn't it Riverbank Restoration Day?" I asked. "How many kids do you think will show up?"

Kameela shrugged. "We've been promoting it on social media for weeks, but only a dozen or so people have said they'll show up. Planting willow stakes on the eroding banks of the Salmon River is not exactly easy work."

"But it's important," I said, wishing I could be there with them. Before Dad died, we'd all spent some time harvesting branches from Plumas sitka willow trees and cutting them into stakes with pointed ends and flat tops. The idea was to insert every stake deep into the riverbank.

Over time, each stake would sprout into a willow tree that would stabilize the river's bank and provide food and cover for small game and birds, as well as reduce the temperature of the water to improve conditions for fish.

"We'll get the job done," Minh said confidently.

"Guys, I'm going to stay here, if that's okay with you, Nora," Will said. "At least for a little while. I'll catch up with you all later. Uncle should be meeting you at the site with the willow stakes."

A sudden wave of relief flowed through me. "That would be great, Will, thanks," I said.

"You might need a little support with Gran. Not that easy to tell someone that their home's gone," he said. "I'm going to go get Gran a cinnamon bun from the cafeteria. It'll give her something to criticize." He smiled and headed down the hall to the stairwell.

"I can stay too," Kameela said.

"No, go save the world, you guys. I've got this," I said.

"I know this probably isn't a good time to bring it up—but it's your birthday tomorrow. Remember?" Kameela said gently.

I nodded. "Right. Great timing."

"I know it's hard to think of celebrating at a time like this, but if you want to honor your birth and your parents in some way, my parents would like to help," said Kameela.

Minh said, "Mine want to help as well."

Then Minh and Kameela squabbled for a minute about whose family offered first. I smiled and tried to keep the peace.

"Kameela, Minh, I appreciate both of you and your families so much. Please thank them for me. Do you think they'd mind if we did something all together—another time?"

There it was again. Kindness. Shouldn't that get at least as much attention as all the crappy things going on in the world?

Both families had their share of troubles, but that didn't keep them from being kind and generous. The Bashirs and Phans had gone through more than any family should and maintained a sense of kindness and generosity, not to mention a healthy sense of humor that I appreciated and admired. Their stories were not mine to tell. But while I had lost almost everything that had value to me, including important people in my life, they had also lost all their possessions—and access to family members, their way of life, and their countries.

It made me shudder to think of the stat I heard awhile back— that in the next thirty years, by the time I will be almost fifty, at least 1.2 billion people could become refugees due to climate-related events. Why wouldn't that prediction get everyone off their butts to do something—*anything*—to keep such disasters from happening? And what about the prediction that all the fish in the ocean, and presumably freshwater, too, would be gone by 2048? Facts and figures like those paralyzed me with an overwhelming sense of doom. But it was better to fight with everything we had to lessen the future devastation then to do nothing.

There was a saying that the best time to plant a tree is 20 years ago and the second best time is to plant one today. We would never return to the paradise Earth had once been, but we could keep it from becoming a nightmare in the future.

After strong hugs from them both, Kameela and Minh left.

I poked my head into Gran's room. She was sleeping. I stashed my backpack behind the door and sat in the chair beside her bed. How was I going to tell her that her home was destroyed? Her eyes fluttered open.

I handed Gran her hearing aids, which were sitting on the bedside table. There was no point starting a conversation without them. She put them in quickly and turned them on with the remote control that was in the case.

"There," she said. "Now get this bed into position so I can see you eye to eye."

I worked the bed controller. When Gran was upright, she scooted over the best she could to make room for me beside her and patted the mattress.

"I don't want to hurt you, Gran."

She blew out a dismissive puff of air and held out her arms invitingly. I lay down and rested in the crook of her arm.

"You're here," she said, and sighed deeply.

I grabbed one of her blue-veined hands and squeezed, her skin papery to the touch.

"You're all right? You weren't hurt in the fire?" she said.

"You know?"

"Of course. The doctor told me first thing this morning. I've been so worried about you."

We both sighed and lay there in a few moments of contentment.

"Am I interrupting?" Will said, peeking in the door.

"Never, Will. You're part of the family. Please join us," Gran said.

I planted a kiss on Gran's cheek and got up from the bed.

"Brought you something to nibble on," Will said, putting a cinnamon roll on her bedside table. "Although they don't taste as good as yours."

"Thanks, dear. I'll eat it soon. Nora was about to tell me everything," she said. "Grab a chair and join us."

Will brought two chairs over to the bedside and once we both had a place to sit, I told Gran what happened. Mostly.

When I was done, she said, "Nothing matters but that you're safe. The house? Everything in it? That's only stuff. It's replaceable. You, however, are not."

"I agree with that," Will said. "I talked to Grandad, and he told me that you both will always have a home with us."

"Thanks, Will, we may have to take you up on that," Gran said, clinging to Will's extended hand, which was a rare and very sweet gesture on his part. Then she said a little breathlessly, "There is so much to take in. So many changes. While a house is only a house, it was *our* house, and it contained a lifetime—many lifetimes—of memories." She leaned back on her pillow and closed her eyes. Tears rolled down her cheeks as her head sank forward.

Watching her, my emotions were in a whirl. I wanted to cling to her and weep with her—for her—for me—for our family and home. I wanted to sweep her up in my arms and promise to make everything better. I also felt anger and resentment toward her and longed to grill her like a criminal for details about what *really* happened with Mom. Did Gran even know the full truth? In the end, I did nothing but love her even though every corpuscle in me ached to dig into our past.

Gran needed time to grieve for her son. I needed to grieve myself. But we also needed to be together and be grateful that we were both alive. "Let's not worry about it now, Gran, okay?" I said, soothing her hair with one hand. "I'll stay here with you in the hospital, and when you're better, we can go to Will's for a while and look for our own place. It'll be all right. I promise."

"I believe you, dear. I'll be okay. We'll both be okay. Look on the bright side—at least we won't have to move all our belongings to another place when Kincade takes possession of his property."

Will and I exchanged alarmed looks.

Gran looked down as her hands picked at invisible lint. "I know as of tomorrow, it's not up to me because everything will pass to you, but I think you'll agree, we must respect your father's final wishes. A deal is a deal, and we Peters never go back on our word."

"You mean you don't want me to even try to find out the truth about what Dad really wanted? And make sure he really signed the papers? What about the easement papers? And his plans for his research center?"

"Nora, promise me, please, that you'll just do what Kincade wants. Please," she begged, looking at me like she'd die if I didn't say yes.

Crushed by her words, I looked at Will with desperation in my eyes.

What was wrong with Gran?

The Queen 🐸 History Hurts

41

One Day Till Pink Moon
Dew Time
The Palay, Hyacinth Hollow

HYACINTH HOLLOW WAS one of the queen's favorite secret places in the vast grounds of the Palay. Gazing down at her reflection in the water from her purple lepidolite throne (designed to detoxify her body), she couldn't help but think she was looking particularly lovely this morning.

The throne, carved in the shape of a water hyacinth, sat on an island in the middle of the pool. A hop-way extended across the water from the bank of the pool so that Simeon could serve her. She was expecting a certain visitor, and a perching stool designed specifically for his unique impediments was already in place not far from the throne.

It was the queen's morning off, so she wore only an intricately woven gossamer robe made from the cocoon of silkworms and dyed purple with the mucus of a rare snail. How light she felt without her crown and the heavy robes of state. How lovely it would be to feel this free always. She took a sip of her morning decoction of herbs, flowers, healing grasses, and honey. She sighed. *This was true contentment. True peace.*

Simeon announced the Grand and Glorious Vizzard.

"Balarius, my dearest brother. You are welcome." She motioned for him to make himself comfortable. At least, as comfortable as he could be.

Simeon helped to seat her guest. When that was accomplished, Ranya filled a dainty calla lily blossom with the morning's brew and handed it to her brother. "You will love the notes of lemongrass and mountain mint. Very invigorating for the circulatory system."

"Sister, you are becoming an even more accomplished herbologist than you were as a metamorph," Balarius said, and he took a sip.

Ranya flushed at the compliment. "I do not like to brag, but had I not been forced to be queen by our dear sister's disappearance, I would likely have distinguished myself in the field."

Then Ranya stifled a gulp. She had told a lie. And they both knew it. For a few moments, the only sound either of them heard was the small waterfall cascading into the pool behind them.

"Simeon, please serve us each some chocolate mint leaf rollups stuffed with worm whip. And do not forget those fungus fingers dipped in wild rhubarb and thimbleberry compote, or our favorite burdock and crumble berry tartlets—exactly like Great-Aunt Peragonia made. And when you have finished, leave us, please."

Simeon prepared a tray of the delicate confections in the length of time it takes to destroy a spider web and departed.

"Do you ever wonder where she is?" Balarius asked.

"She?"

"Our dear sister, of course."

"So, you have come not for sibling camaraderie, but to stir up the past?"

"It is a pot that needs tending," he said.

"Then, in answer to your question, no, I never think of her, wonder about her, or have the desire to inquire about her in any way."

Ranya looked away from her brother's stare.

"Do you ever think that we were wrong to do what we did?" he asked.

"How could it be wrong? We helped our sister fulfill her greatest dream. Who would fault us for that?" Ranya said.

"And we did not betray *her* in the process?"

"Do not be absurd."

"Perhaps you prefer the word *manipulated* better," Balarius suggested. "We should have looked for her. To make sure she was safe. Happy. And in case she really did find the Pearl."

"Maybe she did. Maybe she has it now and is happy with her largetoe love," Ranya said. "But more likely, it was all for naught, and she is long dead and gone."

"That is what I thought as well, until . . ."

"Until what? Until you felt the rumblings of what we *think* was the Pearl?"

"That was the beginnings of it, yes. But there is more. I will tell you in good time. But first I want to know why you are so adamant about not having a true Ceremony of Renewal."

"You know I do not like to discuss such things. But since you never seem to stop asking, I will tell you: It is a myth."

"And yet, you demand this myth be taught at tadschool and at our higher centers of learning."

"Of course. Why would I not? It comforts the masses to think there is a solution to the forces of destruction that seem to be accelerating our demise," Ranya said. "If you think about it, the whole idea that such a thing is even possible is preposterous. We do not even know if the fable of Prince Ponte-Fricani is true."

"You know, I have his journals and used his formulas to—"

"Brother, hush."

"That seems like proof enough," Balarius said. "How do you think I made the potion for our sister to take with her on her quest to find the Pearl?"

"Hush, I say. At the time, I did not care if it was true or not. It only mattered that our sister believed it," Ranya said. "And that her belief made her choose abdication from the throne."

"But why not try for a true Ceremony of Renewal? That might be the only way to find out. Or we could look for our sister, DeLili. She could tell us herself how things turned out."

"Firstly, we do not have the Pearl. Secondly, we do not really know if the potion works. Thirdly, we do not have a largetoe. And given the selfishness of the largetoe species, I cannot imagine that there is even one of them selfless enough to make a sacrifice to a greater cause. And fourthly, who says that what one person learns as a frog will have any impact on the largetoe world when she or he returns? The very idea that a human could change into a frog and learn enough from our frog ways in three days to change their world when they return to it is also absurd. Getting them to change their willfully destructive behavior is beyond improbable. It is impossible. It is a . . . what do they call it? A fairytale. One human being cannot make a difference to the All. Neither can one frog. So why bother?"

"But what does it hurt to try," Balarius said, "if we do indeed find all those things we need?"

"You keep saying that, Brother. I am not risking the disappointment of the masses on frog tales and false ceremonies, and you know that I do not believe in it one bit. If the whole 'kiss a frog, turn into a frog' gambit would work to wake up the largetoe, I would have moved water and wind to make it happen. But it is merely a lie constructed by our ancestors. The only way we know the Pearl even exists is that we feel what we *think* is its effects from time to time. And that might merely be our collective imagination. For all we know, our sister searches for it still. Or maybe she died trying," Ranya said.

"You hoped she would die trying."

Anger flickered in Ranya's eyes. As queen she was not used to being called out on her beliefs or behavior and she let her brother know with one fiery glance that he had pushed too close to the quick. So she pushed back. "Admit it, Brother. You did too. If she had become queen, she would have forbidden your experiments. You know how she disapproved of your radical ideas."

"It is true. I only wished her gone and you queen—for my own purposes, of course. I have made great progress with bodily adaptations that may someday save us as a species. We are so small. It is hard to compete with creatures that are so much larger than we," Balarius said. "I fear, though, that in ignoring the question of what happened to her, we may have overlooked the fact that she might be close. Close, indeed. Close enough to expose our past indiscretions."

"That would be bad, Brother. Almost as bad as talking to my son about sedition."

Her brother looked surprised that she would know this. He would be even more surprised if she told him of her decision about making Linka queen. Had she known that her son was going to propose sedition, she would have acted immediately, and it hurt her to the quick that Azzie would betray her so. Could it be that her declaration to prevent his ascension to the throne had sparked Azzie's disobedience? No, Azzie, not she, was solely to blame.

Recovered from his shock at his sister's knowledge, he said, "If you know of that conversation, you know I am blameless. I rebuffed my nephew's attempts to sway me."

"And yet you did not tell me."

"What do you think brings me here this morning?"

"Convenient excuse. Now tell me about our sister's supposed presence in the area as well as what you know through your new friend, Wink, about Raeburn's visit to the Maw."

"Does nothing escape your ear, fine sister?" Balarius asked, and he helped himself to his favorite dessert.

"While some may deploy roly poly sow bugs as spies, I rely on the earwig. They are everywhere and have what I call a 'distasteful advantage.'"

"And what is that, Sister dear?"

"They are so easily ignored and can go anywhere and everywhere I want them to—as my spies."

"How did I not know that, Sister?"

"Exactly my point."

"There might be one thing you do not know." Balarius brushed stray crumbs from his cloak.

"And what would that be?"

"That I extracted a certain promise from our sister before agreeing to give her the potion to take with her as she set off on her quest for the Pearl."

The queen glared at her brother. "*What* promise?" she asked, her nostrils flared.

"This will explain the details," he said and removed a leaflet from his sleeve. "Perhaps you will feel somewhat differently about your dream once you have read this. It may not have been a portent of the end—as you are assuming it is—but of a new beginning."

Ranya accepted the leaflet and read it with interest. When the implications of the information sank in, she locked eyes with Balarius and said, "What have you done?"

42

Nora ◎ Suspicions Rise

One Day Till Pink Moon
Late Morning
Salmon Falls Hospital

GRAN, WILL, AND I had been quiet since Gran's announce-ment that she wanted Kincade to have our property. I didn't know what to say. My body was still buzzing with what felt like betrayal to me, and I couldn't make sense of it. There had to be a reason that Gran was just giving in like that.

Property—any property—seemed to mean less to me this morning. People were more important. And Gran was the most important person to me. I suppose it might have given me a sense of satisfaction that Kincade wouldn't get the house—or at least the part of it he seemed to want so badly. But, thankfully, I wasn't that petty.

What was really rubbing me the wrong way was the stress Gran seemed to be experiencing when she said what she had to say about the subject. She never talked like that. Again, I got the feeling that she was afraid.

I hesitated to be blunt. But if I didn't ask for the truth, how would I ever know what the truth was? I'd never asked Dad if Mom was really dead. It wasn't a question that would have ever occurred to me. There was a different version of reality out there that I would have never known about if I hadn't dared to ask myself the question, "Is Mom's body in her grave?" I didn't like the answer, but at least I was brave enough to ask the question. So I decided to go for it.

"Gran," I said, gently rubbing her beautifully wrinkled arm, "you seem really stressed out by this whole 'don't fight the sale to Kincade' thing. I'd have thought you'd fight as hard as possible to keep our land, even with the house being gone. Can you tell me why?"

I regretted the question as soon as it left my mouth.

Tears streamed down her face. She began sobbing and buried her face in her hands. I looked at Will with alarm, and we both tried to comfort her.

"Gran, please. Forget about my question. It doesn't matter. Don't cry, Gran. Please don't cry." And then I was crying again with her. Regret, guilt, sadness braided themselves together and twisted around my heart, tugging tight. What had I done? What had I done?

We eventually calmed her down and dried her tears.

Finally, she said, "Nora, there will be no discussion of this. Ever." Her face was still twisted with pain and her breathing was halting and ragged. I took a tissue and dried her tears, then mine.

"You rest, Gran. You rest. You don't have to talk about any-thing you don't want to talk about. Today—or ever," I said.

She nodded and pasted a smile on her face like everything was forgotten. I knew that wasn't true.

There was a knock at the door.

"Come in," Gran called, then took a deep breath, patted her hair as if checking to see that everything was in place, stuffed the tear-filled tissues under the covers, and pasted on a smile.

It was Seth. "How are you, Mrs. Peters?" he asked.

"I'm okay. Thanks."

"I'm really sorry about everything that's going on," Seth said. "The fire, my father—everything."

"Not your fault, Seth. I don't blame you for a bit of it. Not one bit. You've had a rough life, young man. You deserve a break."

Seth smiled.

"Now, why don't you take this granddaughter of mine outside for some fresh air," she said in a way that was overly bright. "I'm going to eat this cinnamon roll and take a nap." She smiled broadly and took a little bite.

I wanted to leave. I had to leave. I couldn't get out of there fast enough.

"I'll stay here until she's asleep," Will said. Gran patted his hand gratefully.

"I'll be back in a while, Gran," I said and gave her a kiss on the cheek. We clung to each other for a moment.

"Take your time, dear. Take your time," she said. "Oh, before you go, can you take my wallet and these papers and keep them safe? There are so many strangers in and out of this room—and I don't trust a one of them."

She reached into the bedside table, took out her wallet and the rolled-up contract that Seth's dad had given us—the very papers that had contributed to her illness—and handed them to me. "And if you need any money, help yourself to whatever's in the wallet. Do you still have the car fob?"

I nodded, patting my backpack. I'd totally forgotten about Gran's car. I'd driven it myself to the hospital after they brought her in.

"Now, you be on your way," Gran said. "Don't hurry back. Have some fun. You're young. But you won't stay that way."

With a wave from Seth and a blown kiss from me, we left the room.

Outside in the hallway, Seth and I hugged. It felt so good to lean against him and take in his steadiness. I wanted to melt into his body and stay there forever. I felt like a tree that had been hollowed out by sorrow.

As we headed for the elevator, I stuffed all the things I'd gotten from Gran into my backpack.

The elevator doors opened. It was packed. "Let's take the stairs," Seth said. I had a flash image of us kissing in the stairwell, our bodies pressed together.

Then some wise guy said, "Plenty of room here." People jostled around to clear a space, but when we got on, we ended up getting separated.

The elevator sank and so did my heart. What did a girl have to do to get kissed around here?

People poured out of the elevator into the cafeteria. I snagged us a table and Seth got himself some food since I'd already eaten. Then we sat as close to each other as humanly possible, while Seth ate in silence. Then he said, "You're not going to believe what my dad told me."

"Probably not, but if it's about something nice or good or kind—I'd love to hear it."

"He's changed," Seth said.

"Haven't you been down this rocky path with him before?" I asked gently.

Seth shrugged. "I know he's made promises in the past. To me. To Mom."

"Yeah, like that road trip to the World Series he was supposed to take you on—among other things."

"I know. I know. But this time, I think—well, I really hope he's changed."

Seth was excited. Maybe a little too excited. I'd seen that excitement before, and I had seen the aftermath of devastating disappointment.

"And I'm pretty sure it's all because of you," he added.

"What did I do? Other than scream at him at my father's funeral." *And think bad things about him*, I should have said in all transparency, but didn't.

"But I think that's what might have done it. He says he's giving me my college money, *and* he's going to see a therapist to help him with his temper."

I let that idea sit with me for a moment. Carl Kincade in therapy? Not a chance in hell. But I could tell by the sincerity on Seth's face and the ache of optimism in his voice that he was taking his dad at his word.

"He's even at your house right now, helping."

"Help? Your dad? That's only because he thinks he owns the place now."

The thought of Kincade on our property doing whatever he wanted made my stomach turn. He was probably pawing through the wreckage looking for those papers Findley had been bugging me for.

"Nora, I know you find it hard to believe your dad sold the property to mine, but he did. And now that Dad finally got what he wanted, he can be more himself. It's kind of like a miracle. And it's sad to say, but part of it's because your dad is gone."

"Gone? No, Seth. My dad isn't gone. Like on vacation. He's dead. His ashes are in here." I picked up my backpack and practically shoved it in his face.

Seth pulled away and seemed unwilling to look me in the eye. "I thought you'd be happy for me," he said.

I shook my head. Not at Seth, but at myself. I was being a total jerk, thinking of the world only from my point of view.

"I know you think he's changed. I don't. But even if he has, it doesn't make up for what *he's* done to *my* family. But as your friend, I'll try to be happy for you. So, tell me, how did this miracle happen with your formerly terrible father?"

"I know this first part is going to upset you, but I have to say it upfront."

Great! What now? I thought, but to Seth, I said, "Go on."

"After I got home from your place, Dad called me into the living room and told me that he had been thinking. He said he knew it was wrong of him to confront you and your grandmother at the funeral."

"Hate to say it, but I agree with him on that."

"I told him as much. He explained that everything had become clear to him afterward and admitted he'd acted like a real jerk. Said he's grateful that he'd had a second chance with his family, and he was going to make the most of it. So he told me about all the positive things he was going to do so that the three of us could have a better life. Isn't that awesome?"

Seth looked so happy. So relieved. I hoped that my face wasn't ugly with some combination of anger and jealousy because that's what flowed through my veins. *Nice.* I wanted to say. *I'm happy for you. And your house. And your dad. And hey, you've got a mom too.*

Before I could think of an alternate reply, his dad, of all people, walked into the cafeteria, his face covered with cuts and scratches.

Head down, dirty red baseball cap in hand, Kincade shuffled over and stood on the other side of the table from us. The nearness of him sent prickles down my neck. I sprang to my feet, tipping my chair backward. Kincade came around to right the chair and I reached for it, too, but I jerked my hand back before our hands touched.

"Dad?" Seth said. He stood up as well, making me 'pickle' in the middle. I grabbed my backpack again and held it like a shield.

"What are you doing here? Is Mom okay?"

Kincade didn't even look at this son. He stared straight at me. "Nora, we're all so glad you're okay."

I wanted to say *I didn't know you cared*, but instead said, "I'm afraid your precious family home didn't fare so well," I said.

"Yeah." He looked at the floor and ground his teeth. "That's unfortunate. But as soon as I take possession and your insurance pays up, I'll start to restore and rebuild. This time I'll mold it into my vision of the place and erase the history of the Peters family."

I wanted to scream at Seth, *Is this the comment of a sane man? A loving husband and father? No. It's proof your dad is a sociopath.*

And to Kincade, I wanted to shout, *You interrupt my father's funeral, call us liars and thieves, practically hand a heart attack to my grandmother in a basket, and you want me to stand here and listen to your plans to erase any memories of my family's existence? And for all I know, you burnt down our house.*

Okay. That part didn't make sense, did it? Why would he burn down something he'd wanted all his life? I couldn't think straight anymore. Especially when it came to Seth's dad.

"Nora, you okay?" Seth asked, placing his hand on my shoulder. "You're just standing there. Staring."

All those words that had been tumbling through my brain froze in my mouth when I saw the pain in Seth's face. I had to dial back my reaction for him. But I wondered . . . would there ever be a time when I could take care of how I felt and not put everyone else's feelings first?

"She's fine," Kincade said with a sneer, and he took a step closer. I instinctively moved back. "Now come on, Seth, we have to go. There were more bears killed on our property up the mountain."

All other thoughts fled my mind. All I could picture was a pile of dead bears. I clutched Seth's arm.

"I said we have to go, son." Kincade grabbed Seth's arm and pushed him harder than he should have toward the elevator. Seth fell to one knee and looked up at his dad, defeat in his eyes.

A love for Seth I didn't realize I had welled up from the pit of my stomach, and I reached out to help him to his feet. Kincade pushed me away.

Seth stood on his own and wouldn't meet my eyes. "Guess I'll see you later."

"I'll go with you," I said without thinking. Seth shook his head no. I stepped back.

"We don't need your help," Kincade said. "Stay here," he added like he was talking to a dog he didn't like.

That set my hackles straight on end. But I didn't move. It would only embarrass Seth further if I did. Then I realized, what did that matter? Seth might be in danger. The elevator door opened. Kincade marched in. Seth hesitated then followed. They faced outward, looking at me.

A spider—another *Eratigena agrestis*—swung right in front of Kincade and dangled there for a moment before he slapped his palms together and crushed it.

With a ding, the elevator door closed.

Fear rose in my throat. And I knew. Seth was in danger. Real physical, life-ending danger from his dad.

I dashed up the nearby stairs in twos and burst out a side door into the parking lot.

I spotted Seth and his dad getting into their relic of a truck. A conspiracy of ravens circled above.

I got the fob out and remembered I'd left the car at the charging station. It should be more than charged by now.

I jogged around to the charging lot, climbed in, and headed for the mountain road I knew they'd be taking. The ravens seemed to be following Kincade's truck, which made it easy for me to track where they were.

But why were the ravens following them? Their cawing and calling and cacophony of it all added *headache* to my list of complaints. At least *nausea* wouldn't be lonely.

A particularly large raven swooped in front of my car as if it were saying hello, then flew ahead. Was that Poe?

I stayed far behind so I couldn't be spotted as they turned right onto the old highway.

When I spotted them again as they wound up the mountain, they had turned in the direction of our sequoia grove.

By the time I reached our parking lot, Seth and his dad had already hoofed it into the woods. I parked Gran's car pretty much where my dad's car had been the night he was shot. There was another truck there—Mel Finley's. Goose bumps rippled across my shoulders and down my arms.

As I got out, my whole body trembled. My breaths were shallow and short, and my heart pounded so fast I thought it might break out of my rib cage. As I put my pack on, a gleam of color caught my eye. I bent over and picked up a small piece of blue paper and tucked it away. Dad would not have been happy to find even one piece of litter on his land.

I surveyed the area, and a buzzy feeling seized my body. My breathing became shallow and quick. Images of that terrible, terrible night surged through my head.

The gunshot . . .

The blood . . .

Dad's whispering voice . . .

The sadness in his eyes . . .

Leaving his body, cold and alone to chase down his murderer. . .

The terror of it all wrenching my heart and gut.

I leaned forward to support myself on the hood. Maybe it was too much for me to be here so soon. But I wasn't here for myself. I was here for Seth. I followed the sound of angry voices. Seth was arguing with his dad.

"I can't believe someone killed all those bears," Seth said.

My heart sank. More dead bears on our land. When would it ever stop?

"Don't be such a wuss, Seth. Those bears don't do anybody any good. They just wreck the trees."

"Yeah, Seth, listen to your dad," Finley said. What a weasel.

"These are our trees now and we have to protect them. We'll be clear-cutting this land as soon as we can, and I don't want to lose one penny to damaged trees."

I couldn't breathe. Clear cut our sacred sequoias? They were living, breathing creatures, not ancient, but in sequoia years they had eons of time left on the earth. What a greedy monster to cut them down. I bit my tongue and clenched my fist and stayed right where I was.

"But, Dad, these trees are over a hundred years old. They're like family members to Nora. It'll kill her and her grandmother if you cut them down."

"So what? Let 'em die," his dad said with a chuckle.

"Yeah, let 'em die," Finley said.

I imagined Finley's mouth stuffed with sequoia seed cones. He was even more annoying than usual.

"You really do hate the Peters family. I don't understand why," Seth said.

"This isn't school, Seth. You don't need to understand a thing, except for what I want you to do."

"What exactly is that?" Seth asked.

"Use your charm to talk that girlfriend of yours into not challenging my claim to the land."

Seth laughed. Not loudly, but enough to turn his dad's temper up a notch.

"You think your old dad's hilarious, do you?"

"I don't think you're hilarious. I think you're evil," he said.

Kincade rushed his son and I leapt out from behind my tree to stop him.

"Nora, what the hell? You shouldn't have come," Seth said.

"I don't need to remind you," I said, "that the so-called sale of this property is not final as of this moment, so technically speaking, you're trespassing and have no right to be here at all."

"If you play that card, you're going to have to clean up the mess over there by yourself."

I whipped around to see Finley standing there, a cocked shotgun resting on his hip. He tipped his head to the east, where I saw the birds flying in circles above where the dead bears must be lying. Some were landing to feed. I wanted to shoo them away, but I had to deal with these creeps first.

I planted my feet firmly on the ground. "I'm pretty sure I fired your ass." Then I added, "Or are you waiting for an engraved invitation to leave?" This was a version of classic Gran sarcasm when I was slow to do what she wanted, and it felt good to say it now, in honor of her and the way she might handle this situation.

"Don't worry. I'm well out of your rat's nest. My new boss over there," Finley nodded toward Kincade, "is keeping his property clean, and it's my job to help."

"There *is* no deal as far as I'm concerned, and there never will be. For all I know, your new boss took advantage of my father's death to cook up that land deal and try to push it off on us as real."

Kincade snickered.

"First thing Monday morning, I'll be talking to an attorney, and we'll be challenging you in court," I said, pushing my story a little past the truth. I would be doing all of that—but first I had to talk to that lawyer Violetta had promised to put me in touch with.

"Maybe. But if you happen to meet with an accident, like the one your dad had, there wouldn't be anybody left to fight the deal."

His words chilled me.

"Dad, what are you saying?" Seth asked, his face looking pinched and hurt.

"Shut up, Seth. I'm not talking to you," his father said without even glancing Seth's way. He continued to talk to Finley like we weren't even there. "I found out that as of tomorrow, her eighteenth birthday, she'll be owner of her dad's so-called land."

"Hell, we didn't see that coming," Mel said.

"No, we didn't," Kincade said. "Now tell her what's going to happen if she doesn't shut her yap and take the deal."

"Dad, leave Nora alone," Seth said, and he moved protectively in front of me.

"I am taking NO deal," I said, stepping out from behind him and standing by his side. Seth looked at me and grabbed my hand. We both held on tight. This was something—someone— we'd conquer together.

Finley twitched. "I don't think you're going to want to refuse this deal," Finley said to me, his eyes nervously shifting back and forth between me and Kincade.

"And why's that?" I asked.

"Because if you don't go along with this deal, your grand-mother will go to jail and rot there for murdering your dad," Kincade said.

His words hit me with a force that buckled my knees.

Seth put his arm around my waist to support me. "What are you talking about?" he said, looking as shocked as I was.

"In a moment of weakness, she confessed the whole sad thing to me," Finley said.

I felt dizzy, sick to my stomach, confused, until I realized— that's exactly how they wanted me to feel. Shaking my head, I said, "Not a chance."

Finley shrugged. "I have proof."

"Show me," I demanded.

Finley laughed. "I'm saving that for our beloved sheriff. If, and only if, you make a fuss about the contract your dad signed with Kincade."

"Go ahead. Tell her," I said. "I'm sure Gran would rather take her chances with her than with you."

Both men exchanged looks that made me feel afraid.

I heard a dog bark. Mickey! There he was, prancing in place over the spot where Dad's body had fallen. Had he been standing vigil where Dad drew his last breath? The thought of him waiting for a man who would never return broke my heart. He kept barking but didn't move off that spot.

The men moved closer.

"Stay the hell away," I said.

"*You* do not tell *me* what to do," Kincade said, advancing relentlessly toward me.

Then Kincade lunged for me, and Finley went after Seth.

We both fought back.

Mickey broke position and attacked Kincade. He nipped at his leg and the man let out a grotesque yowl, then a stream of swear words and epithets ending with, "You lousy mutt, I'm going to kill you." Mickey released one pant leg only to attack the other.

Seth had pushed Finley away from him a couple of times and threatened him with a fist if he tried again.

"That's it, Carl. I want out of here. Pay up or I'm gone," Finley said. "You all are too crazy for me, fighting over trees and land. I'm the one doing the dirty work, and you, Carl, are the one who's going to reap the benefits."

"You leave now, you get nothing from me!" Kincade bellowed.

"I want my cash, Kincade," Finley said. But he headed for his truck.

Kincade roared after him, "Get back here and help me, you piece of shit!" But Finley didn't listen. And it wasn't long until we heard him peel out.

All the while, Mickey snarled and barked to keep Kincade from getting to me. "Tell your damned dog to stand down. You damn Peters. Always fighting dirty to get what you want."

I could have argued. But what was the point? I was more worried that he might land a kick and hurt Mickey, who charged him again and again, nipping first at one leg and then at another as he tried to herd Kincade away from me.

Then Kincade pulled out a revolver. He fired into the ground, kicking up a cloud of dust. I couldn't tell if he missed or if he was aiming at the dog or me. Terrified, Mickey took off through the center of the sequoias. I ran after him, glancing over my shoulder to witness Seth tackling his dad.

"Run, Nora!" Seth shouted.

And I did. I felt like a jerk running away from Seth, leaving him all alone to deal with his brute of a dad, but surely Kincade wouldn't shoot his own son.

Once I passed through the sequoia grove, I kept going. I could hear and see the brush ahead wiggle and writhe as Mickey ran ahead of me and wondered if he was running away or leading me somewhere. Didn't really matter, because I was going to follow him until I caught up and made sure he was all right.

It occurred to me that I might need some help if Kincade came after me, and wondered if Linka was near. I had had that funny 'someone might be following me' feeling on and off all day. So I took the jewelry casket out and opened it. The veins on the pearl's surface began to swirl in its mesmerizing way.

Within seconds, I saw an army of huge flying frogs supplied with an array of nasty weapons zeroing in on me from above. These frogs looked seriously sinister, from what I could see. I didn't study them long and took off again up the mountain. Even from my brief glance at them, I could tell they played on a different team from Linka given their size and the markings.

Their way of getting around was different too. Instead of riding bats, they flew on big-leaf maple leaves supported by what looked like little black clouds.

The flying frogs closed in on me even as I kept moving.

But as I climbed higher, the terrain became rockier and harder to navigate, especially at the clip I'd been keeping. I stopped. I had to. The circle of frogs flying around me tightened. I picked up a fistful of stones and prepared to defend myself.

What the heck did they want with me anyway?

It must be the pearl.

I stood there, staring at it in in my open hand.

43

Linka 🐸 The Path Not Taken

One Day Till Pink Moon
Warming Time (Late)
Mountain Range Beyond Salmon Falls

LINKA WAS RIDING the perfect bird for this mission: a falcon named Creet. Thanks to scouts that had followed Nora from the burnt dwelling to the dwelling of the sick and dying to the climb up the mountain, Linka knew just where to find the girl with the Pearl. And when she and the rest of her Zons caught up to her, the first thing she noticed was the Bulldoggies circling the girl. But how could they have even known she had the Pearl?

Had one of her victims at the girl's house survived to tell the tale? It wasn't the one called Xeron, she was sure of that. Igneo had toasted him nicely. It must have been the other one, that rolled off the roof and she had assumed died. *Drengo*, that was the name he went by. She'd be keeping an eye out for him.

"We have stayed at a distance until you arrived," one of her Zons reported.

"You did well," Linka said in a rare compliment. "Now, break into four flanks," Linka ordered. "One on each side of the battalion of Bulldoggies and two on top. Drive them together from the sides and down from the top. Kill as many as you can and try to crash the rest. Whatever happens, do not let them get near the girl." Linka sniffed the air. "I can smell it now—the reek of dead Bulldoggies. Remember your training. Do not let their size intimidate you. May the Well of White Light illuminate your path."

The Zons shouted their battle cry in unison and dove toward the burfing Bulldoggies who were descending in a spiral over Nora. Over their armor, the Zons had put on mica vests to reflect the sun and make it harder for their enemies to get too close. Their rock shots hung from both horns of their saddles. These slings, woven from vines, had been preloaded with acorn-sized rocks ready to fling at any enemy.

Linka took aim at the closest Bulldoggie and nailed it with a rock. He toppled off his leaf and tumbled to the ground, squawking like a coward all the way. All the Bulldoggies but one broke formation to counterattack. The Zons, however, had the tactical advantage because they always stayed above their enemy, making it impossible for the Bulldoggies to deploy their deadly drop nets, their main offensive weapon. As anticipated by Linka, her Zons inflicted maximum damage and distraction and she watched gleefully as Bulldoggies tumbled snout over rump to the ground, thanks to the Zons' renowned ability to aim true.

Then Linka spotted a problem and ordered Creet to follow the biggest Bulldoggie who was barreling straight for Nora. Linka tried to warn the girl to protect the Pearl, but it was too late. With expert precision, the Bulldoggie whipped past Nora and snatched the Pearl right out of her hand, then banked a turn to head off toward the Maw of Malevolence. The force of the wind blew off the hood of this expert burfer, revealing a face Linka recognized. It *was* Drengo—the Bulldoggie she had battled during Nora's fire. She would recognize his tattoos anywhere. And now he had the Pearl.

Linka whistled for her troops to abandon their battle and follow her. Drengo must not be allowed to keep it.

"Faster, Creet, faster," Linka urged. Her blood buzzed with the desire for revenge.

"Then you had better hang on, Princess," Creet said. He climbed high into the sky but moderated his speed so they were still behind the Bulldoggie. Then he hugged his wings to his body and dove down at the perfect angle to take the big frog out.

"Woohoo!" Linka cried. The speed was astonishing.

The Bulldoggie, and his cohorts who followed him, loomed larger in the sky the closer they got—and then they disappeared.

Creet's head snapped right and left as he searched the air space below.

"I see parts of a leaf," Creet said, and swiftly pivoted to follow the odd sight of leaf tips poking out of blue sky and puffs of cloud.

"Then aim for what you can see," Linka commanded.

With a series of clicks and chirps, Linka relayed the message to her troops that the Bulldoggies had deployed their camo capes. *Sneaky vermin*, Linka thought. But fortunately for the Zons, the Bulldoggies never quite managed to cover their humongous bodies completely. She had trained her troops how to spot what sometimes looked like flying body parts.

Linka commanded Creet to make a pass and rip the camo cape away, then he turned, using the tip of one wing as a pivot point, and went after Drengo. The sun broke through a cloud, temporarily blinding them so that Drengo and his ride never saw the falcon coming.

Creet swooped down on Drengo and Linka, infinator in hand, and sliced his head off like it was made from aphid jelly. Drengo's body remained upright for a moment, his hand still clutching the Pearl, his torso, legs, and feet twitching in the stirrups. Then his body toppled over and plunged toward the ground. Creet dove after the Pearl, which had fallen from Drengo's dead hand.

Linka scrambled down Creet's body and prepared to capture it as it fell. Creet gained on the object and Linka leaned forward, her hand outstretched, the webs between her fingers flapping from the force of the onrushing wind. Creet flew faster and faster in the service of catching the one object that meant everything to the future of the frog queendom—and maybe the world. But just as Linka was about to grab it, a raven swooped past and caught it with its open beak.

Luanne R Peterson

Nora ◎ So Close

A RAVEN, I WAS sure it was Poe, zipped over my head, his feathers cutting the wind into infinite slices of air. Instinctively I put my hand out, and plop, the pearl was mine once more. This was getting to be a habit—Poe's putting the pearl into my hand. It almost seemed too easy. Could the pearl have the power to seek out one person? Or was the raven calling the shots? I sensed it was the pearl and that the raven was doing its bidding. But what did I know?

This time, holding the pearl gave me a different sort of feeling. Like we were friends, like we belonged together. Respect for its power and its will washed over me. What was it that the frog princess had called it? The Golden Pearl of the Forest. A sacred object. When saying its name, there was such reverence in her voice. Like she was spelling it with a capital 'P'. Maybe I needed to start thinking of it like Linka did. It clearly had remarkable powers . . . and good taste in largetoes. I chuckled at my own joke. It was a lonely sound.

A peregrine falcon flew in front of me, back flapping to stop from colliding with the ground. Linka was on its back. Stuffing the Pearl back into its green casket, I shoved it into my pocket instead of putting it the pouch. Felt safer there. When I looked up, Linka had disappeared from the bird's back. Instead, I saw the air where she had been shimmer. She was there all right, but I couldn't see her without the Pearl being open to the air.

The steppes were in front of me, high above to the northwest. I could go back or I could go up. If Kincade was determined to kill me, I might not have a chance to do what my father's spirit had asked: to spread his ashes at the Nexus. Why risk going back down and getting shot when I go forward and fulfill my father's request?

That's when I made my decision to try to give my father's spirit what he asked for. One last duty as a daughter. I would find the Nexus, release his ashes, and return to take care of Gran.

As I looked upward at the steppes, I remembered my father's words: *Take me up there, above the steppes to the Nexus, where it all began. Start at the Flying Demon Tree and the path will open for you.*

I considered going back to the grove of sequoias to check on Seth. That probably would have been the smart thing to do since I could have hidden and waited for the sheriff to show up.

But a force greater than my will pulled me forward. It was time to carry out my father's last wishes and find out the truth about why he died. Maybe his spirit would tell me what happened to my mom.

Then I heard Kincade yell, "Stop!" from behind me. But naturally his order had the opposite impact on me. I ran faster, wondering what he had done to Seth.

For an old guy, he was agile, and he squawked as if he expected me to listen. Breathing hard, legs cramping, I turned hard right and plunged into a thick tangle of sword ferns, salal, and fallen mother logs. The air was pungent with the smell of rotting cedar. The scent comforted me.

I plopped myself on the ground, backpack by my side. As I checked to see if all of me was covered by the ferns, the ground glowed golden for a moment and the ferns themselves rustled their leaves to cover me completely. The golden glow faded, but the leaves remained in place. "Thank you," I whispered to them. Then I quieted my breathing as much as I could and hoped Mickey didn't decide to return right now and reveal me.

The ground vibrated with Kincade's heavy footfalls. He was near. He stopped moving and I froze. A breeze parted the ferns somewhat so I could see him. He was holding his gun. I wondered for a moment what he would do if he caught me. The answer was clear. I would die.

The sweat of fear dripped down my forehead into my eyes. I closed them with the realization I might never open them again.

Bang! He fired. Rehearsing my death, I stopped breathing. If he'd fired at me, he'd missed.

Finally, he moved on up the hill, due east from the sounds of it.

I looked up to see an empty grey sky with clouds traveling in my direction. I waited, wondering if Seth would be behind him. I heard nothing, so I poked my head above the ferns and saw Kincade disappear over the hill.

I jumped to my feet and ran off in the opposite direction. Saving my neck had to be my priority. Mickey and Seth would have to fend for themselves.

Since Kincade took the path, I would have to go off-trail through dense prickle bush to move in the direction of the Flying Demon Tree. My shoulders still tingled with warning. I found some sticks and used them as tools to part the dense, thorny brush and tore off through it.

The tension in my shoulders grew with every scratch to my hands and face until my arms felt so heavy, I could barely hold the sticks up. I couldn't see more than two feet in front of me. It was so easy to get lost in country like this, or worse yet, end up going around in circles and come out right where you began—if you came out at all. The air was still and heavy; I had to work hard to breathe. Blackflies took aim at my flesh like I was a dart board. I put the hood of my sweatshirt up to keep them from dive-bombing my ear canals. The sweatier I got, the more bugs swarmed around me.

"Hey," I called to the bugs. "You leave me alone, and I'll leave you alone." Miraculously, the buzzing stopped.

I trudged on and on and on. The brush was endless, the ground uneven and hard to walk on. I couldn't take it anymore. I had to go back. I swirled around to backtrack, but the brush had already swallowed my path. Tears stung my eyes. I kept moving forward. After a time, the incline of the land increased. I was climbing. The brush thinned out, but the rocks underneath got bigger and harder to navigate.

All I could think about were those scary movies where someone—usually a girl—is being chased by a monster or a bad guy. (In this case, Kincade was both.) For some reason, they always go up in a rickety old house to the attic, or to the top of a lighthouse, or the peak of a mountain. Gran usually sat on the couch screaming "Don't go up!" I could almost hear her screaming that at me now. But up I went, fearing the monsters I would find if I went down.

I have no idea how long I'd been walking when I looked up to see a swath of what must have once been tall, beautiful trees that had been ripped from the land. They called it a clear cut, but there was nothing clear about it. How was I going to get through this tumbled mass of roots, stumps, and dead branches? I sank down, not caring about the scratching brush that was poking me.

45

Linka 🐸 Wooded Wasteland

One Day Till Pink Moon
Fly Time
Mountain Range Beyond Salmon Falls

LINKA AND THE Zons were following Nora at a distance. Linka did not want to spook Nora into doing anything foolish. She was still shocked by the sight of the Pearl falling back into her hands. Unbelievable. It was almost as if the Well of White Light had willed it. Especially since it had almost been hers. And who was Poe serving? Not the interests of the frog queendom, as usual.

"Zons, patrol the area. I do not like that the Bulldoggies all disappeared at once," Linka commanded. "And watch for Poe, the raven. We do not need any more complications."

"Perhaps your deathblow to the Bulldoggie scared them off," Jineta said.

"You did well yourself, Jineta. But Bulldoggies are never afraid. Perhaps they are gathering even more forces for another attack. We must always remain cautious. After your patrols, meet me beyond that wasteland," Linka said as she pointed to the clear cut ahead.

The Zons ventured out in different directions.

When they were gone, Linka said, "Creet, take me there above the clouds so the girl cannot see us. Hurry. We must get there before she does."

They cruised over the destroyed trees, which extended as far as Linka could see. *There must be an easier way to do this,* she thought. She would appeal to the rubble to help her. She instructed Creet to land on a large snag of limbs and addressed the carnage from her position on her back.

"Oh, trees, once you were great. Now you lie broken and useless on the forest floor. You can be part of the Flow once more if you help me immobilize the femtoe who walks this way. Reach out with your roots and hold her in place so that I can take back property that belongs to the queen."

The wreckage of the once magnificent forest answered back in a diminished voice. "We have asked the queen to send Igneo to burn us and take away our pain and she refuses to help. So why should we help you? Besides, our own kind has sent us a message to protect the largetoe if the need arises. Not that we can do much in our sorry state."

"The queen must have her reasons." Linka dared not say more, even though she knew from last night's encounter with the wayward elemento, Igneo, that he no longer did the queen's bidding. Maybe that was why she didn't grant their wish to die in flames—because Igneo would no longer obey.

"How dare she get to decide what is best for us? Tell her to come—to stand here beside us—to stand for us, since we can stand on our own no more," said a trunk that had been mortally wounded by a mechanical device invented by largetoe to kill and torture trees.

"You question the queen's intent? She does her all for the All. And I am acting on her behalf. I command you in the queen's name to wrap what is left of your roots around the largetoe's legs and arms and pull her to the ground. Will you obey?"

"Please withdraw from here, and we will discuss this matter and inform you of our decision shortly," an old, upturned root said.

Linka dipped her snout and signaled Creet to fly to the top of the only towering fir tree left on the desecrated ground. As her Zons completed various patrols, they joined her and together they waited.

46

Nora ◎ Daughter of the Root

*D*AD HAD HATED clear-cutting. He said it was a big waste of wood, destroyed homes for any animal that lived there, caused flooding, and ruined the ground for generations to come. It even had the power to change the surrounding weather. Like a lot of things he said, I hadn't really understood the depth of what he meant. But now that I'd experienced that vision of connectivity of all things using the power of the Pearl, I got a deeper sense of the horror of clear-cutting. Destroying the trees was not only torturous to them, but it destroyed everything else above and below the earth as well.

I had to choose each step carefully or risk getting my foot or leg caught in the crazy maze of wood. My internal clock was already sounding the alarm—*It'll be dark soon and you'll be stuck on the mountain.*

I picked up the pace, but eventually I had to stop to catch my breath and collapsed against a severed stump. This was a terrible place. Maybe I should pour out Dad's ashes right here, right now, and then figure out some other way down the mountain. But the idea of his remains being abandoned in a place he would have hated turned my stomach upside down.

Now that I had started on this journey, I was stuck with my task: find the place my dad's spirit was talking about and carry out his wishes. It was the least I could do. If I did what Dad wanted, maybe he would appear before me and answer my questions. Dad had been honorable in life. His spirit would be honorable as well.

Maybe I should have stayed on the easy path and not gone all Explorer 101. If it hadn't been for trying to lose Kincade and then chasing down the Pearl, that's what I would have done.

I noticed the quiet. Deeply quiet. I closed my eyes to rest, my body heavy. Exhausted.

I put my backpack between my feet, took out the green jewelry casket, touched the golden frog, and opened the Pearl to the air. "Tell me what to do, Golden Pearl," I said quickly, in a gruff voice like I was talking to a genie.

I heard faint moans. Not human moans. Not animal moans. It was more like a creaking floor in pain. I couldn't tell where the sounds were coming from. Was someone hurting?

"Hello? Is anybody out there?"

The moaning got louder.

"Help? Do you need my help?"

The ribbons of color on the Pearl's surface swirled. My body tightened. I clutched the Pearl to my chest.

Instead of seeing the clear cut before me, I saw a field of battle. Man and machine against tree.

And the trees had lost.

They couldn't run. They couldn't hide. They couldn't even fight back. It had been a slaughter.

Arm-like limbs, slain body-like trunks, stumps, tangled roots out of place above soil. It was a jumble of wood woven tightly together by shared suffering. A wooden war memorial with the wounded and dead left on the field.

The moans were sounds of mourning and pain. The twisted limbs, the severed trunks, the crumpled roots were communicating with me. Not in words, but in whole stories that hit my senses like balls of ice. I was filled with a sense of knowing that seemed to spin out from the broken trees:

A sapling, too small to be cut, crushed by the fallen body of its mother . . .

A family of trees growing close to one another for generations, wiped out by men and their chainsaws . . .

A once majestic tree that had lived longer than many generations of humans, reduced to nothing but a big stump.

I wanted to yell s*top*. I couldn't take their pain. It felt like no human had listened to them in a long, long time. So I let them have their say. When the groaning and crying lessened, I softly said, "I'm sorry."

Would the trees understand?

The maimed trees parted on each side to form a path that led straight through the clear cut. The sound of gnarled roots pulling themselves out of the ground raised goose bumps on my skin. The loamy smell of opened earth pinched my nose as limbs and branches crawled, using their smallest twigs like fingers to pull themselves out of my way. Stumps, broken trunks, and large branches rolled when they could or tipped themselves end over end to move to clear the path.

It was a remarkable sight—like the parting of the Red Sea. But I'm no Moses. I didn't make it happen. Was it the Pearl that created this remarkable sight, or did it only help me see things without human filters?

If the Pearl had taught me anything, it was that the whole world was sentient and that every part of it was equally important and had a right to its own point of view.

I thought of that note that had been written to accompany the pond flowers at Dad's funeral. Gran had snapped at me for asking about the All. Linka had explained it before, but sometimes I need to hear things more than once to really understand. I was the All. The trees were the All. The birds, the bugs, the animals, the air, the dancing waters were the All. We were *all* the All. Even the maimed trees were the All, which made their pain my pain.

Then, the ghosts of the trees spoke to me.

Stay and be one with us, oh Daughter of the Root.

Roots grew out of my feet mid-step and plunged into the cool soil, spreading, intertwining with the dead and dying roots of the trees that lay in all directions.

Stay with us from this day forth,
And perhaps your presence
Can alter our course.

The trees' pain at being betrayed and brutalized seeped into my roots. Panic electrified every part of me as the root hairs exploded in size and plunged deeper into the ground. My legs and chest expanded into a tree trunk, and my head, hair, shoulders, and arms morphed into branches with fragrant flowering buds and leaves.

Panic changed quickly to a sense of awe. It was glorious to be rooted in the earth and embracing the sky. Dirt's moist coolness was so comforting, and the earth's vibrations tickled my root hairs and made me want to laugh with happiness, but I had no throat or mouth. Despite that, the leaves on my branches quivered with a distinct pulse. The pulse of me. Then I realized, I wasn't seeing to the blue sky and the clouds meandering across it. I had no eyes! And, yet I could sense a blueprint-like vision of the world beyond my physical presence.

Other sensations overcame me—sensations so strong it was like I could still see without having eyes. I longed to see what kind of tree I was. A stately western cedar, my beloved Sequoia, an oak? I couldn't tell. But what I could sense was amazing. Everything, including the wind, twined through and around my tree body in its own unique energy pattern. And the rustle of my leaves was sweet music, their vibrations felt not heard.

As quickly as I had fallen in love with being a tree, I became terrified of the idea. I wanted to move with my own feet, feel with my own skin, see and hear with my own eyes and ears. For *As a tree, I would be a prisoner of one place—this place—forever.*

I sensed a swarm of activity that took on the shape of frogs riding bats circling my crown. Leading the way was a fierce ball of red energy that could only be Linka, atop a steel-blue swirl I knew was a falcon.

From my tallest leaf to my deepest root, I knew Linka was not coming to free me. She was coming to get the Pearl.

There was a tug inside my trunk, and I sensed that it lay protected over what had been my heart and was now my heartwood, where neither Linka nor her Zons could reach. Relief pulsated up my xylem and down my phloem.

"Will you give it up?" Linka asked.

I shook my branches and twisted my trunk. No. I would not.

There was no mistaking their intention to do me harm as they charged me, swinging their lethal weapons. My tree body squatted, and all my branches, from the tallest to smallest, curled up as they rolled in on themselves.

With a burst of energy, every part of me unfurled at once in an explosive release, hitting the riders and mounts, who tumbled to the ground.

All the cells in my body screamed, "I don't want to be a tree!"

In an instant, my roots dissolved, disconnecting me from the earth, and my body returned to itself with a jolt of red-hot pain. I fell to the ground, grateful to have my ears, my eyes, my feet back. I watched as my attackers shook away their shock and retreated. I checked my feet. My backpack was still between them.

And then the dead trees spoke to me once more:

> *Worry not, little daughter, we release you for now.*
> *In honor of today's root talk, which told us how. . .*

> *. . . You've been kind to trees since the start of your life.*
> *But to stay with us always would cause too much strife.*

> *Princess P'hushtalinka begged us to betray you here,*
> *But as a friend to your home trees, we held you dear.*

Now you're our cousin in fiber and verve,
And if you ever need us, your cries will be heard.

So, wherever you are, if ever you fall,
Put your lips to the ground and give us a call.

And to any that would harm you, we will take on your fight.
And bind the betrayer so they can't harm or take flight.

We will encase them in bark, branch, and leaf.
And from that danger give you relief.

You may invoke this wish by asking for our presence.
Command with two words: Tree essence.

I picked up a twig and poked my arm hard enough to make sure I was in my body. Here. Now. The answer to that was *ouch*. I put the twig into my pocket as a reminder of what I had experienced.

I heard the path close behind me, but I did not turn to watch.

It was probably safe to say that I would never look at a tree—any tree, from sky toucher to twig—in quite the same way again. And after experiencing the pain of the trees for myself, I had to wonder about all the pain we'd inflicted on the ones on our tree farm. Trees weren't a commodity, something to sell. They were living, breathing creatures with a language and a way of life, like us. And if trees felt pain, did that mean every living resource we exploited did as well? What were we doing to the planet we called home? It wasn't only home to humans. It was home to everything that lived here.

There was something deeper that this experience had stirred inside me. Did all the work that I'd been doing to try to save the world hold—at its heart—the rottenness of self-preservation? Was I really trying to help other species for their sake . . . or my own?

In the distance I heard shouting. Maybe Ardith was looking for me because she thought I was lost or in danger. I wasn't going to stick around to find out.

So up I climbed.

47

Linka ⚜ A Debt Paid Forward

One Day Till Pink Moon
Fly Time (Late)
Mountain Range Beyond Salmon Falls

L INKA AND HER Zons were silent until the girl disappeared over the horizon. "Continue following her at a distance," Linka said.

When the Zons had flown away, Linka removed the fire stick from under her saddle. She had put it there the night Nora's house was burned. She instructed Creet to dive off the tall tree and fly low over the desecrated forest. Even though the trees had not delivered the girl, Linka would deliver mercy.

She spotted a large pile of dry brush. "Land there," she said to Creet. Linka dismounted, went to the driest part of the pile, and struck the fire stick across her armor. It ignited.

The flame morphed into the distorted face of Igneo. "We are together once more," Igneo hissed.

"Do your worst, Igneo. Relieve these tortured trees from their pain," Linka said. "You will have my gratitude."

"Your gratitude will have to suffice for now—but one day, I will have you."

Linka touched the flame to the dry branches. It caught and spread quickly.

She leapt onto Creet's back and they flew off as the smoke rose and spread.

"Peace be with you, once-great forest," she said, and was gone.

"She is coming. She is coming," one Bulldoggie said as they coasted on an updraft, having watched the band of Zons fly under them.

"Wait until she is beneath us, then drop the frog catcher," another Bulldoggie said. The small band of Bulldoggies wrestled to spread out the net made from woven ivy vines that served as the frog catcher.

"General Oddbull wants her alive, but if she happens to die in the fall, there will not be any spots off my skin," another Bulldoggie said. "Get ready . . . and . . . drop."

The net fell from the cloud and tangled itself around Linka and Creet and they plummeted toward the ground.

Linka groaned and rubbed her head. She had seen a flicker of the net before it landed on them and forced them to the ground. It took her a moment to realize that she was wrapped in Creet's wings and pressed against his cold, dead breast. He had given his life to save her in their fall.

She poked her head through his feathers and saw the tangle of net snagged on dead branches. How would she ever get free?

Then she heard a voice. "Well, little one, need some help?"

Linka looked up to see a huge frog-like creature like none she had ever seen before and promptly passed out.

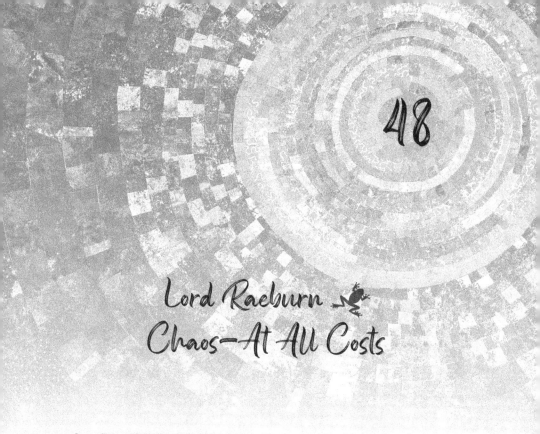

48

Lord Raeburn
Chaos—At All Costs

One Day Till Pink Moon
Fly Time (Late)
The Palay, Lord Raeburn's Chambers

A s PRACTICE FOR the day when he ascended the throne, Lord Raeburn liked to hold court in his own quarters, which featured a large domed room surrounded by a collection of smaller domed rooms.

His large chamber glowed with a soft yellow light from the lumitubes above. This gentle cascade was created by a series of mica reflectors positioned to reflect light from outside the Palay into the dome of the chamber.

Exquisite wall mosaics inlaid with quartz, agate, and tourmaline gave the illusion that the whole room was the shore of a living pond with fat, happy frogs sitting on spacious lily pads and delicious-looking Egyptian mosquitoes and dragonflies flitting about. And under the waterline, nestled among the inlaid jade reeds, a male and female rainbow trout guarded their buried nest. It was all so realistic that guests sometimes hurt themselves trying to dive into the water.

His growing band of young memnuras circled the low divan covered with pussy willow pillows where Lord Raeburn reclined.

"Really, it is hard to believe that the queen dismissed us without revealing her dream," said Kon, Raeburn's aide-de-chambre.

"Now, Kon," Lord Raeburn replied, "let us be kind when we speak of our queen. Who knows the strain that ruling our queendom has on her delicate constitution? Of course, someone who was stronger and more fit would not be prey to such weaknesses as fainting spells."

"Fainting spells?" The room buzzed with surprise. No one had heard that the queen was suffering from fainting spells until this moment.

Raeburn, pleased with his impromptu malady idea, popped nut worms into his mouth and tapped one webbed foot in a languid fashion. "It is probably only a vicious rumor spread by some disenchanted subject," Lord Raeburn said. "Although, we cannot help it if rumors are usually based on some sort of truth. Can we?"

"Does that mean the queen could die?" asked young Wink, who had been invited by Raeburn to join the gathering.

"Let us speak of this no more," Raeburn said. "We all know that to utter ill invites ill. Off with you mudclomps. I must confer with Kon on vital matters of state. By the way, Wink, I want you to stay behind."

"Yes, Your Lordship," Wink said, blood rushing to his transparent face.

The other memnuras made their way out of the chamber, leapfrogging and wrestling in the playful manner of the young.

When the chamber was empty, Lord Raeburn approached Wink with a sigh. "I am extremely disappointed in you, young sir. I expected that your uncle's relationship to the Grand and Glorious Vizzard would net me better information than you have given me."

"I am sorry, Your Lordship, but I find it hard to betray the best interests of my uncle. I have told the vizzard about our previous arrangement and he advised me not to lie to him or to you."

"Very wise advice, but I still expect my due. You already have my instructions. If I am not satisfied with your output, I may have to take you back to the Maw myself."

Wink inhaled sharply.

"You must find out all you can about the queen's dream."

"But how?" Wink asked, his heart visibly beating like rain on rock under his skin.

"That is your problem. Now go," Raeburn said, clearly irritated by Wink's shortcomings.

Wink left the area in one large jump. Then Raeburn drew Kon into a side chamber—a small round room with nothing but two perching stools. The domed ceiling was decorated with quartz panels used to heat the more tropical areas of the Palay. Hidden under the backside of the panels was a grid of interrupter rock. Lord Raeburn pulled a cord and the panels descended, forming a protective circle around the perching stools. No one could spy on them now.

"I want you to arrange a special greeting for our esteemed council members who are making their way to the Palay. And for the prince who is being sent by his mother to greet our distinguished guests. Let us, oh, how do I say this delicately? Let us do away with them all so the queen's allies never reach the Palay. And if we can do away with her son at the same time, all the better.

"I have prepared a note for you to take to the general requesting that his Bulldoggies be available for action at a specific time and place. I want you to accompany them and protect my interests. General Oddbull is the tool I will use to pry the doors open to my kingship. But I cannot let him get the upper hand. Keep your earpads open to any rumblings of discord among his troops. Perhaps I can entice them over to my cause."

Kon nodded in acceptance of his mission.

But before Kon got far, Raeburn called him back and handed him a vial crawling with sow bugs. "And while you are there, release these surreptitiously around the Maw and surrounding area. I must have intelligence to pull this off. And my little beauties will do the job well."

"And, oh, if in the heat of battle, the prince receives a fatal blow," Raeburn added, "all the better. Extra rewards if you drown him."

Nora ◎ Circle of Friends

One Day Till Pink Moon
Sundown
Alpine Meadow

AFTER MY EXPERIENCE with the clear cut, I climbed and climbed until I finally found the beautiful meadow my father had directed me to—the home of the Flying Demon Tree. Huge and very dead, it had been gnarled by forces I couldn't even imagine.

Dad had said a lightning strike must have killed the center of the tree, which was hollow. But roots on either side of its trunk hadn't gotten the message. In a frantic attempt at survival, they had pushed themselves up out of the earth in the shape of twisted angel wings. And in the middle, out of the trunk, a burl became a tortured neck that contorted into the shape of a grotesque demon-like head, with bulbous eyes and a biting beak.

Go to the Flying Demon Tree and the path will open for you, my father's specter had said. Okay. I had arrived. Now what? Wait until the path to the Nexus magically appeared? I still didn't even know what or where that was. What if I used the Pearl? Would it help, or would it be like turning a beacon on myself, alerting armed frogs to come and get me? I needed answers.

Maybe Mom's book could help. I hadn't really looked at it yet, other than to show it to Linka. Where *was* she, by the way? I was pretty furious that she'd tried to ambush me back in the clear cut. That's gratitude for you. Fat chance she'd ever get those webbed fingers of hers on the Pearl again. But what if the only way to find my mother was through her? I'd worry about that later. Once I fulfilled my obligation to my dad.

I moved beyond the Flying Demon Tree into the surrounding field of flowers, including pink-to-purple-to-blue Lupinus, orange and white avalanche lilies (or Erythronium montanum), and orange-to-red-tipped Castilleja. I hid myself on the other side of an outcrop so anyone coming up the mountain couldn't see me. To be honest, I was terrified that Kincade would show up and murder me. If only I could find Mickey, at least I could be sure that he was safe.

The magnificent oranges, pinks, and purples of a Pacific Northwest sunset filled the sky. I took my dad's ashes, the book, and Gran's purse from my backpack and set them all on the grass beside me. Gran's wallet called to me more than the other objects, so I opened it first. It had been my job, since I was little, to straighten Gran's wallet. She was usually the neatnik, and I was the messy one—except when it came to her wallet. Before she had moved in with us after Mom . . . left . . . Gran would walk in the house, wallet in hand, and give it to me to tidy up. It had become kind of a meditation for me to do it. I needed that feeling of peace and familiarity now.

License, credit cards, business cards of friends. I opened the center zipped pocket and took out its contents, which included origami papers in a rainbow of colors.

That Gran. Of course she'd be carrying that around. She was that dedicated to her cranes. "Always have something to do in a flood," she'd say, meaning that if she ever got stuck anywhere, she could occupy her time by folding a few cranes—and usually giving them to the first kid she saw. We'd also both been working with Mrs. Hayashi and other residents of our town to make a thousand cranes for a world peace project.

As I straightened the origami papers, something about the blue ones sent a sudden chill down my arms. I counted the papers in the pack. There were ten of each color. Every color, that is, but blue. I took out the wrinkly piece of blue paper I'd pocketed outside Kincade's truck. Was it only this morning? I compared it to the other unused pieces. It was the same size and color. No printing variations at all.

Had this unfolded crane been a part of Gran's pack? If so, how had it gotten to the site where Dad died? My stomach got queasy. Something wasn't right here, but I didn't know what. Had Gran visited the site of Dad's death on her own?

My eyelids felt heavy. Life weighed on my shoulders like the moon was on my back. I wanted to cry, but my tears were too tired to fall.

The green earth looked so inviting, and the sweet fragrance of the alpine meadow flowers drew me toward them. I tossed aside my backpack and lay flat on the ground. Its coolness soothed my fiery fear and anxiety. The sounds of the forest, which was never silent, calmed me like a lullaby. Maybe if I closed my eyes for a few minutes, I would . . .

Cool moisture pricked my face. My eyes opened to the darkest part of the night—illuminated only by the soft light of the fog-covered moon. Not too far beyond the reach of my arm, I could see a ring of lights glowing in the darkness. Tendrils of fog whirled slowly about, making everything a bit hard to see.

A rough blanket scratched my legs. Wait, a blanket? Where'd that come from? It smelled wild and foresty with a hint of lavender, a strong smell but not a bad one. Despite its warmth, a shiver chilled me. I wasn't as alone as I thought.

"Hello?" My voice was weak and crackly. "Anybody here?"

Branches rustled in the soft night breeze. A twig cracked.

"Who's there? Seth?"

Bushes swished.

"Please, whoever you are, let me see you."

"Eat," said a voice in a gravelly whisper.

I heard a raspy inhale and a low exhale with a painful sounding "haaaaaaaah." The breath blew past me and made the little hairs on my arms stand straight up. It seemed to come from nowhere and everywhere at once and shredded the gathering fog into stringy wisps. The light flickered and danced. There was something at the center of the lights. I got to my feet, clutching the blanket tight around me, and walked over.

The lights were crudely carved cedar bowls filled with burning oil. At the center of the circle, on a nest of boughs, was a collection of big maple leaves, mounded roasted filberts, black walnuts, hickory nuts, and wild blueberries, salmonberries, and blue-leaved strawberries.

I sampled a few. The berries were dried since it was too early in the season, and the nuts were roasted, salted, and seasoned with thyme, wild garlic, and some other dried spice I didn't recognize.

An oyster shell held a white creamy substance. I brought a bit of it to my lips on the tip of a finger. It was yogurt with a gamey taste, like it had been made from the milk of some other animal besides a cow. There was also a small cake dripping in what looked like honey with a pressed wood violet, or Viola odorata, on top. What a lovely little feast. Almost like a birthday party.

The moonlight brightened, and I saw a highly polished wooden cylinder. It looked like it was part of a branch—about a foot long and four inches around. I picked it up. It was warm, almost hot to the touch. Steam trailed out around one end. It was a hand-carved flask with a top. I pulled the top off with a tug.

A steamy fragrance hit my nose: wild rose hips and mint. And another ingredient that smelled of mystery. I let it cool a bit then took a sip. It was sweetened with a fragrant honey, but there was a slight bitter aftertaste. I didn't care. It was warm and quite wonderful as the cool night air closed in.

"Hello?" I called out again.

"Eat," the voice repeated. It sounded close.

"Won't you let me see you? To say thanks?"

"No thanks required. Eat."

Seized by hunger, I added the nuts and berries to the yogurt and sucked the concoction into my mouth. Then I licked the cedar bowl clean. The wooden surface felt rough on my tongue. I could have eaten more, but I was grateful for what I'd been given.

I sighed. That was better. "Thank you," I called out to my invisible host.

The remaining wisps of fog were blown away by a random breeze. The moon shone high in the sky. Tomorrow night was the full Pink Moon, so-called because pink flowers in the phlox family, like moss pink phlox, and wild ground phlox, bloomed during this time.

Fog started to creep in again but before it concealed my surroundings, I saw my host crouched low to the ground. Back hunched, one leg extended to the side, propped up by two arms covered in long raggedy sleeves and draped in a flowing cloak that pooled all around its feet. Two eyes glowed red inside a cavernous hood. Who was this puzzling figure? There was something strange about him. Her? Them?

"You know, my mom and I used to talk about never feeling alone at night when the woman in the moon was smiling down upon us," I said, hoping that my visitor was listening.

No response.

"When I was little, I thought the man in the moon looked more like a woman. Mom agreed. It was our little secret. We had other moon secrets, things we shared about the moon. She taught me lots of names that some Native American nations used for every full moon throughout the year." I heard rustling in the fog, which had grown thicker. It was still listening. I knew it.

"Some nations called February the Hunger Full Moon. March was the Crow Full Moon, and April, according to some of the many Anishinaabe tribes back east, was the month of the Pink Full Moon. Mom loved these names and said they reminded her of where she came from because they had names for every full moon too. I remember asking her what the moons of her childhood had been called, but she'd laugh and say they were words I wouldn't understand since I didn't speak her original language. I asked her to teach me, but she never did. I don't know why."

There was more rustling, but this time the sound moved farther away.

I picked up the bentwood box, returned to the circle of light, and placed it at the center of the circle. I placed a few crumbs of honey cake in front of the box like an ancient Egyptian offering to the dead. I'd learned all about that in school.

"If it's after midnight, this is my birthday cake. Please, come. Have a piece with me," I called out into the darkness, trying to tempt my host. I heard a small shifting of leaves beyond the reach of the light. I waited. But there was only silence.

I took a sip of tea and a bite of cake. There was a sweetness and sadness to the flavors that raised a lump in my throat that led to tears. More cake. More tea. More tears.

By the time the tea and cake were gone, my tears were gone too. My legs and head were heavy and I wanted to sleep, but I was still angry at the world and especially at my parents for deserting me and leaving me so alone. There was nothing I could do to punish my mother, but in case my dad was listening, like a genie inside the lamp, I pushed the box away.

Instantly I regretted my action and scrambled to pull it close. The wood was hard and as cold as my father's hand in death.

A picture stirred in my mind of all my friends in their homes, snug in their beds, with mothers, fathers, grandparents close by. Why did they get to have families? I was even jealous of Seth. Even though his dad was the most repulsive man on Earth, he still had a dad. I didn't.

Miserable, I huddled under my blanket, which offered thin protection against the damp night and the crushing loneliness. I couldn't face my father's ashes, so I pulled the blanket over my head.

Ugh, I'd just had a nap. Why was I still bone tired? Was there something in the tea? Sleep. Forget. That's what I wanted to do. The food I'd been given was one blessing, but sleep would be an even greater one.

I woke up to something licking my face. It was Mickey. "Mickey. You found me," I cried. Then I saw Seth bound toward me.

"Nora, you okay?" Then without waiting for an answer, he called behind him, "She's here. Mickey found her."

Kameela came running next. Behind her were Will and Minh.

"I—we—were so freaked out about you disappearing, Nora," Seth said, a bit breathlessly. "Did my dad hurt you? Are you okay?"

A part of me wanted to kiss him, and another part of me wanted to push him away.

"Okay? Okay? I will probably never be okay again. Your dad was about to shoot my dog before he came after me." I couldn't stop hugging Mickey, and I was getting dog-kissed to death.

"I know, I know. He is such a . . . jerk," he said.

That comment ruled out 'the push.' So only the urge to kiss him was left. But I wasn't about to let Mickey go.

"Deep breaths, Seth," I said, going for cool and calm. "I'm fine."

"Seth told us everything, Nora," Kameela said. "What a terrible experience to go through. How could his dad have threatened you like that? And Finley too. You must still be in shock."

"Shock? I passed through that territory some time ago," I said, trying to lighten my own mood. "And I don't even have a name for where my head is living now."

Everyone piled on for another massive group hug. Mickey pranced in a circle around us barking joyfully. I sighed in a temporary state of bliss. But I had the idea it wasn't going to last. "How'd you know where I was?"

"Last night after the fire, on the ride to the hospital, you told me what your dad said when . . . well, you know."

Good old Seth. How could I be mad at him? He was just too nice. He cared. He was protecting me by not letting the others know about the crazy visions I'd described to him—points in his favor.

"What about you, Seth? How'd you get away?" I asked.

"I didn't have to. After body slamming me to the ground, he took off after you."

"He came after me all right, but I hid and he walked right past," I said.

"So basically, we don't know where he is, and until we do, I'm not going to leave you alone," Seth said.

"Me neither," Kameela said.

"I feel so much better now that you are all here," I said.

Everyone gathered around on the blanket. Seth sat close to me and put his arm around my shoulder. I tossed my worries to the wind and leaned against him.

The moon was setting—it must have been after midnight—but it was light enough so that we could see each other's faces. Then Kameela and Minh pulled out solar lanterns so there was even more light.

"We brought water and food if you're hungry," Minh said. "I even brought your favorite banh mi veggie sandwich from the restaurant."

"Thank you. That sounds delicious." I don't know how I could still be hungry after my last little feast, but I was. Minh handed me a brown paper bag. "I'd also love some water," I said.

Will poured some from his canteen into mine. I took a long swig, which helped wash some of my tiredness away.

"Thanks," I said and dug into the best sandwich ever. "Exactly what I needed. Between this and the food my mystery host gave me, I won't be hungry for days," I said.

Seth looked around. "Who did all this?" Seth asked, pointing to the cedar bowls of oil and the blanket and boughs I was resting on.

"I'd love to tell you, but I don't know. Call me crazy, but I think it was the same person who jumped over my mother's grave and who left all the recyclables outside the door of the church at my father's funeral."

"Whoa, whoa," Minh said. "Two steps back. You never said anything about a grave jumping."

"There's been a lot going on, Minh," I said. "Besides, most of the stuff I haven't told you is just too weird. I need to figure out if I'm crazy first—then I'll give you a chance to weigh in."

"We could make a list," Kameela said, jokingly. "Pros and cons. Is Nora crazy?"

We all looked at her and said in unison, "No lists." Then we laughed.

"Okay, okay," Kameela said. "But if we *did* make a list, what kind of things would be on it?"

"How about a Pearl that makes weird things happen? Like creating colorful visions that show lines of energy running between all living things? And water that dances?"

"What pearl?" Mihn asked.

I took out my pouch and showed them. "It's in here." Then I tucked it away.

"She's right," Seth said. "I saw it for myself."

"Aren't you going to show us too?" Minh said.

"Whenever I open it, trouble follows, and I've had enough trouble today. But I promise to show you tomorrow."

"Leave her alone, Minh," Will said.

Seth and Kameela joined with Will.

"Ok. Ok. I was curious. Curiosity is the foundation of truth. Don't slay me," Minh said.

We all laughed.

"Ask me any question you want to know," I told Minh.

"So, what exactly do you see when you open this thing?" he said, pointing to the pouch around my neck.

"Armor-wearing, tattooed frogs, for a start. No, make that armor-wearing tattooed frogs that fly."

"Ah, Nora. That's weird."

"There's more to this world than most people see," said Will thoughtfully.

"Those are some crazy events," Minh said.

"It's a lot to take in and understand," Kameela said. "But I believe that everything you told us is something you experienced. You're not a liar or an exaggerator. And you're not crazy. This I know. What I don't know is what it all means, but maybe that doesn't matter."

"I agree," Will said. "I think we need to get back to things where we can make a difference, if you don't mind, Nora."

"I don't mind one bit. You're my friends. Not telling you felt like I was lying to you. So now you know. Either I'm crazy or the Pearl makes weird things happen."

"Speaking of weird things," Will said, "can you get out the contract your grandmother gave you?"

"Sure," I answered and rummaged through my backpack and handed it to him. He separated one of the pages from the bunch.

"Since Grandfather is on the Board of Trustees of the foundation your dad formed for his research on the impact of climate change on tree farming, he had copies of all the paperwork your dad put together to form the conservation easement." Will took out two pieces of paper from his own backpack and pointed his phone's flashlight at them. "Look at these two pages." He pointed to a page of the easement papers and a page of the contract Kincade had given to Gran and me. "These two descriptions are the same—right down to the typo."

He pointed out the double periods at the end of a sentence that were in both copies.

Seth took the papers. "Will, can you shine the light through the back of this page?" he asked, and he held up the copy his dad had given me. "One thing I know about my dad is that he's a wily opportunist—like a magpie. He could have found . . ."

". . . or stolen," Will said.

Pain wrinkled Seth's face, but he continued. ". . . or stolen your dad's paperwork somehow and created the contract he handed to you from that. It wouldn't take much. A scanner, a computer and a heart that tends toward larceny. Look here." He pointed to something else. "See?" he said, indicating a shadowy line.

"That's not on the original easement page," Seth said, "But it is on the papers that Dad handed to Nora and her grandmother. That *could* mean that my dad did a cut-and-paste from the original. A sloppy one at that."

"And what about the rest of the property, including the land where the house is? Er, was. That was on the contract too," I said.

"Really, any land info is pretty much available online," Will said. "That's probably where your dad got the property description for the easement papers. Seth's dad could have also gotten your house info there. But the typo, that was your dad's mistake once he copied and pasted it into his documents."

"So what you're saying is that if Seth's dad and my dad *really* had a deal, then there wouldn't necessarily be the same typo that was in the easement papers," I said trying to puzzle the whole thing out. "And that the typo is there because somehow Seth's dad got hold of the easement contract and did some cutting and pasting from there and not from the county website. And neither of them noticed."

"I'm just saying it's a possibility," Will said.

"Saved by a typo?" Kameela said. "Who would have thought? Sounds a bit too easy to me."

"There's one way to check," Minh said.

"What's that? I asked.

"Look up the property description on the county website," Minh replied.

"Not happening tonight," Kameela said, looking at her phone. "As usual, we're out of town and out of luck when it comes to cell service. We'll have to wait until we're back in town to find out."

I stood up and let out a sigh of frustration. "I still don't get why your dad is so hateful toward my family, Seth."

"Dad wants what used to belong to his family. He talks about what he calls 'the theft' a lot."

"Nobody stole anything," I said, with anger in my voice.

"I know, I know, Nora," Seth said, trying to calm me down. "My guess is that when he heard your dad was dead, he saw a chance to steal the property from you and your Gran and just went for everything your family owns—house, tree farm, and all."

"I know you're trying to help," I said, my blood boiling, "but what I hear you saying is that he thought that Gran and I were too stupid to stop him from committing a crime and stealing our property."

"Yes, that's what I'm saying."

I let out a long sigh as I tried to turn my internal temperature down. "And is that what you think?" I said, feeling all red and prickly in my own skin.

Seth jumped to his feet and ran his hand through his thick hair. "No, Nora. Never. I *don't* think it. But that's the way *he* thinks," Seth said. "That he's the smartest and the best and deserves whatever he wants just for being him."

I was still buzzing with anger. The more outrageous his father's behavior was toward my family, the harder it was for me to separate Seth from his dad even though I knew that wasn't fair. I pocketed my hurt feelings. "We've got to get this information to Ardith. It's all we've got," I said.

"I think you're going to have to get a handwriting expert, Nora. Do you have a recent sample of your dad's handwriting?" Will asked. "Tricky, I know, when your house just burned down."

I smiled. I did have something. I pulled out the card that said *Happy birthday to my Nora* and handed it to Will. "Here. I'm sure the bank has a sample but take this. Just in case."

"Nora, I forgot with all the craziness going on—today's your birthday," Seth said. He looked like he wanted to give me a hug. I moved a step back, still feeling like his father was standing between us. A hurt expression crossed his face, but he hid it quickly and said, "Happy birthday," anyway. Everyone joined in with their good wishes.

"Can't say I feel much like celebrating," I replied. Birthdays will never be the same anyway, so why bother.

"That's understandable," Kameela said.

"We'll leave it for a happier time," Minh said. The others agreed, although not enthusiastically. It seemed like we all needed a dose of hope—something to look forward to, to celebrate, to feel joyful about.

"I know, let's plan the biggest party ever—not now—not for me, but for all of us. For the community when my dad's research center gets underway. Hey, maybe *that* can be Mother Nature Commandos' big-deal project. For any of you who want to be a part of it. That *would* be worth celebrating."

"I'm in," Kameela said.

"Done." I declared. "You'd make the best CEO—if you want."

Kameela smiled. "Let me get through college first," she said.

"When I'm a psychiatrist working with refugee kids who were separated from their families, I'll start a camp—in the foundation's forest," Minh said.

"I'll be the chief technology officer and graphic designer," Will said. "We'll have a kick-ass website where people from all around the world can participate in online learning experiences."

"What do you want, Seth?" Kameela asked.

"Right now? I want to help Nora untangle this mess caused by my family. I'll worry about the rest another day. But I do promise to help when I can."

And me? "I'll write about all the cool things the foundation does. But I'll be there too. Nothing seems more important to me now than doing everything we can to keep the forests viable. They may be only one of the systems we have to keep going, but if one system does poorly, all the others will as well. And based on everything I've been experiencing lately, all entities have an unquestionable right to exist as they are created. All forms of water, land, and creatures," I said. "Everything."

The others agreed.

We talked for a while more until I couldn't keep my eyes open. The edge of dawn appeared pink on the horizon.

"Maybe we better get some sleep before the sun comes completely up," I said, trying to hide a big yawn.

"What are you going to do tomorrow, Nora?" Kameela asked. "Or I guess it's today."

"Let's worry about that later," I said.

Kameela handed me an extra sleeping bag and a ground sheet. I snuggled into the sleeping bag with the bentwood box in the crook of my arm. Everyone else pulled out their sleeping bags and gathered around in a jagged circle. It was nice to have the company. A moment before sleep came, I realized how much my life had changed. From daughter to orphan, from having a home to being homeless. But there was one constant through all these changes. I still had my circle of friends.

50

General Oddbull
Delicious Surprises

One Night Till Pink Moon
Deepest Night
The Maw

Gᴇɴᴇʀᴀʟ Oᴅᴅʙᴜʟʟ ʟᴏᴜɴɢᴇᴅ in his massive nest in his ornately decorated quarters. He was even less fastidious in his personal quarters than he was on his throne above the Maw, and there were piles of frog bones around this circular shaped room. The mess didn't bother him much. In fact, it excited him because each bone represented a unique artistic opportunity.

During those times when he couldn't sleep, he would pick one up and consider its shape and dimension. Would it work for piercing a body part? Not that he had many body parts left to pierce. But he was a prodigious gift giver and would often design pieces—executed by others, of course, for his favorite henchmen, who wore them with pride.

He was sorting through one of the larger piles looking for the perfect pieces to fashion into a necklace, or perhaps yoke, for Ranya when Raeburn turned her over to him. What fun that would be. He must outdo himself for this work of art, as he was sure he could.

A Bulldoggie entered, accompanied by a very ordinary frog with a black circle around one eye.

"General, this is Kon, emissary from Lord Raeburn. He has a message for you," the Bulldoggie said.

"Well? What is it?" The general did not like to be interrupted during his rest time, and he was somewhat tempted to eat both the Bulldoggie and this Kon. But first he would find out what Raeburn wanted from him now.

"General, I am honored," Kon said, dipping his head so many times he was probably making himself dizzy.

"The message? Please?" General Oddbull asked, surprised at himself that he was being so polite.

Kon moved forward and handed the leaflet from Raeburn to the general, who touched it to his head. As the imbued message transferred itself from leaf to noggin, it was like a shadow worming its way into the general's head.

As the general contemplated Raeburn's message, he couldn't help but notice that Kon was struggling with something behind his back—not an easy place for a frog to reach. Kon was clearly not the smartest frog in the pond because he didn't seem to notice all the mirrors in the room. That meant that Oddbull could see what Kon was trying to get the top off a vial of sow bugs. Kon's lack of stealth was shocking indeed.

The general knew immediately that Raeburn had sent his spies in a bottle with Kon. Sneaky fiend. No matter, they would make a tasty snack as soon as Kon left.

He called the Bulldoggie over—not by name, of course. The general didn't believe in naming something that someday might be food and had a strict personal motto: *Never eat anything with a name.* He tried to adhere to it but sometimes he failed.

"Soldier, give our visitor some firefly nectar. He must be parched from his long journey here."

"Oh, I am, Great General. You are too kind," he replied.

While the Bulldoggie distracted the little frog with a glowing drink of juice made from ground-up fireflies, Oddbull rifled through a basket that sat on the floor close to his side and palmed a vial of his own specially trained sow bugs from it. From another basket, he withdrew a Bulldoggie flycape left over from a feeding frenzy he had last week. He made a point of never ingesting fabric. Such indigestion it caused.

While Kon was struggling to find the courage to drink the glowing (and quite bitter) drink he was served, Oddbull inserted the vial into a secret pocket all Bulldoggie capes had.

When Kon got back to the Palay, if he survived the ordeal that surely would follow the execution of Raeburn's plans, the sow bugs would be released within the confines of the queendom. Soon, given their reproduction rates, he would have a steady and permanent supply of intel delivered to his door without having to rely on Raeburn. What fun that would be!

As Kon choked down the last swallow and the general's mission was completed, he said, "Worry not, Kon. My Bulldoggie here will ready the troops Raeburn has requested and, of course, you can accompany them. I even give you this disguise, your very own Bulldoggie fly cape." Then he called the Bulldoggie over and whispered the cape's secret into his ear.

"I've just instructed my soldier here to make sure this cape is altered for you before leaving the Maw."

"You are too kind," Kon said again.

The general laughed. No one had ever accused him of that before.

51

Nora ◎ Mourning Breath

Day of the Pink Moon
Dawn
Alpine Meadow

"Nora, time to wake up."

I sat straight up, still half asleep.

"Coming, Mom, I'm coming."

I stretched and smiled and opened my eyes to find that I wasn't in my comfy bed in my tidy bedroom in my home sweet home. Instead, I was in the middle of a grassy steppe covered in blooming flowers lying on a bed of cedar boughs surrounded by my sleeping friends. The cold air of a mountain morning made me shiver, so I tucked myself into a ball and burrowed back into my sleeping bag, leaving one arm out to feel around for Dad's ashes. But there was only empty space.

"What?" I scrambled out of my sleeping bag and stood up. Mickey, who had slept beside me, was also gone.

"What's wrong?" Seth said. He went from sleeping on the ground to standing on it.

I was too busy scrambling around looking for Dad's ashes to answer. I couldn't find them anywhere. I wrenched apart the intertwined boughs of my little nest and flung them aside. It didn't take long to search the tiny space where I'd slept.

Maybe the box sprouted legs and ran off into the forest. After the horrible things I'd said to my father's remains last night, I wouldn't be too surprised.

"What's going on?" Kameela asked, sitting up, still sleepy-eyed.

Will and Minh woke up as Kameela was asking her question. Soon everyone was on their feet.

"My dad's ashes," I said. "They're gone."

An empty feeling gripped me when I noticed my backpack with its contents scattered on the ground. I groped for the pouch around my neck. It was missing as well. As we all searched our sleeping ground, I discovered other things were missing, too. Among them, my mother's book. Gran's wallet was still there, as was the packet of origami papers and the unfolded piece of blue origami paper. The only other things left were some of my personal items.

"You know what this means," Kameela said.

I looked at her blankly.

"It means that while we were sleeping, someone . . ."

"Like whoever helped me last night," I said.

"Or maybe someone else?" Kameela said. "Whoever it was, someone crept past all of us to get to Nora," Kameela said.

"Some Commandos we are," Seth said.

"Some watchdog Mickey is," Minh said.

"He must have taken off before the thief arrived. Otherwise, he would have barked his head off," I said, adding, "I don't know what you guys are going to do, but I'm going to find my dog and my stuff."

Seth, Will, and Kameela wanted to come with me, but Minh had to work and promised to come back in the late afternoon to pick everyone up at the bottom of the mountain.

After saying goodbye to Mihn, we cleaned up our sleeping spot. Kameela told me to keep the sleeping bag and ground sheet, so I rolled them up and tied them onto the bottom of my backpack. Then we took off in different directions. Kameela took a faint path that led up the mountain. After a few minutes, she called out to us and we raced to her side. She'd found one of the small cedar bowls used last night by my host.

"I'd say your thief went that way," Kameela said, and pointed up the pathway. She took the lead, and the rest of us followed, as above the sky greyed over with clouds.

52

Nora ◎ Strange Territory

Day of the Pink Moon
Late Morning
Up the Steppes

WE TRACKED THE trail of the thief up the last steppe and into dense forest that covered this part of the mountain. The trail frequently disappeared and then reappeared several feet beyond. Who made a trail like that? It was almost as if someone were swinging through the trees then pushing off the ground and up into the air again like Tarzan. But the canopy of the forest was too dense and low to swing through and there were absolutely no vines. I would call for Mickey from time to time in case he'd come this way, too. I wasn't as worried about him, though, as I had been before. He'd proven he could take care of himself in the woods. And maybe that's where he preferred to be.

We had been silent for quite a while when Seth asked, "Who would want your father's ashes?"

"And why?" Kameela said.

I shrugged. I had no idea.

"It's more likely that the person is simply a thief and took everything they could get," Will said.

"That makes sense, but why feed me and keep me warm, then steal all my stuff?" I asked.

For a minute I wished the frog princess were around. She could do some scouting for me. But without the Pearl, I couldn't even get her attention.

We passed out of the soft morning sunlight into the giant shadow cast by the mountain. The trail had disappeared, but really there was only one way to go, and that was up; so up we went.

The climbing was tough, the slope slippery in places with shale shards.

We moved on together until we reached a rocky outcrop with paths going to the left and right.

"These paths are great for mountain goats," Seth said.

Will let out a goat bleat that made us all laugh.

"Why don't you and Seth take one path and Kameela and I can take the other?" Will said.

"I think we should stick together," I said.

"Okay. Then which way do we go?" Will said. "Right, left, or back down?"

I closed my eyes and waited. The path to the left tugged at me.

"I'm going to go this way," I said. "Wait here for a minute while I check out what's ahead."

"Whoa, whoa, let's go together," Seth said. He caught up to me and followed as the path narrowed and we had to face the rock wall and side shuffle along the path.

After a bit, Seth said, "I think we should turn back. This is way too dangerous." The tension in his voice grew. "And there's nothing to tell us this is the way your thief took."

"Just a little farther, Seth," I said, still being pulled in this direction.

He followed reluctantly and we continued until our friends, who were cheering us on, were out of sight. Then we came to a curve in the rock wall and heard our friends cry out.

"Kameela? Will?" Seth called out. And what he heard back sent panic coursing through my body.

"Seth, get back here, now," his father bellowed. The anger in his voice vibrated the air and sent a cascade of pebbles skittering down the mountainside.

Seth and I looked at each other, both of us shocked.

"I have to go back," Seth whispered.

"No, Seth. Come with me, please," I said, my fear for Seth's safety growing.

Seth inched his hand forward to cover mine. The warmth of his touch was comforting. But I couldn't let go of the rock face to return it. "I can't," Seth said. "He'll shout the mountain down and kill us both if I don't obey. I'm not going to let him hurt you. So keep on going. Find your things if you can, then hide. I'll come and find you. I promise."

Seth withdrew his hand and started back. I wanted to cry, but there was no time. I was so ready for this to be over and to get back to Gran, who must be frantic by now. Just a little farther. Maybe the thief would be just around the next curve. If not, I'd turn back and help Seth.

I moved forward as quickly as I could and rounded the curve in the path. Then I ran into a wall of mist.

I closed my eyes and focused on the feel of the rock, which was slippery. With each inch of progress, I paused and waited for the mountain to invite me to go further. My hands acted like magnets going to the right spot. My feet also felt the mountain encouraging me to move forward, while around me the mist swirled.

Then, as quickly as it had appeared, the mist was gone. I'd passed through it into the bright morning sun. The rock was dry. The path was wider and easier to navigate. But no sign of any of my stuff or the person who stole it. With a deep sigh, I let go of any hope of getting my things back. I had been crazy to have come even this far. And now my friends were risking their lives to protect mine.

I had to go back, to make sure he didn't hurt Seth and the others and deal with any venom he'd be spewing my way. It was the right thing to do. I couldn't let him take out his hatred of my family and me on his son and our friends. But when I tried to move back through the mist, I couldn't. There was a force like a bouncy mattress that kept me from moving through.

Without thinking, I called out to Seth, and all I got back was a shower of pebbles and a fierce ringing in my ears. What was going on? I tried again. No go.

As there was no going back because of whatever force was blocking me from returning to my friends, I had to go forward. And truthfully, I felt a tug in that direction.

So I took the broader path that spiraled up and around a curve for a short way. I scrambled up the last few feet of the path and up on an outcrop to survey the surroundings with the hope that I'd spot my stuff or the person who took it. One thing was for sure: I would have to find another way down.

Apparently, I had summited a peak because when I looked around me, I saw the path I was on continue down a steep and rocky slope that led to the oldest, most magnificent forest I'd ever seen. Was this the Nexus? I paused and drank in the place. No it was not.

The trees were huge, much taller than our modern redwoods and wider around than sequoias. I couldn't tell from here what species they were, but I was excited to tramp down the slope toward them.

When I got to the edge of the forest, I realized I'd totally forgotten about my immediate mission. Concern for Gran overwhelmed me for some moments, but the best I could do was complete my father's task and get back to her as quickly as possible.

Oh, I wish Dad was alive so he could see these magnificent trees, which remained a mystery to me even up close. They towered above me in such splendor that it took my breath away and brought tears to my eyes.

I picked one, ducked under the skirt of branches that brushed the ground, and walked to a trunk. I felt like an ant in the presence of a dinosaur. I took my backpack off and set it on the ground. It was slightly lighter because Dad's ashes were gone but bulkier to carry because of the attached sleeping bag. It felt good to be free of it for a moment. Then I leaned against the trunk of the tree and inhaled its splendor. It smelled like hope.

Looking up the trunk at the densely whorled branches that stretched above made my throat swell with emotion. I shut my eyes and tried to paint a picture in my mind of all this beauty so I'd always remember it.

My fingers traced the deep, wide grooves on the tree's massive trunk. The air hung heavy with a densely rich, cedar-like cinnamony smell. And I listened to the tree dance as a gentle breeze caressed every needle on every branch. It made a music all its own. When I listened harder to the tune, I realized it was harmonizing with the trees around it. Together, they were a beautiful symphony.

I turned and embraced the tree. I drank in its beauty and it drank in my sorrow, and for a few blissful moments, I simply was. I had no past, no future, only now. When I finally released my grip on the magnificent being and walked away, the rips and tears from all that had happened to me were soothed. My heart knew peace.

I thought of Kikko's mom, the kind Mrs. Hayashi who practiced the art of Sashiko, an embroidery style used to fix worn fabric. Like her needle repairing holes, the tree had repaired me. I felt mended. Once again, when life's hardships tore me down, Nature was there to renew me.

I picked up my backpack and as I walked away, my feet ploughed through the thick layer of forest duff that covered the ground. Before I left the protection of the tree, I silently asked if I could take some needles and a seed cone so I could identify the species later. I felt resistance, like the tree was saying no.

Respecting the tree's wishes, I moved back onto the faint path and followed it as it wound more downward into the forest. It was then I noticed a medley of bird song I didn't recognize and saw bursts of every color of the rainbow as birds I couldn't identify flitted through the canopy of the trees.

What a treasure trove of nature this place was—and I would keep it forever secret to protect its pristine state. But, oh, how I ached for my father to be here with me. If I had to let his ashes go, this would be the place I would choose. But it wasn't the Nexus, and I didn't have his ashes.

I left the tree behind and walked and walked, thinking that the forest would go on forever, when it ended just as abruptly as it had started.

The view in front of me was like yet another world—different from the forest I'd left behind, but of equal beauty. So pristine everything sparkled like it was new and untarnished. Every shade of green glimmered in golden light. It was like a painting where the brushstrokes had been painted by a divine hand. There was a stunning green glen with a crystal-clear stream meandering through it. This place felt like magic. Maybe *this* was the Nexus. I paused again, waiting for an answer from the place itself. And unfortunately, the answer again was no.

A soft, sunny light danced off the clusters of large dark-green sword ferns covering the glen's hills. And I'd never seen a prettier shade of shamrock green moss that covered the flat, squared rocks that lined the stream's bed and jutted up the creek's banks, like building blocks of various heights.

Looking for signs that the thief had come this way, I walked through a swath of waist-high sword ferns that cut across my blue jeans with a *sworsh, sworsh* sound.

When I got to the water, a stiff breeze ruffled my hair. I looked up to see puffs of ominous black clouds moving toward me. I shivered. Someone was going to get wet. Me. I leaned over to fill my water bottle when something surprising happened. Frogs wearing parachutes made from glistening threads (spider webs?) fell from the sky like rain, landing on the rocks and in the water, where their parachutes collapsed and fell away.

The frogs were all various colors, sizes, and shapes. Where had they come from, and why were they here? I looked all around. I'd heard that sometimes frogs did rain from the sky—but I'd never heard of them parachuting. Could these frogs have anything to do with Linka?

And still they fell, even as the sky darkened. The menacing clouds that had only moments ago been on the horizon were now directly above, coming together in the shape of a ring, almost as if there were a purpose to their movement. The closer the puffs got to each other, the lower they dropped toward the ground. The barometric pressure dropped, too, until my temples pounded.

When the clouds had all joined to form a circle, more frogs, bigger frogs, flew out of the cloud, riding large leaves with a thick layer of black cloud under each one. These were the same frogs who had attacked me back on the mountain.

Okay. What were *they* doing here? The bigger flying frogs instantly answered my question as they attacked the smaller parachuting ones. Some of the flyers swooped in and swallowed the wee frogs in their mighty mouths. Others used a sword-like weapon to cut the threads of the delicate parachutes mid-air, sending the smaller frogs crashing to the ground.

I ran down the hill to the creek, wishing I had my catcher's mitt. I stuck my hand out and caught a cute little leopard frog and then a huge yellow frog that almost broke my hand. Unlike the other falling frogs, he was sitting on a platform of sticks, which broke into pieces when it hit the ground.

I gathered up the bottom of my shirt and used it like a sack to hold all the frogs I caught. And when that was full, I tucked frogs into the crook of my left arm. I tried my best, but there was no way to be everywhere—the rocks, higher on the hill, the shallow parts of the stream—at the same time. I hoped that those that fell in the middle of the stream would have deeper water to cushion their fall, but the splat factor might still kill them or knock them unconscious, leaving them to drown.

It was chaos. It was bedlam. It was a frog-killing hell.

When I reached the banks of the creek, I put down my shirt full of frogs and coaxed them into the water, where I hoped they'd be safe. As I bent over, I came eye to eye with the corpse of a little green tree frog. What a loss. What a shame.

That task done, I stood up and saw that the frog falling had stopped and the big flying frogs were circling at the other end of the glen. One by one, they broke out of the circle and headed down the length of the creek toward me. Their plan was obvious. Kill as many little frogs as possible. But how were they going to do more damage now that the little frogs were on the ground?

It took two seconds to figure it out as they flew a strafing run, dropping stones the size of jawbreakers on the frogs below like deadly hail.

I had an idea of how to stop them and ran to get my sleeping bag.

As I loped up the hill then down again, I wondered how it was that I could see all that was happening before me without the Pearl. Had its power seeped into my bones so deeply I didn't need it anymore? Or was it this place?

Ever since I passed through that funny, bouncy mist, it was like I'd entered a different dimension or time—a magical place where giant trees grew and frogs flew through the sky. In all ways that count, I didn't really care what the answer was at this moment. There were too many frogs to save.

When the flying frogs reappeared, I was ready. Which was good because they looked just as ready as me. Not only were their little black cloud flying platforms thicker, like they'd been refueled from the bigger cloud, but the sacks where they kept their ammunition were bulging too.

Who knew frogs could be so diabolical?

Well, I could be just as diabolical as they were. I found a long branch and used it to create a flag by sticking it into the sleeping bag. I stood on a high rock at about the same level they'd flown the last time. When the flying frogs came barreling down over the stream just before they got to where I was standing, I dropped the flag down like a parking lot gate and stopped them in flight.

It was a terrible pile-up as one after another crashed into the sleeping bag and fell into the water.

I had managed to stop them all with my unexpected play. Except one.

A much smaller frog, with a black spot covering one eye, came flying straight for me and poked my hand with something sharp, which made me drop the sleeping bag. But I managed to stomp a foot on the bag to keep it from falling into the water.

When I looked for the frog, he was gone, and I was left with a puncture wound on my hand. I thought the worst was over, but then more flying frogs arrived. This group was riding on purple martins. Were they friend or foe? This frog-fighting stuff was about to get even more real. I picked up my sleeping bag and prepared to defend my life.

53

Azzie Enemy? Friend?

Day of the Pink Moon
Warming Time (Late)
The Gathering Glen, Inside the Veil of Mist

AZZIE, HIS FLYCAPE rippling in the wind, circled the Gathering Glen with Frago and his FAFA behind him. He was still contemplating the return message he had received from Linka yesterday and could hear his cousin's voice as he reviewed it in his head.

"Cousin," she had said, "I am alarmed by much that I see in the world beyond the Veil. And yet, I cannot bring myself, no matter the stakes, to betray your mother, our queen. My orders were to recover the Pearl and destroy the girl. I cannot in good conscience do otherwise, although I see the wisdom in your words. I, too, hope that from this day forth, we can behave more as family members should. Your Cousin, Linka."

He had been disappointed, of course, deeply so, but he had tried and would keep trying if the opportunity presented itself to proceed with a real Ceremony of Renewal. Time was running short, however. The Pink Moon would be at its fullest tonight.

And, as usual, he was already late to receive his mother's guests. Among the many council members were frogs that Azzie considered true friends, and he would be happy to see them. He was hoping his mother wouldn't shame him in front of her council by announcing her change of heart as to who would succeed her. He needed time to recover from recent blows to his confidence before suffering the biggest one of all.

Cook had prepared a sylvan feast for the council members so they could regain their strength before traveling on to the Palay on the backs of a cadre of birds who had volunteered for the mission.

The Veil of Mist had been opened by a Royal Decree from his mother earlier in the day to admit her council guests—as previously agreed upon by Aquatessa and Bortos, who both held dominion over the Veil. Once all her guests were accounted for, Azzie was to close it. But first he had to make sure that all had safely arrived.

Something that looked the opposite of "safely arrived" was happening below.

There was a largetoe standing on the bank of the creek. A largetoe! There shouldn't *be* a largetoe behind the Veil of Mist. How had she even gotten there? And then he saw something that knotted his stomach tighter: Bulldoggies. They didn't belong behind the Veil either. How could it have happened?

Nausea twisted his stomach when he realized that it was *his* fault. He forgotten to close the opening to the Veil of Mist. That would make this debacle his responsibility. His mother would have his hide. But more importantly, friends had died because of his carelessness. It was an unforgiveable error. Oh, why was his memory like cottonwood fluff in the wind?

Descending closer to the ground, Azzie recoiled at the sight of the lifeless bodies of his brethren scattered in and around the stream. Not only was there a femtoe standing in the middle of the water, it seemed to be attacking the frogs burfing around her.

He motioned Frago and the others to follow. The closer he got to the largetoe, the higher his breakfast of raspberry stuffed with minced mosquito larvae (served on a bed of watercress) rose in his throat. She bore a strange resemblance to the flower-covered statue that had been at the faux Ceremony of Renewal. But then maybe all femtoes were that . . . interesting.

Judging from the carnage below, the viciousness of the largetoe demeanor had not been exaggerated.

Azzie gave the attack sign, indicating the femtoe as the target, and directed his new mount, Trill, further downward. But Trill didn't respond. Frago and his mount appeared at his side.

"Might I suggest a second look, Your Highness?"

Azzie's throat tightened in anger. Who was Frago to countermand his orders—again?

Still, Frago had been right in the past. Suddenly, Azzie regretted a lifetime of rejecting the leadership lessons his mother had tried to gift him. If only he had paid more attention. If only he had been heroic enough in his true nature to care the way Frago obviously cared, he might not need to be coddled into doing the right thing.

With the dead and injured council members, a femtoe, and Bulldoggies loose behind the Veil of Mist destroying perfection, this was shaping up to be a catastrophic debacle far worse than the faux Ceremony of Renewal. He had to save every frog he could save and defeat every Bulldoggie, or they would return to the Maw and report on the weaknesses of his mother's queen-dom.

"Airtilliers away!" Azzie cried, and he urged Trill to plunge toward the ground. Frago and his corps followed.

54

Nora ◎ Good Samaritan, Bad Idea.

Day of the Pink Moon
Late Morning
The Gathering Glen, Inside the Veil of Mist

THE FLOCK OF purple martins shot down from the sky and banked a wide circle around me. They were flying so fast I got dizzy trying to follow them.

Apparently, I wasn't as much of a threat as the leaf-on-cloud flying frogs because the bird riders abandoned me and took off to do battle with them. I watched for a moment as they sparred in the sky.

The black cloud the bigger frogs used for refueling had dissipated so much that they couldn't replenish their flying power, and several of them dive-bombed into the surrounding rocks below. Good riddance. I had the feeling it was time to make my exit, especially when I saw some of the birds land so that the frogs on their backs could tend to the injured and dying.

The sun was almost overhead, which meant it was practically noon, and I was still no closer to finding my father's ashes. It didn't matter. I was going home. *Dad*, I said silently, *I've tried my best, but Gran needs me more.* Maybe if I walked along the ridge, I could find another way down. I headed up the hill to survey the area. I would choose a destination from there.

I'd reached the sword fern–covered hillside when I heard a twig snap. A shadow fell across my path and a deathly chill ran through me. There, standing not six feet away, was a man with murder in his eyes: Kincade.

"I've been trying to find you since yesterday. You can thank your little boyfriend—that worthless son of mine—for helping me find you."

His words stabbed me like a knife—Seth?

"You're lying. Seth would never . . ."

"Doesn't really matter now," Kincade said with a sneer. "There's only one way to bring this all to an end."

I was frozen with terror. I knew exactly what was about to happen. I was going to die. But I wasn't going to die until I spoke my truth and defended his son.

"You want to hurt me, and I can't stop you. But you could stop yourself. You want me to believe that it's Seth's fault that you found me. Even if that's true, which I doubt, it doesn't matter. You're the one doing the evil here, not Seth. And for what? A piece of land? A burned down house? Generations of resentment at what the Kincades don't have? Go ahead and do it. But it's all on you. Nobody else. You have a magnitude of hate when you could have chosen a magnitude of love."

There was something truly evil in Kincade's eyes, a shadow so deep and so dark I knew there was no hope for him or for me.

And then he said something I couldn't hear clearly because of the pounding in my ears. Something snarky about target practice.

Kincade stuck his hand into his jacket pocket, pulled out his revolver, and shot me. The shot hit me like a freight train and tore through my chest. I collapsed on the ground. The last thing I felt was the warmth of my own blood as it spurted out the bullet hole.

Azzie 🐸 Save Our Saver

Day of the Pink Moon
Warming Time (Late)
The Gathering Glen, Inside the Veil of Mist

AZZIE HELPED GATHER the wounded and tried to ignore the crushing grief of losing so many friends when he heard the loudest noise he had ever heard in his life. It sounded like a crack of thunder, and it thankfully scattered the enemy flock above. It was not thunder, though, because the sky above was clear and blue and free of the flying, murdering fiends who had attacked his friends.

Then the earth shook as it absorbed the shock of some great object falling. A tree somewhere close? But there was something not quite right about that guess either. He shoved the thought from his mind. There was simply too much to do.

Council members who could still move hid. Those who were unable to move because of their injuries cowered in fear.

"Come out, come out!" Azzie called. "There are many here who need your help. We cannot let a falling tree deter us from tending to the wounded."

The hiding frogs emerged. "Your Highness," one said, "I do not think that was a tree."

Azzie hardly heard the comment. His attention was riveted on his friends.

Lord Shaba, dead.

Lady Ranocchia, dead.

Lord Oscarfroskur, dead.

His mother would be devastated. Others on the council would be devastated. He was devastated.

In addition to the dead, there were those who were wounded—some badly. Their moans and cries of pain were breaking Azzie's heart. He must bring them relief, now. But what could he do?

He called Frago over. "Is there an earth healer among you?"

"I have some skills in that area. I have already sent one of my frogs to gather the leaves of the balsam poplar, bark of the willow, and beeswax. I will prepare a soothing poultice to start the healing process where possible," Frago said, bowing his head in deference.

A feeling of jealousy crept into Azzie's heart. Was there anything Frago couldn't do? Earth healers, who used the bounty of nature to heal the mind, spirit, and body, were rare as hair among frogs, unlike dream healers.

Water healers healed relationships. Air healers healed the mind and heart. Fire healers instilled or regulated passions. Healers of these types could restore well-being across all species, including their own. The only power frogs could not use for themselves was dream power. Some suspected it was the sacrifice required by the Well of White Light for the granting of their many other gifts.

Enough. Azzie declared to himself. He would whine no more about anything, especially someone else's greater skill set. If he were going to learn to be a true and just ruler, which he was now more determined than ever to be, despite his mother's decision that he would never rule, he would try to earn the privilege back—without envy. His subjects were more important than his frayed sense of self-worth. They came first, especially in this dire situation where so many had been harmed.

Future king or not, the welfare of his friends still mattered. Some might recover. Some wouldn't. Such a staggering loss.

One thing they needed immediately was transport back to the Palay—but how would they get all the surviving and the wounded frogs there? Given their state of trauma, burfing was unthinkable.

He couldn't and wouldn't rely on his mother or Frago to solve this problem. And he needed for his own pride, and of course for the sake of those in need, to come up with the answer quickly.

He paused before Gindjurra the Magnifico, who looked stunned but otherwise unhurt. "You all right, Ginny?'

The large yellow toad nodded.

"May that grotesque femtoe who tried to kill you churn forever in the Maw," Azzie cursed.

"It was not the femtoe. It was the Bulldoggies and their putt-putt burfing leaves. They snipped off my chute." Ginny struggled to get the words out. "I would be frog mush if it were not for that femtoe. She caught me and saved my life."

"She caught you?" *A largetoe ally! Was this the same girl Linka had been sent to kill? Had the forces of the All conspired to bring her here?* It seemed unlikely, and yet his cold blood thrilled at the thought.

"Naturally she assumed I was a water-loving frog and brought me safely—although not gracefully—to the stream. If you could get me back to the Palay, Your Highness, where I could burrow into some lovely loose dirt, I will be fine."

"Hang on, friend. We will get you there."

Azzie moved through the crowd of injured, who were being gathered into one spot by Frago's airtilliers, and those frogs who had survived the fracas. From everyone he talked to, he got the same story: The largetoe had been helping them. She had caught and saved many falling frogs and tried to get others, who were so stunned they were paralyzed, to safety.

Azzie closed his eyes and sent a silent plea to the creatures of four legs and fur.

> *Friends of the Forest hear my plea*
> *We have an urgent request for thee.*
> *With wounded and dying we must go*
> *To the Palay immediately, where healing flows.*
> *The Veil of Mist will let you pass,*
> *So come now, please, and make it fast.*

He knew that in making such a request he was inviting criticism from some of the injured who would not like being carried by creatures whose bodies were warm. But hopefully getting back to the help and safety of the Palay would temper their complaints.

Azzie jumped up to a high rock on the banks of the stream to address the wounded and shaken. But first he'd have to reopen the Veil of Mist so the animals he had summoned could enter.

"Ochi, ochi, all. I have summoned help. Creatures of four legs and fur are on their way to transport the wounded to the Palay. Commander Frago, create groups by size and injury. The smallest, most critically wounded frogs will be transported by you and your airtilliers immediately. I will stay to supervise the loading of the wounded, respectfully dispatch the dead, and then meet you back at the Palay. Hurry now. We must be sure that all who can be saved are saved."

Frago nodded and immediately commanded his airtilliers to carry out Azzie's orders.

Azzie jumped down and returned to helping with the wounded. Frago approached him with an acorn cap filled with a greenish-yellow paste.

"Your Highness, here is the poultice I concocted. Place it on open wounds. For broken limbs, we have some twigs and twined ivy vines to hold them in place."

Azzie accepted the mixture. "Thank you, Frago. Now, please take the most wounded and go straight to the Palay."

"Your Highness, it is most unwise for you to be left without someone to assist you with these tasks."

"I thank you and understand your concern. Now go."

Frago tried to speak again, but Azzie commanded silence. Frago withdrew.

Azzie bustled about applying balm and setting broken limbs. When the last frog he could help had been attended to, he looked up and saw Frago and his airtilliers taking flight, their mounts carrying as many of the severely wounded as they could strap to the bodies of their birds. But there were still dozens of them left.

"May the Well of White Light protect you," Azzie whispered, watching until they were out of sight.

When he looked down, he saw a bear sitting on the bank of the stream, with marmots, foxes, weasels, a coyote family with three young, and a pack of pikas lined up on either side—and more.

"We are here in answer to your call, Your Highness," the bear said.

"We are honored by your presence. Thank you all. We have many injured to carry back to the Palay, so please take as many as you can carry," Azzie said.

The animals loaded up with as many frogs as they could hold.

The pikas, led by their matriarch, Pym, were the most helpful of all. Because of their small size and relatively great strength, they were able to ferry smaller frogs onto the bodies of the larger animals. They all helped each other load the injured onto backs, shoulders, and even heads.

"Do you wish me to carry the wounded largetoe?" asked the bear.

"Wounded largetoe?"

"Yes, the one who lies among the ferns. The one who once carried the Golden Pearl of the Forest—although now it is gone."

Azzie was dizzy with confusion. It *was* Linka's largetoe.

"Show me," he said.

The bear extended his arm, and Azzie, along with several other curious frogs, hopped on.

Ginny insisted on accompanying them, even though he was hardly fit to do so. The bear offered his upturned paw as a travel perch.

"Thank you," Ginny said and heaved his large body into the bear's palm.

Azzie and the other frogs traveled up the length of the bear's long arm and came to rest on his shoulders.

The bear ambled up the bank of the stream with his passengers. He was followed by the other mammals and their riders.

Then they all made their way partially up the fern-covered hill until he came to the body of a femtoe.

How strange this giant looked lying among the ferns.

"Is she dead?" asked one of the frogs.

"Poor thing," said Ginny. "She saved my life."

"She is not dead," said the bear, "but she soon will be. One of her own kind wounded her."

"Was that the loud sound we heard?" Azzie asked.

"Yes. He used a weapon made from unearthly things," the bear said.

"And the shaking of the earth—that was her body falling," Azzie said. It was not a question. How often, he wondered, did he misinterpret events out of ignorance or lack of concern? What he thought was a fatal crack in the trunk of a dead tree was really some largetoe killing device.

"Her enemy has left, but who knows if he will return," the bear said.

"My apologies. I should have listened more carefully," Azzie replied. "I have never seen a real largetoe before, and the shock of the experience rendered me rude. Forgive me please."

The bear nodded curtly, perhaps still a bit hurt that Azzie had not paid closer attention to what he had said in the first place.

"We must give this largetoe a frog healing," Azzie said, barely believing that he was uttering those words. If this was Linka's largetoe, they might still go through with their plan. But dead, she would be good to no one.

"You must direct us, Prince. Your grand master chorale skills will be required to get the job done," Ginny said.

The forest creatures placed the frogs they carried onto the largetoe's body and then drew back as the frogs who could still move on their own scrambled to join the others. Azzie moved onto her forehead and lifted his arms to direct the frogs in the chant of an ancient healing song. The larger frogs began first. Their deeper voices laid down a rhythmic beat that tapped into the healing energy of the earth: dark, rich dirt layered with red clay and yellow sand. And as they sang, healing mycelium to match the colors of the frequency of this layer of healing energy rose dancing from the ground and twisted themselves around the largetoe's body pulsating with healing vibrations.

Then the medium-sized frogs added a melody that summoned lifeforce from the surrounding forest, drawing in effervescent green particles that appeared out of thin air and danced above the girl.

The frog chorus broke into a three-part harmony as the smallest among them added a sprightly counterpoint, drawing bright white energy from the heavens, infusing the girl with an all-over glow.

Azzie conducted the frogs, his body swaying expressively to the sound. He rose on his legs as the music crescendoed. His expressive hands dipped and swept the air and pointed at notes as they rose, as if he could see their physical embodiment. In those moments, not only did the singers live, but the song lived, too. And the conversion of these forces wove itself into a warp and weft of golden light that hovered right on top of the prone body.

Azzie teased the air with the tips of his fingers, touching to hold the last note of their song as these golden threads of energy wrapped themselves around her.

He ended the singing with a swift motion of both hands and settled back on his legs, arms resting at his side.

The singing was done. But the healing continued: The girl's body seemed to drink in the energy like water, absorbing the golden warp and weft into her bones. Would it be enough to reinvigorate the lifeforce of this fallen giant? Azzie, deeply moved by the power of the chorus, found himself hoping that it was.

Then a thought nagged at him. The Veil. He breathed a sigh of relief that he had finally remembered, then bid the Veil to close.

56

Nora ◎ Back from the Dead

Day of the Pink Moon
Warming Time (Late)
The Gathering Glen, Inside the Veil of Mist

I DON'T KNOW HOW I knew I was dying, but I did. It's not like I saw a white light at the end of a long tunnel or heard angels calling my name. I listened for Dad's voice calling me from beyond as my lifeblood poured out through the hole in my chest, puddled on the earth, then sank into the darkness. But I heard nothing.

Had Dad suffered like this before he died? Maybe we'd be able to compare notes before long. A tear trickled out of my left eye, ran down the side of my face, and pooled in the opening to my ear. It itched like crazy, but I couldn't move to scratch it.

The itch faded. Everything faded. There was nothing more. No more pain, no more cold, no more regret. Death—one big dark bubble of nothing—forever and ever. Amen.

Then I heard the most beautiful, delicate sounds, a choir of voices both strange and intriguing. Each note of the complex melody seemed to send out a lifeline of light that hooked into my spirit and stopped me from falling so far into dark nothingness that I'd never be able to crawl back up.

Slowly I rose out of the darkness using the lines of harmonic singing like rungs of a ladder.

As darkness became light, vibrating weights pressed down on me, sending waves of energy to every cell.

Then, a tunnel of red-hot pain flared in my chest. I wanted to force my hand through my ribs to rip the pain out at its source. What had happened? What was causing that pain? I couldn't remember a thing.

Then the pain subsided, and once more weights shifted on my skin. Again, the beautiful song seeped into my ears, my skin, my bones with vibrating highs and lows, harmonic thrills and chills. It was the song that saved my life.

It seemed as if a heavy blanket was covering my body, including my torso and legs—but the blanket wiggled. I lifted my head and came eye to eye with the big yellow frog I'd rescued earlier. And he wasn't alone. There were frogs crawling all over me. Spots of bright color everywhere. I sat up, and the frogs on my chest fell into my lap. Had it been the frogs singing to me—singing me back to life?

My head pounded. I was dizzy. My throat was dry. My chest hurt. I was covered in frogs and blood—cold, wet, cakey blood. So much blood.

And the blood was mine.

How had I survived? I unbuttoned my shirt and looked at my chest. There was a massive black-and-blue mark over my heart.

Then I remembered. Kincade shot me and left me to die. And now I was alive, with little evidence I'd even been shot except for the blood that stained my clothing and a deep bruise over my heart. I was mystified but grateful. The frogs had sung me back to life.

The frogs slowly moved away from me, and the next thing I knew, they were on the backs of the animals that formed a semicircle around me. Bear, marmot, fox, coyote—they carried many frogs. Even a cute little pika had a tiny yellow frog on its back. This should have shocked me, but after all I had gone through, nothing would ever shock me again.

"Thank you," I called out with a feeble wave. But did they understand or even hear my words of gratitude?

A sudden mist appeared and swallowed the creatures up. When it cleared, they were gone.

I struggled to my feet. Where was my backpack? I stumbled through the ferns and found my stuff spread all over once again. The straps were slashed, the canvas soaked with my blood. It was empty.

Memories exploded in my mind like old-fashioned flashbulbs. The frogs: fighting, flying, dying. Being shot. And then the wonderful frogs with their vibrations. It all ran in a loop through my brain.

By the time I had collected everything I could easily spot, I needed a drink of water. I made it to the creek and, moving upstream from where the fighting had been, filled my water bottle.

I took off my shoes and stuck my feet in. Ahh. Relief. I sat on a rock and drank.

I heard splashing—not rub-a-dub-dub fun-in-the-tub splashing, but a more frantic "I'm drowning" kind. I looked along the creek bank and saw two frogs locked in a death hold fighting for their lives.

57

Azzie 🐸 Till Death Do Us Part

Day of the Pink Moon
Warming Time (Late)
The Gathering Glen, Inside the Veil of Mist

*A*FTER THEIR DEBT of gratitude had been paid to the large-toe, everyone departed for the Palay as Azzie commanded. He neatly folded his flycape, left it on a rock, and went about the sad task of launching the bodies of the dead down the creek in one of the time-honored funeral traditions of the frog world. Azzie rolled each body in a big maple leaf and wrapped it with vine and flowers Frago had collected before he left. Then, he gently rolled each body into the swift current with the ritual words, "Water to water, into the Great Pond Beyond."

It had taken more time than he would have liked, but there was only one more beloved council member to lay to rest. Azzie released the body of Lord Oscarfroskur into the water, and seconds later he was viciously attacked from behind by an unseen foe who put him into a choke hold. Unable to expand his throat to speak, he had no way of asking why he was being killed. It would only be a moment until he passed out.

Pinned to the ground by his unseen enemy, Azzie couldn't use his powerful back legs. His arms thrashed in the air. Resistance was futile. The more he struggled, the weaker he got and the stronger his opponent seemed to become. It was almost like Azzie's strength was being directly absorbed by the frog who was trying to kill him.

Azzie had one choice. Give up. Surrender. Let go. It was an ancient frog fighting technique taught to him by the Grand and Glorious Vizzard. The trick was to convince your opponent that you were dying bit by bit, then wait until the right moment to spring back to life and overcome the enemy. So, after Azzie struggled a bit, he went limp. Then he waited and waited, willing himself not to panic, realizing that there were two types of fear: imagined and real. Surely this type was real. With a burst of energy, he fought as hard as he could for a moment, then went as floppy as a dead worm.

He held his breath for as long as he could and then slowly released it through his skin. Soon his lungs would be empty and still the assassin did not release him. Instead, he was being dragged over rocks, then sand.

Azzie willed himself not to yelp from the pain of having his belly scraped raw. He managed to gasp a few shallow breaths as his aggressor pulled him forward.

Azzie saw what was coming next. It was the creek. His opponent was dragging him into the creek to drown him. It was like a bolt of lightning had struck Azzie. Every nerve was on fire with fear. He kicked his powerful back legs to flip his attacker on his back. But his opponent's weight and momentum were too great to overcome.

Panic surged through him. His worst nightmare was about to come true. The attacker hurled Azzie and himself into the water from a high spot on the bank, and they landed with a splash.

Oh, Great All, send me the strength I need to defeat the one who would have me dead.

And like that, his strength surged. With a powerful kick and twist, Azzie managed to roll over, pinning the mystery frog beneath the water. His success did not last long—the other frog quickly reversed their positions. Locked in the fierce embrace of a faceless opponent who was on top of him, still gripping his throat from behind, Azzie's face was forced under the water. Water seeped into his mouth, down into his throat, into his lungs. If he couldn't stop his lungs from filling with water, he would drown.

Azzie gave one last attempt to free himself, but it was futile. He was too weak and had no air. This time he went limp for a reason. He would soon be dead.

His last conscious thought was of the irony of it all. There was a reason he was afraid of water. It had been trying to steal his life from him since birth. In the end, water would win. It always did. His lifelong fear of it had been warranted. It was how he had entered the world, and it was how he would depart from it.

58

Nora ◎ To the Rescue

Day of the Pink Moon
Late Morning
The Gathering Glen, Inside the Veil of Mist

I WATCHED AS ONE frog dragged the other into the creek and held him underwater. The captive frog thrashed, then went limp.

I took a few giant steps, plunged in, and plucked them out of the water. The bigger frog flipped around with a mid-air twist and began to devour the other one, right there in my hands.

"Hey. Cut that out." The frog didn't pay any attention to me. I sank to my knees. With one hand, I managed to pinch the attacker on both sides of his jaw and pop it open. Then I pulled the victim's leg out.

I tossed the attacker into the water and picked up the other frog. His body felt cold—but then, he was a cold-blooded amphibian, so what did I expect? I rubbed his belly with my thumbs. Nothing.

I held his little body up to my cheek, but I couldn't feel any air coming out. I must have been desperate to help him because what I did next was plain weird (and I *don't* recommend it to anyone). I put the frog up to my lips, blocked off his nasal passages, and blew into his mouth—very gently. Nothing happened. I pumped his chest with my thumb. Still nothing. I blew again. Pumped. Blew. Pumped. Blew. Nothing.

Suddenly, the frog drew a croaky breath and opened his eyes. He looked at me and blinked. Then he drew in his limbs, flipped over, and jumped off my hand. The leg that had almost been devoured seemed to drag a little.

"You're welcome," I said, and watched as he recovered more fully and with a healthy leap, hopped away. I got up, washed off my hands and mouth, and was ready to go when the frog I rescued picked up a twig, leapt onto the back of the frog who had attacked him, and plunged his weapon into the back of the frog's head.

That was it for me. Nature was too rough. Time to get out of here. I climbed up the bank of the creek and stood up. Breathless. Stomach cramped. Black spots before my eyes. I looked at the rocks below. Boulders with sharp edges. Do not faint. Do not fall.

Do . . . not . . .

59

The Queen — Worse to Worser

Day of the Pink Moon
Fly Time (Late)
The Palay, Fern Grotto

HE QUEEN BROKE the water's surface with a sense of urgency
flowing through her veins. If she didn't hurry, she would be
late to her own council meeting. But it was hard to tear herself
away from the tranquility of Fern Grotto.

Floating on her back, she gazed around her at the ancient
ferns growing up the walls and hanging down from the top of
the grotto. Lovely, luscious ferns. Tickly ferns. She giggled as
she swam under a patch of them along the grotto wall, their tips
dragging along her great belly.

The grotto was another of the queen's private escapes peppered
about the Palay. Ask any frog for directions there, and you would
receive no answer because no one knew of its existence outside
the queen and her confidants. Of the few who did know of

its location, none of them would ever break the strict rules of privacy.

That is why when the queen saw Simeon creep into her space, she knew: *Something is terribly, terribly wrong.* Ranya fought against the urge to sink back down and stay underwater forever. Her heart fluttered in her chest like the wings of her beloved hummingbirds who were no longer with her. She had lost so much. And was certain she was about to learn she had lost more.

"Say it, Simeon. Just say it." She could barely whisper.

"There is news of the most terrible nature, Your Majesty . . . the Bulldoggies . . . Prince Azzumundo . . . all dead," Simeon could not go on.

"Calm yourself, Simeon. Calm yourself. Then tell me every-thing, although I do not want to hear one word of it."

60

Nora ◎ Down Under

Day of the Pink Moon
Late Afternoon
The Creature's Lair

WHERE WAS I? The room was dark. Strange smells came from everywhere. I drifted in and out of awareness. There was singing. Different this time. One voice. Unfamiliar. A gentle touch on my forehead. That song. What was it? That touch. Whose?

I had a splitting headache and what felt like a hole in my chest. When I felt it, I realized it *was,* or had been, the hole in my chest that Kincade had put there and the singing frogs had healed. There was already, miraculously, a scar. I couldn't see it, but I could feel it and it felt like a swirl.

And oh, how it hurt, and not just physically. It felt like Kincade had shot a big dark hole in my soul as well. I had always trusted that things, no matter how bad they got, would eventually work out for the best in the end. But getting shot had changed that. The blanket that covered me seemed weighed down with despair. I wanted to pull it over my head and die in my sleep.

But that seemed unfair to those frogs who had saved me. The frogs had worked so hard to conjure that song, the healing energy it pulled into me. And it also seemed unfair to Gran. She had lost everything. Her son. Her house. Her health. Losing me would be the end for her. And my friends would miss me as well.

Do you miss the ones you love when you're dead? I didn't know, but I decided it was probably best to wait a few decades to find out.

But really, where was I? Who brought me here? At least the air was warm, thanks to the open fire that blazed against the curve of the round room. But the firelight only went so far. There remained a ring of shadows at the edge of the space that hid any clues as to where I was.

A mixture of smells piled into my nostrils. *Cedar*—both the full smell of the green leaves I had been sleeping on and the throat pinch of its smoke. *Damp earth. Rotting wood. Mint. Oregano. Dried berries. And the scent of wild animal.* And dog? It smelled like no place I had ever been, but not in a bad way. Simply different.

Tree roots formed a canopy over my head. Tied to them, and dangling down, were bundles of herbs, branches with drying berries, and bouquets of long-stalked dried flowers. I was underground, lying on a nest of cedar boughs. There was another smaller bed of cedar beside mine and stuck to the cedar leaves were strands of animal fur. I teased a tuft of the fur off the brand and examined it, rolling it in my fingers and giving it a sniff. This was Mickey's fur. I was sure of it. I had brushed him almost every day of our life together, cleaned it off his bed and my clothes. Is this where he'd been? I shook my head confused and pulled the threadbare quilt covering me up to my chin. It took a bit to pull the name of its pattern into my muddled mind. Wedding ring. My parents once had a quilt like that. Gran had made it for them when they got married.

Cloth dragged across the earth with a halting slither. I had heard that sound before. It was the sound of both savior and thief. As my eyes adjusted to the firelight, I saw it. Her? Him? They? I still couldn't tell by appearance, voice, or manner. Whoever, or whatever, it was moved around the dark circumference of the room, settling in a place that put the greatest distance between us and the arc of firelight. Only its tattered cloak stuck out into the soft yellow light. I stared at the rough cloth. It also looked familiar.

"It *was* you," I said, sitting up. "At the church—with the note and the pond flowers. And the sorted junk. It *was* you at my mother's grave. And it was you last night in the meadow. It was you who stole my stuff."

"Yes. It's true."

"That's why Mickey didn't bark when you stole everything. He knew you."

"Yes. We are friends and he comes and goes here as he pleases."

Part of me felt relieved that Mickey had somewhere to come on his roamings, so I didn't argue about that. But then my host said, "Those things you claim as yours? I am keeping them. They are the price for the help I gave you before in the meadow where you cried. And for the help I give you now."

It sounded like it was speaking through bubbling water.

"But those things are mine. They're all I have," I said in a whisper, tears rising.

"Are they? Are they really yours?"

There was no meanness in the question—simply pointed curiosity.

I laid down and drew the quilt back up to my neck and rested a moment before I said, "If they don't belong to me, then why do they belong to you?"

"They belong to no one. I can keep them safe. Safer than you ever could."

"Safe from what?"

"Your ignorance."

"Ouch. That's a little harsh. You don't even know me."

"I am only being honest. You are dealing with forces here that you could not, at your green age, have any idea of how to cope with. The Pearl will only bring you ruin. As beautiful as it is—as tempting as it is to own—it is not yours. It belongs to another world."

"I don't want to use it."

"Then it will use you."

"It belonged to my mother," I said.

"It belongs to no one."

"If it didn't belong to her, how did she get it?" I wanted to know.

"As stories go, she stole it."

"My mother never stole anything. She was the kindest, most honest person in the world."

The creature coughed. It sounded like a punctured garden hose. "I knew her in another life. I wasn't always as you see me."

"You? Knew my mom?"

"Yes, Nora. I knew her well."

A cavernous space opened inside my already aching chest, and I longed to fill it with details about my mother. I didn't care where I was or whom I was talking to. This creature knew my mom. And through the creature, maybe I could get to know her better. Then I remembered. My mother hadn't died. She had left. She didn't care enough to stick around to know me. Why should I . . .

"You know my name. What's yours?" I asked.

"Some call me the Watcher," it said.

Watcher? I got a funny feeling in my gut. Could this person be my ghost in the forest?

"What do you watch?"

It shrugged. "The world as it crumbles."

"How well did you know my mom? Can you tell me about her?" I asked quietly, trying to sound casual. Like I almost didn't care.

"She was a woman, like any other. At least that's all she ever wanted to be, but it doesn't matter now."

"It does to me. Please, won't you tell me one thing?"

"She liked tulips."

"Yellow and blue ones," I said, remembering the flowers embroidered on the buckskin pouch.

"Yes."

"Were those her favorite colors?"

"She liked more colors than I could say."

It seemed hard for my host to talk. And there was loneliness in its voice. I stopped asking questions for a moment. Then, I couldn't help myself.

"What made you leave your home to live up here?" I asked, assuming my host must have once lived in town if she had known Mom.

"That is in the past. No point discussing. You are welcome to stay here for the night. There is food beside you. Now eat. And drink the tonic in the cup by the food. Your body has been through much. Then sleep. In the morning, you must go. And never come back."

I drank the tonic first, wiping my mouth with the back of my hand to catch the dribbles. Then I pounced on the food, the same fare from last night's feast. As I ate, I vowed to myself that I wouldn't let these little kindnesses distract me. I *would* get my things back. My things could be hidden in the shadows of the room. Somehow, I had to distract my host so I could look. "Couldn't you come out into the light so I can see you? It's hard talking to a shadow," I said.

"People talk to shadows all the time."

"What will you do with the Pearl?"

"There is nothing you need to know about the Pearl, except that in your hands, it is a dangerous thing."

"What do you mean?" I asked.

"It is not for you to know."

I swallowed a burst of anger. My host seemed way too bossy to me, but I would, as I was taught by my parents, be polite. At least for the moment. But there were still things I *had* to know. "And why do you want the box?"

"Why shouldn't I want a thing of beauty for myself?"

"It's not just a box. It contains my father's ashes," I said.

"Yes, I know. Last night—I heard you talk to him."

My face grew red. "That wasn't nice. To eavesdrop like that."

"I grow lonely living in the forest with only other injured creatures like myself for company," my host said.

"Injured creatures?" I asked.

She pointed beyond the curtain. "I have a special hospital-like room I've set up beyond where you can see. I do what I can to save those who couldn't survive without intervention. I will show you tomorrow before you leave."

"You still haven't answered my question. Why do you want my father's ashes?"

"And my answer is, I don't. I want the box."

"Then give me the ashes and keep the box," I said.

"I will think about it. Let us not discuss it any further for now."

I nodded. Again, my curiosity got the better of me. "How did you come to live here? If you don't want to say, that's fine."

"An accident. Of my own making. Made it impossible to live normally."

"And the doctors can't help you?"

"A healer—doctor, as you say—is the one that did this to me. Aided by my own greed for more than life intended me to have."

"I'm sorry. Maybe there's some other doctor that could help you."

"No, little one," my host said with a sudden swerve toward kindness. "There is no one who can help. If I asked for it, I would only be locked up—prodded, poked, experimented on. Treated like a freak of nature, which is exactly what I am. I live here because I can live as freely as my body will allow me to. Now sleep. I can't talk anymore. In the morning, you may go, like I said. But without what you call *your* possessions. And don't try to find your way back to this place or bring anyone along with you. Even if you got back here, I will be gone. It is time I find a place that is deeper in the forest. You will be the last human I will ever see, and I am glad that it was you. Your mother . . . you must go back to her. She has lost her husband and now she must think she has lost you. That would be awfully hard for any parent."

"You don't know?" I said, torn between asking more questions and revealing what happened to Mom.

"What?"

"My mother has been gone for a long, long time. We thought she was dead. But she tricked us. She ran away."

There was a long silence. Then the Watcher cleared its throat and said, "Always remember, she loved you very much. With all her heart."

"Do you . . . *did* you have a family? Someone to miss you?" I asked.

"Thank the All, I do not."

"The All. Yes. I've heard that before."

"It's only a saying. It means nothing."

But I knew that it did.

"Funny thing about families," I said. "You complain about them, you fight with them, but when they're gone, it hurts. And it's lonely."

"You must sleep now," my host told me.

I was too tired to argue.

"There is tea waiting for you to the left of your bed. It has steeped long enough."

I looked to the side and saw the same cedar container I'd used the night before. I opened it. It smelled the same. A little funky and foresty, like its taste. That bitter aftertaste was familiar too. Last time I had it, I could barely stay awake.

I realized *my tea had been brewed with something to make me sleep.*

But I didn't want to sleep. I wanted to find my things and go.

"Won't you have some tea with me?" I asked my host.

"I have some waiting for me by the fire. I will drink it when I return with more firewood."

I looked over and saw a similar container.

The shadow moved through the curtain, and I heard my host's trademark dragging sound. Some moments later, a blast of cold night air entered the room.

I took my drink and scrambled from my spot over to the fire where the other container lay. I grabbed it, opened it, and took a whiff. Same tea. But without the funky smell. I dove for the edge of the room, pushed away some bags, and poured the tea right onto the dirt floor. I shoved the bags back in place and spotted the bentwood box containing my father's ashes. I reached for it, but then I stopped. If I took it now, my host might know and take it back.

Cold night air skidded across the floor and rustled the curtain that separated this room from the entrance. The Watcher was back.

I quickly poured my tainted tea into the Watcher's now empty container. I fumbled with the lid, which wouldn't go on straight.

I heard the rustle of the Watcher's cloak and listened to the drag of its feet getting closer. I was running out of time.

My heart pounded as I kept trying. Beyond the curtain, I heard wood being piled. Success!

I tucked it back where I found it, grabbed my container, and lunged onto my bed of boughs.

The curtain that hung between the entrance to the room and the outer door swished. The Watcher was back in the room.

"Did you drink your tea?"

I pretended to sleep, curled up in a ball, my back to the fire, my sweating face hidden from view. The now-empty tea container that had been intended for me was tipped over at my feet.

Minutes ticked by. I wanted to chuckle. To laugh at my trick. But I managed to control my delight. Even without the sleeping potion, I fought against the soothing warmth of the newly stoked fire. I would not fall asleep. I would not.

I heard the Watcher stoke the fire and saw orange flares on the inside of my eyelids from the bright flames. Good. The extra light would make my search easier.

I listened to the sounds of my host gulp the tea. Would the same bitterness I had noticed be obvious to the one who made it?

It took a while, but at last I heard the rhythmic rasps of sleep slow down and get deeper. I waited and waited as patiently as I could until I had to move. I rolled over to find the Watcher sitting up next to the fire, back hunched against the wall, face covered by a hood.

Muscles screaming, shoulder burning, my gunshot scar pulsating, I moved to a crouching position. I'd found my father's ashes. I would look for the Pearl and the pouch first, then get the bentwood box before I skedaddled.

I searched the handwoven baskets filled with different herbs and dried flowers, and through a stack of rough-woven blankets. But no pouch or Pearl anywhere.

There was only one place left to look. On the body of my host. The thought unfurled a ribbon of dread in my stomach. I didn't want to invade its privacy, but I had to do it. I tiptoed toward the sleeping form and touched the cloak. It was scratchy and as dry as the skin of a lizard. I looked closer.

The cloak, different from the hood, was a patchwork of dried skins and hides woven together in a rather ingenious way with strips of fabric that were embroidered over with the most accomplished stitching I had ever seen.

I can't say that the design itself was beautiful, but there was a dark and angry quality to the collection of symbols. None that

I recognized. Laid out in almost a grid, it could be a kind of foreign writing, but from what country? I didn't know. It was mesmerizing but also disturbing.

I probed under the cloak for the pouch. That heavy feeling of wrongness paid my shoulders another visit. I would hate it if someone did this to me.

But the Watcher *had* done it while I was sleeping in the meadow. Two wrongs don't make a right, but I did it anyway.

I gently pulled at the cord that tied the hood around its neck, listening for any changes in its deep, heavy breathing. I had to see if the pouch was there. When I had just loosened the bow, a hand grabbed me.

Webbed talons the color of rotting pea soup encircled my wrist. It looked like no other hand I'd ever seen before or ever wanted to see again.

My heart pounded. I pulled back.

My captor's hand fell away with a tortured-sounding snort, which settled into an uneven snore. I held my breath for a beat, hoping it wouldn't awaken.

I opened the cloak to search for the Pearl, and the hood slipped back a little to reveal a remarkable-looking face. I managed to silence a gasp.

I carefully peeled the cloak away, and what I saw filled my heart with compassion: This loose-fitting garment (a long skirt or baggy pants?) was designed for maximum coverage. But under the rough fabric, I could still see the outline of haunches, like jack rabbit legs, with large feet bound with narrow rags. Could they be webbed like the hands? Curved spine, no neck, and a head shaped like a wedge. There was no nose, just a wide mouth with two nostril-like holes that opened and closed in a quickening rhythm. I had gone too far. Been too invasive. But I couldn't help but wonder . . . Where did such a person come from? And what did it have to do with me and my family? I wasn't sure I ever wanted to find out.

My fumbling fingers found the pouch, and I could feel that the casket with the Pearl was inside. I still had the pocketknife my father had given me and used it to sever the cord.

I quickly secured the pouch around my own neck by tying the cut cord then pocketed the knife. Fortunately, I found my mother's book right away, tucked in a large inner pocket of its cloak. Next, I grabbed the box that contained my father's ashes. I stuffed it and the book into my backpack, which was lying beside my makeshift bed. The slashed straps had been repaired with hand stitching. I had my things. Now—to get out.

I headed out through the curtain and found myself in a short corridor with another curtain at its end.

Off to the right was a smaller room. I should have run out the door. But instead, I took out the flashlight I still had in my backpack and turned it on. The room was filled with mostly small sleeping nests filled with all kinds of creatures, from birds to frogs—with one thing in common. They were hurt. A bandaged wing, tiny poultices tied on with young green vines, even a splint on the broken leg of a baby marmot. Most of the creatures were asleep, uncaged, except one—a frog. Perhaps the creature had drugged these animals too.

The frog in the cage looked like Linka. No armor. No tattoos. Yet I was sure it was her. Unfortunately, I had lost my ability to see the other world without the help of the Pearl. Or maybe I was no longer in the magical place I had been before—the land of beauty and pain. I could have opened the Pearl to make sure I was right. But that might have woken everyone. I couldn't risk it.

So instead, I followed my instincts and grabbed the caged frog to take her with me. I had one or two things to say to that traitorous little princess. I hadn't forgotten how she'd tried to get the trees to betray me. And as soon as I got the chance, I'd let her have it.

61

Wink 🐸 The Council Convenes

Night of the Pink Moon
Sundown
The Palay, Council Chambers

W INK COULDN'T TAKE his eyes off the ceiling of the great dome in the sacred council chambers.

"Spectacular show, do you not think?" Lord Bumbleberry said.

Wink was attending the ancient frog as his new job within the Palay. "Yes, My Lord, this is the most spectacular sight I have ever seen."

The ceiling glowed with iridescent worms that took the shape of frog constellations in the sky above the Palay—constellations of various star systems that only frog eyes could see. There was the Queen's Cape; the Fighting Staff of Whodora, an ancient hero to the world of frogs; the Vizzard's Cauldron; the Golden Leaf; the Bloody Infinator; and many, many more.

Wink knew he was lucky to even be here. Lord Raeburn had volunteered Wink's services to Lord Bumbleberry at the meeting of the Frog Council. Wink was also supposed to keep an eye on him so that Lord Bumbleberry did not topple off the perching stool once he was up there, given his current state of decrepitude.

His other orders from Raeburn were of a darker nature, and they were the cause of Wink's constantly churning stomach. He was to memorize and report every meeting Bumbleberry engaged in and every missive he received. Raeburn said it was to protect the old fellow from advantage-takers. But it sounded more like spying to Wink. He had, in all honesty, told the vizzard this—and everything else—except Raeburn's threat to return him to the Maw. But that made him feel like a traitor. Clarenso had assured him that complete honesty was the best course of action under his difficult circumstances. And he trusted his uncle more than anyone to have his best interests at heart. So, here he was. Spying for both sides in a battle he did not quite understand.

Wink was grateful for the soothing sounds of the water that flowed through channels along both sides of every perching stool so attendees could refresh themselves at any time. The lone exception to this was the perching stool that sat to the right of the queen's throne. That was Prince Azzie's place—poor tragic prince, feared dead and gone—and those channels had been blocked to accommodate his aversion to water.

Wink's eye followed the water as it cascaded down each channel, following the decline in the room's floor to pool at the bottom, where the queen's throne was located. This lower position was symbolic of the queen's service to the All.

Wink had been asked to squat at the base of Bumbleberry's perching stool and be as still as possible so he did not attract any attention during the proceedings—and, of course, he was to keep his ear pads on the alert.

His stomach grumbled. All this excitement was making him hungry. Hopefully tasty, exotic tidbits like soufflé of snail and crispy fly bits would be served if the proceedings went long, or so he'd been told.

Wink heard a slight snoring sound. Lord Bumbleberry was dozing again. Wink was never sure how much His Lordship was able to comprehend, but he treated him with the utmost respect as was His Lordship's due.

The room was filled with local council members. They all sat silently under brightly colored ceremonial capes that were elaborately embroidered with their family symbols and stories. Soon the queen would ascend from the depths to take her place at the center of the room. A stream of spittle leaking out of the corner of Lord Bumbleberry's mouth fell onto Wink's shoulder. The younger frog dipped a web kerchief into the water and wiped the older frog's drool away.

"Sorry, Taddy," Lord Bumbleberry said, slurping up the rest of the long, mucousy drip.

"Not to worry, sir, not to worry."

"Where is everyone? They are late. In my day, this would not be tolerated. And why is everyone so glum? Faces are as dark as toasted snail shells. What is going on?"

"Your Lordship, word came earlier today that the council members traveling to this meeting from the outlying areas are missing and presumed dead, including our most beloved Prince Azzumundo."

"Dead? What do you mean, tadpole? Explain yourself."

"They were supposed to arrive some time ago, according to the Schedule of Comings and Blowings, and when they did not, Simeon sent out several search parties."

"Well? Well? What did they find?" Bumbleberry sputtered.

"There was one report by a crew who saw signs of a bloody battle at the Gathering Glen."

"The Gathering Glen? That place is as safe as a Hatching Pond. Distressing. Very distressing, indeed. Say more."

"Well, Simeon has widened the air search, but my sources tell me—"

"*Your* sources? Upon my word, you are exceedingly well connected for one who has recently arrived here." Bumbleberry chuckled and wiped his perpetually drippy snout with a web kerchief. "What do these sources of yours say?"

"That the council meeting will start now—but the agenda has been changed. Hope dims, My Lord, that any survivors may be found. A terrible event must have occurred. But we know not what."

Movement at the entrance distracted Lord Bumbleberry, who turned to see Lord Raeburn enter.

"What is he doing here? The young upstart. Why, he has not been a member of the council since he was kicked off for unbecoming behavior."

"He is a member, My Lord, and has been for quite a while. Perhaps you are thinking back to another time. As second hop-cousin thrice removed to the queen, he is still in the line of succession, which empowers him to be here, I believe," Wink said.

"Quite right you are. You are learning, young one. You are learning."

Wink watched as Raeburn entered the chamber with an air of ownership. Something had changed, and it was something dangerous from the look on Raeburn's face. Wink's empty stomach twisted a few turns tighter.

Next to enter was the Grand and Glorious Vizzard. Wink struggled not to divert his eyes in a way that would appear rude and fought hard to assume a face of respect and nonchalance as the great frog walked by on two legs with the help of his walking sticks. Wink's uncle, Clarenso, had schooled him in how to act, and he was grateful. He also knew how it felt to be looked at with disdain because of one's appearance. It hurt, and he had no wish to hurt the feelings of his and his uncle's benefactor.

Then came the Frogoon of Zons who had stayed behind to guard the queen—they marched into the chamber and set up a line of defense around her throne. Bacareno, the court caller, appeared before the throne and announced the queen.

"Ocie, ocie," he called. "Let the 10,937th gathering of the Royal Frog Council begin. All members salute, Ranya, Majesty Within the Veil and Magnificent Queen of All Frogs That Flourish in the North, South, East, and West and in Water, Sand, and Mud."

Normally, according to his uncle, council members would have erupted in a full chorus of croaks, wails, screeches, whistles, barks, and high-pitched peeps as each paid deference in her or his own way to the queen. But given the grim circumstances, the room was silent.

The sound of stone upon stone was heard by all as the queen rose on her pillar dressed in her mourning cloak, a simple piece of frog cloth woven from the humble dried stems of a flower Wink knew was called Queen Ranya's lace.

"This is indeed a dark day for us all," the queen said. "We have grave problems that face us and many difficult decisions to make without the benefit of our dearly departed friends.

"I can scarcely believe we will be able to carry on without him—excuse me—without *them*. Painful as it is, urgency demands that we put aside our sorrow for now and turn to the matters at hand and address the problem that forced me to call this gathering together. Let us do the best we can and do it in honor of those who are no longer with us—"

Just then the doors to the grand council chamber flew open. Simeon rushed in. "Your Majesty, Your Majesty! We have been blessed by the Well of White Light. All is not lost. There are council members who live!"

Those gathered in the chamber erupted in hoots, croaks, and hollers of glee as Simeon poured out the news.

"By Prince Azzumundo's command, the surviving council members, many of whom are wounded, have been transported to the Palay by our own airtilliers and other friends of the forest who came to their aid. The council members, who are extremely grateful for the prince's valor, are all determined to appear before your Majesty as soon as possible to report what happened and to get to the work at hand."

"Blessed be the Well of White Light," the queen said. "No, please, do not bring the council members here first. Take all the wounded directly to the Frog Hospital. They must be treated and helped immediately. I will visit them shortly."

"But, Your Majesty, they insist on coming to the council chambers. They will be here in two flaps of a fly wing."

"Then let them come," the queen said.

62

Nora ◎ The Root of the Matter

Night of the Pink Moon
Creature's Lair
Early Evening

W HEN I LEFT the warmth and soft light of my strange host's nest, I found myself in a tunnel that twisted upward. The smell of deep earth was the strangest perfume. I didn't remember coming down it, but I'll never forget going back up this narrow passageway which wasn't tall enough for me to stand.

Once I let the curtain fall behind me, there was no light for me to navigate by, so I took out my flashlight and immediately dropped it, breaking the lens. I fumbled in the dark but couldn't find it.

At first, I wasn't too worried. I would 'feel' my way out. Bent over and shuffling along, fine root hairs brushed against my face like cobwebs.

With one hand on the earthen wall, I felt my way up the passage until the walls receded and I was left with nothing to guide me through the blackest black.

Disoriented, I accidentally dropped the cage that Linka was in, then fell to my knees to search for her using my hands. I found nothing. I hoped I hadn't crushed her. My throat tightened at the thought.

I didn't know up from down. In the darkness of the tunnel, I had no point of reference to use as orientation. Afraid, I remembered those tree-words from my mad vision.

> So, wherever you are, if ever you fall,
> Put your lips to the ground and give us a call.
> To help and right you, we'll give it our all.

Afraid to reach for the Pearl and fumble it away, I lay my head on the earth and whispered, "Help."

At first nothing happened. Then I heard little scratching sounds, like something crawling out of the ground. My body tensed. I ground my teeth together, this time to keep myself from screaming. I heard a whispering sound that made the back of my neck prickle.

Little threads of light appeared above like dangly stars in the sky and snaked their way toward me. From below, similar threads of light emerged. I couldn't tell what they were. Worms? Or worse: snakes? But as the threads got longer, they split, then split again. And I could finally see that they were fine bioluminescent root hairs.

Within seconds the root hairs entwined themselves around my arms and shoulders, and then my stomach and legs. At first, I felt only a tickle. But as the roots crawled along my skin, they expanded in size and brightness until I could spot Linka in the light. She was getting away.

I wanted to speak to her but didn't have the Pearl open, so what was the point? And then, it occurred to me that maybe the rules of the Pearl were evolving. Or maybe it was me that was changing under the Pearl's influence. Had being shot and healed in that magical place by those magical frogs done something to my DNA? Did it even matter? Linka had said the rules of the Pearl were mysterious.

I dared myself to find out and spoke.

"Linka? You okay?" I said, while not quite believing I would be heard and answered.

I was surprised when she said, "I am. No thanks to that creature who put me in a cage. A cage!" She sounded incensed.

"You're free now, thanks to me," I said, not afraid to claim credit for her rescue. "How about returning the favor and getting me out of this tangle?"

"Give me the Pearl, and I'll see what I can do," Linka said.

"Help me first, and we'll talk. Then, I'll trade you for it if you tell me where the Nexus is."

"The Nexus? How do you know about the Nexus?"

"None of your business. Is it a deal?"

"You asked for help from your precious trees. Now take it," Linka said.

"Sounds like you're a bit bitter from your lack of influence with dead wood," I said, a bit smugly.

"Don't fight what's about to happen to you," she said.

"Don't fight what?" I asked. But Linka was nowhere to be seen. Roots from above and below wrapped around me and pulled me to the ground. Then thicker roots farther up the tunnel shot out and pulled me forward. I felt like a mummy on a conveyor belt being wrapped and rewrapped as I moved up the line.

At first, I struggled to be free of the pressure the roots exerted on my body. Ultimately, I just gave in to the process and closed my eyes to lessen the dizzying effect of the spin. I *had* asked for help. It would only be gracious of me to accept it.

The crisp night air oozed down through the tunnel to meet me. I looked up. I was at the bottom of a shaft, on my side, staring at the legs of a makeshift ladder. The roots retreated. I was free. I rolled onto my back and stared up at the moonlight streaming into the shaft.

I rubbed my arms and shoulders to brush away the spidery feeling the roots had left on my skin and eased myself into a standing position. Sensing they were still nearby, I whispered my thanks to the roots and scrambled up the ladder to ground level to find myself in the middle of a hollowed-out cedar tree.

I stepped off the ladder and felt for an opening in the trunk. Like a conch shell, the hollow core of the tree spiraled outward. Finally, I stood outside in front of a gnarled root with the head of a demon and the contorted wings of an angel.

The creature lived under my family's Flying Demon Tree.

A short way off was the field in which I had slept the night before with my friends. I looked for them with a sliver of hope that they'd decided to wait here for me to return. I was back all right, but it wasn't where I wanted—or needed—to be.

The full Pink Moon was rising in the sky. There was more than enough light for me to see where I was going—even if I didn't know where that was. I had to get out of here, to someplace the creature couldn't find me.

I heard a noise, maybe from the tunnel below. My trembling legs didn't wait for orders from my head. I ran as fast as I could away from whatever or whoever might be chasing me.

63

The Queen
A Mother's Sorrow

The Night of the Pink Moon
Swarm Time
The Palay, Council Chambers

THE SURVIVORS OF the Gathering Glen massacre began to straggle into the grand council chambers. The queen's heart beat a little lighter, even though that horrible, mangled feeling remained. Could the Well of Light be so gracious to grant her son's safety among all of those who did survive?

Many of the council members rushed forward to help the arrivees, including the Grand and Glorious Vizzard, who sent Clarenso to fetch his treatment satchel and other supplies.

The queen suppressed the urge to cry out a welcome to her dear friend Ginny when she saw him lean against Frago for support as he made his way toward her throne.

"Your Majesty, we are saved," Ginny said, double-dipping as best he could with his injuries. Frago struggled to keep them both upright. "It was the courage of your son and—"

"My son?" The queen held her breath. Her heart cramped again. Could she bear to hear the story of her son's demise?

"He should be coming soon, Your Majesty," said Ginny. "He stayed behind to make sure that all were evacuated from the site of the massacre."

The sorrow that had weighed down her heart took flight, and she was filled with gratitude. "I am so happy that so many of you are saved," the queen said. "I do want to hear what happened— every detail. But first, we must treat those who are injured, feed those who are hungry, and care for those of you who are tired. We must delay the meeting until these things are done."

A voice boomed from the back of the room. "The time to meet is now."

The queen's heart beat faster. Everyone looked toward the back of the room. A shadow fell across the entryway.

"Enter, my son," the queen said, her voice choking on the words. "Enter."

And Azzie did.

64

Linka 🐸 Loose Threads

Night of the Pink Moon
Early Swarm Time
The Creature's Lair

"Let me go!" Linka cried as the root hairs that bound her in place tightened against her struggle. "She's getting away—and she has the Pearl. Why are you helping a largetoe anyway?"

"We promised to help her when she asked," the roots spoke as one. "And she asked. That's the way it works with trees. We promise to stay in one place and take care of many things on both the physical and metaphysical plane, and all we desire in return is compassion and respect. She is a rare largetoe, indeed, to have given us both. But you? You have tried to boss us and hold the power of the queen over our heads. So, we will hold *you* tight until the girl is too far from here for you to easily catch up to her."

Linka tried to relax her muscles. There was no fighting against the will of even one tree, let alone the collective root system. And maybe the sooner she surrendered, the sooner they would let her go. She longed to be out in the air, to be free.

Finally, the roots loosened their grasp, and she was free to go. She made it quickly outside the gnarled tree and heard a sound she'd been longing to hear.

"Princess, I am here," Myth said.

She looked up and saw him hanging upside down from the gnarled knot at the top of the tree.

"I have never been so happy to see anyone in my life," Linka said.

Myth swooped down, and Linka jumped onto his back.

"Are you well enough to fly?" Linka asked.

"Yes. To wherever my princess and commander wishes to go," Myth replied. "And how are you, Princess Linka? I mean no disrespect, but you seem in need of a long float in a Pool of Restoration."

"That is exactly what I wish I could do," Linka sighed, "but that pleasure will have to wait. There is much to report to the queen and to my father."

As Myth launched into the sky, Linka searched for the vial of Golden Death she had tucked under her saddle when she and Myth were attacked by the Bulldoggies. To have lost that would have brought shame upon her. She would return it to her father, and he could do with it as he liked. She would not deploy it against anyone—most especially not the largetoe . . . if they ever met again.

The trees had taught her a lesson. Not even a queen could hold dominion over the compassion and respect that must be shown to all energetic matter. No one had the right to impose their power over the rights of others.

"Home, Myth. Let us go home," she said.

Myth banked a turn and headed off in the direction of the Palay.

Azzie & Treachery, Treason, From Within

Night of the Pink Moon
Swarmtime
The Palay, Council Chambers

THE SMELL OF change was in the room when Azzie entered and heard council members murmuring as he moved down the ramp to the throne. He stopped at Lord Bumbleberry's perching stool and said, "My Lord, I may need a fighting rod. May I borrow yours?"

Instead of answering, Bumbleberry's head tilted to the side, a sign of deep sleep in frogs. But a small glass frog, Bumbleberry's aid, grabbed the nearby fighting stick and handed it to Azzie.

"I'm sure my lord would be honored for you to have this."

Azzie tipped his head in thanks and continued toward his mother as all around him the cries of the crowd celebrated his presence.

"Praise the Well."

"I thought he was dead."

"What's that he's carrying on his back?"

They would soon find out.

Azzie stopped before his mother's throne and double-dipped as best he could while searching the room for someone.

He threw down the burden in front of his mother. It landed with a sickening thud. With a flick of his hand, he unfurled his flycape to reveal the dead body of the frog who tried to kill him, disguised in the cape of a Bulldoggie, but tailored to regular frog size. Azzie tore it off and tossed it to the side.

The crowd gasped, no one louder than his mother.

"This is my would-be assassin and the leader of those murderers responsible for the carnage at the Gathering Glen this day." Azzie rolled the dead body over so everyone could see its face.

"Who is it?" the queen asked.

Azzie reached down and ripped off the eye patch his assailant had been wearing.

"It's Kon!" someone shouted.

All eyes turned to Raeburn.

"Yes," Azzie said, advancing on his target. "It's Kon. What do you have to say about that, Raeburn?"

"Surely there is some mistake," Raeburn said. "It must be an impostor. Why, I think I saw the real Kon before I entered this chamber."

"Liar." Azzie said, seething.

"To tell the truth," Raeburn said, "I've been suspicious of him myself for quite some time."

"I call you a *liar*," Azzie said, moving ever closer, fighting rod in hand. "And a barbaric murderer of your own kind."

"My Queen, may I speak with you in private?" Raeburn asked. "There are things I could divulge, but only to your royal ear pads."

"Zons, seize Raeburn and detain him in the dungeon," the queen said.

"Your Majesty, I protest," Raeburn squealed, but it was useless. With false dignity, he let himself be escorted away.

"Mark my words, Mother. Raeburn has more in store for you than we yet know," Azzie said, and his mother shuddered at the thought.

"He will tell me everything," the queen said.

"Your Majesty," Simeon said. "Look."

He pointed to the grand door. Another unexpected visitor had arrived.

66

Nora ◉ And the Pink Moon Rises

Night of the Pink Moon
After Dark
New Territory

I T WAS DARK. I was out of breath—and almost out of options. If I couldn't figure out where I was supposed to go or how to get there, I would have to abandon my quest to make amends to my dad. And I would never know what he had intended to tell me when I set his ashes free.

Should it seem weird to me that I was going to all this trouble on the word of a ghost, even if it was the ghost of my dad? Probably. But something deeper had taken over my desire to do this, and I didn't know what that was. Maybe I was simply avoiding all the real-world pain I was going through by pretending or imagining there was a world beyond my usual dimension.

I ran quite some distance from the Flying Demon Tree in the opposite direction I'd gone earlier this morning. I had no desire to end up back at that frog-killing and almost-Nora-killing place. How could Kincade hate our family enough to kill us? For I was positive now that he killed my dad. I knew it in my bones.

I felt like I had a thousand fishhooks in me pulling in different directions. It was exhausting. I had to catch my breath and get my head right. I sat down on a knee-high rock and took out the book I'd retrieved from my mother's coffin. But looking at the pages made me realize there had always been holes in my heart even before I got shot. Not really knowing who my mother was and why she didn't share more about her family had put those holes there in the first place, and they were made even bigger when she faked her own death and disappeared. Without knowing those whys, how could I ever really know who I was? And why hadn't she trusted me with the truth?

Inside the book, my mother had drawn lovely pictures of plants and places I didn't recognize. That she came from a different country was clear. You only had to listen to her speak to know that English wasn't her first language, although she spoke it extremely well. She also spoke French, German, and Spanish fluently. But she'd made it clear that those were languages she'd learned at school, and in her "travels around the world," as she used to say without adding details.

She had hidden her truth from me. I knew she wasn't the only person to do things like that. Kincade kept his secrets from his son. Corporations, governments, politicians, officials—elected or otherwise—did the same. Lies protected the liars. It made me mad and sad at the same time. But I guess I was guilty of it too.

I flipped through the rest of the book. I didn't understand a word, so if it had a secret message telling me which way the Nexus was, I wouldn't have understood it anyway.

I shook the book at the rising pink moon and caught a glint of gold on the edge of the pages. I looked more closely. A miniature panoramic picture stretched along the gilt-covered edge of the pages that appeared when I shifted the book just so under the waxing light of the Pink Moon.

From one angle, the page edges were simply gold. From another, there was a delicate, detailed miniature of a waterfall between two worlds. The normal world was a forest on one side of the waterfall. The other side showed pooling at the base of a mountain—a stone amphitheater guarded by standing frogs wielding weapons. It was a coming together of two worlds. The Nexus. I was sure of it. I had a destination.

How to find it was my next question.

Waterfall. Entrance. Statues. Were they really frogs? Frankly, I was more than tired of this whole frog thing. But now that I knew where I was supposed to be going, maybe the Pearl—and the trees—could work together to help me.

I took out the jewelry casket, touched the frog, and exposed the Pearl. It seemed bigger in the light of the Pink Moon. I'd have to do this fast or risk signaling my location to the Watcher and every other creature who cared to know.

I pressed my forehead onto the nearest tree and asked it and its brethren to show me to the place I must go.

The mycelium carpet and tree roots that ran above and into the ground began to glow with a golden light, creating a pathway for me to follow.

Once I got my bearings, I shut the Pearl and only opened it occasionally to make sure I was going the right way. I wasn't willing to risk discovery by leaving it open to the air for too long.

After some time, I passed once again through a wall of mist. Was it a continuation of the wall of mist I'd encountered earlier in the day? It had the same bouncy quality, but I didn't even check if I could go back through it because I felt the need to push on. Would it let me back out when I finished with this business? The creature had brought me back through after I was shot. I was positive I'd find a way to return.

Soon after, I heard the rushing sounds of water. I was almost there. I could feel it. A few more paces and then, there it was—a huge waterfall beyond the path.

I checked the book's covert image by the moon's light. Clearly, I had to go through the waterfall to get to the stone amphitheater behind it.

I climbed up a stack of rocky boulders to get closer to the edge. Thankfully the moonlight brightened as it rose. It was almost as if the moon herself wanted to light my way. The closer I got, the louder the rush of water sounded. Spray hit my face and clothes. I pulled back. If I kept on, I'd be drenched and colder than before, thanks to the chill that had crept into the night air.

I couldn't make my legs move and I had the odd sensation of both wanting to move forward and going back at the same time. Was I turning into that animal in the Doctor Dolittle book—the pushmi-pullyu, with the head of a gazelle going one way and the head of a unicorn going opposite? My inner gazelle wanted to move forward to the Nexus. I would scatter Dad's ashes, wait for his spirit to share its secrets, and get down the mountain to whatever empty life awaited me. But my inner unicorn wanted me to choose another direction and go off with his remains clutched in my arms—away from here, forever.

I swallowed hard. I had come so far. Why couldn't I find the courage to keep going? My eyes widened with the realization. It was because I didn't have the guts to let Dad go.

I closed my eyes and counted to three.

I stepped through the waterfall, gasping when the frigid water hit me like a blow. I was drenched. Somehow the waterfall was absorbing the moonlight and casting it inward, so it was like stepping into a bright cave. The damp air had a chilled bite and smelled like sheets that had been dried outside on a sunny day. Could this be my destination? Intuition said no. I pushed deeper into the cave, examining its walls for the outline of a door or hidden chamber. But there was nothing. I had hit a dead end.

I touched the rock. There had to be a door leading somewhere. There had to be. I ran my hand over the lower part of the cave wall. The rock felt dense, like it would take a bomb to get through it. Nothing. I reached up and quickly found a small outcrop that was hard to spot in the low light. I stepped back to see what was above and witnessed a spectacular sight. There on the stone wall, glowing in a shaft of reflected moonlight, different colored fungi and algae grew in an uneven and convoluted design in the shape of a frog with an open mouth. And inside the mouth was a small, round indentation chiseled into the stone.

Curiosity rippled through me. Had that indentation been created especially for me? Had I been any shorter, my hand would have missed discovering the spot. And I would never have been able to do what I was going to do next, which was to place the Pearl into the indentation on the wall. I pushed it in and heard it click. When I took my hand away, the Pearl stayed where I'd placed it. Moments passed. And then . . .

The sound of stone grinding on stone filled the air, and a chilly breeze from somewhere back in the dark of the cave carried a fragrance sweeter than any I'd ever smelled.

I followed the breeze toward the back wall only to see a portal pivot open. If I stepped through, would the opening close? How would I get out again if I didn't take the Pearl with me?

There was only one way to tell. I ran back and grabbed the Pearl and raced through the open portal. It did not close. There, below me, was the most beautiful valley I had ever seen awash in moonlight. Gently rolling hills covered with a breathtaking array of flowers. Their scent tickled my nose and drew me forward. In the distance I could see an amphitheater carved into stone. Surrounding it, like guards, was a circle of six frog statues, each taller than a two-story house: The Nexus. It must be. For the third time, I asked that question. And the Nexus replied *yes*.

I had found the right place and held back a sob of relief. I had persevered and done it. I didn't give up. I was proud of myself and excited to get this huge task done and off my shoulders. Everything—including getting back to Gran—should be downhill from here. And I'd be taking information with me that I could use to get justice for my father. This nightmare was almost over. Although technically I didn't have a home to return to, I had Gran and my friends. They were all home to me. I pushed thoughts of my mother's faked death out of my mind. Perhaps I would just let her mystery go and get on with my own life.

I looked at the short distance I had to cover to reach my destination. It wouldn't take long to get to the amphitheater, scatter Dad's ashes, and return. I was excited to 'see' my father once more. But I was also bewildered by all my new feelings and perceptions. I felt more connected to the world of nature than I ever had before, and I longed to know more.

I entered the Nexus, my curiosity rising.

Azzie 🐸 Making the Case

Night of the Pink Moon
Early Swarmtime
The Palay, Frog Council Chambers

"Linka. You are most welcome," said the queen as Linka entered the room.

Azzie was ecstatic over the safe arrival of his cousin. Relief was on the faces of his mother and uncle, as well as the usually stoic Zons.

"With you both here, both safe, I am hopeful that we can deal with the devastating issues and losses we face. Your wisdom, combined with that of my council, will make it so."

Azzie was a bit surprised to learn that he had been feared dead by his mother and the others. Is that why his mother was greeting him so warmly? A dead son must be far worse in her eyes than a son who failed to be wise enough to one day rule in her place. Or was he being unfair?

"Your Majesty." Linka double-dipped to the queen and then to her father. She handed him the vial of Golden Death she'd been safeguarding. "I return this into your care, Father."

"What is this?" the queen demanded upon seeing the exchange. "You did not execute my specific order to destroy the largetoe with the Pearl?"

"Your Majesty, please," Linka addressed the queen, "I did not want to act precipitously before you had all the facts at your disposal."

Azzie could tell that his mother was extremely vexed by the 'courteous yet contrary to orders' behavior on his cousin's part. *Good for her*, he thought. Perhaps there was hope that she would come around to his way of thinking after all.

"Very well, Commander, I will hear you out," his mother said to Linka.

"I have come with amazing news, Your Majesty," Linka said. "I know the location of the Golden Pearl of the Forest."

"Where is it?" the queen asked.

"In the possession of the femtoe Nora, and instinct, based on the girl's determination to find the Nexus, tells me that she should be at the Old Renewal Grounds as we speak."

"And she knows of the consequences of the ceremony and is still willing to participate?" the queen said.

"No, I do not believe that is the case. But she has proven to be a compassionate largetoe and may be open to the case we make to participate in the ceremony, if we put it to her properly."

A hush fell over the court.

"Do you not see? This is the opportunity of a thousand lifetimes," Linka said. "With a little persuasion, we might be able to convince her to participate in the Ceremony of Renewal."

The crowd raised a ruckus and the Court Caller had to calm them down.

"It could be propitious," the vizzard said, when all was quiet again.

Azzie swallowed his lingering anxiety about, well, everything and said, "We must do this. It is our only hope."

"We do not know for sure if it will even work," said the vizzard. "Although it did work, a long time ago—and perhaps even more recently."

Azzie looked at him with confusion. "Would you be referring to what happened to your older sister, our former queen DeLili?"

"What do you know of that?" the queen said sharply.

"Just what I saw on the contract between herself and the two of you," Azzie said. "You know, Uncle, the one you had in your study."

His uncle and his mother's mouths dropped open in shock and they exchanged a quick look that was laced with fear.

"I swear to you, I was not snooping. But once I caught a glimpse of it, I had to see more." Azzie wondered if he should retrieve the contract that he had 'borrowed.' It was still in the pocket of his flycape and was probably worse for wear. But then he thought better of it.

"You see, Majesty," said Linka, "if we could convince the girl to participate, it might be the beginning of a solution to the continual downturn in the stability of nature. It could reconnect largetoes to the earth. And unless *that* happens, our march toward destruction will only continue."

Again, silence dominated the room.

"What say you, my queen?" Linka asked.

Azzie's heart swelled with hope. This was his chance to redeem himself in his own eyes. To risk it all. No matter how fear weighed down his legs and feet. Kicking his uneasiness aside, he leapt in front of his mother's throne and faced her.

"I stand ready to do your bidding and the bidding of your subjects." He bowed down to the mosaic floor and touched his nose to its rough surface, his heart pounding in his chest.

The queen rose briefly and surveyed those assembled.

"Thank you, my son. But first, beloved Azzie and Linka, and my faithful frog council, I must tell you of my dream. If, after hearing it, you still want to proceed, it shall be done."

The room was so quiet one could hear the water breathe. The queen began.

"In my dream, I saw the beginning of time—and the end of it. I saw the moon crash down from the sky, my face etched across its surface, and crushed our home, the Palay."

Everyone expressed shock.

"No, no, it was not me who caused the destruction of our home—it was a girl. Energy pouring out of her like the sun, she stood within our magical circle and destroyed our defenses. Her power was so great she shattered not only the Golden Pearl of the Forest, but the Palay."

Sounds of dismay rippled through the room.

"Sister, dear. What a terrible experience for you. I better understand now that your order for the Golden Death was an attempt to save us all. But might I suggest another interpretation?"

"As if I could stop you, dear brother."

The vizzard spoke up loudly for all to hear. "What if the destruction of the Palay was precipitated not by the girl, but by your unwillingness to open up your mind to other ways of doing things? You resisted the enactment of a real Ceremony of Renewal. What if that is the reason for not only your portended death, but the destruction of the Palay?"

The hush that followed was thick with fear. Azzie was astounded that his uncle would say something so offensive to his sister in public. And the queen was obviously astounded too. She inhaled sharply as the weight of her brother's words sank in, then sat silently as if stung by the truth she had secretly known all along.

Soon the other frogs started babbling about the audaciousness of it all, although Azzie wasn't listening to their words. He was more concerned by his mother's distant look and pained expression and approached her to extend some comfort. "Mother? Are you okay?"

The vizzard moved back to his original position. It was obvious from his expression that he did not regret what he said.

During a long moment where the Council Chambers were as silent as death, Azzie watched the light of change ripple across his mother's face.

Looking younger and less burdened than before, the queen addressed her son, her mouth slightly upturned in what on a largetoe might be mistaken for a smile. "Yes, Azzie. A good gust of honesty has the power to blow the shadows in one's heart away in an instant. My brother has shared a truth. And the truth has touched me. I will no longer lie to myself or to my subjects. Let the vizzard's wisdom prevail."

The room erupted with jubilant cheers at this surprising development: The queen had admitted she was wrong.

"What say you, my subjects?" she asked, with the hint of a smile on her face. "Shall we risk it all?"

Azzie rose and faced the court, watching as the courtiers around him looked to each other to measure reaction. Shoulders shrugged. Mouths mumbled.

"Shall we risk the well-being of my son, who could die from the potion he must apply to his lips?" the queen asked.

Die. Yes. He could die. Azzie shuddered at the thought. But for the first time in his life, he was prepared to do his duty. Azzie addressed the throng.

"Worry not about me. If I die, it will be for the greatest of causes. But there are other risks. Shall we risk that the girl will say no?" he asked.

"Risk it," some of the courtiers began to chant.

Azzie drew in a deep breath through nostrils and skin, inhaling energetic white waves from the earth and red-hot waves from the heavens. *Strength, conviction, courage. Strength, conviction, courage.*

"Shall we risk that the power of the Pearl may fail us?" Azzie asked. Earth energy permeated his feet, pushing the fear out.

"Risk it." The room rumbled with the power of many speaking with one voice.

"Shall we risk that, once done, the girl's body will not survive the difficult transition?" A jolt of sky energy infused Azzie's voice with calm as words rose in his throat from a new place of strength.

"There have been times when weak largetoe flesh—though willing—has not possessed the vigor to withstand transmogrification," the vizzard said. "And if the largetoe dies, her connection to the Pearl might render it useless to us forever."

"Shall we risk it?" Azzie asked the crowd.

"Risk it." The courtiers' cries were accompanied by whistles and squeaks. And some frogs began to stomp in unison.

"Shall we risk that even if the girl's physical heart can withstand the stress, the nature of her true heart will be such that she will not sympathize with our cause and embrace it as her own?" Azzie asked.

"Risk it." they chanted in a unified rhythmic beat.

Those in the room continued to chant. "Risk it . . . risk it . . . risk it . . ." The volume and intensity of their cries made the very rock the room was carved from rumble.

Azzie faced his mother. "I think we have your answer, Majesty. I await your command."

The crowd in the sacred council chambers was so distracted by the historic event that had just occurred in this very room that no one noticed an intrepid band of sow bug spies crawl out from under the discarded Bulldoggie fly cape and disappear into the cracks of the Palay.

68

Nora ◎ Waiting for the Morn

Night of the Pink Moon
Evening
The Nexus

WITH EACH STEP toward the amphitheater, my amazement grew. It was covered in moss, almost camouflaged. There was a sacred, untouched aura about the place. The air was clean, crisp, and fragrant. The meadow I had to walk across was full of night-blooming flowers that made me want to pick a bouquet, but that seemed wrong. Everything was perfect as it was. This place had an otherworldly quality to it. I took some care where I stepped, not wanting to ruin the perfection.

The amphitheater was such a strange place. It was a place of ceremony, but there was no one to witness what I was about to do.

I had planned to quickly ask my questions and cast his ashes to the wind, sending him off with my love. But there was no wind to cast them into. The night was perfectly calm, which is exactly the opposite of how I felt inside.

I plopped down on the stonework-covered ground, resting with my back up against one of the giant frog statues. Still soaked from walking through the waterfall, the earth's chill crept up through my body, carrying on its cold fingers thoughts of what might have been.

I dug out the day-old remains of the sandwich Minh had given me and ate a few bites. Clearly the Watcher didn't know a good sandwich when they saw one. Or maybe it purposely left it for me.

A dog barked in the distance—or was it a coyote?

Looking at the Pearl, I wondered: Was there any magical property it had that could change the past—let me go back in time and fix all the wrongs that had added up to my not-so-right present? So far, the only thing it seemed to do was cause me wild visions and summon every animal and tree in the area when it was open to the air. Linka had said something about its unknown powers. After all this was done, I planned to hide it somewhere and never look at it again. It was too unpredictable.

Something rustled through the flowers and tall grass. For some reason, my body was relaxed. It could have been anything coming to eat me or steal the Pearl, but I felt no fear. Calm glided through me as Mickey burst through.

He ran up to me, wagging his tail, and licked my hand.

"Mickey, you found me." I buried my face in his neck.

I ran my hands over his fur and scratched his neck just the way he liked.

"Happy to see you, too, NaNa."

Come again? My dog *was using words to communicate with me.* But if frogs and trees could communicate, why couldn't dogs, who were practically the cleverest creatures around? I was beyond thrilled. And he had a special name for me. That warmed my heart.

But once we'd greeted each other, Mickey behaved strangely. He pawed the ground, then danced around me, barking, like his words weren't enough to communicate. "What's wrong, Mickey?" But my question seemed to agitate him more, and if he was sending thoughts my way, I couldn't pick up on them.

"Okay, boy. You've got to calm down. Are you hungry?" I asked, then took out the remains of the sandwich. He wolfed it down. Then I poured the last of my water into one hand and he licked it up.

"Okay. Come here, Mickey. Sit by me and rest for a moment," I said, sitting down on the ground. I patted my knee, trying to entice him closer. "We've both been through a lot."

But Mickey wasn't having it.

"You must come home, now."

"As soon as I do one thing, I will." I answered.

Mickey yelped, shook his head, then pulled on my sleeve, trying to make me get up. "Men. Bad. They will hurt Gray Mother."

Gray Mother? "You mean Gran?"

Mickey barked.

"But who?"

"Seeh—pa."

Oh, why is it that those we are closest to are the hardest to understand? Mickey spoke in a way that was more difficult for me to figure out than the frogs. It was like he was living life at a faster speed and didn't have enough time to say all the in-between words that gave human speech the flow I was used to. Or maybe it was because we didn't usually need words to communicate.

"Seeh—pa," I said, and repeated it out loud a few times. "Seth's pa? Seth's dad? Kincade? Is that who you mean?"

Mickey barked again.

"But how do you know?"

"Heard them. Talking. In woods."

"Them? You mean Finley too?"

Mickey barked his *yes*. "Now. Come. Can't wait. Must keep Gray Mother safe."

"Mickey—I can't go as fast as you. But please, take this note to the sheriff. You know who I mean? Ardith Wakeen."

"Star woman. Yes."

I had a feeling Ardith would like that name.

I grabbed a scrap of paper out of my backpack and used the pen attachment from my Swiss Army knife to scribble down the message that Gran was in danger. To give some context, I wrote the date and the time at the bottom. I folded it around Mickey's collar with a tight tuck. "Stay safe, Mickey."

With a bark and a nuzzle, he was gone.

I watched the tall grass flick back and forth as he ran in a direction I hadn't expected him to go. Maybe he knew a short-cut—or another way around the waterfall.

Now was the time to summon Dad's ghost, find the answers to my questions and get back to town.

I tucked the Pearl in my pants pocket, got out the bentwood box, and stood up, looking up to the sky hoping for the right words to come to me. I had to make this moment count. Dad deserved that.

The moon grew brighter as it rose in the sky, and the stars flickered like faraway fireflies navigating the heavens in familiar formations—the Big Dipper part of the Big Bear, the Little Dipper part of the Little Bear, Orion's Belt.

Bands of the Milky Way whipped through the heavens, begging me to consider what might be out there in the depths of space. If I could have great conversations with ghosts and trees and frogs and dogs, what possibilities might be lurking beyond the pull of this planet? I snorted at the silliness of the question at a time like this. I had my hands full with the here and now. There was no time for the great *what if.*

A branch crackled nearby, sending a bolt of fear through my body. Then fog rolled over the ground, and I knew immediately that the Watcher was here.

"It's me," a hoarse voice called out.

I placed my hand protectively over my pants pocket, sticking my thumb into my belt loop to keep my hand firmly in place.

"Go away," I said.

"I'm not going to hurt you. I could never do that."

I didn't say a word.

"You left without saying goodbye."

"And you drugged me and stole my things," I snapped.

"I was sorry to see you go."

"You mean you were sorry I got my stuff back."

"As I said, they are not *your* things. The Pearl belongs to no one. It is not even of this earth, and I must have it back immediately. You cannot have it here, of all places, and on this night, of all nights. You have no idea the danger you have put yourself in by coming here."

"My father led me here."

"He could not. He would not. This is the last place he would want you to come."

"Is this called the Nexus?"

"It is."

"He told me to bring his ashes here."

"That is impossible. He knew the consequences of having you come here, especially now." The Watcher glanced up to the sky. "There. I see them. They're coming," it said, sounding terrified.

"I won't let them hurt you," I said. "I'll make sure you're okay."

"It's not me who will be harmed. It's you!" It moved closer. "I am trying to protect you. That has been my primary goal—always and forever—to protect you."

"You are not my mother, so why should you even care?" I barely recognized my own voice. It was so contorted by anger.

"I told you, your mother and I were once friends."

"Is my mother still alive?"

Silence.

"Tell me if you know, please." I hated the desperation in my voice.

"We must leave *now*. They are almost here."

I really didn't want to hang around there anyway, but I still hadn't spread Dad's ashes here like he wanted me to do—and I had to get back to Gran. But I'd go nowhere with the Watcher, that was for sure.

"If I give you the Pearl, will you tell me the truth and leave me alone?"

"The only truth is this—if you will not come with me, I must take the Pearl and go. If you do not have it, they can do you no harm."

It reached out to snatch it from my neck, rough skin scraping against mine. I grabbed its wrist and held tight.

"You won't find it there," I said.

"Where is it? I must have it. I must," it said desperately.

A shadow undulated like a dragon across the rising pink moon. Something dark and ominous was coming our way. Even from this distance I could see their silhouettes. There were frogs on bats, and they were coming for the Pearl.

The Watcher and I struggled for it and its hood fell back, revealing its face. No, it was *her* face. And under the brightening light of the Pink Moon, which was now almost as light as day, I could clearly see that the creature looked half woman, half frog. I hadn't been able to tell this in the pale firelight of her lair last night. And as we looked at each other, I realized something more. It was the first time I had seen her eyes . . . and it was *like looking into my own.*

Our eyes were the same blue color. And we had the same shock of white hair—only hers was long, and it was braided with bone and shell, while mine was more of a stub since it had been cut off.

She sucked in her breath with horror when she realized I knew who I was looking at and she pulled her hood up over her flat, broad head.

I wanted to ask her how she'd gotten this way, why this had happened, but I was overwhelmed by the feeling that we didn't really know each other well enough. And while I really wasn't repulsed by her looks, I could tell that she was sensitive about it. So I said nothing.

She violently jerked her hand away. I shoved my hand into my pocket and pulled out the Pearl. But I felt no satisfaction at frustrating her. My body buzzed with a dawning shock, leaving me feeling as hollowed out as the Flying Demon Tree.

"Mom?"

I could barely believe that word was coming out of my mouth. How could this . . . this . . . be my mom? An angry fire in my belly burned so hot, my skin felt like I'd been coated with oil and broiled.

I held my breath, vowing silently not to release it until the answer came. And yet under that fire, even though I didn't want to admit it to myself, bubbled a feeling I could only call joy beyond joy. My mother was alive. I wanted to rush to her, hold her close, feel her touch.

"Mom, is that you?"

"I am not your mother."

But she was lying. And we both knew it.

"If you're not my mother, then you won't mind if I do *this*."

I grabbed the box of ashes, stepped away from her, undid the lid and threw the ashes into the air.

"No!" she cried. "That's all I have of him!" Her hand shot up and she tried to grasp the ashes as they danced in the breeze. Then her hand dropped to her side as she realized the futility of trying to capture dust in the wind. She slumped, throwing an arm across her face and sobbed, deep and desperate tears.

What had I done? Regret immediately washed over me.

"Oh, Mom, I'm so sorry."

The temperature dropped suddenly. I looked to the sky and saw a dark fast-moving cloud in the distance. The wind quickened and twisted Dad's ashes into a narrowing gyre that took on the shape of the man loved by me—and my mother.

My mother gasped. "Henry? Is that you?" she said. A smile bloomed on her face.

"Nora, Reggie, you're together. It's one of the reasons I brought you both here," he said.

"Henry, here? Now?" she said. "You know the risks to her. You know how I suffered. How *we* suffered. We both vowed since the moment of Nora's birth that we would never let what happened to me happen to her. You promised."

"I am sorry to break that promise," he said, "but the risks to the world are too great to keep it. We must risk everything, even our daughter, to heal the rifts within the All."

"Wait, wait," I said, confused. "You said something about that before, when you died." My blood boiled. "You mean you put me through hell just to get me here to meet Mom? Couldn't you have just said, 'Nora, your mom isn't really dead. Instead, she's turned into a half-frog, half-human creature. And I really want the two of you to meet and get to know each other again.'"

"You miss the point," Dad's specter said. "It goes beyond that. Way beyond. Although how far, I didn't understand until I died and saw it from the other side. The state of the world is dire. The energetic bonds between things are frayed and broken. We must take this chance. We each must do everything we can. That's what I've come back to tell you. There's no waiting. If it's not *now*, there will be no *when*. You are the *hope*, Nora. You."

"Wait, Dad, what are you talking about?"

"You'll soon learn what you need to know," he said. "I trust you'll decide what's best for the greater good of the All. Now I must go for—"

"But you promised to tell me everything, who shot you and why. And the land. What about the land?"

"Those are such small problems when the fate of the world hangs in the balance."

"They are not small things to me," I said, feeling dismissed and abandoned.

"Nora, you have every scrap of information you need to answer those questions already," he said. "And when you do, promise me you'll get on to bigger things."

"Was it Gran who shot you? Was it?"

"Don't let her think that she did anything wrong. I forgive everyone. Goodbye, my loves, goodbye."

With a rush of air, my father's specter circled my mother and me and I swear I felt a hug. Then, with a soft whoosh, his spirit was gone.

My mother shuddered and let out a low sob.

I sank to my knees, the air sucked out of me. After a few moments, I asked, "So Dad knew that you were still alive and never told me?"

"Yes, he knew," Mom said, sinking down beside me and placing an arm around my shoulder. I cuddled into the curve of her body, and for a moment felt like I was home.

"That's why he brought you to the Flying Demon Tree," she whispered softly in my ear. "So that I could see you at least once a year on your birthday and hear about your life in your own words. I treasured every moment of those visits." She hugged me closer. "But it wasn't enough. I took to following you sometimes while you were roaming the woods."

"So you were *my* watcher in the woods," I said, wondering why I hadn't put it together before.

She nodded.

"I wish so hard you would have let me know. All those years without you. All those years feeling so alone. At least I had Dad and Gran. You had no one."

"It was a price I had to pay for what I'd done."

"And what did you do?" I asked gently, wanting desperately to know.

"It's a story for another time," she said firmly, so I didn't press.

"And did you see him at other times?" I asked.

"No, never."

"Why not?"

"Nora, look at me."

"I'm looking, Mom," I said, staring back into her eyes. "I see nothing here not worthy of our love, and I bet Dad told you that."

"He did, but I could not inflict *this* . . . on the man I love, on you." She rose to her feet, threw off her cape, and held her arms out wide.

The moon silhouetted her body, the flat wedge-shaped head, the bent spine, thick thighs, narrow calves, and the webbed feet of a frog, forced within the confines of a human female form. And stretching on both sides of her body between her wrists and rib cage, were translucent webs of skin.

I muffled a sob, but it wasn't a sob of horror. It was a sob of deep sadness. My mother had gotten it wrong. Far from thinking she was something unworthy of love, I loved her even more, just as she was. "Mom, Mom. Dad would never have thought you were ugly. I don't think you are ugly either. You are beautiful. Magnificent even in your unique form. We would have loved you and thought you wonderful, but you never gave us the chance."

"No, no, that can't be right," she said. "You *would have* loved me?"

I nodded.

"We still *could have* been a family?"

"We still can," I said, ready to forgive her because it would help heal both our pain.

She shook her head slowly, her face wracked with agony as she seemed to realize that she *had* been wrong. Heart-crushingly, soul-smashingly wrong.

The sky above us darkened. I looked up to see an approaching flock block the light of the moon.

My mother grabbed my arm and helped me to my feet, pulling me close to whisper urgently in my ear.

"Nora," she said. "I need you to listen to me. There's not much time. They are going to ask something of you that they have no right to ask, and you must say no."

For some reason, my mother's instructions seemed to set my destiny. Because if she wanted me to say no, how could I say anything but yes?

69

Azzie 🐸 The Contract

Night of the Pink Moon
Late Dark Time
The Nexus

AZZIE HAD BEEN leading the Palay contingent of frogs and was the first to land on the ceremonial grounds with Linka beside him. Together, they saw the femtoe who had saved them both—Nora. She was there with that strange, hooded creature he had met at what he now thought of as the Lake of the Dead.

They dismounted and waited.

"Leave right now!" the Watcher cried, a protective hand on the girl's shoulder. "You have no claim on this girl."

Then, the femtoe opened the jewelry casket that contained the Pearl. It encased her with a pink glow, like a translucent bubble, breaking the Watcher's hold on her and repelling the Watcher away.

Every time the creature reached out to touch the pink bubble, the bubble grew, pushing the creature farther and farther away from the girl.

The femtoe, with the Pearl resting on the palm of her hand, moved to the raised platform in the middle of the ceremonial grounds and sat in what looked like a bench carved out of stone.

With a few mighty leaps, Azzie reached a column positioned at the side of the stone bench and willed the column to rise so that he could look the girl in the eyes.

The moment they were in that position, the pink bubble that had encased the girl ballooned out to include Azzie and cover the whole of the amphitheater stage, but not the semicircle of tiered perches that ringed their way up the side of the hill that formed the back of this sacred place. These perching stools were now filled with field frogs who had been drawn to this spot from near and far to see the unfolding spectacle.

The creature was forcefully pushed back to the outer edge of the area. Only Azzie and the girl were left within the protected circle the pink bubble had formed.

Azzie was stunned. No one had told him that this would happen. Linka looked puzzled as well. *Was it the quixotic nature of the Pearl?* Or perhaps, no one knew how the whole thing was *really* supposed to work.

Azzie's heart pounded. *All is well. All is as it should be*, he repeated to himself. Speaking loudly enough that his voice reverberated throughout the theater, he recited the words to invoke the start of the ceremony.

"It has begun," Azzie said. A hush fell over the crowd. "Greetings from my mother, Ranya, Queen of Frogs, and from me, Prince Azzumundo," Azzie said, dipping his head forward. "We ask you to join us in an effort to save the All."

Again, the Watcher tried to break through the pink perimeter, but the greater the force she used to try to penetrate the light, the harder she was repelled.

"Let me in, let me in! Nora, please don't do this. You have no understanding of what they want and what it will do to you!" the Watcher cried.

Nora turned away and looked straight at Azzie.

Azzie cleared his throat. "We kindly request that you come to our aid, to the aid of the world, by participating in the Ceremony of Renewal. The state of the world's environment is dire, and we must work together to save it."

Nora shivered and said, "Your words echo my father's before he died. I thought you just wanted the Pearl, but it seems that you have something different in mind."

Her mother was pounding on the pink barrier between them. "They want *you*! They need you to do their bidding—don't! Please!"

"The Watcher is right. We do need you. But it is not to do our bidding. It's to follow the ways of the ancients to enact the Ceremony of Renewal."

The femtoe looked like she was contemplating whether she should stay or run.

"Oh, please, do not worry," Azzie said kindly. "We mean you no harm. But we need your help."

"You do?"

Azzie nodded. "And we do not have much time."

She seemed less afraid. And more willing to listen.

Nora took a deep breath, released it, and nodded her head. "I'll listen."

"From time immemorial, until the Pearl was stolen by one of our own, Prince Ponte-Fricani (curses on his name), an annual ceremony was held to renew the connection between largetoe and the All with the goal of reversing your kind's perspective on their assumed role in the world. The ceremony gave them a sense of what things are like from the point of view of others. It was our gift to your kind, along with your power to dream."

"I'm sorry? Are you saying that we owe our dreams to you?"

"If you come with us, you will understand."

The girl stared at him blankly. Oh, that's right. He needed to *tell* her more of the story.

"We are inviting *you* to participate in this ancient ceremony designed to remind your kind of their humble role in the world."

"Humble? My kind is hardly humble. Unfortunately."

"We can agree on that!" Azzie said and wondered if he'd gone too far too fast.

"Please, tell me more."

"Here is the situation. Together, we have the chance to accomplish the remarkable. Come with us and we can work together to come up with ways the largetoe can live more respectfully on the earth without wielding your kind's talent for creating destruction.

"While you are one of us . . ."

"One of you?" she asked.

"I will get to that. Please, bear with me. While you are one of us, not only will you learn to see things from our point of view, you will have the honor of participating in the Confab for the All, an extremely rare meeting of all the elements of the world—plant, animal, as well as the forces of nature—where everyone can participate equally in creating a vision of what it would look like if we honored earth and every form of life on it."

"I would love to participate in such a gathering. Truly, I'd be honored."

"There's a catch!" the creature bellowed from beyond the pink dome. "Tell her about the catch."

"Yes, what is the catch?"

"You have to become a frog," Azzie said.

Her eyes widened into little full moons, like the one in the sky. "Could you repeat that, please? I didn't hear you right."

"You have to become a frog. Otherwise, you are too big to visit the Palay."

The girl clutched the Pearl more tightly in her hand.

"And I want to visit the pa-lay because?"

"To learn about what your kind is destroying. To see things from our point of view. To celebrate with us the glory of all things frog! And to take back that message to your kind. They do not value us or the All as a whole and that lack of awareness and respect is destructive."

"I don't disagree that we largetoe are all kinds of horrible. But I kind of like being me. I really like being me. Well, maybe things suck now, but not so much that I would want an interspecies transplant. How is anything like that even possible?"

"With the power of the Pearl, and our mutual intention, anything is possible."

"I don't know about this."

"It is only three days. And you will automatically turn back to yourself."

Azzie could tell he was losing her. That she was closing her mind to the idea.

"Ah, sorry, I have to get back home to help my gran. She is in danger, and I promised I'd go to her."

"The world needs you, Nora. You are our best hope that we can come together, truly as one mind to find a way forward that makes the most of what we have left."

She thought about it for a moment. "That's what my dad said - that I was the 'best hope.'"

"It sounds like your father would have wanted you to go through with it," Azzie said.

"I think he would, but you're a little vague on all the details," Nora said. "Can you be more specific?"

"I swallow this potion. You and I kiss in the presence of the Pearl. And then—"

"Right. The kissing thing." She didn't sound like she thought it was the greatest idea. But then, neither did he.

"We kiss. As I recall, we have already done it back at the Gathering Glen when you breathed life back into me."

"That was no kiss. I was trying to save your life to repay you for saving mine with your song. I'm still not sure about the kissing part, but say we do. Then what happens?"

"You change into a frog."

Nora laughed and shook her head in disbelief. "Okay. Stop there."

"A frog. What kind of frog you will turn into we do not know for sure, but we will soon find out."

"Oh, no we won't! I'm not changing into any frog."

The Watcher sighed with relief. "Tell them, Nora! Tell them you won't do it."

Nora looked at the Watcher with confusion, then shook her head as if she couldn't make up her mind.

Azzie saw a change come over her face. She took a deep breath and returned her gaze to him.

"Tell me more," Nora said.

"No, Nora! You mustn't. Do nothing the frogs ask of you!" the creature pleaded from outside the bubble.

"You, beyond the pink dome," Azzie said, addressing the Watcher. "You are the one who warned us not to land at the Lake of the Dead. Thank you."

"In return for the favor, I beg you, do not ask my daughter to do as you have requested. I—"

"Your *daughter*? How is that possible?" Azzie asked.

"It is a story you should ask your mother," the creature said.

"What has my mother got to do with this?" Azzie asked.

"Your mother has everything to do with this, Nephew."

The word struck him like a slap, and Azzie could feel his heart beating.

"There is only one frog who could call me nephew. My Aunt DeLili. But she is dead."

"She is not dead. She is right in front of you. I am DeLili, former Queen of Frogs, and elder sister to Ranya, your mother, and Balarius, your uncle." She then looked at Linka and said, "Greetings to you, my niece."

Linka did a double dip of her snout, eyes wide in amazement.

Azzi, too, was stunned as he followed Linka's example and bowed before his aunt.

"DeLili?" Nora said.

"The human name Reggie was my little joke," DeLili said. "A daily reminder that I had given up my rank as Regina, as they say in Latin, or Queen of the Frogs, to be your father's wife and your mother."

"The Queendom of Frogs thinks that you are dead, Aunt," Azzie said. "That is why my mother is the queen. She took your place." But his aunt was not paying attention.

"You . . . you were a frog?" Nora said, at this point beside herself. "The Queen of Frogs?"

"That is how I started off life. Until I fell in love with your father, Nora. The first time I traveled outside the protective Veil of Mist, I saw him working in the woods. And fell instantly and forever in love with him."

"I didn't know such things happened," Nora said.

"They aren't supposed to. But in my case, it did, and that love sent me on a quest around the world to find the stolen Golden Pearl of the Forest so I could do what Prince Ponte-Fricani had done so long ago. Instead of using the power of the Ceremony of Renewal to change a largetoe into a frog, he conspired with the then vizzard, Darcillus, to change the formulation of the potion so that he, Fricani, would change into a largetoe. If he could do it, so could I.

"After much searching on my part, that is exactly what I did. And Azzie and Linka, your parents helped for their own reasons. Ba helped so he could continue his experiments of which I most heartily disapproved of and had forbidden. And Ra helped because she wanted to be queen and could never achieve that with me on the throne. The transition was agony, Nora. Pure agony. But when it was through and your father and I were united, we were happy. Your dad and me—and then you. Truly happy. But there is a cost to breaking the laws of nature."

"Oh, Mom!" Nora said and rushed from her bench to the edge of the pink bubble, shoving the Pearl in her pocket as she ran.

Azzie immediately feared that she would break through, and the magic of this moment would be lost. But she only went up to the bubble, not through it, placing her hand on its see-through surface.

When his aunt placed her hand up there, they matched the spread of their fingers—Nora's webless, human fingers and her mother's webbed and gnarled ones. Bending forward, they touched their foreheads to the pink field of energy, causing a rainbow of soft pastel colors to ripple outward, shaking the dome.

When the ripples had subsided, they looked into each other's eyes.

"Nora, my child, that is why you must not do what the prince, my nephew, would have you do," she said. "It will change your body forever in ways you can't anticipate now. That's what happened to me. When you were eight, my body began reverting to its original form. That's when I got stuck in this monstrous shape, half one thing, half another."

"You mean, the potion that you took changed you into a human—but it wore off?"

"I don't know what happened. I have never spoken with the one who made the potion—my brother, Balarius, the Grand and Glorious Vizzard—to find out what might have gone wrong."

"Maybe he could help," Nora said.

"I cannot go there like this—and he cannot come to me, so it is pointless. There is no hope. There is no cure."

"But Dad said there's always hope! Maybe he wanted me to do this to help not only others but to save you as well." Nora kissed her mother's forehead through the dome, causing another ripple. "Don't worry, Mom. I've got this." Then she broke away and returned to the bench, where she sat down and faced Azzie with a look of determination in her eyes.

"What comes after the whole 'becoming a frog' thing?" she asked him.

"You come back with us to the Palay . . ."

"Where?"

"Home of all things frog. Oh, it is a magnificent place, Nora," said Azzie. "You must see it. And you will. For three wonderous days, you will be gifted with many astounding things and learn secrets about life that exist beyond the spectrum of your largetoe senses so you can truly comprehend the beauty of the All. You will meet with many different lifeforms and forces and together we will work out a plan of redemption for you to execute when you return to your human form. And you will also have time to explore your roots and meet your relatives."

Nora's eyes brightened at his words.

"Then we will return you here, and you will change back into your human form and take what you have learned from our world into your own—to open the eyes of those who were once ignorant like you. Your act of trust in us would be the beginning. It would help re-instill the understanding that all life forms—including the earth itself, and the air and the water—depend on each other to survive and to thrive."

"But look at what happened to my mom. How can you promise that won't happen to me?"

"With all due respect to your mother, what she did was try to reverse-engineer a sacred act. That is bound to have grave consequences."

Nora looked at him with skepticism in her eyes. "Are you blaming my mother?"

"Not at all!" Azzie said. "I am explaining why things could have gone awry with her."

Nora looked upset.

In a manner as calm as he could muster, Azzie said, "This must all be so very hard for you to take in—and to trust that my kind has your best interests, as well as ours, in mind. But you need not worry. For us to continue to live, you must continue to live. So we will do nothing to jeopardize that. Just hear me out as I explain the rest."

Nora nodded.

"The Grand and Glorious Vizzard, your uncle, has given me two vials." Azzie held up a vial that was bejeweled with amethyst and taurine. "This one, in case our discussion led me to determine that you were part frog." Then he held up a second vial of aquamarine and ruby. "Or this one, if it seemed that you were a mere largetoe."

Curious, she moved a step toward him. She raised an eyebrow at him as if repeating his words in her head, *mere largetoe?*

"The formula in the first vial takes into consideration your special circumstances—that you are already part frog—and my uncle has engineered a variation of the ancient formula to protect you from aberrations," Azzie said.

"And what about helping my mom become human again? What if I demand help to make that happen as a condition of helping you?"

"I do not want to mislead you. There might be a way. The vizzard, my uncle, is a clever frog who knows many things. If there were help to be had for your mother, he would be the one to do the helping."

"Help the world and maybe save my mother," Nora said. She closed her eyes in contemplation for a few moments, then said, "You have made me an offer I can't refuse."

Relief flooded through every corpuscle in Azzie's body. At last, he had succeeded at something of value to his mother, his kind, and to himself.

"Of course, there will have to be a written contract that we both sign with witnesses. I've learned the importance of a good contract lately," Nora said.

Azzie wasn't exactly sure what she was talking about, nor did he want to slow things down by asking questions. They only had until the Pink Moon was at its fullest to make the impossible happen. "By all means. We have a contract. Let us look at it," Azzie said.

Azzie retrieved the contract from under his flying cape and handed it to Nora.

"Uh, this looks like a rolled-up leaf," Nora said, examining it.

"Look at it with the light of the Pearl."

Nora removed the Pearl from her pocket and did as he directed, holding the glowing Pearl up to the leaf so that she could see it better. Her eyes widened as the veins of the leaf pulsed with golden light. Shaking off their natural form, the marks meandered along the tissue-like surface to form words in both the language of largetoe and frog. The twin lines danced across a misty screen that formed in front of her, spelling the agreement out word for word.

"Nora, please allow Princess Linka to read it out loud to you."

"I don't ever want to hear any words come out of that frog's mouth ever again," Nora said. "She wanted the Pearl and wasn't afraid to hurt me to get it."

Linka moved forward, her eyes defiant. "I would love to apologize for my actions, but I was under orders of the queen."

"You are lucky Linka disobeyed my mother's orders, which were to kill you," Azzie said.

"Kill me? Maybe it's too dangerous for me to visit an aunt who wants me dead," Nora said.

"No worries there. Mother has changed her mind. Thanks to both Linka and me. We insisted that you not be harmed."

"Lucky me," Nora said. "I'll read the contract for myself."

"The party of the first part, the Frog World, represented by Prince Azzumundo, respectfully requests the party of the second part, Nora, the largetoe, to undergo the following sequence of events powered by the Golden Pearl of the Forest, which is still in her possession. Within the glow of the Pearl's light, the following events will take place:

> *The Party of the First Part will drink the potion prepared for him by the Grand and Glorious Vizzard.*
>
> *Then, the Party of the Second Part will exchange a kiss with the Party of the First Part under the glow of the Pearl.*
>
> *The Party of the Second Part will undergo a rapid transformation to frog. The changeling will return to the Palay*

where she will stay for three days. The changeling will learn
many wonderful things about the world of frogs and the
All. After this time, she will be returned to this place and
to her original form. She promises to go out into the world
with her new knowledge and bear witness to what she has
learned to persuade other largetoes to live as allies of nature
and not as enemies."

The mist dissipated, and the words, golden and shimmering, flowed back into the leaf.

Nora looked at Azzie. "Will it hurt?"

"It will be agonizing!" her mother screamed.

"Yes, there will be pain," Azzie said.

"And what guarantees are there that I'll be put back into this form I was born into?" Nora asked.

"Absolutely none," Azzie said. "But other than your mother's experience, history tells us that it is possible to return to the person you once were."

Nora faced Azzie again. "I have some demands. I will write them into the contract."

"Demands?" Azzie asked, alarmed at the sudden change in plans.

"Yes. Do you have something to write with?"

Linka handed Nora a porcupine quill.

"What's this for?" she asked.

"Use it like a pen. To sign the contract. But you must use your own blood as ink."

"My blood?"

"More binding that way. Now, write your demands in the air and they will be absorbed into the Vein of Truth," Linka said. She pointed to the main vein that ran through the leaf.

Nora stuck the quill into her finger and drew blood. The air in front of her grew misty again. Nora wrote out her changes, drawing more blood from various fingers to keep up with the flow of her writing.

Azzie read the words aloud as they appeared on the misty screen.

"'Number one: There will be no kissing.'"

"That's right," said Nora. "I decide who and when and if I kiss, as well as anything else that involves actions to or changes to my body. No one else decides that for me. And besides, it looks like we're cousins, so that's just gross."

"But we do not know how the potion will react to these changes," Azzie said.

"We won't know until we try it, will we?" Nora said. "But if the whole point of the kissing exercise is to get me the potion—I can swallow it myself."

Azzie and Linka looked at each other and shrugged.

She returned to writing.

"'Number two,'" Azzie read. "'When the P2P' . . . wait, what is the P2P?" Azzie asked.

"Party of the Second Part," Nora said. "Too much blood to write it all out."

Azzie nodded and continued. "'When the P2P turns into a frog, she gets three requests that must be honored.' Hang on a second," Azzie said.

"That is my condition," said Nora.

"But wait—what *are* your requests? We have to know to make sure we can honor them," Azzie said.

"I will tell you the first one. We must go immediately from here to see my grandmother."

"Absolutely not," Linka said.

"I am not asking permission. Grandmother, plus two other wishes, or it's a no-go," I said, extremely confident I would have my demands met.

Azzie withdrew to confer with Linka out of Nora's earshot.

When they returned Azzie said, "There is something you must know. Something that negates our obligation to grant any requests from you."

Nora's eyes squinted in confusion. "What are you talking about?"

"I think you had better ask your mother," he said, "about the contract she signed before undertaking her transformation."

All eyes turned to Nora's mother, the creature and former Queen of Frogs who still stood helplessly outside the pink bubble.

"Mom?" Nora asked. "What is he talking about?"

70

Nora ◎ Metamorphosis

Night of the Pink Moon
Late Dark Time
The Nexus

AZZIE TOOK ANOTHER rolled-up leaf from his pocket. It had a tag hanging from its stem that I couldn't read. He unrolled it and showed it to Linka. They talked some more—somewhat heatedly. But I couldn't hear a word.

"There is a belief on our part that we do not have to give in to any additional demands by you. In truth, signing this contract was a courtesy to you, since your agreement in this matter was already granted by your parent," Azzie said.

"What?" I yelped. "My father wanted me to do this—but how could he agree to anything without my permission?"

"It was not your father," Azzie said, and he looked at my mother. "It was her—and the agreement was made before you were born."

My whole body shook with anger. I was set up—since before birth. No choice in the matter. It wasn't fair. I almost walked off through the pink bubble in protest. But a few things stopped me. If I left, I couldn't help my town or perhaps the broader world. Nor would I be able to help my mom. A few deep breaths—and I let go of the anger, for now.

Azzie handed me the leaf, and I unrolled it and read its contents on the screen of mist. The point of the older agreement was clear: the signer, my mother, had agreed that her firstborn, whether female or male, would become a renewee and participate in the Ceremony of Renewal once she/he was of age. In return, my mother was given the potion she required to turn from frog to largetoe, *if* she found the Golden Pearl of the Forest.

Every deed has its price, and in this case the price was me. But I wondered, who would I be kissing if I'd turned out to be a boy?

"How did you get that contract?" my mom cried. "No one but the parties involved were ever to see it."

"I found it in your brother's library and brought it along—out of curiosity and for reference if needed. I really had no idea that it would apply to this situation, but here we are. And here the contract is—so I do not think we have to agree to any additional demands," Azzie said.

"Mom?" I said, walking to the edge of the pink bubble. I felt doubly betrayed, hurt, and just plain sad.

"Nora, you have to understand. When I signed that . . ." She broke down and wept.

Azzie spoke. "According to the contract, we can name the date for the ceremony. And we so name this day."

My senses were swirling. "You mean to tell me that you agreed I would go through this torture, as you describe," I yelled at my mother, "before I was even born?"

"I had no idea if my quest for the Pearl would be successful, or that I would turn into a human—let alone give birth to a largetoe child," my mother said, tears the size of dimes falling from her eyes. "It's not an excuse, but I didn't realize the implications of what I was agreeing to, or the pain I would go through, as well as the hurt I'd impose on others. It's that pain and hurt I'm trying to spare you from now."

"Yet you signed my life away—to get the life you wanted," I said. "What kind of mother does that?"

"I've been trying to protect you from just this thing ever since I knew I was with child," my mother said. "Everything I've done since you were born has been aimed at trying to keep this from happening—even if it means the whole world suffers."

"And you, Frog Prince, you would hold me to a contract that I didn't even sign," I said, my cheeks burning with anger. "What's to stop me from leaving here and not agreeing to anything?"

"You could try," Azzie said.

I thought about putting the Pearl back in its case and disappearing from this bizarre world forever.

I moved to shut the casket so I could go, when Azzie said, "No. Wait. We agree to your demands—whatever they are. Forget about what your mother did. We cannot allow ourselves to be ruled by our parents' mistakes. Let us, you and I, undertake this to try to make the world better for the All."

I sighed. What was the use of fighting something that seemed at this moment to be my destiny since before I was even conceived?

"Let us begin," I said, and I poked my finger again with the quill. I stared placidly through the dome and signed the leaf while my mother beat against the wall of pink crying.

Azzie moved back in front of me. He stuck a quill in his thigh, drew blood, and signed. The leaf glowed with bright golden light as it absorbed his signature. "The deal is done," he said.

Azzie removed two amulets from the inside of his cape.

"You're sure this is the right one?" I asked.

"Pretty sure," the prince said with a wink. "Yes. The amethyst vial is for this situation. Definitely."

I held it up to the light. Whatever it was that roiled inside like a phosphorescent rainbow storm looked *alive and potentially lethal.* I had second thoughts.

I looked at my mom. I understood her fears, but that didn't mean I had to live them out. I was making this decision. I wanted to do it. I hoped, *really* hoped, that I could find a way to help her—but the Earth needed help as well, and the lives of billions of living things had to count as billions of reasons to do this—not just one.

To help her. To help the world.

I fumbled with the tiny cover. When I got it off, I held the amulet up, stuck my tongue out, and turned the amulet over. A single drop of liquid hit my mouth. I smacked my lips.

And waited, my body tense, my nerves on fire.

"Why isn't anything happening?" I asked. I looked around. Would I ever see such beautiful sights again? A slight tingling over every inch of my skin felt like it was raining tacks.

I stood up. My heart pounded. My head ached. My tongue burned. *Everything will be okay*, I told myself, remembering the lessons I'd learned from my recent experiences. I had already experienced turning into a tree and survived that. Surely I could turn into a frog and back again.

A haze settled over everything. Had I already grown a second set of eyelids? My mother beat at the pink light of the dome, which now appeared in oh so many colors, some I had never seen before. With each blow of her fist, the pink light changed to a pulsating rainbow of colors that blossomed into concentric circles.

A searing pain passed through my body. I screamed. But I couldn't hear it. I couldn't hear anything.

The air brushed against me, whirling in circles so fast around my head that I was dizzy and weak. My stomach knotted so tightly the pain pitched me to my knees. What little I had eaten for the past day came roaring out of my mouth.

And then I couldn't see.

The beautiful light, gone. My mother, gone. I tried to sit up, but I didn't know what direction up was. I reached out my hands, flailing for anything, anyone, to hold me and make it better. But there was only blackness and nothingness until the bone-crushing pressure hit. It was like an oil tanker was slamming me against a wharf and flattening me as thin as the leaf the contract was written on. My entire mass retracted, slowly, into itself. Fire and ice alternated in every cell.

My hands, legs, torso, were no longer as they had been.

A pressure was building, surging, flooding me with an even deeper darkness that sucked every ounce of life—my life—into it.

My back ached, no, *burned*, like a slab of raw flesh laid out on a cutting board, pounded by a meat mallet and sprinkled with chili peppers and salt. Meanwhile, I was drowning in the smell of burnt chicken feathers, or more like cow hide, no . . . *my* hide, which sizzled, snapped, and popped as the chili pepper worked its way in. Only I didn't hear the sizzles, snaps, and pops—I *suffered* them. My flesh, bone, and cartilage broke form, discarding my mass and reforming me into something entirely new.

A wheel mad with color appeared before my eyes. And as I watched, the colors fused into the shapes of various body parts much smaller than my own. There were arms with webbed hands and legs that were long and powerful and covered in skin that was textured and colored differently from the skin I'd been born with. There was a rounded back and flatter head and bigger eyes but no real nose and no ears. I could hear again but only a giant, high-pitched hissing sound that, if it went on for too long, would drive me crazy.

I passed into unconsciousness as I was eaten by the night under the light of the Pink Moon.

71

Azzie 🐸 First Swim, Last Breath?

Night of the Pink Moon
Late Dark Time
The Nexus

THE STONE BENCH where Nora sat sank into the ground as she changed size until it was flush with the ground. As she became smaller, the space she occupied became smaller as well, until Nora was a perfectly amazing purple frog. She was the richest purple Azzie had ever seen. Golden sprinkles the shapes of stars lightly brushed her skin from her brows down the sides of her body. And out of the top of her head grew a tuft of pink hair. Remarkable.

Relief flooded through him, followed by a sense of awe. That which he secretly desired for the sake of the All and dreaded because he was too weak to play his role had happened. He was seized by wonderment at the power of intention mixed with alchemy and metaphysics.

It was over. What a harrowing sight it had been to see the torturous reduction in scale and form the girl had undergone. Now all they had to do was get back to the Palay. Right? He heard a sound that froze the relief running through his veins. It was a drip. Of water. And it was remarkably close.

Azzie's gut tightened as each drop rang out like a bell.

One drop.

Then another.

Of course! This was the dreaded water part. Every fiber of his being burned with flames of fear. It was like some precognition of disaster had seized him. Things had gone horribly wrong during the faux ceremony. This was his chance to remake a past wrong into an immediate right.

Instead of berating himself as a coward, he began to encourage himself to succeed. *You can do it. You can do it*, he repeated to himself and willed himself to ignore the familiar frazzled buzz of fear that nipped at his nerves.

He spotted more dripping from the open mouths of the gigantic frog statues—a sign they were portals for water. This theory was quickly proven accurate as the drops turned into trickles, the trickles into streams.

Soon water was gushing forth, filling the floor of the amphitheater, which was ringed with a lip of stone to form a pool. The water level was quickly rising to the level where Nora's new frog body lay still.

The crowd joined in as Linka began to chant, "First swim, first swim, first swim," like they were all waiting for Nora to rise, dive in, and show off some strokes.

Why didn't Nora move? The rising water level would cover her soon.

And now the water pooled around her. Pacing the perimeter of the now full pool, Azzie quickened his step, swallowing the urge to turn his back on the whole thing and hop off into the night. There would be no forgiveness for that disgrace.

Every muscle and nerve in his body sizzled with lightning. He had to be the one to save her. It was the only way to save himself.

The water had covered Nora's body completely. Flashbacks of the faux Ceremony of Renewal hit him. Would he fail again?

It was now or never. A few more moments and she could be dead. Drowned. Because of him.

Go. "Oh, Well of White Light, help me," he begged out loud. "I am nothing without your strength."

A ray of hot white light shot up from the earth and engulfed him. And he heard one word: *breathe.*

Taking in the deepest of breaths, he jumped.

The water burned his skin at first. Then, with each powerful kick of his back legs, layers of shame about his infirmity washed away as he dove toward the bottom of the newly formed pool where Nora the frog sat like a stone at the bottom of a lake.

He dove down to fetch her. Grabbing her by the tuft of white hair that still stuck out of her head, he pulled her upward, kicking his strong back legs with all his might toward the surface.

With a final thrust of power, he pulled her onto the stone perimeter of the pool and turned her over on her back.

She wasn't breathing.

He poked her.

Still her chest didn't move. Then he pressed on the lower part of her abdomen, willing air into her lungs.

One push.

Nothing.

A second push.

No movement.

A third, fourth, fifth push, each one a little harder and faster.

He leaned over her and whispered, "Breathe." And finally she gasped for air, along with coughs and sputters.

One day he would compose an ode to this moment of joy, when he felt fear no more. All would be well. He would be well. While the water had yet to bring him comfort and joy, like his brethren, perhaps that would one day come too.

Raising his snout to the sky for a croak of gratitude, he stopped, choking on his own tongue. For there, circling the dome, was the biggest flock of flying Bulldoggies he had ever seen.

And the already wildly cheering crowd flew into a panic at the sight.

Nora 🐸 In the Beginning

Night of the Pink Moon
Late Dark Time
The Nexus

I N THE BEGINNING of my life as a frog there was . . .

Pain. Salt. On. Raw. Flesh. Pain.
Darkness. Buried in the earth black.
Terror. Starting as one thing. Ending up as another.
Silence. Sound muzzled by the void.

And then there was . . .

Deeper pain.
Bone-grinding, stuffed-in-a-bag-too-small pain.
Light. In vivid colors I didn't know existed.
Water. A vibrant medium with unimaginable

depths.

Terror. Yes. Terror of the complete unknown.

As my reconfigured senses came to me, the world seemed so very big. At the same time, I was aware of my former size and felt confused by the difference between what I had been and what I now was. But there wasn't time to be confused. There wasn't time to adjust.

I patted my skin and recoiled. It had the ice-cold, rubbery feel of death that reminded me of my father's body. I held my hand up to the moon and spread my fingers. The pink moonlight glowed behind the translucent purple webs between my fingers. Purple!

I looked down into the water that still surrounded us and saw my reflection in startlingly bright and vibrant color. I was popsicle purple with a peppering of golden freckles that ran down the sides of my body like racing stripes. And there, on the top of my head, was my tuft of straight white hair turned shocking pink. Even though it was a different color, the shaft of hair was a comforting sight. That, along with the whitish raised swirl in the center of my chest, the scar from Kincade's bullet wound, reminded me of my old body, my body of origin. I touched the scar. It still hurt. But then I realized, while *everything* on my new body hurt, *this* part of the new me hurt more.

A wave of sadness engulfed me. What had happened to my blondish hair, my blue eyes, my pale skin? Where had my longer arms and legs, my squarish big toe, the mole on my right thigh gone? My mind, my heart, my feelings, my passions, and convictions seemed to be the same—it was still me inside. But the outside me was gone. Where, I didn't know. And I had to wonder if that me would ever return. Would I ever be the same again? A wrenching sense of loss twisted tightly around me.

The sky went dark. Where'd the moon go? I strained to focus, though I seemed to be seeing things in still pictures that shuddered from one to the next. But there was nothing but a whirl of shadows in the air.

"Those are Bulldoggies, Nora, more than we have ever seen before. And they are all here for you. General Oddbull wants the Pearl—and he wants you—thanks to Raeburn's treason. And he will kill us all to get what he wants," Azzie said. "We have to leave now."

I gulped and almost swallowed my tongue, which was way bigger before.

"Here, take my armor," Linka said.

I tried to protest but I couldn't speak. I still had a lot to say to that frog princess, but now was not the time.

They dressed me in Linka's armor. It was light, but it didn't make it easier to move. I needed a course in how to be a frog, but with no time to study, I'd have to jump into the deep end of the pond.

They also fitted me with what they called an arachnachute. When Linka explained to me what it was and how to use it, I said, "Yes, I have seen them in action," remembering the frogs who had deployed them at the battle before I was shot.

As my eyes grew more accustomed to the dark and adapted to the herky-jerky workings of the frog eye, I saw that there was a battle raging around me. The outer ring of flying Bulldoggies had swarmed around the amphitheater, attacking the observers as they tried to flee.

"You are going to ride with me," Linka said.

"Never fear, Princess Nora. I will see you safely to the Palay," Myth said.

I cocked my head at the word *princess*.

"When a clear spot opens, we will take it," Linka said.

I noticed that the pink dome was fraying in places, thinning, but not yet enough to let the Bulldoggies in.

"We have placed the Pearl, which is spent for the moment, inside a new amulet around your neck," Azzie said.

I clutched my neck, remembering that the Pearl fell from my hand as I changed into a frog and peered down to see a beautifully hand-wrought celestine amulet hanging from a gold chain that was perfectly scaled for my new size. I shook it and heard the Pearl rattle inside. "Thank you," I said. "But what do you mean by 'spent'?"

"Notice how much smaller in size the Pearl is now that your transformation is complete?"

It was!

"That is because all its powerful energy was used for your transformation," Azzie said.

Wait a minute. If its magic is all used up, how's it going to be able to fuel back up in three days' time to get me back to normal? It was a question that I'd ask when I had the strength to accept the answer.

Still, I was grateful to have the Pearl, in any size, around my neck. It had become like a mysterious ancient friend. I had the feeling it was trying to teach me to be wise, to believe in my own powers, not just the Pearl's. But it also kept me guessing. What could I do on my own and what did I need the Pearl for? The Pearl had become my partner in this adventure, and I knew there was much still to learn.

"Mount up, Your Highness," Linka said. And I moved awkwardly toward the bat, tripping over my own webbed feet.

I was finally able to choke out some words. "Why is everyone treating me like royalty?"

"I see you do not realize the repercussions of your mother being our former queen," Linka said.

I tried to shrug my shoulders and almost tipped forward. A frog's body did not work like a human one.

"That makes you royalty. With my father being your uncle, we are cousins."

Does every girl have to be a princess? I was quite content to be plain Nora. Or at least I had been until I decided to become a frog. I was never sure why so many girls wanted to be princesses. Maybe it was because as a princess you get to tell everyone what to do. I'd have to try that out.

"Hang on now. I am wrapping a flyrein around you so you do not fall off," Linka said, showing me how to climb up on the bat. I inserted my feet into a saddle-type seat. Once I was settled, Linka hopped on in front and we took to the sky, bursting through the pink dome, which crumbled as we passed through.

"It keeps others out but does not keep us in," Linka said.

As we climbed into the sky, I wondered how all this could be. But there was little point in asking that now. It was done. I only hoped it could be undone in three days' time.

Leading the way was Prince Azzie, with flyers on either side of him in a *V* formation. Linka and I were tucked in safely behind the point of the *V*.

"I am going to take you to see your grandmother," Linka said, "and Azzie is going to lure the Bulldoggies away to give us time to escape."

Below I saw my mother battle Bulldoggies who had either fallen or landed. My heart beat faster as hundreds of them surrounded her. But they had no interest in her when they saw we were escaping and quickly took to the sky after us.

Goodbye, Mother, I said silently. *I hope to bring back a cure that can return you to me.*

73

Nora 🐸 Forgiveness

Night of the Pink Moon
Deepest Night
Salmon Falls

I WAS FAR FROM comfortable in my new body. The armor didn't help and chafed in places that I didn't want to think about. Myth's soaring bob-and-weave flight pattern was also a problem, and I was sure he would see me hurling before the night was through. Azzie distracted the Bulldoggies while we flew through a bank of clouds as we zipped across the sky.

I wasn't afraid. I was simply discombobulated. The night wasn't dark like I expected it to be. It was a kaleidoscope of brilliant new colors. Oh, if only everyone could see the world this way, they'd feel it was way too precious to be harmed.

Linka handed me another vial, this one carved from fire opal. "My father wanted you to drink this if you made it through your change."

"You mean there was some doubt?"

Linka shrugged like it didn't matter to her one way or another.

"Drink it. It will fortify your mind and spirit and reduce the shock of transition to your body."

That sounded good. I drank its contents eagerly. Even though I had changed size, the amulet hadn't, so this time it was more of a swallow than a drop.

"Father was concerned that any strengths or weaknesses you had as a human would impact how you would be as a frog, and he told me to warn you that your body may do strange things—that you may have unusual powers other frogs do not have, even before the gifting," Linka said.

"The gifting? What is that?" I asked, trying not to focus on the 'unusual powers' comment. Being a frog was unusual enough for me right now.

"You will see when you arrive at the Palay," Linka said. "Although I am beginning to wonder if we will ever get there at this rate."

We passed through that curtain of mist. (I'd been right. I found a way out! I hadn't been expecting, however, to leave as a frog.) I drank the moisture into my skin. On the other side of the mist, the difference in the air quality was noticeable and not in a good way. I could feel the dirt in the air. It hurt my skin, burned my eyes, and weighed heavy on my chest when I breathed it in.

As my eyes adjusted, I began to perceive the strings of energy running between everything. It was spectacular. And dizzying. And disturbing. But as we neared civilization, I noticed that more and more strings were frayed and broken.

I sensed other birds following us. Ravens they were. And leading them was my father's raven friend Poe. He flew by Linka and me with a nod.

"Do you know that raven?" I asked Linka.

"I do," she replied. "And a real scoundrel he is. Stole the Pearl right in front of me."

"And gave it to me," I said. "Another time too. Guess that makes him my friend and your scoundrel."

"Never trust a raven. That is what I always say."

I could not take her advice seriously. Poe had proven to be my friend. He didn't have to be hers.

"I suppose I could have adopted a more positive attitude when I realized we were probably related. . ."

"And when was that?" I asked, suddenly wondering why I was the last to find out about my unusual relatives.

"When you showed me your mother's journal. I immediately felt the tugging of a familial webstring and I did not like it one bit. So, of course, I did not like you either."

"Me? Irritating?" I said with a scoff. "The feeling is mutual, cuz. Too bad all this 'being connected' stuff doesn't actually lead to liking each other and getting along."

"Hold on, Princesses," Myth said. "Turbulence coming up."

I wanted to tell him not to call me that, but that seemed a bit rude since he was taking me to Gran.

After we bounced through a bit of sky, Linka picked up our previous conversation.

"And, I've got to say, I'm not too fond of your mother. She put me in a cage! Humiliating."

"I suspect she did not want you anywhere near me. She desperately wanted to stop what happened back at the Nexus."

"I guess I cannot blame her for that—but a cage?"

"I hope that is not what you are planning for me when I get to the Palay," I said. A longing for the past squeezed me like a vice grip. Would things ever be normal again?

When we finally arrived in Salmon Falls, I was shocked to see how buildings and cars and asphalt disrupted the connecting strings between earth and sky, and everywhere else in between. Instead of a lovely colorful spider web of connection, there were ropey strands of dingy cobwebs. It made the air look spooky and grim.

I instinctively clamped my eyelids down twice and the connecting lines went away. I blinked again and they came back. I appeared to have an on/off switch for them, which was a relief and eased the queasiness in my stomach caused from seeing, firsthand, how broken the environment really was. This fraying reminded me of what my father's spirit had told me when I released his ashes.

When we got to the hospital, we circled around it a couple of times, scouting for a way to enter. There were transoms on the windows on the upper floors, but they were all buttoned up tight. The only way in was through the front door.

Myth did a flyby as I explained how things worked in my world.

"If we can hit that button there really hard," I said, pointing to the wheelchair access by the front door, "the doors will open."

"Leave it to us," Linka said. Myth came in high above the button and banked a sharp turn. Linka leapt from Myth's back, did a somersault in the air, and hit the button with her powerful back legs. Myth pulled a tight pivot and came in almost at ground level. Linka landed expertly on his back, and we flew right through the door.

"Well done," I said. Their precision was remarkable. I told Myth to fly alongside the fluorescent lights so we didn't cast a shadow. I also warned him away from the sprinkler valves that dotted the ceiling.

The stairway door would be impossible to open. The only way up was the elevator. I wanted to try Linka's trick but wasn't sure I was in full control of my new legs and arms, so Linka used a stone from a bag that hung off the saddle and threw it against the elevator button. Bullseye. The doors opened and we flew inside.

It was time for me to be a little brave, so while Myth treaded air in front of the elevator buttons, I jumped at them, hitting the floor number we needed. Myth repeated his quick pivot, but I missed and dropped to the floor with a thud. Myth flew up to the ceiling and hovered nervously.

When the elevator doors opened on the wrong floor, a woman tried to get in, but when she saw a flapping bat, she screamed and ran away. I urged Myth to remain calm until the elevator doors closed and we got to the right floor. This was my world, and I knew how to navigate it.

When the doors opened on Gran's floor, I saw Seth snoozing in a folding chair in the hallway. Bless his heart, it looked like he'd fallen asleep guarding Gran.

I signaled Linka to head into Gran's room, and they glided past as I hopped behind. Turns out I was getting pretty good at this hopping thing and could quickly travel quite a distance (for a frog). Maybe hopping was one of my superpowers.

Once inside Gran's room, Myth landed in the corner by the curtains and hung upside down, his wings wrapped protectively around Linka as she peered out to keep watch on what was happening below.

The bed looked awfully high, and the surface appeared uneven to me from where I sat on the floor. So, I decided to try for the bedside table. One giant hop and I was almost eye to eye with

Gran, who was asleep. That hop had been a bit of a thrill, but it was even more thrilling to see that Gran was alive and sleeping peacefully.

I had landed on a piece of paper that skidded a little across the table. When I looked at the paper I was sitting on, I saw it was something I'd only heard about. It was a telegram from Recycle Rick in Rwanda. I had to jump up on the tissue box to get far enough away to see the words. It said:

> *Got your message. Devastated by Henry's death. Gave me his conservation easement papers to mail. But forgot. Still in my possession. Will return to you when I'm back in two weeks. Love, Rick*

Good! Maybe we would be able to prove that Kincade was a liar. At least that was one problem potentially solved.

I bet Gran was relieved. Or maybe she hadn't seen it yet. I made the short hop from the tissue box to the bed and scrambled as close to Gran's ear as I could without tumbling down the pillow onto the mattress.

As a frog, would I need the Pearl to communicate with humans? I decided to try without opening it first. "Gran, it's me. Nora." I spoke with thoughts, not words.

Gran moaned in her sleep and mumbled my name out loud. Okay, maybe she was hearing me. Maybe she wasn't. I said more.

"I have a message from Dad to us both. He forgives us . . . both of us . . . for the part we played in his death."

A tear trickled down her face and she thrashed a bit in her bed.

"But what did you do, Nora?" she asked, not in words (she still slept) but in thoughts like I had.

"I was there, Gran," I said. "And that's why Dad came. That's why he died. And I think you were there, too. But I don't know why or when."

Gran, becoming increasingly agitated, said, "It was my fault. Mine."

"Tell me what happened that night—the night Dad was killed."

And then, I don't know quite how, but my consciousness meshed with hers: separate, but together. I could see and feel her memories as she saw and felt them.

"By the time your dad listened to your phone message, it was in the wee hours of the night. We were frantic about where you were and were about to call Ardith when your dad thought to check his messages. We were both shocked. Why would you do something so foolish, girl? Risking so much to save some bears.

"Sometime after your father had left, Mel came to the door and told me that Henry needed me up the mountain. Something had happened. Something terrible. Said he didn't know what. So he loaded up a couple of guns from the house, and we drove to our grove of sequoias, where you and Henry were supposed to be."

There was something here that didn't quite make sense. Why would Dad need Gran? If anything, he would have gone out of his way to keep her safely at home. My blood ran a little colder at her words.

Then I saw her standing at the edge of the gravel road in front of the giant trees. The sky was growing lighter with every passing minute. She kept shifting from one leg to another like her feet hurt, and I saw that she was wearing her house shoes with the thin soles. She was wringing her hands and shivering. She reached into her pocket and pulled out her gloves, accidentally bringing the blue origami paper along with them. The paper fell to the ground. She was about to pick it up when Finley came around from the other side of the truck and handed her a gun.

"Got to be ready to protect the people you love," he said with a lopsided grin that was a bit demonic.

"Talk louder," she said, and I realized she wasn't even wearing her hearing aids.

There was a noise in the woods.

"It's a bear!" Finley cried.

"I don't hear anything," Gran said.

"Trust me."

There was a noise in the distance, its sound hard to hear. But I knew it was the shot that had killed my dad. Who fired it though?

"Over there," Mel pointed and called out, "It's a bear. Attacking Henry!"

Finley tried to fire his gun, but it appeared to jam. "Shoot, Ellie, shoot—save Henry!" he screamed.

Gran was panicky by now. Her breath quickened and it was like I could hear her heart pounding with uneven beats. "What am I aiming at? Where?" she asked, scanning the horizon.

Finley pointed the way. "Shoot. Shoot," he said frantically, whipping up Gran's anxiety to a fever pitch.

Gran planted her shaky legs and fired.

"You got it," Finley said. "Come on, let's go see."

"I don't think I can walk," she said, feeling faint and quite ill.

Finley helped her into his truck and drove a short distance through a roughed-out logging road to the other side of the lot.

Wafts of mist wove between baby beams of sunlight and tree shadows, weaving this dawn into a sinister tapestry. Finley helped Gran down from the truck as she wrung her hands and mumbled words of worry and regret.

My heart quickened. I knew exactly what Gran was going to see: Dad's dead body, bathed in a pool of morning sun. And I couldn't bear to feel the intensity of her loss as she reached his body, knelt on the ground, and cradled his head in her lap, keening his name.

Finley slunk forward. "You shot your son."

"Bear, it was a bear. You said . . .you told me to shoot!" Gran cried.

"Your secret is safe with me. But you will owe me. Big time. There's something I'll be telling you to do—*and you must do it.* Or I *will* tell the sheriff what happened here tonight. And then you will go to jail. For a long, long time. It would be a shame for Nora to be left homeless on her own."

"Homeless?" Gran said. "Why on earth would she be homeless?"

"No time for questions. When I say the word *favor,* you'll give me whatever I ask for. Understood? Or it's off to jail you go."

She was staring at my father's face while Finley blathered on. Dad could have been sleeping, but he wasn't. He was dead. She kissed Dad's forehead and rose with difficulty. Then she marched over to Finley and pulled herself up to her full five-foot-five height and slapped his face. Finley didn't miss a beat. He drew his hand back and connected with her cheek. She staggered backward against a tree.

"Consider yourself officially under my thumb," Finley said, laughing. "Now get in the truck, old woman. Time to go."

Her dream faded and our connection broke. I was horrified by Finley's cruelty. He was every bit as evil as Kincade. Was there a special stream of hate they were drinking from around here or what?

What I'd just experienced explained so much, especially when I thought back to Ardith's drawing.

And now I finally understood why Gran didn't fight Kincade. That was the obvious favor Finley had asked for. I heard him use those very words more than once.

So even though Finley was guilty of being a low-life bottom feeder, he couldn't have been the person who shot Dad. It had to have been Kincade. If he was heartless enough to shoot me, he'd be heartless enough to shoot Dad. If only I could remember what Kincade had said to me just before he shot me. It felt important but I had no recollection past the word *practice*, which was hardly a clue.

Besides, he really was the only one to benefit directly from that favor Finley had asked of Gran, and hadn't they been as thick as thieves up the mountain the day Kincade chased after Mickey and me?

What I wasn't clear about was why Kincade had to humiliate us at Dad's funeral by making the whole thing public. I also didn't know how I was going to be able to prove any of this as a frog.

Convincing Gran of the truth before I had to leave was my only hope.

"Gran, you did not shoot Dad—you did not. I was there before you. I heard the shot that hit Dad. I was with him as he died."

"I didn't shoot him?"

"No, Gran. You did not."

"Henry didn't die alone?"

"No. I was there."

She let out a deep sob, still asleep.

"Finley set it up so you would think you killed him," I said. "But it had to have been Kincade who fired the gun. He wanted our land—and he killed Dad to get it. He is the only one who benefited from Dad's death. We cannot let him win, Gran. We cannot. You have got to tell the sheriff what we know. The truth is the only way to keep you safe."

I felt danger approaching. What could I do as a frog to protect Gran?

I had to get help. But how? I looked around and saw a potential answer. Jumping back over to the bedside table, I did a kind of roundhouse kick to the receiver of the phone, pressed "o" with my nose to get an outside line, then punched 9-1-1 the same way. I thought of what I would say when the call was answered and then remembered—I was a frog. I couldn't say anything.

Someone entered the room and closed the door. I dove behind a box of tissues on the bedside table. Peering around the edge, I froze like a piece of porcelain. I could clearly hear the phone ringing—would the intruder hear it as well?

Then I heard the emergency operator say, "This is 911. What's your emergency?" The intruder walked over and hung up the phone. I gulped when I saw who it was.

"Wake up, Ellie, wake up."

Gran opened her eyes. "Nora? Is that you?" she said, confused at first.

"It's me. Mel. I'm leaving town. Things are getting too hot around here. Damn snoopy sheriff asking too many questions. I need money—a lot of money. And Kincade reneged on his promise to pay me for helping him."

Gran used the beside controller to raise the bed. "You'll get nothing from me," Gran said. "You lied to me. I didn't kill my son. I think you did."

"How is that possible? I was with you." Finley said.

"Yes, you were, but you could have shot him before you came to get me and tried to make me think I'd done it," Gran said.

"You're crazy. It wasn't me," Finely said.

"I think we'd better get Ardith here and let her figure it out," Gran said and reached for the phone.

I peeked out to see a wave of nastiness ripple across Finley's face. His expression terrified me.

"Hold on there just a minute," he said, lunging toward her and ripping the receiver from her hand. "I guess I can tell you this. It isn't going to make any difference in a few minutes anyway," Mel said, and he grabbed a pillow from a nearby chair, and slowly walked his way back to Gran in a threatening manner.

"It was *Kincade* that killed your son. And I happily helped— from creating that note that your interfering granddaughter found to orchestrating that business up the mountain to convince you into thinking you'd killed your son."

Gran inhaled sharply, "You evil son of a bitch. To think I once considered you a friend."

"What about that money?" he growled and twisted the pillow in his hand.

"You're not getting one cent," Gran said. "Now put down that pillow before I get out of this bed and thrash you."

Mel laughed. Not a pretty sound.

"You don't scare me, Mel," Gran said. "And you got your favor. I let Kincade humiliate Nora and me in front of all our friends at the funeral. I didn't fight the sale, although I *knew* you were lying. And I didn't report you for threatening me. You're not getting another thing."

"That favor was for Kincade. I got nothing from it."

"Boo hoo," Gran said.

"Listen, I can still make the sheriff believe *you* were the one who shot Henry. I can be very convincing when I want to be." The venom in his voice thickened with every word.

"Get out of here."

He laughed coldly and with a swift move pounced on Gran, forcing her backward, the pillow smothering her face.

I called for help from Linka and Myth.

Myth was there in a second, circling Finley, while Linka flung stones at his head.

From my hiding place, I jumped onto one of Finley's temples and struggled to cling to his sweaty face. I grabbed a piece of his stringy hair to hold on to, and I kicked him in one eye repeatedly.

Finley roared with anger and grabbed me, dropping his hold on the pillow to do so, and flung me into a corner of the room. I landed with a *splat*, the wind knocked out of me.

Seth rushed in and immediately charged Finley. Seth connected with a grunt and took them both to the floor. Gran screamed instructions to Seth from her bed. "Kick him in the shins! Grab his arm! Punch him!"

Finley was older and wilier, but Seth was younger and stronger. And Seth had Myth, Linka, and me on his side.

I hopped alongside as the two of them rolled on the floor. Whenever I could, I took aim, jumped in the air, and executed a twist so I landed a blow with my back flippers right in Finley's eye. I'd seen Linka do this move, and although I wasn't as smooth as she was, I made an impact and it hurt him.

Myth and Linka swooped around their heads, pelting Finley with more stones, while Gran continued to coach Seth on where to hit Finley.

Eventually Finley's endurance faltered, and Seth pinned him to the ground.

Then, to add another ring to this circus, Ardith and her deputy arrived.

"He tried to smother Mrs. Peters. I saw him." Seth said and they jumped in to help.

"We've got this, Seth. Step away," Ardith said, but Seth wouldn't let go.

Linka and Myth had darted to the ceiling, and I shrank into the corner behind the leg of a chair to watch.

As I hunkered down in my corner, hoping no one would see—or step on me—a prickly, icy sensation rippled across my skin. I looked at my arms and belly. My body had turned from deep purple to hospital green to blend into my surroundings. And my armor changed color too. At least I'd be hard to spot.

"Seth? Ellie? You both okay?" Ardith asked, once they got Finley quieted and cuffed.

"I will be when Nora comes back. Where did she go?" Gran asked. "I thought she was here—I, I must have been dreaming."

"I found Mickey outside my office," Ardith told her. "He had this note from Nora warning me that you were in danger. And it looks like she was right."

"That can't be right," Finley said.

"What can't be right?" Ardith asked.

"Nothing. Never mind," Finley said.

"Better to tell me now than to end up doing time for Carl's sins," she said.

"You can't pin anything on me."

"Doesn't mean I'm not going to try. If I were you, I would be as clear as you can be about what you didn't do."

"I did not murder Nora. That's on Carl. Not me," Findley said forcefully.

The room was silent, taking that in. I wanted to yell that I was still alive to spare them the pain I saw on their faces. But how could I?

"No." Seth lunged for Finley. "What are you talking about?"

Gran had a look of horror on her face that left me hoping that she didn't have another heart attack. "Seth, stop," Ardith said, ready to step in. But she didn't have to because Seth pushed Finley away in disgust and sat on a nearby chair, his head in his hands.

"Now, Mel. Tell me more about when Carl supposedly killed Nora," Ardith said.

"I don't have an exact time," Finley said. "But it was yesterday for sure."

Ardith went over to Gran and showed her the note I'd written.

"Ellie, someone here is wrong. I can't say for sure until we locate her, but I suspect Nora is alive. The note she wrote me was dated two hours ago, not yesterday. Can either of you confirm this is Nora's handwriting?" She shared the note with them both.

"Looks like her writing," Gran said. Seth agreed, then combed his fingers through his hair, relief beaming from his face. And Gran also looked relieved.

"So, what was the reason for this story Carl told you," Ardith asked, "about shooting Nora?"

"According to your dad . . ."

"Don't call him that. He's no father of mine," Seth said.

"According to Carl, Nora attacked him, and he had to shoot her to defend himself."

I wanted to hop up and shout, "I'm here, I'm here." But I probably would just get stomped on.

"Well, there you go. That says to me there's a pretty good chance that what Mel is saying is designed to draw attention away from what he's done wrong," Ardith continued, "or maybe he's less informed than he thinks he is."

Finley's face darkened.

"Not only are you a liar, you miserable bastard. You tricked me into thinking I'd killed my own son while he was already lying dead on the ground by someone else's hand." Gran looked at Seth and said, "And I'm sorry to tell you this, young man, but I believe it was your father who did it."

Seth's face drained of color. He leaned against the wall and slowly sank to the floor, a blank expression on his face.

"I can explain," Finley said.

"I'm sure you can," Ardith said. "Down at the station."

"Read him his rights and get him out of here, Deputy," Ardith said.

"None of this is my fault. It's your dad's," Finley said to Seth. "He's the one who hired me to kill the bears. He's the one that promised me a better paying job as *his* foreman if I helped him get his deal through."

So, I was right about who was killing the bears. Now maybe that would stop. What a creep Finley was—he played my dad and poor Gran and he even played me.

"What about the forged real estate contracts? You have anything to do with that?" Ardith asked.

"Not one thing," Finley said.

"What about trying to get Henry's original paperwork from Nora?"

"That's no crime," Finley said, hotly. "And you can't pin the fire on me, either."

"We'll see about that," Ardith said. Then she placed a comforting hand on Seth's shoulder. "Son, we're looking for your dad. For all the reasons Finley said—and more. Do you know where he is?"

Seth shook his head. "I'll definitely let you know if I hear from him. What'll the charges be?"

"Forgery and fraud for now," Ardith said. "We don't really have enough to pin the arson on him yet—and it was arson. And we'll have to investigate Mel's accusations for sure. So I can't really fully say now."

Seth looked ill. I wanted to hug him. And more.

"Mrs. Peters, I'm so sorry for everything my dad did to you and your family," Seth said, his eyes spilling over with tears. "I wouldn't be at all surprised if in the end he did burn down your house. But whether that's the case or not, I swear I will find a way to rebuild it as good as new."

"Well, son, it was the old parts that we liked best. But I greatly appreciate the offer. You go home to your mom now and comfort her," Gran said. "What I *still* don't understand is why he would have burned down property he was so eager to own. I guess there are a lot of things about hate that don't make sense."

It was time for me to get out of here and on my way, as much as I hated to leave Gran. A promise is a promise. But how were Linka, Myth, and I going to get out?

I tried an experiment with Seth and sent him a silent request. *Seth, it's me, Nora.*

Seth looked around the room, a puzzled expression on his face. "Nora?" he said out loud.

"Shush," I said in my head. And he heard me.

But no one was paying any attention to Seth anyway. Ardith and her deputy were too busy getting Finley out of the room. And Gran looked exhausted.

"I need your help, Seth. The Pearl has turned me into a frog, and I am in the corner of the room."

"Which corner?" Seth, inside his head too.

"The outside corner. I need you to open the window on the other wall—the top part."

Seth heard me and didn't hesitate, although he did have an "I must be going crazy" look on his face. He walked right over and opened the window. A shadow passed over the room as Myth and Link flew out. I breathed a sigh of relief that no one seemed to notice.

A nurse tried to get in the room, but Ardith blocked him.

"We were just leaving," she told the nurse. Then she turned to Gran. "As soon as we get this guy down to the station and process him, we'll look for Nora. You take care now, Ellie."

"Thanks so much, Ardith. Please let me know when you find her," Gran said. "I'll be worried sick until then."

"Nora's a fine girl, and I'd take her at her word that she'll return. So don't worry. Just get better for when she's back." With a nod of her head, Ardith and the deputy ushered out Finley, who was still making noise about the travesty of justice he was experiencing. Man, that guy talked a lot.

All the commotion, not to mention the shock of my complete transformation to another species, was making it hard for me to focus. I had to get out of there, as much as I didn't want to go. But I'd made a promise to my new frog family, and it was one I would keep so I could get back to *this* family. While the nurse checked on Gran, I gave more instructions to Seth.

Seth, pick me up at the corner by the curtain and take me outside.

He rushed over to where I said I was and looked around. But I was the same color as the walls and floor. He took out his phone and turned on the flashlight, which he shined right in my eyes.

He picked me up and looked at me quizzically. "Nora?"

I nodded my purple head.

And then we were on the move. Being held closely against Seth's chest had its advantages. He smelled better than ever, but I have to say I wasn't keen on the amount of body heat he was putting off.

The next thing I knew, we were out in the hallway. Seth opened his hand and stared at me.

"Nora? Is that really you?"

I nodded. The elevator opened and the other Commandos poured out.

"We can't find Nora anywhere," Kameela said. "Is she here?"

"Kinda," Seth said with some hesitation, then opened his hands slightly to let our friends peer at me. I looked up at their beautiful faces as the elevator doors closed and we descended to the lobby.

74

Nora 🐸 The Truth Does Burn

Night of the Pink Moon
Deepest Night
Salmon Falls

WE HAD REACHED the parking lot of the hospital and were standing (well, they were standing) under one of the lights and peering at me through Seth's fingers, which were arranged in a protective dome around my body.

"Where'd you get such a unique specimen?" Kameela said. "I don't think I've ever heard of a purple frog with pink hair."

"She was in the room upstairs," Seth said to the others. He then whispered to me, "You're safe now, Nora."

I could see our friends exchange looks of concern.

"Uh, Seth, are you all right?" Kameela asked.

"He is okay, but he did get hit in the head by Finley," I said to my friends.

"Nora?" Kameela whipped her head around looking for me. Will and Minh did the same.

"She's right here!" Seth said.

"Where?" Will asked.

"This is Nora. She's changed into a frog," Seth said.

At first, they laughed. But after a few moments they seemed to realize Seth was serious.

"Uh, Seth?" Minh said, obviously thinking his friend had gone crazy, "You okay? Did that head injury Nora told us about knock you silly? Where is she anyway?" He spun around looking for me.

Seth didn't respond.

"Okay, Nora, wherever you're hiding," Mihn said, "you can come out now."

"I know what you're thinking," Seth said looking at our friends. "That I'm nuts. That I've flipped out because I just learned that my dad probably killed hers." He nodded in my direction. "And that he also shot Nora."

I nodded my head.

"Wait just a minute here," Minh said. "Did you guys see that frog nod its head—like it was answering Seth's question?"

"She was! This frog *is* Nora. I don't know how. Or why. I just know what is."

"Hi, guys," I said, this time trying to use my frog mouth to say the words.

They all stared at me intensely, like they were hearing things, then said as one, "Nora?"

"Let us go over to that patch of woods where we can talk," I said to them, suspecting that Linka and Myth would be waiting for me there." My words sounded slightly scrambled, but they seemed to understand.

"You heard her," Seth said. "Let's go."

We arrived in the woods, where it was dark—to everyone but me. I guess that's why they turned on their flashlights and trained them on me. I shrunk into the shadows cast by Seth's fingers.

"Don't do that. Can't you see you're hurting her eyes?" Seth said with some force. We all stared with some shock at Seth, who hardly ever raised his voice. But I guess anyone would have to agree that having your almost girlfriend turn into a frog was reason enough.

"We have to use at least one light," Kameela said, a little exasperated.

"Then don't shine it directly at her," Seth said.

To see the expressions on my fellow Commandos' faces was a riot. They looked like they'd been slapped with a piece of seaweed.

"Okay, Seth," Kameela said in her calming and rational way. "Let's start over and take this slow."

"Tell us more about, uh, Nora—the frog," Will said.

I could have explained myself, but Seth had already launched in, explaining about what had happened up in Gran's hospital room. Not just what happened between him and me but all the Finley and Gran stuff as well.

When he finished his explanation, they were all still staring at me, waiting for me to do a frog trick or something to prove what he said was true. Wasn't speaking to them enough?

I tried again to make them realize it was really me.

"Kameela, Mihn, Will—Seth is right. I am a frog."

A big smile broke out on Seth's face. "You see, it *is* Nora."

But our friends still didn't seem convinced.

"So, when did you become a ventriloquist, Seth?" Mihn said, poking Seth in the arm.

"Nora?" Will said, staring at me intently. "Are you—the frog—really Nora?"

I did my best to nod. The three of them gasped and stepped back.

"Nod three times to prove it's you," Will said.

I did as he asked. One. Two. Three. I could tell Will was convinced, Minh was pretty much just terrified, and good old rational Kameela was not ready to accept any fact as weird as this.

"Sorry to be the skeptic here," Kameela said, "but there's no way this is real, and I for one am tired of the joke. I'm out of here. First thing tomorrow morning I'm going out to look for my friend."

"Well, do not look for me by the stand of dying salal," I said.

Kameela froze, then turned around. "Did Nora tell you about that patch of dying salal down by the river?" she asked Seth.

"She told me nothing," Seth said.

"And how about that time when we were nine and you spent the night and ate so many of my mom's cinnamon rolls you threw up?" I asked, certain she'd remember that. "You were so embarrassed you begged me not to tell anyone, and I never did."

"Okay, okay!" Kameela said, looking straight at me. "I get that this voice we're hearing knows things that only Nora would know and *keep to herself*," she said with emphasis. "But that doesn't necessarily mean that this purple frog *is* Nora. We could all be hallucinating, or . . . something. Maybe we got a poison plant in our system when we were up in the mountains and it's messing with our minds."

"Or maybe I am really a frog. Look, I cannot make you believe me. And I will never get back to my human self if I do not go."

"Go where?" Will asked.

I explained most of my story as quickly as I could. I mostly talked about the Pearl, how that worked to change me, and that the whole point of this was to meet with other stakeholders in the natural world to come up with a way to fix the terrible problems we were facing right here in Salmon Falls. And if we were able to make a difference here, then maybe others would learn from what we did and help make their own little parts of the world healthier for all. This was a cause I knew—or at least thought—they would get behind. All of them, that is, except for Kameela.

"I'm sorry, I can't—" Kameela struggled. "What about, you know, the laws of science and nature! No, it's impossible. It's a trick of some kind. This purple frog can NOT be Nora. You're playing a cruel joke on us. I don't like it one bit. And neither would Nora."

"Kameela, think about it. It may be that what I have just told you goes against the laws of science and nature that we know about at this time," I told her. Maybe if my lips moved when I talked, it would be more believable, but I was still communicating using my thoughts. "But I am right here in this form, so something is going on that we did not understand before."

"It's a lot for anyone to take in, Kameela," Seth said. "But we can't spend any more time talking about it. Nora has to go—so she can come back—and I have to find my dad and convince him to surrender to the sheriff."

Those words scared me. I said, "Seth, you have to be careful. Promise me."

He shrugged unconvincingly.

I heard a whistle. It was Linka. I *had* to leave.

"Look guys, I *really* have to go." And it was true. Staying wasn't an option.

"Be sure to come back. Please," Seth said. Were those tears in his eyes?

"I will try my best. And meanwhile, if you make sure Gran's okay, I can go with a lighter heart."

"If it's true . . .," Kameela started. "If you really are this frog I see here, and this is not a trick"—she gave Seth a suspicious side glance— "and you're going where you say you're going to do what you say you're going to do, it's an opportunity like none other to make a real difference."

"If for some reason I do not come back, promise me that you will be the hope," I said, looking at them all in turn.

"The hope?" Kameela asked.

"The hope for the future. The hope for the planet. The hope for all the plants and animals and ecosystems that can only be saved if we do something now," I said.

"*We* are all the hope," Will said.

And then they all reached out to place their hands, palms up, on top of one another and Seth added his hand, holding me, to the top of the pile. And together we said, "We are the hope." The moment passed, hands were withdrawn, but a new conviction had been born.

"We all must do our own special thing," I said. "Apparently becoming a purple frog is mine." Everyone chuckled. "But everyone has something unique to add to the fight and it is the only way to move things in a more positive direction."

"If anyone can pull this 'turn-into-a-frog-and-make-it-better thing,' Nora, it's you," Kameela said, warmly. "So, I'm willing to officially declare I believe in purple frogs."

"That's right," said Will. "We've tried marching. We've tried signing petitions. We've tried so many ways to change people's hearts and minds, and not one of them has worked the way we hoped it would. Doing this might make it possible to figure out the secret to saving what we can of our little town. So, I believe in purple frogs too."

Minh added, "And if what you do can help others save their parts of the world, I guess I'll believe at least in *this* purple frog."

I heard that high-pitched whistle again and saw Linka and Myth circling.

"I *really* appreciate the votes of confidence and will do my best. And, uh, well, would you mind if I had a moment with Seth?"

"Good luck, Nora. I'm counting on one heck of a story when you get back," Kameela said.

"Me too," Will said.

"I don't think I want to know anything—but I reserve the right to change my mind," Minh said. "See you tomorrow, Seth. Nora? Three days?"

I nodded and they wished me goodbye and good luck and headed off.

Once they were out of sight, Seth raised me to his face, and we looked intently at each other. Finally, I said, "If I ever get back to my human form, there is a lot we will have to talk about. I will not lie. Knowing that your dad killed mine and tried to kill me makes everything harder," I said. "Cannot quite see spending holidays with your parents. Know what I mean?"

"I don't see me spending holidays with Dad, either, if that's any comfort. And I want you to know how sorry I am that he's hurt you and your family so badly."

I could tell that he meant what he said.

"Did . . . did it hurt when you got shot?" he asked.

I shrugged. "The whole experience has left its mark." I rubbed the scar on my chest.

"Is that where the bullet hit you?"

I nodded, wondering if it would always hurt.

"Oh, Nora." He bowed his head, I think in shame, and let out a stifled sob, quickly wiping his eyes with the back of his other arm. "I don't even know how to say sorry anymore. I've said it so many times. But I'll tell you one thing. Next time I see him, I'll make sure he pays the price for his unadulterated evil."

"No, Seth. Leave it. He will get what he deserves. I do not know how, but he will, and you cannot play any part in it. He is your father. Let others do that job. Besides, I am afraid he might hurt you now that he has been discovered."

"If I didn't have such a crazy family, none of this would be happening," Seth said.

"That is not quite true. A big part of this story happened before either you or I were even born. The stuff with your family's land ending up in my family's hands. The stuff with my own mother and dad. That is not on us. We are left to deal with it. And make the best of it we can."

There was one more thing I wanted to say, even if it was weird coming from my frog form. But I decided to say it anyway. "Seth?"

"Yes?"

"Would you mind giving a frog princess a kiss?"

He smiled his broad, wonderful Seth smile. "Not if that frog princess is you," he said, and he brought me up to his lips. Our mouths touched and lingered. It felt oh so nice. And then what I'd waited for so long was over. Kisses could be many things, or so I figure. This one was comforting, made me like my real self for the moment, and held the promise of more pleasure to come.

"You are a good guy, Seth."

"And you're just plain weird, Nora."

We laughed.

"But that's what I love about you," he said.

Did he say *love*? Before I could reply, Myth landed behind Seth.

"My ride is here," I said, and asked Seth to put me down on the stump behind him.

His eyes were wide. "These your new friends?"

I nodded and hopped on Myth's back.

"Uh, where is this prince guy?" Seth said.

"You sound a little green, Seth," I said jokingly. "He is my cousin. So no worries there," I said.

"Come back to me, Nora," he said.

Then he spoke to Linka. "Please take good care of Nora," he said with a catch in his voice. "She's very precious to me."

With a wave goodbye, Seth stepped back and watched as I settled behind Linka for what I assumed would be a long ride to the Palay.

"Well, that was a different kind of experience," Linka said.

"Yes, it was," I replied, the corners of my mouth turned upward in a frog smile.

Myth stretched his wings, about to take off, when I caught a sight that nearly stopped my heart. Kincade emerged out of the woods. What now? Was he checking to see if Finley had done the job on Gran? Frantic, I whispered to Linka to stay put when I heard him say, "Son, your mother and I have been looking for you."

75

Nora 🐸 Reckoning

Night of the Pink Moon
Deepest Night
Salmon Falls

MYTH TOOK OFF despite my request to hang around, so I pulled the princess card on him. I insisted that we circle about the little clearing as Seth and his father talked below.

"You have had your wish—now it is time to get back to the Palay," Linka said.

"Look, I have an arachnachute on. I can jump and you can go on without me."

"Anyone tell you that you are even more annoying as a frog than you were as a human?" Linka said. "I am not wearing Myth out by flying around while those two memtoes spar below," she said.

I had never heard that term before, but I knew what she meant. Linka instructed Myth to land in a nearby tree and we watched the drama below us unfold.

"How'd you find me, Dad? I've been working hard at avoiding you," Seth said.

"Heard your name on the police scanner. Seems like Mel finally admitted his crimes."

"And what about your part?" Seth said heatedly.

"We're not talking about it. Come on. We gotta leave," Kincade said. "Your mother's waiting in the car."

I hopped off Myth's back onto a sturdy tree branch.

"Where are you going?" Linka said.

"To help my friend," I said. "And if you could help me, I would be very grateful."

"That is not part of our deal. You got to see your grandmother. It is well past time to go," Linka said.

"I am not leaving until I know Seth is safe," I said and kept watching the action, unsure of how I could help but determined to do so. The wind rustled the branches where I sat, and I found myself clinging to them as hard as I could.

"Do not get too close," I tried to warn Seth. But it didn't seem like he heard. Instead, he took out his phone and pressed the screen a few times.

His father laughed. "No calls. This is between you, me, and your mother," he said.

Seth put his phone away.

"We're leaving and she insists on taking you with us. Then after we've laid low for a while, we'll be back. I found a remarkable stand of lumber. Trees I couldn't identify they are so rare—and old. They're giants. And they're all comin' down. Add that to Henry's sequoias and we'll be rich. Rich!"

Was he talking about the huge trees I'd passed through before I rescued the parachuting frogs? He was going to cut down our sequoias—and those remarkable trees too? A level of rage I've never known boiled inside me. He had to be stopped. But how?

When I tuned back into the conversation between father and son, I heard Seth say "So, you *only* want me to go 'cause Mom wants me along."

Kincade nodded.

"Since when did Mom's opinion carry any weight with you?" Seth said.

Kincade laughed. "The point is it carries weight with *you*. Now you can come on your own or I can drag you."

"I'd like to see you try," Seth said.

"Please do not antagonize him," I called out. Again, he didn't react to what I said.

"I'm going to talk to Mom. She doesn't need to be caught up in your forgery, murder, and arson games," Seth said. "Fine family legacy you're passing on."

"They might have me on forgery. But arson? No way."

"And what about murder?" Seth asked. "Nora says you killed her dad and shot her."

His father's eyes widened.

"Nora? You talked to Nora? That's impossible."

"Why? Because you left her for dead? She was here. A few minutes ago. She just left."

"Impossible!" he said again.

"Why? Because you think you killed her? Well, you didn't. Nora is still alive."

Kincade said nothing. But I could see his body seethe red with anger. I noticed that as a frog I could see strong emotion in colors, some of which I'd never seen or have names for.

"Whatever it is you've got to say, you're going to say in front of Mom so she has a full understanding of how low you'll sink," Seth said, his body glowing red just like his dad's. "Then I'm going to the sheriff's office and turn you in for all your evil. For forging those land deal papers, burning down Nora's house, killing Henry Peters, and for trying to kill Nora. And then I'll never speak to you again."

"I told you—I didn't burn her house down. And to be perfectly truthful . . ."

"As if you could," Seth said.

"Why would I want to burn down something I've wanted my whole life?"

"I don't know why you do most of the things you do, Dad," Seth said, and he walked past his father.

"Worthless kid," Kincade muttered. He picked up a rock and drew back his arm.

My whole body tingled with fear. No way I could hop the distance to Kincade quickly enough to try to stop him, so, using pure instinct, I blinked—twice—so I could see the lines of energy that ran between all things.

Grabbing the energy line that ran between Kincade and me with both hands, I jumped off the branch I was sitting on and used it to slide down toward Kincade.

Linka cried in alarm. "Nora, stop!"

But it was too late. My body buzzed with electricity the second I grabbed it. My infinitesimal weight, which seemed to be some-what magnified by the current the line of energy possessed on its own, seemed to be enough to spoil Kincade's aim. Instead of delivering a deadly blow, he only managed a glancing one. Still, Seth sank to the ground, moaning. His father grabbed him by the arm and hauled him to his feet.

"Come on, kid. Off we go."

The cobweb-like darkness that dripped from the energy line I was using slowed my sliding time, but because it seemed to permanently connect me with Kincade, where he went, I followed. By the time I reached him, I'd gathered enough momentum to pack a punch when I slammed into the side of his head. I hopped onto Seth's chest to see if I could feel his breath rising and falling. He was okay. It was then I realized that my body was buzzing with all the pure energy I'd absorbed from the line.

A shadow glided over me. I didn't have to look up to know it was Linka and Myth. They dive bombed Kincade, with Linka releasing a weapon that resulted in several small arrows being embedded in a circle on his forehead.

"And that is how you do it," Linka said a bit too smugly for me as they circled around and came in for another blow. "By the way," she called out, "you should be dead from grabbing so many web strings."

So that's what you call them. Makes sense I suppose. Web of life, web strings. "I am not dead, but I am definitely tingling," I told her, then hopped to a nearby rock.

Kincade grunted as he sat up, shook his head in confusion, then got to his feet. He leaned over Seth, who was still lying on the ground. "Get up, boy! Get up."

Seth's mother charged out of the trees with a baseball bat in hand. "What have you done to him?" Sarah screamed.

I hopped from the rock to a tree and clung to the bark. I wasn't sure what to do. But getting out of the way seemed to be my best bet for the moment.

"Shut up, woman, and help me get him to his feet," Kincade said. But Sarah didn't listen. Instead, she walked straight toward her husband, baseball bat raised and ready.

"You think you're so smart, don't you?" she said, snarling with disgust. "You set everything up to your advantage. You killed Henry and set up the old lady to think she did it."

"Yeah, so? I told you what I'd done—and you didn't have a problem with it when you thought you'd get to live in their fancy log cabin."

"No, Carl, I didn't say a word because I thought you'd kill me, too, if I did. And I'm here to tell you that I did do something. Something to make you regret all you've done to others, including our son and me."

"And what could someone so simple and ignorant do to me?" Kincade said, his hands on his hips.

Seth sat up, rubbing the back of his head. "Mom? What's going on?"

"Seth, get out of here. This is between me and your dad," his mother said.

"I'm not going anywhere unless you come with me," Seth said, and he got to his feet.

"It's too late for that," Sarah said. "Now go, I don't want you to see what I'm about to do."

"What?" Kincade said mockingly. "You gonna hit me with that thing?" Then his voice deepened into a snarl. "I'd like to see you try," he said, then stuck his hand into his jacket pocket.

I had a bad feeling. I'd seen him do that before, and it hadn't ended well for me.

Linka and Myth landed above me in the same tree. Linka was furious. And I couldn't blame her, but I wasn't leaving until I knew Seth was safe. Then I told her why. "I think Kincade has a gun in his pocket. He used it on me, and I am afraid he will use it on Seth or his mom."

"Farp and fiddleheads," Linka said. I wasn't sure what *farp* meant, but her disgusted tone led me to believe it was a swear word of some kind. Do all languages have bad words that start with *F*?

Sarah ignored him, in a trance of anger as her body glowed a darkening red. "People feel sorry for me because I'm married to your dad, but feeling pity isn't the same as caring. It's the opposite. If they cared, they'd say something. Try to talk to me. Try to be my friend. But no one cares, Seth. No one besides you."

"I do care, Mom. You know I do. Now please, put the bat down. Let's get out of here. Leave him to the sheriff. She knows all about him."

"That's not enough. Your dad will worm out of it. I know he will. He always does. No, I gotta make him pay now because soon the sheriff will catch up to me as well."

Seth walked slowly toward his mom. "Give me the bat. Please."

"Did you hear me, Seth? I said I was going to be arrested too."

"I heard you, but you're really upset now and worried the sheriff will make you pay for his crimes—or maybe even that he'll blame you for what he did. But I won't let that happen."

"But it will—because I burned down Nora's house."

Her words almost shocked me out of my frog body.

Seth stopped. "That can't be right. You *couldn't* have. You were at the Legion that night."

Sarah gave an amused snort. "That's what I wanted you to think. And nobody, including the sheriff, thought I was threatening enough to even check. But I want your father to know what I've done. He always gets what he wants. And he's always wanted that house. It was up to me to make sure he didn't get it."

"You bitch, you ruined everything," Kincade said. He rushed his wife.

From above, Myth swooped in between the two of them, and Linka pelted Kincade with stones.

Confused, Kincade looked up. He pulled his revolver out and fired.

Myth knew what was coming and expertly dodged the shots.

Kincade focused on his wife once more and moved so fast she froze. He shoved his gun back into his pocket, grabbed the bat, and ripped it out of her hand. Then he twisted her arm behind her, spitting words into her ear. "Why? Why'd you do it? Just when I almost had it all?"

"Because I wanted to stop you from having it all," Sarah said, her eyes defiant even while she winced in pain. "And I'm not sorry I did. You hated Henry's family because they had your property. That stupid log cabin. But why? Why was that so important to you? More important than Seth? Than me?"

Kincade let go of her arm and struck her in the face. She fell to the ground, knocked out. He pulled the gun back out and aimed at his wife. Seth jumped him and nailed him with blows. But one of Kincade's return hits landed smack on Seth's chin and knocked him off his father.

I blinked twice to see the line of connection between the gun and me. I reached for a webstring.

Linka called out to me, "Do not do it. It is too dangerous."

I could feel its raw energy run through me. It was like each time I touched one, the zing got stronger. I snapped the line to the gun and used it like a rope to flick the gun out of Kincade's hand. It fell to the ground and I jumped on top of it. The only way Kincade would get to that weapon would be to stomp on me, which appeared to be exactly what he was about to do.

It was amazing how terrifying the worn-out sole of a work boot could be. There was only one thing to do. Be equally terrifying back.

"You did not kill me, Carl Kincade," I said in my deepest voice.

He lowered his boot and frantically looked around for me.

When it became apparent that the only conscious thing around was the frog at his feet, he said, looking down at me, "Nora? Is that you?" His face was contorted by disbelief, and he stunk with fear. "You're supposed to be dead. Or did my pathetic son kiss you and turn you into a frog?"

"I want to tell you two things first," I said.

"First?" he said with a sneer.

"Before I take my revenge against you for killing my father," I said.

He laughed.

"First thing. We have Dad's original conservation easement papers. And they prove that he had no intention of selling anything to you."

"Where are they?" Kincade said desperately.

"Somewhere you would never guess," I said. "And secondly, I remember what you said before you shot me."

"And what's that?" he said, like he wasn't much interested in my answer.

"You said, 'Your dad made good shooting practice, and so will you, just like all those bears.'"

He shrugged. "Can't fault your memory," he said with a sinister chuckle.

"Let me share something else I remember. It is a little poem some friends taught me."

"No time for poetry. It's frog-stomping time," he said. He raised his foot over me. I jumped to the top of a tree stump and recited these words, which seemed to hold him spellbound:

So, wherever you are, if ever you fall,
Put your lips to the ground and give us a call.
And to any that would harm you, we will take on your
fight.
And bind the betrayer so they can't harm or take flight.

We will encase them in bark, branch, and leaf.
And from that danger give you relief.

You may invoke this wish by asking for our presence . . .

A yell rumbled in my throat, and I croaked out two words with all my might. "Tree essence!"

Kincade roared with laughter and shot out a hand to snatch me. But I sensed what was coming and jumped as high and as far as I could. Just in time, too, because right then roots shot from the ground and wrapped themselves around Kincade's legs, then his torso, arms, and head. Within seconds his whole body was wrapped like a mummy, and he was screaming and clawing at the roots, trying to get them off his body and cursing my name.

Some of the roots plunged back into the ground, expanded, and twisted into gnarls. Continuing their transformation, they morphed into heart wood and then bark. Kincade's torso torqued into a twisted trunk, and his arms, flailing in terror, split into limbs that branched out and produced leaves. His neck and head elongated and sprouted more branches like a crown.

Within seconds, he was a full-fledged leaf-bearing tree with a burl where his face used to be. And in the fading light of the Pink Moon, the burl took on the look of a man's face frozen in a silent scream of terror. It looked so much like the Flying Demon Tree but without the wings, and I wondered who else had been *treeified*?

Seth missed seeing his father's transformation. He'd been protectively hugging his mother. And by the time he looked around he saw nothing and was so traumatized, he didn't even notice that a new tree had sprung up out of nowhere and was standing where his father had stood.

But Sarah had opened her eyes as I made my request of the trees and had seen the whole thing.

"He's gone, Mom," Seth said. "We're safe now. I hope he gets thrown in jail and never comes back."

His mother said nothing, her eyes wide in disbelief. All she could do was stare at the tree. Then a relieved smile crossed her face and she wept with relief.

I had done the only thing I could to make Kincade stop, and if I hadn't done it, Seth might be dead. Like my dad. Would I tell Seth what I'd done? Not now. Or maybe ever. It would be a secret between Sarah and me.

I barely had enough energy to motion to Linka that I was ready to go. She and Myth had landed on the tree stump and I jumped to them, then climbed back into the saddle, feeling like—well, like I'd never felt before.

"Nice work down there," Linka said begrudgingly.

"Trees, he was going to cut down *my* trees and *your* trees. I had to do something drastic."

"As if turning into a frog is not drastic enough," Linka said. Was that a smile on her face? "And, oh, by the way, trees do not really belong to anyone. At least in my world."

Linka signaled to Myth who took off, circled Seth once, then headed north and west as the Pink Moon faded in the sky and the promise of a new day hugged the horizon. I did not look back.

I had three days to spend with the frogs. And to find at least one thing that might save the world, my mom, and me.

Three days.

Starting now.

The End

Acknowledgements

USUALLY, FAMILY COMES last in the acknowledgments, but for me, family has always come first.

I would like to thank my husband Thomas S. MacBriar for his support and encouragement. Tom, every time I falter, you lift me up. Thank you for always believing in me. And for your willingness to read "just one more version."

To our beloved children, Kate MacBriar and Ryan MacBriar, you have always inspired me to make the world a better place for all. Thanks, too, to my son-in-law, David Wien and daughter-in-law, Tishina Sutton MacBriar, for your ongoing interest and support.

To my adored grandchildren, Miguel, Lili, Joaquin, Carter, Makenzie, and Orion, I wanted you all to have a 'grandma story' that would inspire resilience and optimism.

And to my nieces, nephews, their spouses, partners, and children, including, Nicholas, David, Nora, Max, Freya, Gwen, Arwyn, Michael, Lindsay, Zoey, Simeon, Sarah, Logan, Myketa, Alex, Diana, Jaime, Sam, Wesley, Ali, Luanne, Justin, Cameron, Erin, Ben, Margo, and the precious little ones on their way.

To my siblings Neal Brown and Elizabeth Paschuk, we were lucky to come from such loving parents, and pass that love onto our children. I know Mom and Dad would be proud of us.

To my brother-in-law, Myron Paschuk and sister-in-law Robin MacBriar and her husband Craig Hutchinson, I am grateful for your friendship.

To my dozens of Brown, Elburg, and Sorensen cousins and cousins-by-marriage, in the U.S., Canada, and Denmark, you inspire me by the interesting lives you lead.

Friends

To my friends who have supported me through this labor of love, most especially Amany El Shazley, Marc Freeman, Cheryl Hatch, Martha Holmes, Betty Kim, Pamela Jo Ledbetter, Olive Lefferson, Nancy Luce, Janis Marziotto, Trish McGuire, and Mona McAllister. You are all amazingly talented people and you helped make this task more fun. Without the encouragement that each of you provided, this book would never have been completed.

Editorial and production team

- Caroline Clouse, editor, you have my deepest thanks. You elevated my writing, and I'm grateful.
- Kelly Wise, associate editor, thank you so much for your significant contribution to the final polish.
- Rudy Ramos, I am grateful for your work on the cover and other pieces.
- Thanks as well to Brittany Yost for your sensitivity read, Warren Layberry for your story development advice, and Beth Jusino for sharing your industry knowledge.

- Colleen Sheehan and Ampersand Bookery, you did an amazing job on the design of this book. Thank you.
- Natalie Faghri, I am beyond grateful to you for your work on my various websites and marketing efforts, as well as your support and encouragement.

Subject matter experts

I appreciate everyone's time and expertise.
Thanks to:

- Paul Armbrust, retired Captain, Lake Forest Park Police
- Alice K. Boatwright, author
- Jeffrey D. Briggs, author
- Alan Chafie, with Whatcom County, Washington, Public Defenders Office
- Roxie Star, Home Baker and Blogger
- Edna Czaplewski, artist
- Michelle Lichter, author
- Kate MacBriar, Creative Consultant
- Mark Phillips, Environmentalist
- Dave Robbins, Hama Hama Tree Farm
- Dørte Sorensen, artist
- Matt Stark, real estate agent with Windemere Realty
- Steve Sutton, retired Chief of Police, Lake Forest Park, Washington
- Charlotte Stuart, author
- Don Stuart, Expert on Conservation Easements

- Philip Stielstra, NWPropagationNation
- Marianne Sweeny, Search Information Architect
- Lisa Wathne, Senior Strategist at The Humane Society of the United States
- Janis Wildy, author

Other wonderful groups

- The American Eagle Foundation, Pigeon Forge,TN (Home to the real rescued raven, Poe.)
- The 15th Avenue Marketing Group, you are such great writers and friends.
- Refugee Welcome Mat Group, your warm hearts and generous nature always fills me up.
- Puget Sound Sisters in Crime, I love to hang out with you all even though I write YA Fantasy!
- P.S. I Love You, Power of 8 Group, thanks for your kindness and insights.

Local Volunteer Environmental Organizations

Change at a local level leads to change at a regional, national, and international level. I'd like to acknowledge the following local groups of environmental volunteers in my community for giving your time, energy, and dollars to protect and preserve the City of Lake Forest Park, Washington, and surrounding area.

- Five Acres Woods
- King Conservation District

- Lake Ballinger/McAleer Creek Watershed Forum
- Lake Forest Park Community Advisory Board
- Lake Forest Park Stewardship Foundation
- Lake Forest Park StreamKeepers
- Lake Forest Park Tree Board
- SnoKing Water Shed Council
- WRIA 8 Salmon Recovery Council

For a list of youth-oriented environment organizations, please visit www.sequoiagrovebooks.com.

In Memoriam

I'd also like to acknowledge my parents, Virgil N. Brown and Evelyn B. Brown. Although you are no longer with us, your passion for imaginative living inspires me every day. You are the heroes in my personal story.

And to the many other family members and dear friends who have left us behind, I am thinking of you as well, most especially my husband's parents, Susan and Wallace (Mac) MacBriar, my cousin Carolyn Richardson, who saved me from drowning when I was six, my sister-in-law Barbara MacBriar, my foster sister Eve Schocket and her son, Eric Neal Schocket, and Dustin Canham, who I used to call my littlest proofreader.

All opinions and errors are my responsibility.

Characters

Aquatessa: the elemento of water

Prince Azzumundo: "Azzie" (As-ee) son of Ranya who would rather be composing chorales than ruling.

Balarius (Bah-LARRY-us): Grand and Glorious Vizzard to the Court of Ranya (and Ranya's brother)

Lady Batrachas (Bat-TRA-kas): council member from Many Islands in Bright Blue Waters

Bacareno (Bah-ka-RAY-no): court caller

Lord Bumbleberry: elderly frog lord

Bortos (Bore-TOES): the Elemento of wind

Violetta Bravo: Nora's attorney

Bulldoggies: frog guards of General Oddbull

Lord Byang (by-ANG): council member from Bangla

Clarenso (Clare-EN-so): aide to Balarius

Creet: a peregrine falcon

Aunt DeLili: Elder sister to Ranya and Balarius, formerly, Queen DeLili

Lord D'graff: a frog lord

Drengo: a Bulldoggie

Mel Finley: tree farm foreman

Commander Frago: Commander of the FAFA (Flying Army of Frog Airtilliers (Air-till-e-ays)

Lord Fountainblower: a frog lord

Dofedi el-Gabal (Doe-FAY-dee El GAB-el)**:** council member from the land of the pyramids

King Garruchian (Garr-OO-che-an)**:** exalted monarch (long dead)

Gindjurra (Gin-JUR-ah) **the Magnifico:** desert frog from Down Under, member of council

Kikko Hayashi(Key-co Hay-ashi)**:** friend of Nora

Mrs. Hayashi (Hay-ashi)**:** cleaning woman at hospital and mother of Kikko

Sheriff Ardith Heinze (Hin-ze)**:** Salmon Falls sheriff

Idillons (EYE-dill-lawns)**:** Zombie frogs produced by the Maw

Igneo (IGG-knee-o)**:** Elemento of fire

Jineta (Gin-ET-ta)**:** Zon

Kameela Bashir (Ka-meal-la bah-SHEER)**:** friend of Nora, member of Mother Nature's Commandos. Her family are refugees from Somalia.

Lady Keewada (Key-WAH-da)**:** council member from the Ouaddaï Highlands

Carl Kincade: who wants Nora's family tree farm, no matter what the cost.

Sarah Kincade: Carl's wife

Seth Kincade: Carl's son, and Nora's friend

Kon (Con): Lord Raeburn's aide de chambre

Pastor Lackerby (LACK-er-bee): pastor in Salmon Falls, Washington

Lem: commander of Chantry Cavern

Lady Li (Lie): Malaysian tree frog (member of council)

Lucia (Loo-CHEE-ah): mate of Gindjurra the Magnifico

Magmo: Elemento of rock

Mickey: Nora's Sheltie

Minh Phan (Min Fan): friend of Nora, member of Mother Nature's Commandos. His family came from Vietnam.

Milostonae: (MEE-low-stone-a): exalted king (long dead)

Mura (MIR-ah): a Squad One Zon

Myth: fruit bat mount of Linka

Noble: a snowy owl

Nunya (NONE-yah): femnura Azzie meets at ceremony

General Oddbull: one of the Queen's nemeses who rules over the Maw of Malevolence.

Lord Oscarfroskur (Os-car-FROS-kur): council member from the Land of Ice

Great-aunt Peragonia (Per-a-GON-ya): great aunt of Ranya and Balarius

Ellie Peters: Nora's paternal grandmother

Henry Quentin Peters: Nora's father

Nora Peters: environmental activist

Reggie Peters: Nora's mom

Pender: Azzie's temporary replacement as supervisor of Dream Pod Centurion.

Princess P'hustalinka (Push-TAH-link-ah): "Linka" Commander of the Queen's personal guard—the Zons.

Pym: matriarch of the pikas

Prince Ponte-Fricani (Pon-TAY-frick-CON-nee): ancestor of Lord Raeburn who stole the Great Pearl of the Forest generations ago

Lord Raeburn (RAY-burn): ne'er-do-well frog lord

Lady Ranocchia (Ra-noo-CHEE-ya): council member from Peninsula of the Boot

Ranya (RON-yah): "Magnificent Queen of All Frogs That Flourish in the North, South, East, and West and in Water, Sand, and Mud", Azzie's mother, and sister to Balarius and DeLili

Recycle Rick: Henry Peter's friend and fellow environmentalist

Roya (Roy-yah): a Squad One Zon

Sage: purple martin mount of Commander Frago

Sajay (SAH-jay): Linka's second in command

Lord Shaba (SHAW-ba): council member from Ruska

Simeon (SIM-e-in): majordomo to Queen Ranya

Soffinatta (Soff-in-ET-ta): an exalted queen (long dead)

tad or taddy: familiar names or slang for tadpoles

Trish: First Aid attendant in ambulance

Trep (Ter-ep): a Squad One Zon

Wink: nephew of Clarenso

Virgil Wallace Peters: Nora's great-great-great-grandfather

Will Wakeen: friend of Nora, Mother Nature's Commando a member of the local tribe.

Whodora (Who-DORA): ancient frog hero, with a constellation named after her.

Xeron (Zer-ON): a Bulldoggie

Lord Yan: member of frog council

Glossary

Airtilliers: members of the Flying Army of Frog Airtilliers (Air-till-e-ays)

All (the)**:** the connected entity that includes everything

arachnachute (a-RACH-na-chute)**:** spider-spun parachute

Auraventricalus (Aura-VEN-tri-callus)**:** the heart of the Plais

Bulldoggies: troops of General Oddbull

burfers: frogs who burf; also burfets (burfers in training)

burfing: breeze surfing

Centurion: a dream pod

Chronicle cape: a garment allowed only to frogs of the court depicting important life-events in embroidery

CODERs: converters of dream energy

Elementos: elemental spirits of Water (Aquatessa), Wind (Bortos), Fire (Igneo), Rock (Magmo)

esbue: a natural color only seen by frogs

FAFA: Flying Army of Frog Airtilliers(Air-TILL-e-ays)**:**

femnura: female frog

femtoe: human female

flaktal: (flak-tul) a sharpened flying disk used by FAFA

flycape: a protective cape, with inside pockets, designed for burfing

flyrein: a rein for flying

frogklath (frog cloth): durable fabric handwoven by frogs from materials collected in nature. Comes in edible and inedible forms.

furd: cross between a fur-bearing animal and a bird

hopalometer: frog measure of distance

Golden Pearl of the Forest: an object of great metaphysical power, revered by the Frog World

Idillons (EYE-dill-lawns): Zombie frogs produced by the Maw

Infinator: the figure-eight-shaped fighting blade of the 'Zons

Lek: collective noun for a group of fireflies

Liths: giant frogs that guards the Maw, true goliaths of the frog world

Largetoe: the frog term for human

Lumitubes: Tubes carved into Frog Mountain to admit light to the interior of the Palay

Maw of Malevolence: the Maw, where captured refugee frogs, fleeing their homes are turned into idilons

Memnura: male frog

Memtoe: human male

Mounthorn: frog equivalent to saddle horn

Palay (pal-LAY): Seat of the Frog Kingdom, located within Frog Mountain, which sits atop the Well of Light, behind the Veil of Mist

Plaza of the Blazing Sun: the outdoor hub of commerce and social life, located on Frog Mountain, behind the Veil of Mist

Pule: a natural color only seen by frogs

rink: a natural color only seen by frogs

Ruling Room: the cavern from which the queen rules

Shibshibs: frog slippers for poisonous frogs (only Simeon is exempt from wearing these while attending the queen because other frogs are afraid of stepping on his 'trail, which deters them from approaching the queen.)

snerd: cross between a snail and a bird

snish: cross between a snake and a fish

Stellarus: a dream pod

squirtle: cross between a sea squirt and a turtle

tadschool: tadpole school

tuw: a natural color only seen by frogs

Trinitarium: a dream pod

twisp: a thread of energy

umba: a natural color only seen by frogs

underfrog: equivalent to the largetoe usage of 'underdog'

Veil of Mist: protective layer of mist that surrounds Frog Mountain and environs

vizzard: Frog wizard

Watcher: mysterious creature that keeps watch on Nora's part of the world

webstring: connective energy

Zons: Queen Ranya's all-female personal guard

Equivalent Times in the Largetoe and the Frog World

Largetoe World	Frog World
Before Dawn	Sing Time
Sun Rise	Sun Rise
Early Morning	Dew Time
Morning	Warming Time (Early)
Mid-Morning	Warming Time
Late Morning	Warming Time (Late)
Noon	Fly Time (Early)

Early Afternoon	Fly Time
Late Afternoon	Fly Time (Late)
Sundown	Sundown
After Dark	Swarm Time (Early)
Early Evening	Swarm Time
Evening	Swarm Time (Late)
Late Evening	Dark Time (Early)
Midnight	Dark Time
After Midnight	Dark Time (Late)
Deepest Night	Deepest Night

Dear Readers,

We hope you enjoyed reading Luanne C. Brown's novel, "Once in a Pink Moon."

Would you mind taking a few minutes to post a short review on Goodreads or Amazon? Reviews are the best way to help authors reach a wider audience.

And don't forget to look for the second book in the Frog Tale Trilogy, "When Frogs Dream." This volume will be published in 2024.

And please tell your family and friends about this book too.

Thank you,
Sequoia Grove Books

CPSIA information can be obtained
at www.ICGtesting.com
Printed in the USA
LVHW010149220922
728942LV00001B/22